Other Waters

Also by Eleni N. Gage

North of Ithaka

Other Waters

ELENI N. GAGE

ST. MARTIN'S PRESS

NEW YORK

OTHER WATERS. Copyright © 2012 by Eleni N. Gage. All rights reserved. Printed in the United States of America. For information, address St. Martin's Press, 175 Fifth Avenue, New York, N.Y. 10010.

www.stmartins.com

Design by Omar Chapa

Library of Congress Cataloging-in-Publication Data

Gage, Eleni N.
    Other waters : a novel / Eleni N. Gage. — 1st ed.
        p. cm.
    ISBN 978-0-312-65851-9 (hardcover)
    ISBN 978-1-4299-4149-5 (e-book)
    1. East Indian American women—Fiction.   2. India—Social life and customs—Fiction.   3. Family secrets—fiction.   4. Domestic fiction.
    I. Title.
    PS3607.A3573.O84 2012
    813'.6—dc23

                                                            2011033232

First Edition: February 2012

10 9 8 7 6 5 4 3 2 1

For Amalia, who didn't exist when I started writing this.
I'm sure I will adore, annoy, and embarrass you as much as
the mother in these pages does her daughter. I apologize in advance.

And for Emilio, who set sail with me into uncharted waters.

You could not step twice into the same river
For other waters are ever flowing on to you.

—Heraclitus

PART ONE

Chapter One

"He says he's there to keep an eye on her doctors, but that's just not true." Maya looked up at Dr. Bernard; he had on his usual listening face, forehead crinkled, blue eyes peering nearsightedly, one finger resting along his nose, the rest of his hand scratching his beard. She had been seeing him for only six weeks; it was a requirement that all second-year psychiatric residents undergo their own course of therapy, to see what it felt like to be a patient, and she'd chosen Dr. Bernard for both his sterling reputation and the fact that he charged residents on a sliding scale. Did he even remember what her father did? Had she ever told him? "My dad's not in medicine, it's just the girls—me, my mom, my sister. He's a civil engineer, or was before he retired," she said. "He's just saying that to placate us."

And that was the problem; since when did Pops think she needed placating? Her mom might need careful handling; although Seema was strong and she could handle the hardest, most uncomfortable truths, not being there to oversee the situation personally would be maddening to her. And her sister needed to be sheltered, definitely. Priya had her hands full with the kids and her practice; disrupting her carefully calibrated existence was only acceptable in the most extreme of circumstances. But Pops always said that Maya was level-headed; he never had to worry about her overreacting.

"So why do *you* think your father went to India?" Dr. Bernard tugged on his beard again. It was sweet of him to grow a beard, such a reassuring sight for his patients. With his graying orange hair and camel-colored jackets, Dr. Bernard looked like an old-time analyst, or some white girl's grandfather who took her to ride carousels when she was little and helped her apply to his alma mater when she turned eighteen. When he pulled on his beard, it was a sign that he was thinking about something Maya had said. He probably thought she felt abandoned by her father's departure, but that wasn't the issue.

"He went because he thinks my grandmother is going to die. He's her only son, he'll need to be there to be her chief mourner," Maya said. "So why not tell me that? He's trying to protect me, but from what? The inevitable? I'm an adult. A medical professional."

"And is it inevitable? Is your grandmother going to die?"

"I guess so." Maya sighed. "She's ninety-six or something, no one's really sure, the records were lost, during a fire maybe, who knows." She smiled, buying time to regulate her breath. Dadiji wasn't dead now; it would be ridiculous to start crying before anything tragic even happened. She needed to stay in good spirits for tonight; Sanjay was only in town every so often, and this time he was bringing his girlfriend. Maya couldn't remember the last time her cousin had wanted to introduce a girl to her, not since they were in college, maybe. In any case, when her grandmother did die, she wouldn't want Maya to be sad; Dadiji viewed her own death as a release from mortal existence, a step bringing her closer to moksha, spiritual liberation. "After all," Maya said out loud, "ninety-six is old, even for India, and living long is a competitive sport there."

Dr. Bernard leaned forward. "But it can still be hard to accept. It sounds like your grandmother is a very dynamic person to you."

Maya stared at Dr. Bernard. He really was good if he could tell how large Dadiji's presence was in her life, how out of proportion to her stooped, shrunken body. Dadiji was her strongest link to India; she was as vibrant and mysterious as the subcontinent itself.

"Dynamic is a good word," Maya said. "Although maybe not in the traditional sense. I mean, she isn't very active. She just sits on her bed in her blue room, looking out the window. But when she speaks, it's like she's been watching the whole universe."

Dr. Bernard wrote something in his notebook.

"She almost never gets up; I remember the last time I saw Dadiji get out of the bed," Maya continued. She had been five, or maybe seven, on a trip to India, they'd gone both of those years. Her parents were off at the bank or the consulate, and she was waiting in the doorway of the house for her sister to get out of the latrine when a man stomped into view, pulling a small figure behind him. The man was filthy; Maya could smell him from across the dirt road. He was yelling in Marwari, she could only make out a few phrases; the rest must have been bad words she didn't know at the time. In one hand he held a ragged red velvet bag—it was strange to see a man holding a purse—and with the other he was yanking the arm of a little goddess. Maya knew she was a goddess because of her whitened face and the crown on her head. She was bigger than Maya, maybe as old as Priya, who was still in the latrine. Twelve, maybe. Or already a teenager.

The dirty man took his hand off of the goddess's arm, raised it in the air, and brought it down onto her face; it landed with a cracking noise. The goddess crumpled into the dirt but didn't say anything, didn't cry or make a sound. A trickle of blood, darker than the red velvet of her dress, dribbled from her nose down the white paint on her face.

"Dadiji, come quick, hurry up!" Maya ran up the slippery stairs, taking them two by two. "He's killing the goddess!"

She could hear Priya's footsteps behind her, then Priya yelling, "Dadiji's resting! Ma said don't make noise! And gods don't walk around on earth anymore, stupid!"

They arrived in Dadiji's room at the same time, Priya's legs being so much longer than Maya's.

"Maya thinks there's a goddess in the yard." Priya snorted.

"And is there?" Dadiji asked.

Priya laughed. "It's just a girl, like me. Maya's just being stupid."

"Isn't Krishna a baby sometimes, and then a man?" Maya demanded.

"Of course he is," Dadiji said. "There is no reason a god cannot be a child, or be outside our home." She gestured toward the window. "Have another look."

Maya elbowed Priya, triumphant as they walked toward Dadiji's bed. This was why she loved Dadiji so fiercely, because her grandmother treated her like a rational human being, not a whining pest or an adorable moppet. Even as a child Maya felt that Dadiji understood her essence, knew who she was, whether Maya was in India or in Michigan. Whoever that little person was, Dadiji had decided that she mattered; she was someone whose words were worth hearing.

"You girls do not yet understand India," Dadiji continued. "It is different from Michigan. There is room for gods to walk the streets; it is not for us to disturb them."

Dadiji spoke as slowly as always, one word rolling leisurely into the next; Maya felt her chest was going to explode. "But the bad man is hurting her!" She pointed out the window behind Dadiji's head.

"There is room for evil, too, and for good." Dadiji dropped the mala she had been meditating with before being interrupted and turned to look out the window. Over her shoulder they could see the man pulling the goddess to her feet.

"It's a beggar girl, Maya," Priya whispered. "And he is hurting her, Dadiji."

"Just because evil exists does not mean we should sit by and watch it," Dadiji said, pushing herself to her feet.

This all happened over twenty years ago, but Maya could still remember the feel of Dadiji's hand on her shoulder as they made their way downstairs. Dadiji always moved slowly, but somehow it seemed like they were on the dusty street in seconds.

"I can see the man now," she told Dr. Bernard. "But I only remember a few things he said; I was so scared of him, I must have been dissociating, seeing it as a dream, because the reality was too upsetting. I remember he had a lot of spit in his mouth, and when he talked it would collect where his lips met, sometimes spray out onto his cheeks."

"Who was he?" Dr. Bernard asked. He must have been engaged in her story, or impressed at her self-analysis; they'd just reviewed dissociation in her seminar last week. Otherwise Maya would have expected him to comment on her fixation on the spit.

"The girl's father," Maya said. "At least that's what he told us. Whoever he was, he made her beg—the goddess outfit was supposed to inspire pious people to give more—and he felt she wasn't earning enough. He told Dadiji that soon he would have to seek other employment for her, he had so many other mouths to feed. It made Dadiji mad, I could tell, but I didn't get it at the time."

"Prostitution?"

"I guess. But Dadiji would never acknowledge that, she's a lady; she pretends everyone exists on her level instead of stooping to theirs. She played along and said how convenient, she happened to need an apprentice for her cook. She pulled out cash from the waist of her sari, and handed it to the man." Maya could see the wad of rupees in Dadiji's hand, the man's fingers, crusted in dirt, as he took them. She glanced up at Dr. Bernard. "The first month's salary, I guess." She had no idea what the arrangement was, really, but she didn't want Dr. Bernard to think Dadiji bought the girl, at Maya's request. That's not what happened at all, of course, but it had to be made clear. Dr. Bernard couldn't be expected to understand India; he didn't have Dadiji to explain it to him.

"Did the man ever see his daughter again?" Dr. Bernard asked.

"I don't know. I never saw him again, but I suppose that doesn't mean she didn't bump into him, or even go visit him. I wouldn't know; I never really hung out much with Parvati. She seemed so much older at the time, and so remote. I guess I was a little afraid of her." Maybe she should have asked if Parvati ever saw her father, at some point over all those trips to India, Maya thought now. Parvati and Priya must be roughly the same age, although somehow that was hard to believe. Six years older, Priya always made it clear she considered herself superior to Maya in every way, but she still spent more time with her than anyone else. She wasn't above playing UNO or even Barbies. Once, at Dadiji's house, Maya left her Barbies on the kitchen table, and when Priya marched her back in there to clean them up, they found Parvati holding one, twirling the doll's blond ponytail with her free hand. The dolls were actually just Skippers, their mother wouldn't buy Maya Barbies even though their clothes were so much nicer, but Parvati was staring at this Skipper as if she were Christmas Dream Barbie or Malibu Princess.

"Do you want to play with us?" Maya asked.

At the sound of her voice, Parvati dropped Skipper on the floor, then bent at the knees to pick her up, bringing the doll up to touch her forehead before reaching her out toward Priya. Parvati's downcast eyes were full of tears.

"It's okay." Priya took the doll in her right hand and touched Parvati's shoulder with her left. "They're babyish, I know, but I still play them with Maya. It can be..."

Parvati rushed past them both, holding her arm where Priya's hand had been, as if the touch had hurt. The sound of Parvati's skirts swishing drowned out whatever Priya had said; Maya never got to hear what Priya thought playing Barbies with her could be.

That night, in the dark, Maya asked Priya why Parvati had acted so weird.

"She doesn't want to play with us," Priya said. "Not everyone does."

Maya opened her mouth but Priya said, "Good night, Maya," before she could ask why not. She had been excited at the thought of another person joining their games, but lying in the dark Maya realized she was a little relieved Parvati didn't want to play Barbies. Priya was her sister and had to love her. Why would someone as beautiful and mysterious as Parvati want to play with a baby like Maya anyway?

"I guess that for a long time, I still thought of her as a goddess," Maya said to Dr. Bernard now, laughing at how limited her point of view had been as a child; she'd just accepted what she'd seen, questioning so little about the world around her. "That might not even be her name, maybe it was just the name she used when she begged."

Dr. Bernard looked at his notes. "Parvati?"

"Girls can be called Parvati, but it's a goddess's name, originally. Parvati was Shiva's consort, the perfect wife. First he was married to Kali, this black, terrifying goddess who wears a necklace of men's skulls. But he was scared of her, so one day she peeled off her dark skin to reveal a gentler incarnation. Parvati is Kali's lighter side, both literally and figuratively." Maya paused for Dr. Bernard to ask questions, but he was apparently uninterested in Hindu theological genealogy.

"And Parvati, the girl, I mean, she still lives with your grandmother?"

"She's a woman now; married a guy, has a baby girl crawling around upstairs. I'll ask Parvati if that's her real name when I visit in December," Maya said, to please Dr. Bernard. But she knew she wouldn't. She would never remind Parvati of the day they met. It would be too painful; a father that abusive, that eager to abandon her.

"Something always made me keep my distance from Parvati," Maya said. "I knew she wasn't really a goddess, but I also felt she wasn't a kid like me. And her story was so sad. Maybe I thought sorrow was contagious, that her bad luck could attach itself to me. Whatever it was, I wanted no part of the life I had seen, that awful man."

Even now, the memory frightened her. Before the man left, walking unsteadily, his hand around the rupees creating a bulge in his right pocket, Dadiji had whispered to him, softly but steadily, "I do not want to see your face here again; do not come looking for her," and put an arm around Parvati's shoulder, an arm Maya liked to think of as her own.

"Come back? For her?" He spat on the ground. "You think I am a sinner, a bad man. But you will see, that girl will try your patience, too. That," he said, pointing at Parvati, "that is a wicked child. She has evil in her."

Maybe that's why she had steered clear of her for so many years, Maya thought, but didn't say. To Maya, at that age, evil meant wicked stepmothers and poisoned apples and princes trapped in frog's bodies. Maybe she was simply scared of Parvati.

Maya didn't share this insight with Dr. Bernard. It was too new, and she was embarrassed to think that instead of pitying the poor girl, she'd believed that sadistic man, had been afraid of attracting Parvati's attention and bringing all that evil crashing down on herself.

.   .   .

"Congratulations!" Heidi mashed Sanjay's face into her lips, distorting his grin for a good four seconds before she pulled away, leaving a red imprint of her mouth against his right cheek. Heidi had been Maya's college roommate for four years at Dartmouth, which meant that she'd known Sanjay for almost as long as she had known Maya herself; Sanjay was only a year older and had done his undergrad at Middlebury, visiting them at least once a semester. Still, Maya had seniority here.

"He's *my* cousin!" Maya yelled. "Let me at him!" She pushed back her chair and walked around Heidi's so she could lean over and hug Sanjay. This was why he'd come to New York a night early and asked Maya to arrange dinner; it wasn't just that he wanted her to meet Amrita, he was going to marry her. She glanced at Amrita, who was sitting demurely, staring at a radiant-cut engagement ring Maya had failed to notice before. She seemed a little quiet so far, but she was definitely beautiful, with a thick mane of glossy black hair framing a face that seemed to glow in the dim light. Her skin was the color of caramel and it looked even smoother and richer, even more delicious because she was sitting next to Scott, whose pale skin had flushed pink in the overheated Italian restaurant. Their family would think Amrita was perfect. Maybe that's why Maya hadn't warmed to her on sight; she was almost too perfect, not one of her manicured nails chipped, not a speck of lipstick on her teeth, and her turquoise button-down didn't gape at the chest despite her shapely figure. Maya made herself relinquish Sanjay and walked over to Amrita's chair to embrace her, too. Amrita squeezed Maya's back but pulled away so quickly that Maya was left standing next to her chair with one arm still on Amrita's shoulder, wondering how to gracefully reclaim her limb.

"This calls for champagne!" Scott motioned to the waiter, then grabbed Maya's free hand, pulling her onto his lap, rescuing her from the one-sided embrace. She sank onto his knee and leaned against the warmth of his body.

"So my parents know, of course, and yours, Seema-auntie, Ajit-uncle," Sanjay said.

Maya kept smiling, and told herself she was glad they knew, glad that Sanjay was giving her parents—and his—what they wanted, a pairing of two successful desi kids who would have children who looked just like them and who could afford to fly the adorable moppets to India once a year. And, even more than that, confirmation that the family could continue to live their in-between lives with ease and unity.

"Mohan knows, too, and Priya," Sanjay continued. "But I swore them to secrecy—I wanted to tell you in person."

"You told my brother and sister before me!" Maya gave her most dramatic sigh. "They get to do everything good first. And you're supposed to like me best."

"I'm sorry, you're a psychiatrist? An adult?" Sanjay shook his head. "Look, I knew I'd be coming to New York and I wanted to tell you in person. All of you. The wedding's in January—that's when we could get the most time off—and you're all invited."

"Great! Obviously, we're going early to buy appropriate clothes." Heidi was now a fashion editor at *Glamour* in charge of their "real women" coverage, stories like "The Best Bathing Suit for YOUR Body," which made every June issue a bestseller. She had been on some talk show this morning, overseeing ambush makeovers of audience members; Maya had woken up early to watch her. Heidi had removed her heavy TV makeup, but Maya could see a smear of dark lipstick had made its way onto the tip of her tooth. It looked a little like blood, but her expression was too joyous to be scary.

"Fix your lipstick, Hei," Maya said, but Heidi kept right on talking, scheming how to get more vacation time out of her top editor.

"And will you dance with some of my friends from home at the sangeet, Maya?" Amrita asked. "It turns out only three of them can make the trip, but the dance is choreographed for four; Sanjay says you're a fabulous dancer."

"What's a sangeet?" Heidi asked.

"It means 'music together' in Sanskrit, but it's the night before the wedding, kind of like a rehearsal dinner," Maya explained. "Only the guests dance and sing and do skits to entertain the bride and groom."

"Way better than a rehearsal dinner!" Heidi crowed. "Good thing we've been taking those Bollywood dance classes."

"You take Bollywood dance?" Amrita asked.

Heidi looked at her evenly. "Don't be racist."

The caramel color of Amrita's skin flushed more toward corn syrup.

"Just kidding!" Heidi picked up a now-filled champagne glass and raised it toward Amrita. "It's a great workout. Cheers!"

"Watch it, Hei!" Sanjay hit Heidi on the shoulder. "Amrita's not part of the family yet—you can't bust on her until after the wedding."

Amrita was smiling again, but Maya could see she was clasping her hands together under the table. Poor girl; this crowd could be tough to break into. If Maya had suspected the big news, she would have insisted they have dinner just the three of them, so that she could get to know Amrita better. Sanjay hadn't talked much about her, he had been so busy trying to establish himself at work. He and Amrita had been at Wharton together, but didn't start dating until the last semester of their MBAs. They'd moved to Chicago, where each had landed a consulting job, about four months ago, right after graduation. They couldn't have been together more than eight months. That seemed awfully fast, Maya thought. And not just because she and Scott had been together, off and on, for almost seven years. She pulled Scott's pale hands close around her waist.

The engagement might seem sudden to her because Amrita was a stranger; all Maya knew about the girl was that she was a year younger than Sanjay. And that she was Indian, which was all that her parents, and Sanjay's, too, would have needed to know. Maya would have liked a chance to talk to her in a less rowdy setting. But Sanjay was in his glory. He loved sparring with Heidi, and made it a point to hole up in some obscure bar to watch far-flung soccer matches with Scott whenever he was in town. Sanjay had specifically asked that both Heidi and Scott be present. They'd all known each other for so long now, they could be a bit insular, even if they didn't mean to be. She'd make an effort to be more welcoming.

"Don't worry, I'll tell you all Sanjay's embarrassing secrets." Maya smiled at Amrita.

"Show some respect," Sanjay warned. "I'm your elder."

"By ten months!" She turned back toward Amrita. "But Sanjay was a year ahead at school, so I always thought he was so cool. And he used to tell me all the things he learned from the big kids, like he'd been doing recon."

Scott, who knew where this story was going, was already laughing; Maya could feel his body shaking beneath hers.

"So this one time," she continued, "I remember it so clearly, I can see the Members Only jacket he was wearing! Anyway, we were on the swing set at Arjun-uncle's house, and Sanjay makes this announcement. He leans over and says, 'So. There's this thing called 'fuck.'" She took a breath, then added, "Now, keep in mind that we weren't even allowed to watch *Sesame Street* growing up because Kruti-masi—your future mother-in-law—wasn't sure what the Spanish words meant. It's like she always sort of suspected they were dirty."

Heidi was chuckling so hard she choked on her champagne. Maya looked at Amrita. Nothing. Not even a smile. So maybe it wasn't high comedy, but anyone who really knew Sanjay, who saw how his whole urbandaddy persona was a reaction to the extreme geekiness of their shared childhood, would get how the story so captured his essence. Maybe not a belly laugh, but a little smile for the earnest, dorky boy he once was? Amrita just sort of stared. And now Maya had gone and cursed in front of the perfect Indian bride.

Amrita took a sip of champagne. At least she drank alcohol.

"What about you, Scott, are you in for the wedding?" Amrita asked.

Was that a dig? Had Sanjay told her Maya's parents didn't know she was dating Scott?

"I go where the boss tells me," Scott said, and kissed Maya's cheek.

"Really?" Maya asked.

"Really?" Heidi echoed.

"Your wish is my command."

"Well, there is one thing I'd like to do right now, something Sanjay and I used to do when we were little," Maya said. "You know, in moments of great joy, and when our parents weren't around to watch."

"And what was that?" Scott asked.

"'Summer Lovin'.'"

"No!" Sanjay groaned, just as Heidi decreed, "Genius!"

"Karaoke it is," Scott said. "I'll call and see if we can reserve a private room."

Maya stood to let him leave the table and smiled at Amrita in a way that she hoped seemed genuine. "You can be Sandy," she said.

"In honor of the occasion," Heidi supplied.

As they left the restaurant, Sanjay leaned over to Maya and whispered, "Great idea—the singing. Amrita was the soloist at Wharton graduation."

"She's lovely."

Sanjay was looking over his shoulder to hail a cab so Maya wasn't sure whether she actually heard, or imagined, him whispering, "You haven't done so bad for yourself."

Chapter Two

Maya shifted onto her side and exhaled deeply so that Scott would think she was still asleep. She could feel his arm brush past her; he was performing the usual stretching and groaning that preceded him opening his eyes. She resisted the urge to roll over and settle in under his arm, to let the sound of his heart beating lull her back to sleep; she had to get on with the day. Finally he kissed her, his lips soft against the pulsing vein in her temple, and stepped over her onto the floor toward the bathroom.

Maya could feel her heart beating as if it were somehow synchronized to the sound of the water running as Scott showered. A couple of years ago, when she'd moved to the city and they'd first gotten back together, Maya taught him how to use conditioner; she'd just seen *Out of Africa* and thought a feminist interpretation of the hair-washing scene was in order, and besides, it was time for Scott to step up the grooming routine that he'd developed during Boy Scout camp. But she wished he'd skip the conditioner this time, and go back to the days of the three-minute shower. Scott wouldn't be able to hear her if she made the call now, but there was no way she could do that, not with him in the apartment, naked, even if he was behind a closed door. Last night had been the perfect blending of her family with her life in New York. But Sanjay was young, he had his own life, with no expectations of her. There was no place for Scott in this morning's situation.

She rolled over violently so she could no longer see the alarm clock flipping its red digits, and started the pranayama breathing Nanaji had shown her on the first visit to India she could remember. Maya had been five or so when her mother's father pulled her onto his lap and brought her hands up to his nose. "Feel my breath," he said, teaching her to regulate her own. Now she did this breathing at the hospital when things got tough. It wasn't conspicuous; the psych patients were too concerned with their own internal dramas to notice and the attendings just thought she was taking deep breaths, which, basically, she was. But this morning the pranayama wasn't calming her. The water quieted and Scott was standing over her, adjusting his glasses, his wet hair dripping onto her skin.

"You okay?" he asked.

"Just tired," Maya said, her eyes still closed, her voice hoarse from last night's karaoke extravaganza. Maya had performed all her signature songs: "Midnight Train to Georgia" with Heidi, Scott, Sanjay, and even Amrita acting as the Pips, then a reprise of "Summer Lovin'," with Scott singing Danny Zuko's part. And Maya had even come up with a brilliant business idea, flipping through the pages of Korean songs at the back of the songbook: Bollywood karaoke, with all the hits from the classics and new films, too. It would cater to a desi crowd, of course, but there could be phonetic subtitles on the videos for non–Indian Americans; Scott and Heidi both said they'd do it in a heartbeat. The idea still held up in the glare of the morning sunshine. But Maya herself wasn't doing so well. Last night Heidi had said Maya was on fire; today she felt like ashes, gray and insubstantial. "I'm not ready for the psych ER," she whispered.

"I'll reset the alarm for fifteen minutes from now." Scott let one hand rest on her sheet-swaddled hip as he fussed with the clock; she wanted to seize his fingers and pull him back into bed. But med school had taught her discipline and time management skills. So instead she grabbed his hand and kissed it good-bye, before mumbling "call you later" and rolling over to his side of the bed. She waited for his footsteps down the hall to stop and the elevator button to ring before opening her eyes, then pulled the afghan her mother had knitted up from the foot of the bed, wrapped it around her naked body, and dialed.

"Are you there?" Maya curled her knees up to her chest. "Come on, Ma. Something happened and you're not telling me."

Maya had been expecting the news since Pops left for India three weeks ago, after Dadiji had a syncopal episode and had been taken into the hospital to be monitored. Aside from sessions with Dr. Bernard and the occasional sharp pain when she saw something in the face of a newspaper vendor or a lady sweeping the stoop of her import shop that reminded her of her grandmother, Maya had made an effort not to ruminate on Dadiji's illness; last night she hadn't thought of it at all. But sometime in the early morning she'd opened her eyes and felt weighted down with the heavy certainty that something terrible had happened. And that she hadn't been there to help when it did.

The feeling had grown stronger each second she waited for Scott to leave the apartment, the hall, the building. But she had to be sure he was gone before calling. Otherwise, Seema would have known that her daughter had awakened next to a naked man, his white flesh sticking to hers in the overheated studio, minutes earlier. She would have been able to sense it through the phone line, and Maya couldn't even imagine how she would react. Aside from Dadiji, her mother was the strongest woman Maya knew, quiet but powerful. Maya was not entirely convinced that if her mother learned of Scott, Seema wouldn't turn into a fierce black goddess like Kali, and vaporize Maya, or Scott, or the world, with one fearsome glance.

She could hear her mother breathing through the phone line, could picture her standing in the kitchen in Kalamazoo, waiting for the water to boil for chai, pulling her cardigan tight against her sari. Seema had picked up the phone on the first ring, but still she said nothing. Finally, she wailed softly. "I was going to call your sister first, before she took the girls to day care," Seema said at last. "Your Dadiji died in her sleep. Your father was with her; it was a good death; she lived a long life."

Now Seema was crying into the phone, between sobs saying she needed to call Priya. Maya heard the phone click as Seema h   g up, dropped it onto the floor, and knelt in front of the altar on her windowsill, a brightly patterned tin box filled with flowers; a statue of Ganesh, remover of obstacles; her paternal grandfather's mala—she had inherited the prayer beads when he died; and photos of her ancestors, both dead and living. There was a snapshot of her maternal grandfather as a young lawyer, and a recent black-and-white of Dadiji smiling her toothless, gaping grin. Losing Dadiji was not unexpected, but it still felt like a shock, to know that their family was without a matriarch. And Maya herself was now without the one person who had always taken her seriously. Along with her grandmother, she had lost some of her own certainty that she had a place in the world, and that it was a good one.

Maya had first realized that Dadiji had quiet, but unshakable, confidence in her seventeen years ago, during the last summer they'd all gone to India together. Priya and Mohan called it "The Worst Summer." Mohan had been eighteen, about to go off to Penn, and bitter about missing his last summer before college to accompany his parents and little sisters to India. Priya hadn't wanted to be there either; she had some AP classes coming up and said she wanted to work on bio and French over the summer. But really, Priya at sixteen hated India, hated the dust that ruined her shoes and got under her toenails, the showers so cold she could only stand to wash her hair every other day, and the way all the relatives felt it was their right to comment on her weight, skin, and clothing. "So much slimmer than last summer, but then last summer you were almost a little too-too, hey?" "Priya, how did you make the spots go away? If only my Bubloo could get rid of his spots, I would happily update his biodata photo."

Maya was the only one of the three who was thrilled to be going, filled with uncomplicated joy. In India she could run around with the neighborhood kids and eat bhutta, fire-roasted masala corn on the cob she bought on the street with rupees Dadiji pressed into her hand. Grown-ups didn't have to drive her everywhere or watch her all the time. She could lie on the roof terrace and read the entire Anne of Green Gables series if she wanted, and no one would tell her there was homework to do or cooking to help with. And in between chapters she could watch monkeys swinging on the power lines.

Pops was glad, too—he'd taken a two-month sabbatical from his job with the city and had been talking for months leading up to the trip about all the things he needed to bring to show "the fellows"—photos of Mohan's graduation, and the car right after he'd waxed it, and gifts, cologne maybe, or, for his best friend, Timberland shoes. He'd talked so much about it that Seema had insisted, "Not one more word about your playmates! You're worse than the children." The scolding drove him outside to wash the car again.

At the time, Maya thought her mother was, just a little bit, jealous. Seema could only come for three weeks—her partners in the practice wouldn't be able to get along without her much longer. But even when they got to India, Seema didn't seem as relaxed as Ajit. She was always with Dadiji, adjusting her meds, or overseeing Parvati.

"Go out, enjoy the town, enjoy your children," Dadiji said to her one morning. "This summer will not last forever." And Maya put *Anne of Windy Poplars* away, because she knew there would be no reading that day. Pops was off with his friends, so Seema led the kids on a walk up to the fortress. On the way, she smiled more than Maya had ever seen her, and pointed out things. "This is where Nanaji would take me for kulfi when I got top marks at school," she said, indicating a sweetshop. "Every term!"

"Was it good, Ma?" Maya clung to Seema's hand and chattered at her, so she wouldn't notice that Mohan wasn't listening; Maya could hear the Grateful Dead coming from his Discman even walking three steps ahead of him. And Priya kept swooping down to wipe dust off her red Reeboks with a tissue. At the temple, Mohan took off his earphones long enough for the pandit to wrap mauli around his wrist, but put them back on right after. Priya pushed her holy bracelet back up her arm, as if to keep it from contaminating her tissue-clutching hand. But Seema dropped Maya's hand and stood very still as the pandit wrapped mauli around her wrist, as if she were thinking hard.

After, they walked down the back side of the fortress and Maya could see the reservoir below them. Leaves and litter bobbed along the edges, but in the middle it sparkled. Maya ran ahead, trying to pull Seema behind her.

"It is time to be preparing lunch," Seema said, but she followed. They were ahead of Priya and Mohan, so they saw Ajit first, strolling with his friends on the other side. Maya was about to shout "Pops" out to him; he had shown her that the lake was an ellipse, and, in the right place, you could hear someone talking all the way from across the other side. It was geometry, he had said. But Seema tugged her hand. "Some people do nothing but gallivant," she whispered, but Maya heard and stood still.

"That was my first wedding, right here." Ajit's voice floated over to them and Maya felt like she might fall down into the dust; Priya wouldn't have enough tissues to wipe her clean. "To a rag doll!" Ajit laughed. "Imagine the things they made us do back then! The astrologer said my chart and Seema's were inauspicious together, that mine showed my wife would die young. So the pandit had me marry a doll, and then we threw her in the lake here. Boom, dead wife. The problem, it was solved."

Maya was relieved that Pops hadn't had a real wife before, but she could feel Seema standing even more rigid behind her.

"And it's a good thing the pandit insisted," Ajit was saying. "What if the charts were right? To raise three children alone would be impossible. There are moments of pleasure, like us here together now, but life is work. A man needs a wife. I try to tell that to Mohan, it doesn't matter who catches your eye now, what is important is who is your karma, whether you like it or not. With me…" But they had started walking again and her father's words were lost as they left the magic spot on the lake—the foci, he called it.

Maya could hear her siblings' footsteps and then the music from Mohan's earphones: "Riding that train, high on cocaine."

"Mohan, will you never turn that racket off?" Seema demanded. She turned and yanked the square body of the Discman out of Mohan's hands and shoved it onto her hip, as if to secure it in the waist of the sari she wore daily. But in anticipation of the dusty field trip, she had put on one of Dadiji's old salwar kameez—Maya had helped her pick it out that morning. The Discman slid down the front of her top, bounced off the dirt, and landed with a splash in the reservoir. No one moved for a moment and then they heard footsteps and the booming voices of Pops and his fellows.

"Who is this cutesy?" one of the men said, patting Maya on the head. Seema reached out as if to swat the man's hand away, then started braiding Maya's hair instead, her hands moving briskly.

"She is cute, but she is intelligent, too, this is what counts," Pops said. Turning to Seema, he added, "Don't wait for me for lunch, I'll be along later."

Maya could feel the braid getting tighter.

As the men moved on and Pops passed Seema she looked at him and said, "You will be buying your son a new CD player when we get back to Michigan. This one was no good."

They walked home in silence that seemed even louder without the music from Mohan's earphones, which he had shoved in his pocket. Maya tried to think of something to say. Finally, almost at the house, they passed a boy Maya's age working at the shoeshine stand, mending Dadiji's slippers as Parvati waited.

"We're lucky, Ma, right?" Maya said, repeating a statement her father made every time he saw a child laborer. "Lucky we were born as us, that we live in Kalamazoo. Not like that poor boy, like the kids who need to work."

Maya meant to cheer everyone up, to remind them to be grateful and optimistic, like Anne of Green Gables herself. But Seema looked hard at the boy and finally said, "Yes and no. That boy, and Parvati, too, they work hard, but they belong here."

Inside, too anxious to read, Maya asked Dadiji where she belonged. When she was here, she realized, even though it felt as if her life back home ceased to exist, her friends and teachers were all still there, going to the park or the library, getting ice cream, continuing to live without her. But in Kalamazoo, she didn't have Dadiji, or the monkeys.

"That is an important question." Dadiji motioned for Maya to come sit on the bed. "But it has a rather easy answer." She paused to consider. "Easy and hard at the same time. It is not where your body is that matters, but where your mind is." She pulled Maya closer. "And because of this, Maya, wherever you are is exactly where you need to be."

The abandoned phone beeped insistently. Maya set it as a backup alarm in case she slept through the clock. Now it demanded attention, bringing Maya back to her apartment and her adult life, which had just become more uncertain. She wasn't convinced that right now she was exactly where she needed to be. Maya picked up the cell, pressed the Off button, and lay down on the couch with her hand still gripping the phone, thinking that this emptiness must be how her newly atheist patients felt when they decided there really was no God. That they were alone.

The light shifted; somewhere, beyond the high-rises, the sun was setting. Maya stood on the curb, her duffel bag swinging slightly from the straps she held in the crook of her elbow, bumping into her calf. Her sister had decided everything by the time Maya had spoken to her between patients. With a medical practice, two daughters, a husband, and a house with guest rooms, Priya was the one who got to stay put in a crisis. Their mother would fly to Boston from Kalamazoo, Maya would take the evening JetBlue from New York. They'd all converge at Priya's home in Chestnut Hill, which she described, when giving directions, as a Colonial, but which sparkled with newness on the inside. Priya had taken something old, gutted it, and filled it with the shiny cleanliness she considered life's highest virtue. If only she could do the same to the entire subcontinent of India, she might consider bringing the girls there someday.

A town car rounded the corner, and Maya knew if she looked up, she'd see Heidi peeking above a tinted window rolled halfway down. Heidi was heading to Chicago, a major market, to celebrate the massive September issue by hosting a fall fashion show at an upscale mall in a northern suburb tomorrow. When Maya texted her earlier, to tell her about Dadiji, Heidi said the only thing that could redeem the whole heinous mall trip would be if she could give Maya a lift to JFK. Maya had been glad to save the sixty-dollar cab fare, but when the car service pulled up, she wished she hadn't agreed to the ride; the black Lincoln looked so funereal.

Which was ridiculous; Dadiji's funeral would have no heavy black cars, no mourners in new dark suits. Dadiji's body would be wrapped in a white widow's sari, then draped in red cloth, covered in orange marigolds, and carried through town by Pops and the other men, moving in time to their own chanting. Maya wished she were with them all in India, instead of on this incongruously bright New York sidewalk, about to slide into a villainous-looking car.

"I'm so sorry, My." Heidi reached her long, tan arms toward Maya as she opened the door, causing a row of gold bangles to jingle together on her wrist. Maya let herself be hugged, then slid into the car, lying across the broad backseat, her head in Heidi's lap.

"I'll never get to meet her." Heidi's voice floated above Maya's ear.

"She already loved you; ever since you sent her that perfume from the office."

"But she's a Das family legend. And when I think of India and imagine Sanjay's wedding, I picture her grinning in that photo on your windowsill."

"Yeah, I know."

"The wedding's still on?"

Maya nodded. "She wasn't his grandmother." Sanjay was a cousin on Seema's side, so mourning Dadiji wouldn't cast a pall over his wedding in January. It was good he was getting married; the ceremony would give her parents something to look forward to, it might even make India without Dadiji seem less empty. Thinking of India without her grandmother made Maya feel tired and achy, as if she had the flu. But she couldn't fall asleep yet; she still needed to check in, go through security. She pulled Heidi's hand in front of her, making the bracelets clink against each other. "These are fancy."

"Graft. From the Bergdorf's PR girl I had lunch with. Take them."

"No, no. I'll borrow them sometime." She pushed Heidi's hand away into the air above her head. "No one I work with brought me presents today. Poor, poor Maya."

In fact, Maya felt lucky to have spent the day working in the Emergency Psychiatric Unit, where it was a safe bet most people were undergoing worse crises than hers. There had been lots of busywork, making notes, consulting files, so it was distracting on a practical level as well as a psychological one, calming the same way running along the river was, concentrating on putting one foot in front of the other. The universe didn't seem to notice that Maya's life had changed, and the EPU was the same as ever. She'd written prescriptions, admitted patients brought in by the police and the outreach docs, and refused admittance to two of the regular border-lines who were always hanging around, relentlessly trying to get sent to the psych ER where they'd get a warm bed, a peanut butter and jelly sandwich, and the attention they desperately craved.

"I did see this one interesting woman." Maya sat up, suddenly wanting to talk about something besides Dadiji's death, and began describing a schizophrenic patient who had been doing well for years until she went off her medication. The woman was in her mid-forties and from California; there was no way Heidi would know her. And besides, Heidi could be trusted, she really seemed to care about Maya's patients. Maya didn't describe the woman she'd seen today, but she could visualize her clearly. The patient was a redhead, except for a few wiry strands of gray, with light green eyes, and a history of self-destructive behavior. The circles under her eyes were the dark-est color on her face.

"So I asked why she does things to hurt herself," Maya told Heidi, remembering the puffy pink scars on the woman's milky arm. "And she says she's a terrible person, has done some really bad things. Finally she tells me that she *used to* think she was the reincarnation of Hitler, and she feels really bad about the Jews."

Heidi snorted, shocked, but Maya continued. The patient and her problems were more sinister, but also infinitely more fascinating, than Maya's own. "She's not stupid," Maya continued. "She's seen enough therapists to know that you can't tell a doc you still believe you're Hitler or you'll never get released. But obviously, the situation's not resolved. She's lucid, back on the meds, but—"

"You're perfect for her!" Heidi interrupted.

"Because?"

"Because you can just say, 'Look, I'm Hindu. I know all about reincarnation, and that's not how it works. You'd have to be born the day Hitler died. There's no way you're him.'" Heidi folded her hands in her lap with a clang of bracelets.

Maya laughed hard, for the first time since "Summer Lovin'" the night before.

"Seriously!"

Maya leaned toward the carry-on bag at her feet, peeling the backs of her knees off the soft leather seat. "I couldn't do that; if you take away schizophrenics' delusions, they can crumble." She pulled out her e-ticket printout and driver's license as the oyster-shaped terminal rolled into view. "Besides, that's not how reincarnation works."

"Too bad." Heidi sighed. "It would be such a relief to know you're not Hitler."

Maya wished there was something Heidi—or someone— could say to relieve herself of the guilt she'd been carrying all day, the feeling that she should have skipped the start of her second year of residency to go see Dadiji once more. The last time she'd actually seen her grandmother, in January, Maya had been prickly, sweaty and dusty from running around Jodhpur, annoyed at the cramps making her stomach twist. She was missing Scott, they had just celebrated their one-year anniversary of getting back together, and she had wanted to tell Dadiji about him, she felt sure Dadiji would say what she had in the past, that Maya was exactly where she needed to be, that she was a smart girl who made good choices. But what if telling Dadiji worried her? She couldn't think of one mixed-race couple Dadiji knew, maybe it was just beyond the scope of her imagination that such a thing could work. And when they had shown Dadiji pictures of Priya's wedding in Kalamazoo, no one mentioned that Priya had also had a small, Muslim ceremony in New Jersey with Tariq's family. Maybe telling Dadiji about Scott would be handing her a burden she would feel obliged to keep secret from her son and daughter-in-law. And if Dadiji didn't give Maya her blessing, then what? If she categorically refused to consider Scott as Maya's future, that meant Maya would either have to lose the support of the one person who had always believed in her, exactly as she was, or consider the fact that maybe Scott wasn't the best choice for her future, if not for herself, then certainly not for her family.

In the end, she was just too tired and irritable and nauseated to tell Dadiji anything about Scott; she wasn't up to presenting the situation in the best light. Now she wished she had taken the time to talk to her, to get her point of view, to share a final confidence. She hated that the last image Dadiji had of her was as a PMS-riddled, sweaty American. She should have gone to India and taken care of Dadiji in her old age, been holding her when she died. It should have been Maya, not Parvati, who was the last person Dadiji saw; her real granddaughter, not a hired substitute.

"I come back right after the event tomorrow, but I can easily arrange for a car service for when you get back?" Heidi offered, bringing Maya's thoughts back to the airport, where the sun was glaring off the glass-and-steel doors.

"Scott'll come get me; he'll probably have to work on Sunday, so he can use a car service anyway." Maya unfolded her e-ticket printout so she wouldn't have to look at Heidi. "He offered not to go in this weekend, to rent a car and drive to Boston after work, so he could be with us. But it's so not the time for them to get to know him."

"You're going to have to tell them at some point." Heidi reached out and stilled the ticket Maya was fluttering in her hand. "I totally got it when we were in college, it would have been really awkward. I mean, at that graduation dinner, when you insisted on bringing your 'friend' Scott…"

"Ugh! And they were *so* nice to your horrible date—what was that guy's name?"

"Jon. Jon with no *h*. The missing *h* is for his missing sense of humor."

"Yeah, they loved Jon with no *h* but they didn't say a word to Scott all night."

"Your dad did ask him the score of the game after he got back from the bathroom."

"But that was Pops trying to impress Jon with no *h* with his regular American manliness, not trying to bond with Scott."

Heidi laughed. "Okay, but now you're adults. It's serious. Your parents have all kinds of rules, I know, but they just need time to get used to him. He loves you."

"I love him, too!" Looking at Heidi in the sunlit window, Maya shaded her eyes with her hand. "But he's been so busy starting at the firm, I couldn't inflict them on him." Seema was the only person Maya knew who was more stubborn than herself. If she kept bringing Scott around, Seema could easily keep ignoring him. Or, worse, what if Seema started ignoring Maya? Her mother was annoying, but Maya still talked to her daily.

"Once they see how good he is to you, Ajit-uncle and Seema-auntie will come around!" Heidi insisted. "They're fine with Priya's husband, and he's not Hindu."

But he wasn't white either, Maya thought, but didn't say. And they weren't so fine with him. They hadn't gone to the Muslim ceremony, just to the dinner after. Priya told Maya she'd better not attend either, just bring Ma and Pops to the restaurant and try and do some damage control. Not that she saw what the big deal was, Priya had said. Neither their family nor Tariq's were superreligious and they were culturally so similar, that's what mattered. His doctor parents dragged him to India every summer, too, and he'd never been to an R-rated movie until college either. These were the things that shaped you.

Still, as they sat alone in the empty function room of the restaurant, waiting for the guests from the ceremony to stream in while Pops pretended to watch a football game and nursed a Diet Sierra Mist over at the restaurant's bar, Seema had leaned over to Maya and whispered, "Promise me you won't disappoint us, too." Maya never told Priya.

Things had gotten better since the girls were born; Seema adored them. But Heidi didn't see the way her mother looked at Tariq when he wasn't facing her, hear the disapproving clicks she made with her tongue when Priya mentioned plans to go to her in-laws' house for Eid. Maya wanted to tell Heidi she was being naïve, that her family wasn't a made-for-TV movie that would end with everyone coming together in peace, love, and understanding. But, really, she wanted to believe that Heidi was right. "They're going to have to come around at some point," she said finally. "I can't imagine giving him up. Or them." Maya opened the car door, shading her eyes with her e-ticket, and pushed her bag onto the curb in front of her. "But it wouldn't be doing him any favors to out him as my honky boyfriend now, while the whole family's grieving. They might even dissemble, associate him with this trauma. Maybe around the holidays, or in the new year, but not—"

"Of course. You'll know when it's time," Heidi said. The driver opened her door as she pulled a second pair of sunglasses out of her bag. "Take these; they were free."

"I have glasses, I just forgot them." Maya stepped out of the sunshine.

"So borrow." Heidi got out of the car, walked around the driver pulling bags out of the trunk, and slid the glasses onto Maya's face, plunging her into comforting darkness.

It wasn't until Maya had already settled into her window seat and looked at her watch that she realized two gold bangles encircled her left wrist. She pushed them back to expose her watch face. It was seven thirty. In an hour and a half she'd be in Priya's house, with most of her family. A tear slid down her cheek as the portly, suited man in the aisle seat looked at her, then looked away.

Maya brought her legs onto her chair, crossing them like a kindergartner settling in for storytime. A plane was like the subway, a public version of private space, but she wanted to hide as much as she could, to make herself invisible. She reached into her shoulder bag for her lab coat, which she'd shoved in before leaving work, and pulled it around her shoulders. Turning her head to the dark window, she inhaled the comforting, antiseptic scent of the freshly laundered garment. She hadn't worn it today—she only got to wear a lab coat when she did consults on the medical floors. The supervisors felt it was too intimidating on the psych wards, creating distance between doctor and patient. It hadn't created distance her first year when Maya forgot to take it off and wore it on the subway, not realizing that by doing so she was inviting every straphanging businessman and homeless panhandler to show her his swollen glands or black toes.

Heidi always gave money to barefoot panhandlers; their exposed feet made her think, *Any one of those guys could be Jesus.* If Heidi had been a patient, this comment might have concerned Maya. But since she was her best friend, Maya wrote it off as magical thinking rooted in the three years of high school during which Heidi taught Sunday school to first graders at St. Demetrios Church in Keene, New Hampshire.

Despite the subway incident, Maya occasionally thought that the fact that she didn't wear a lab coat daily indicated that she should have chosen a different specialty, pediatrics or ob-gyn. She loved psych, but she might love the lab coat even more. It functioned as a shield, protecting her from the anxiety, anger, and fear that seemed to assail so many people she knew, not just her patients, but sometimes her friends as they tried to figure out their next steps, and, especially, her family as they protected the fragile world they had built, trying not to notice the things they had lost in building it.

Growing up, Maya thought that the reason her mother insisted on wearing acrylic-blend, hip-length cardigans over even her most beautiful saris was to hide her exposed stomach, which tended to fold into three comfortable rolls of flesh. Now she suspected that her mother's cardigans were lab coat substitutes, an attempt to bring home some of the control Seema felt at her family medicine practice, a place where people did what she said, took the medicine she prescribed, and followed her instructions instead of shutting her out with earphones or lives of their own that she was not invited to join.

It hadn't worked; she hadn't been able to control any of them. Mohan, Seema's beloved eldest, her only son, resisted medicine, going into advertising instead, which, to Maya's parents, was akin to renting a hovel and attempting to write the great Indian-American novel. Priya, the pretty daughter, was a doctor, and a real one, not a psychiatrist, but she had married a Muslim and seldom visited the temple anymore. And despite Priya's protestations that they were exposing their children to both religions and, besides, she was passing on all her parents' cultural traditions, along with a few of their religious ones, Priya's world was not a replica of Seema's, the compromise-life she created when she came to this country.

Now Maya, the youngest, was Seema's last chance at getting this right, at proving that the decision to leave India for America was a smart one, that a good—no, an even better—Indian life could be lived here. But Maya didn't seem to be making that happen any time soon. Stubborn and opinionated, Maya resembled her mother most, but she was still unmarried at twenty-seven, as alone in the world as Seema herself must have felt all these years, following her husband to a new country where she didn't know the rules but still had to abide by them. Even Seema's degree had been challenged; she was required to take the boards and complete a whole new residency, despite the fact that she'd had a spotless record and the highest grades of her year in India. The lab coat had restored her authority.

It usually did the same for Maya, made her feel in control. But tonight, as the plane started its descent and the lights of Boston grew larger, she felt lost and unprotected.

Chapter Three

By Saturday afternoon Seema and Maya had settled in to Priya's house in Chestnut Hill. The initial tearful hugs and Seema's polite greeting to and tight-lipped appraisal of Tariq, Priya's husband, had taken place on Friday. By now the new furniture had been admired, samosas had been fried, dal prepared, and Nisba and Yasmin were down for their afternoon nap. Tariq was at their practice, organizing the mess he and Priya left when they ducked out early on Friday. The women were finally alone together.

"I know Shalini has a conference, but I really think Mohan could have come, even if his wife is busy hanging out with all the other bright, beautiful stars of pediatric oncology." Priya was reclining on one of the couches that lined the walls of her living room, kicking her left foot against the arm of the couch with a rhythmic knock.

"So you think, Lovely, so you think," Seema said, and Maya saw her sister cringe at the childhood nickname. "Your girls are five and three, you no longer remember what it is to have a newborn at home." Seema shook her head back and forth slightly, the way she always did when she scolded her children.

"It's not like he's a single dad." Priya rose up onto her elbow, finally silencing her foot. The movement rippled the surface of her shiny bob, knocking her bangs into her almond-shaped eyes, and Maya stopped herself from reaching over to smooth them off her face so that she could watch Priya scowl more clearly. "Why can't Shalini's parents babysit? And six months is not exactly newborn."

"Her father is at the conference as well, to see Shalini get her award." Seema raised her voice. "It is right for Mohan to spend time with his children. Perhaps if Tariq—"

"Should we call Pops?" Lying on the couch perpendicular to Priya's, her feet in Seema's lap, Maya turned to face her mother. She felt a need to protect Tariq from Seema's criticism, however veiled. After what Heidi said in the cab, Maya was starting to see Tariq as a test case, paving the way for Scott, although, in the end, Tariq was, at least, Indian, even if Seema considered him the wrong kind. If Seema couldn't get through a day without making sharp, quiet jabs at Tariq, she'd never be able to get through a Thanksgiving sitting next to Scott. "What time is it in India, Ma?"

"It is too early there to make a call!" Seema's fingers tapped softly on Maya's ankles, figuring out the time difference. "Besides, your father is busy with preparations. Soon he will be taking Dadiji's ashes to Haridwar, returning them to the Ganges."

"I keep thinking about that funeral we saw the December before Nisba was born, remember, Priya?" Maya asked. "Those men carrying a body down the street, chanting?"

Seema leaned back against the couch. *"Ram nam satya hai."*

"The name of Ram is the only truth," translated Maya, who had studied Hindi in college to supplement her knowledge of Marwari, the local language the family spoke at home. Now she could speak both more fluently than her siblings, even though, or perhaps because, she was the only one who had been born in the U.S. Priya kicked the arm of Maya's couch, just below where her head rested.

"Yeah." Priya turned toward Seema. "Pops went to see who died, but you wouldn't let us follow him."

"Chee, chee, chee!" Seema raised her shoulders toward her ears as if she'd just poured hot tea into her lap. "Of course not! Women never go to the cremation ground. A man must be the chief mourner, to perform the kapal kriya."

Priya shut her eyes. Seema's eyes were shut, too, but not because she was sleepy; instead, Maya suspected she was trying to more fully imagine the scene at every cremation she'd missed since she was a curious, sheltered girl growing up in India. Seema smiled and said, "The chief mourner takes a pole from the pyre and cracks open the cranium of the deceased, so the prana can escape."

Priya sat up. "Pops is going to do that to Dadiji?"

"It is what the chief mourner does."

"That's disgusting!" Maya yelled.

"It is not disgusting," Seema insisted. "It is what Dadiji would want. It is necessary for the soul to move on."

"Well, necessary or not, if you think I'm going to whack you over the head when you die, you've got another think coming," Maya said over her mother's explanations.

"Mohan will do it," Priya interrupted them both.

"Priya!" Maya yelled at the exact moment that her mother shouted, "Lovely!"

"No, it's true." Priya sat up and winked at Maya so quickly that Maya wondered if she'd imagined it. "I mean, if you or Pops die here, we'll find one of those crematoria that have Hindu funerals, and they'll make up something more tasteful Mohan can do instead, breaking a symbolic pot or whatever."

"These children!" Seema inhaled deeply enough that it was

clear she meant for her daughters to hear her, the sigh equivalent of a stage whisper.

"But if you want to die in India, like a good Brahmin, then I guess Mohan will have to be your chief mourner and whack away—if Shalini isn't at some conference."

Seema's head bobbled back and forth even faster.

"I know, I know, *she saves children's lives!*" Priya intoned. "She cures leukemia!"

"You cure sick kids' diseases, too," Maya said; she could afford to be momentarily gracious, knowing that Shalini was the one person who made her almost-perfect sister feel inadequate. "Or at least their diaper rash."

Priya snorted a laugh and sank back down into the couch cushions. "Well, there's a lot more diaper rash in my future."

Seema was too busy glaring to understand, but Maya jumped off her couch and ran over to Priya. "Really?"

"Yup! Only Tariq knows. It's just six weeks, but I thought we could use some good news."

Maya leaned over to hug her sister, kicking her feet in a victory dance that shook the couch.

"Stop jostling my grandchild so!" Seema yelled. "A woman who is pregnant must be more careful!"

"Come on, Ma, you worked overnights when you were pregnant with me," Priya complained, but Maya stopped jumping.

"I had no choice! Now come here." Seema opened her arms, but instead of waiting for the girls to move, she stood and walked over to their couch. Kneeling on the floor she spread her arms across her adult daughters, squeezing whichever limb she could grip. Trapped by her mother's forearm, Priya sputtered, "I'm asphyxiating here," but Seema didn't release them until they heard Yasmin squalling "Mom! Mom!" down the hall. Finally Seema retreated, moving slowly back toward her armchair. Priya sprang off the couch and jogged off to investigate, leaving the room noticeably silent. Seema was beaming. Maya was happy for Priya, she really was. But a small part of her wished that she could be the reason her mother let herself relax briefly into a moment of pure joy.

Dinner that night was almost festive. The girls behaved, Tariq praised Seema's cooking, and she was unusually friendly to him, almost flirty, an adjective that no one would normally use to describe her, especially not her son-in-law.

"I hear that you are giving me another big-big gift, Tariq," Seema said after he complimented her dal. "I'll be back in eight months or so to collect it!"

The adults laughed and so did the girls, who had no idea what was funny.

"I wish Pops were here." Maya raked furrows in the remains of her rice.

"It is good that your father is in India," Seema said. "He is fulfilling his duties." Seema still worked in her family medicine practice three days a week, but since Ajit retired from his job with the city he spent at least three months of the year in India. No one begrudged him his time there; they knew that being in Jodhpur made him feel like the young man he had been when he left. Seema went back to India, too, but not as often, or for as long. She'd go for a wedding of one of her nephews or nieces, or the celebration of a child's birth, if it was the grandchild of one of her girlhood friends. Otherwise, she let her husband be the one to go. When Maya was growing up, Ajit had been the fun one, bringing home model planes and Legos to build fortresses in the basement on weekends, while Seema returned home from her practice so exhausted that it was a strain to supervise Maya doing her homework, and Priya cooking dinner. Now Maya suspected that Seema looked forward to these times when Ajit was away and Seema had her children all to herself, when she could be the fun parent. Whatever the reason, unless they were traveling with their children, Maya's parents saw no reason to return to their hometown together. They had already been fellow travelers, changing countries. But they weren't soul mates who delighted in each other's company. They were colleagues, getting the job of family-building and child-raising done, as their karma had decreed.

That's not what I want, Maya thought, and wondered how long it would be before everyone went to bed and she could call Scott, tell him about the baby, about how happy it made her, and also, a little bit envious. Scott wouldn't care that she was jealous; he knew how maddeningly perfect Priya was, how hard Maya tried to make her parents happy. He'd love her no matter what she felt. But he still couldn't help her please them.

"Maya, Nisba is telling you how much she likes the Hanuman video you brought," Priya said. "Are you even listening?"

"Sorry, Nis!" Maya said. She pushed her chair away from the table, stood up, and scooped the five-year-old out of her seat. "Why don't you tell me the Hanuman story?"

Nisba opened her mouth, about to launch into the saga of the monkey god again.

"Too late!" Priya stood and reached for her daughter. "Time for the girls' bath."

Seema got up to clear the dishes, Tariq stood to help her, and Maya started picking up plates, too, until she heard the bhangra song she had programmed into her phone playing in the guest bedroom down the hall. Scott only called after everyone was asleep, so it was probably Heidi. But when Maya retrieved the cell from her jacket pocket, an Indian number flashed on the screen. She had spoken to her father daily since Dadiji died; the calls were brief, but he sounded like he was coping, losing himself in the details of funeral preparations, glad to be useful, doing what he needed to do.

"Pops!" Maya yelled into the phone. "How are you? Did the funeral go okay?"

"Oh yes. It was beautiful. Just what your Dadiji would have wanted."

"Are there a lot of people at the house?"

"Yes, Radha-bhuasa, Parul-bhuasa."

This wasn't news; it was only natural his sisters would be there. Maybe it made him feel better to say their names, to remind himself that he wasn't the only one who lost his surviving parent. He exhaled, a breath Maya could hear quivering over the phone.

"Are you okay, Pops?" she asked. "Isn't it early there?"

"It is, but I could not sleep. Although, I am tired."

"Of course you are." But he didn't sound tired. He sounded nervous.

"I have had to put many affairs in order to prepare for the trip to Haridwar so that Parul-bhuasa and I can release your Dadiji's ashes into the Ganges."

"I wish I were there to be with you. And to see everyone."

"Not everybody here has been pleased to see me, beti."

"What happened?"

"Are you alone?"

"Yes. Why?" Maya's stomach muscles tensed, as if awaiting a punch.

"It is so foolish. In all likelihood, your mother and sister would laugh at me if I told them. On the other hand, they might be scared. I do not want to upset them. They are so excitable. That is why I called your mobile. You are levelheaded, you can talk some sense to me without creating a fuss. What is it Sanjay calls you? A mental health professional. I know I should not feel so unsettled by this, but if you could have heard the voice of that crazy woman, I think you would understand."

"Pops, I deal with the psychotic all day, every day; lay it on me."

"All right, then." He paused. "Our family has been cursed."

"What?" Maya laughed, then held her breath, forcing herself to stop.

"I told you it was foolish."

"It just wasn't what I expected." She sat on the bed. "I'm listening, I promise not to laugh. Start at the beginning."

"Well, I have been helping Parul-bhuasa pack up your Dadiji's things, and you know what it is to be in her house—it fills the heart."

"Uh-huh." Maya pictured her bedside altar, with the photo of Dadiji smiling a grin that was powerful in spite of its toothlessness, or maybe because of it.

"Parul-bhuasa and I have been talking about what to do with the house now, whether to rent it out or have one of your cousins move in. Either way we must renovate somewhat. So I told Parvati and her husband that since Dadiji is gone, we need to improve the third floor, and they must move to the first."

"That's good; they turned that room into a pit." Maya pictured her family's narrow, blue house in Jodhpur's Old Town. It was built in the fifteenth century, its stairs were smooth with age, and plaster was falling off the walls in some places, but it retained much of its original elegance, with carved arches around the windows and built-in cabinets and niches that had once been filled with statues of gods. Renters lived in most of the first floor, which also housed a small kitchen and the communal latrine; Dadiji's room had been on the second with the family's kitchen and the new bathroom; and Parvati, her husband Chotu, and their daughter lived on the third. Maya never liked Chotu—his too-wide grin made her instantly look away from him for reasons she could never articulate. But there was never any question of Parvati moving her new family into their own house once she married; Parvati had lived with, and taken care of, Dadiji, for over twenty years now; Chotu had been with her for almost ten working as a general handyman. Parvati even called her Mataji, "mother." Maya and Priya had made gagging faces at each other when they overheard this, but Dadiji was sincerely touched. And in the end, Parvati had acted as a daughter to Dadiji; it was she who eased her transition into her next life.

The third floor was the nicest apartment, with a view of the fort from the arched windows. And Parvati deserved it, Maya had to admit. She knew they should be grateful Dadiji liked her, and Parvati clearly cared for Dadiji. But ever since Dadiji had handed the filthy man that wad of rupees and Parvati moved in, Maya had felt just a tiny bit uncomfortable in her ancestral home. Parvati was so coy, always hiding her face behind her sari, as if she were whispering something she didn't want you to hear.

At first Maya thought she was the only one who felt uncomfortable around Parvati, an abandoned girl who, by rights, should be an object of pity, not fear. Originally, she thought her discomfort might be rooted in jealousy, that she resented Parvati's air of ownership over Dadiji. Parvati was always the one who fluffed her pillows, handed Dadiji her mala when it was time to meditate, and braided her hair. But as Maya got older she realized that Dadiji always made it clear that her love for her grandchildren was special. When Maya was twelve and visiting she heard Dadiji's rumbling laugh and rushed into the room to see what had caused it. Parvati had been there, leaning over Dadiji's bed, braiding her hair. A hot, prickly flush rose from Maya's stomach to her face, but Dadiji had calmly said in Marwari, "Move over, Parvati," and gently put her hand on the girl's arm. "Make some room for Maya to sit on the bed, I have her with me so rarely."

Eventually, Maya also realized she wasn't alone in wanting to avoid Parvati if she could help it. She and Priya and Mohan had often discussed how they hated being caught by Parvati's stare. "She looks at me like I've done something wrong," Priya had said when she first admitted that Parvati made her want to back out of the room. It happened to Mohan, too, just not as often. He went to India the least—there were all those years he'd been wrapped up in college, then work, and their parents felt much more comfortable leaving Mohan behind to get a summer job and fend for himself than they would have had Priya or Maya not known better than to bring the idea up. Plus, modesty decreed that Parvati not look a male member of the family directly in the face. But it had happened once or twice, when Mohan had to ask Parvati a direct question. After she had answered and left the room he'd covered his face with his hands and moaned, "My eyes, Maya, she burned my eyes!"

Parvati always looked down the minute she saw you notice her, but in the moment of eye contact, there was something in her searing gaze that made Maya feel she was a guest in the goddess-girl's house, not vice versa. Last winter, when Maya ran up to ask Parvati for Dadiji's meds and saw they had turned a corner of the apartment into a newspaper-lined makeshift latrine so their toddler, Dimpy, wouldn't have to go down three flights of stairs to use the bathroom, she didn't say anything.

"It's good they're moving to the first floor," Maya told Pops now. "Dimpy can play with the renters' kids. And they'll be closer to the main toilet."

Maya's father laughed, a hard, rough-edged noise. "They did not think it was so good. Parvati said Dadiji promised they could live in the third floor forever, that it would become theirs when she passed. But Dadiji never told me such a thing, I swear to you, Maya, I would honor her wish if she had, of course. Then Parvati yelled that once we fixed the house we would sell it and make them leave. I told her I have no intention of selling my mother's home—although it is true, beti, that I was thinking we might be able to find Parvati and Chotu work with some of the cousins, now that we no longer need them. But I did not tell them that yet, I would have waited until I found them the right place. And still Parvati threatened to curse me if I insisted they move—you know, she's a Brahmin, too, Maya—though her father drank, which is why she had to beg."

Maya remembered the strong, sour smell of the man; at the time she'd just thought he reeked of dirt, but it must have been grain alcohol.

"Your mother always says, Brahmin curses work. And she tells the truth always, even if it is ugly."

"Maybe, but Ma also says Brahmins can't eat onions because they're too stimulating, and I have onion rings all the time. So what happened with Parvati?"

"I was angry. We have supported them for years; I felt they should show more respect for Dadiji's family." But Pops sounded weary, not angry. And confused, like he wasn't sure what he had done that led to this point, to this girl, now grown up, scolding him as if he were an unruly child disobeying his mother's instructions. "I said they had to move or get out." He stopped abruptly.

"And she cursed you?" Maya prodded. Maybe Parvati really believed she was a goddess, Maya thought.

"She cursed the whole family," Pops said softly but so quickly that it sounded like one long word.

"Oh."

"It is nothing, right, beti? A silly superstition. I should not have told you but I do not know what to do. When she said the words, I felt actually frightened."

"Look, it's natural the curse got to you." Maya searched for words to alleviate her father's bizarre new stress. "Dadiji just died! That's huge emotional trauma. To have someone curse you adds insult to injury. But you don't have to *do* anything. Didn't you tell me sticks and stones might break my bones, but words would never hurt me?"

Her father laughed, more genuinely this time.

"Don't worry about it, Pops. Liminal stages like death or moving, even marriage, make people anxious. It's human nature. Parvati is upset because of all the change." Maya paused. "Not that it makes it okay for her to lash out at you."

"You are right, of course; it is a difficult time for everyone."

"Are you really worried about the curse?"

"No, just tired and, of course, sad, and … what was it … liminal, as you said." He laughed again. "Even your old father gets overwhelmed sometimes, beti. Even I."

"I know something that will cheer you up," Maya teased.

"Do not be stingy, then. Out with it."

"I promised I wouldn't tell. I'll get Priya." Maya was not about to bring her phone near a bathtub full of water and her squirming nieces, so she yelled "Lovely!," as loud as she could, trying to suppress the realization that even though Pops had called Maya, Priya would be the one to give him real comfort, the happy distraction he sorely needed.

Priya appeared in the doorway toting a suds-covered Yasmin. "Trade?" she said.

Maya opened her arms to grasp the wet child, but didn't relinquish the phone yet. "Okay, Pops, I'm about to give you to Priya," she said. "I love you."

"I love you, too, beti." He lowered his voice to a whisper. "And keep what I told you a secret. I knew you would not believe; you are strong and modern. No need to worry the others."

Maya wanted to stay to hear Priya deliver the news. Maybe Seema would get on the phone next and talk to Ajit, gloat in this shared joy, something good that was about to happen, something they put in motion together, long ago. But Nisba was in the tub alone, so Maya hurried down the hall where her oldest niece sat waiting, hair piled on her head in imitation of a crown, calmly pouring a bottle of Mr. Bubble into the water.

"Give me that, you little minx," Maya said, plopping Yasmin back into the tub.

"Maya-masi, I'm a princess," Nisba announced.

"Just like your mom." Bathing the girls, Maya thought about her conversation with her father. This curse thing, it was rude, but ridiculous. Having her astrology charts done when she went to India, that was bona fide tradition, and splashing herself with Ganges water from the bottle Seema kept above the fridge in Kalamazoo before she took her MCATs, or if she felt a flu coming on, that was just covering her bases. But believing in curses had to be as asinine as believing Brahmins can't eat onions.

Still, Maya had seen some angry patients; she knew hatred was a palpable force. And she felt her pulse quicken, her cortisol rise, as she talked to Pops. The thought that someone on the other side of the world cursed her family, directing vile energy their way, made her anxious. As she scrubbed her nieces' shiny skin, Maya felt marked somehow.

"Okay, girls, time to rinse off and go to bed," she said, over their duet of protest.

"It's not bedtime yet; it's not even dark," Nisba whined. Maya bargained, "Finish up fast and I'll read you a story." The sooner she got the girls to bed, the sooner Maya could shower herself. She felt dirty, eager to rinse off the grime of someone else's anger.

Chapter Four

Things were so hectic in the psych ER that Maya hadn't been able to get to the cafeteria until three, and by then the only vegetarian option left was a squashed peanut butter and jelly sandwich she picked up to eat in the break room. The deformed sandwich made her think of the summer that Priya, determined not to give up her favorite lunch, smuggled three loaves of Wonder Bread, some peanut butter, and a jar of marshmallow fluff into India, and forgot one plastic-covered loaf in the back of her grandmother's closet. Dadiji found it after they left, and, since the bread's pillowy consistency repelled her, spent the next two weeks feeding it to the cows roaming the streets in the morning. That story always made Maya laugh—it highlighted Priya's stubbornness and Dadiji's sweet practicality. But today, after giggling quietly, Maya cursed, then looked around to make sure no attendings heard her mumble "Shit!" She'd forgotten that Pops was due back to Kalamazoo that morning, and had meant to call him much earlier.

As she rummaged through her bag, she wondered, a bit more anxiously than she knew was necessary, why he hadn't called. The harder she rooted around, the more the phone seemed trapped in the depths of her bag. On her twenty-fifth birthday, Maya had vowed to herself that she would now become an adult, the kind of woman who, when she reached into her purse for a pen, didn't end up pulling out a tampon. But now, at twenty-seven, her palm at the bottom of her bag was getting sliced by the sharp edges of envelopes, her fingertips crushing damp mints. Once she finally felt the cool metal of her phone in her hand her beeper erupted, summoning her to a consult room to settle a dispute between a screaming old woman in a balding fur coat and two doctors from Project AID, the hospital's outreach arm. They had been called by the old woman's neighbors, who complained about the smell of her apartment.

"So I'm not the best housekeeper anymore!" the woman screamed. "I'm eighty-six!"

Maya looked at her more closely; in her fur coat and disheveled orange-dyed hair she resembled a wild cat. Maya tried to keep a professional distance from patients, but she couldn't help but realize this sputtering, shaking woman was ten years younger than Dadiji. The two couldn't be more different; Dadiji was always so serene.

The woman stepped closer to Maya. "I can't be scrubbing!" she yelled, standing so near that a fleck of spit hit Maya's chest.

"Apartment's full of rotting food, piles of newspapers, all kinds of animals," one of the outreach docs yelled over the woman's excuses.

"A few cats!" she screeched.

"We called her son in Philly," the doctor continued. "He's on a fishing trip, said bring her here until he can come straighten things out this weekend."

"He's a bastard," the woman yelled. "My landlord, too. Wants me out of the apartment. I'll kill that communist!"

Maya scanned the report and told the outreach docs to wait outside while she did a physical and interviewed the old lady, found out what meds she took. But they all already knew that Maya would commit Mrs. Esleck. The hoarding behavior and her raving indicated she was thought disordered or demented—probably features of both. In any case, she was unable to care for herself; she'd be better off in the hospital for a few days, while they did a full workup and waited for her son. According to the neighbors cited in the reports, the apartment was a health hazard. Mrs. Esleck was lucky she hadn't tripped over a newspaper, or a rodent, and broken a hip. It was an easy call, a way to help a woman who was someone else's dadiji, maybe. And it felt good to bring a little order into this stranger's chaotic life. Working in a hospital was nothing like the prime-time shows in which blond lady doctors roamed the halls making out with sadder-but-wiser male surgeons and saving women from domestic violence and children from sexual abuse, all without having to pull their hair back into ponytails. There were so few clear-cut solutions in Maya's work that she relished cases like Mrs. Esleck's, in which she could be helpful and efficient, moments that made her feel like rubbing her hands together briskly, the way Seema did after completing a step in a particularly complicated recipe.

"Das residence." Seema's voice sounded even more formal than usual coming through Maya's phone when she was finally able to call, just after getting off the subway near Dr. Bernard's office.

"Hi, Ma."

"Hello, Maya." Seema was still using her phone voice. "Prashant-mausa and Kruti-masi are here, so I cannot chat right now."

"Tell them I say—"

"Oh, but you are calling to talk to your father, of course," Seema interrupted. "Do not be keeping him too long." Her voice was drowned out by Pops's booming through the phone: "Hello, beti!"

"Hi, Pops! How was your trip?"

"Just perfect! I bought the ticket so at the last minute that I did not specify anything, aisle seat, vegetarian meal. So I got a middle seat. But in the end, the other two turned out to be empty and I stretched out like the maharajah," he said, sounding happier than he would have been if he'd booked a good seat in the first place.

"Lucky! Was your flight late? I thought you would call when you landed."

"Oh, no. My battery was dead. And your mother can never find her cellular in the bottom of her pocketbook."

"I was worried."

Pops paused. "Not . . . because of anything I said, I hope."

"What, the curse?" Maya turned onto Dr. Bernard's street. "No, I don't think so. I doubt that caused any extra anxiety, but I'll have to reflect on that."

"Do not reflect, beti." Pops's voice was so bright, Maya could hear him smiling. "Do not pay attention to a gossiping old man. There is nothing to worry about, okay?"

"I never thought there was, Pops!" Maya laughed.

"I am safe at home," her father continued. "I am a little wonked, that is all."

"Zonked, Pops."

"What?"

"I think you mean zonked."

"Really? I have heard wonked." The sound of chattering in Marwari rose in the background and Maya stopped walking in the middle of the pavement, straining to hear what was being said. "Okay, then, I will be going; your masi and mausa want to hear what is the news back home." Pops hung up before she could say good-bye.

Maya was in front of Dr. Bernard's office, anyway. At least she told herself it was just his office. She knew some psychiatrists worked out of their homes, and it looked like the top three floors of this building were residential. But she tried not to think of Dr. Bernard's life outside of the time and space of their forty-five minutes together; it was natural for the patient to wonder about the therapist to a certain degree, but anything more than a fleeting thought was, she felt, unprofessional. She didn't want to fantasize about his life the way her patients did about hers; Maya didn't have a Facebook or MySpace account because many of them admitted that they searched for her online. It made her proud to think she had never even Googled Dr. Bernard. But did being proud of that fact indicate that Googling him was something she wanted to do? Did it make her more like her patients than like him? Or, by stopping herself from wondering, was she blocking a key part of her therapy? Was this resistance? She couldn't perseverate on this now; it would make her late. Maya turned off her phone, satisfied that her parents were now in the same house, and after their guests left they'd be padding around in their slippers, not speaking to each other. Everything was back to normal.

"So it *was* a good weekend, and important, I think, in terms of processing my feelings about Dadiji's death," Maya said, halfway through her session. "I just talked to my dad, and he seems okay. Everyone's thrilled Priya's having a baby." Her voice rose. "Still, it's like I can physically feel Dadiji's absence. Like I know she's gone and therefore the world is a less safe place. Which is idiotic because I have a great life, right? I mean, Dadiji passed on, but we all knew that was inevitable. Even her. Sure, she wanted me to be settled before she died, married, a mom maybe. But she always said whatever my karma was, it would come to find me when it was meant to. She didn't make me feel like it's my fault I'm not married with two adorable Indian daughters like Priya. She said karma is karma and it's a mistake for men to force it." Maya looked up at Dr. Bernard to make sure he was still following her. "Of course, she meant women, too."

In fact, on Maya's last visit, Dadiji had hinted that she might have been guilty of forcing karma herself. Maya had been sitting on her bed, telling Dadiji about the hospital, when Pops breezed in to say good-bye to his mother before heading off to meet the fellows for chai and a photo exhibit at the university. A few minutes later, Seema rushed in with her checkbook in her hand and a wad of dollars stuffed into the waist of her sari.

"Where is your father?" she asked, breathless from having run.

"Gone." Maya nodded toward the window. "He already turned the corner. I'm not sure if he's going to the chai shop first or the university."

"But he said he'd go to the bank before it closes! Now I'll have to go and skip Hanuman puja at the temple. And I leave tomorrow."

"I'll go, Ma," Maya offered. "I'm sure he just forgot. He just got here, he's eager to see his pals."

"No, one of us two needs to sign, this is not just a simple deposit, there is much to arrange." Seema turned to look in the slightly warped mirror that hung on Dadiji's wall, and smoothed her braid around the hairline. "And I so wanted to meditate at the temple one last time this year," she said softly, talking to herself.

"Your mother is a good daughter-in-law," Dadiji said once Seema had left the room. "It was I who chose her. My Ajit was such a smart boy, but so lively, too, almost flighty. I wanted him to have a mate who was as smart as he, but more serious, to steady him. People married so young then, and he already talked about going to America. He needed someone who would respect the old ways, keep them there." She turned to Maya and slowly raised her forefinger to tap at the side of her head. "So I asked who was the top girl in the college and then your dada spoke to your nanaji about his esteemed daughter." Dadiji's eyes left Maya's and she looked ahead as if she were staring out the window. "I never wondered what it would be like for her, such a smart girl, to become a wife to one who was also so strong as herself." She turned to Maya again. "But perhaps I was right, because you children are the result. And right now—"

"I know, Dadiji," Maya interrupted, putting a hand on her stomach to ease the cramps she felt beginning there. "Right now I'm exactly where I need to be."

Maya looked at Dr. Bernard. This memory of her grandmother made her feel safe, and a little bit sad, wistful. But she didn't want to share it with him, she wanted to keep it for herself. "Anyway, Dadiji aside," she continued, "I know I'm lucky. I have an interesting job, sweet boyfriend, family who cares about me, maybe too much. But I still feel . . . nervous. Like I have free-floating anxiety. It's fu— I mean, messed up."

"You can curse in here, Maya." Dr. Bernard, sitting across from her in his leather chair, scratched his salt-and-pepper beard.

Did he want her to swear? Did he think she should be tougher, that she was too much of a people-pleaser? Or was it his problem, did he like his patients to talk dirty?

"Fine, Dr. Bernard, fucked up. I'm fucked up." She twisted the om-shaped ring on her right hand. "Is that better?"

"If it's more natural for you, Maya, then it's better. Let's get back to how you felt while seeing your family this weekend." He shifted in his chair, leaning forward. "That seems to be when the anxiety, as you call it, started. Is there a reason for that?"

"Well, I wished we'd all been there, for one," Maya said slowly. Her words started picking up speed. "Without having everyone in one place, and, I guess, with Dadiji gone, I kept worrying about the people who weren't right in front of me. Like my dad, for one." She took a breath and Dr. Bernard started to open his mouth, but another thought struck Maya. "Also I wish my brother had come instead of paving the way for his miracle-working wife to raise the dead like Jesus in Jimmy Choos."

Dr. Bernard suppressed a smile. Normally, Maya would have

considered this a victory. On the Thursdays she felt she had nothing to say, she made it a game to get him to laugh, giving herself a point each time he did. Now she was so caught up in her own words that she forgot to check if his nasolabial folds were struggling behind the beard.

"And, I guess," she continued, taking off her cardigan as she grew warmer, "what was wrong with this weekend is that Dadiji wasn't there, which is crazy because she hasn't visited the U.S. in twenty years. But I could feel her absence. I even felt, a little, like I'd lost India, too, like the whole country sank into the Arabian Sea." Tears boiled over onto her face, and she pulled a tissue out of the flowered dispenser on the table, wiped her cheeks, and started twisting it in her hands. "I'm fine outside of this office, I swear. I know Dadiji is on her way to moksha and that I have way too much attachment, but…" She paused to take a breath, wiping her nose on the back of her hand, forgetting that it was curled around a crumpled tissue she could have used. "I'm still sad sometimes."

Maya felt the soggy ball in her hand, tried to flatten out the tissue, and brought it up to her nose. She blew, long and loud. And then she laughed.

"My sister can't blow her nose, did I ever tell you that?" Maya laughed again. "She's physically incapable of it, she says, but of course it's psychological." Maya had tried to teach her how on a long car trip through the Rajasthani desert, but Priya just kept making honking noises into her Kleenex. She was not good at release, apparently. It wasn't her thing. Maya wondered if Priya had ever had an orgasm. She laughed and a tiny gold object shaped like the letter *B* fell into her lap. She swatted at her nose. All she felt was smooth, damp skin. She unballed the tissue in her lap to look inside.

"What is it?" Dr. Bernard asked as she brushed her hands up and down her pants.

"My nose ring." She felt around in her chair. "I guess I knocked it out when I blew my nose. You didn't see anything fly off my face?" Her cheeks burned, although her skin was clammy when she touched it. "I bet this is the first time a patient projectile-snorted a diamond stud in your office." Maya was standing now, shoving her hands into her pants pockets, then unfolding her shirt cuffs. She pulled the cushion out of the chair, but there was nothing on the seat. With her back to Dr. Bernard, Maya shimmied a little to see if the stud had fallen into her button-down shirt and lodged in her bra.

"I didn't see anything," Dr. Bernard reassured her. "It can't have gone very far."

When Maya turned around the doctor was crawling on his gray-checked carpet. "Dr. Bernard! Get up!" she yelled. The sight of him crawling around on the polyester carpet made her start crying again; on the floor, he seemed to be one more person she had to worry about, as if she were here to help him, not the opposite. "It's not important!"

She noticed a bald spot on the top of his head, and wished she hadn't seen it. She wanted to grab his shoulders, to stop his crawling, but, except for their introductory handshake, she'd never touched him. "I'll get another one. It's not important." She closed her eyes to concentrate harder on making him stop. Then, suddenly, he did. The noise of his corduroy pants rubbing against the stiff carpet ceased and the room was still.

Maya opened her eyes as Dr. Bernard rose onto his knees, smiling. He held up his right hand, the diamond glinting between his fingers. She stretched out her palm. He dropped the nose ring into it and pressed against his chair to stand. "That nose ring is a part of you, Maya," he said, sitting down. "Why do you think it's not important?"

"I don't think it," Maya insisted, quietly. "I just said it."

"Why?"

"I wanted you to get up, off the floor," she said, still standing. "Thanks, though." She brushed her hand against her nose again. "Are we done?"

He looked at his watch. "We have a few minutes. Do you want to be done?"

"Yes," Maya answered. "I want to go put this back in."

Aside from being the day she saw Dr. Bernard, Thursdays were also when Maya met Heidi for their weekly night out, a tradition meant to guarantee that the girls got enough red-wine-provided antioxidants to stave off heart disease, and enough self-centered conversation to ensure that they weren't leading unexamined lives. And, since a fashion editor's job was, apparently, never done, every third Thursday or so Maya ended up being Heidi's "plus one" at an advertiser-sponsored fashion show, product launch, or presentation. Tonight's event, Heidi had informed her, would be a celebration of the groundbreaking merger between Lucky brand jeans and Seven jeans into a new, even more form-fitting creation, a premium denim line called Lucky Seven. The proud corporate parents were marking the event with a cocktail reception/fashion show featuring several perpetually drunken celebutantes modeling the new works of wearable art. And since the fashion fest was taking place at the heliport that juts out into the East River, the event was within walking distance of Maya's apartment. Outside the heliport, dressed in a paisley embroidered shift (when in doubt, go ethnic, Heidi had once advised her), Maya picked out Heidi from a line of women who stood waiting for their plus ones, shivering in flimsy silk tank tops and jeans that cost more than an hour with a top analyst.

"You know you could never wear that to a real job." Maya kissed Heidi hello.

"Hey, we don't all work with deviants and sexual predators." Heidi lowered her voice. "Actually, our art director, he keeps women's shoes in his file cabinet, and we're supposed to pretend we don't notice them disappearing from the fashion closet."

"Interesting. Is he wearing them? Selling them?"

Heidi leaned in and whispered, "His assistant caught him licking them. Sick, huh? Maybe I should give him your card." She led Maya into the cavernous hangar, promising, "Once the PR girl checks my name off the list and the show's over, we're out of here."

But Maya didn't mind being there. She loved the din, heels clacking, ice clinking, bass thumping, so different from the noise at the hospital. This was happy chaos. She looked around, trying to take it in, but kept getting distracted by male model/waiters brandishing trays of grilled-cheese-and-truffle sandwiches shaped like the number seven. "Your job is over the top," Maya said, then took a bite of grilled cheese and pressed it against the roof of her mouth, to extract as much truffle oil taste as possible.

"Yours is, too," Heidi said. "How's last week's schizophrenic? Hitler?" She flagged down a farm-raised, all-beef cocktail wiener in a puff-pastry blanket.

"Gone. We released her into the custody of her sister. That's how it goes."

"I hope she'll be okay." Heidi sipped her champagne. Hearing about mental illness made some people nervous. But Heidi seemed to find it cheering, as if being armed with knowledge of all sorts of psychiatric maladies would protect her from acquiring any. Just by listening to Maya, she had learned enough of the terms in the *Diagnostic and Statistic Manual of Mental Disorders* to have diagnosed her assistant with every disorder in clusters A through C of Axis II at one point or another. "So, how are you sure someone's having a psychotic break?" Heidi asked now, tugging at Maya's arm.

"Trust me, if it ever happens, you'll know. The person can hear voices, usually does a lot of mumbling to themselves, often has bad self-care. You've seen them in the bus station; they tend to seek out loud, crowded places."

Heidi plunked her glass on a passing tray of empties, then turned to Maya and rested a hand on her arm. "Okay, we should plan where we'd go if either of us suffered a psychotic break," she said. "That way, if it ever happens, we can find each other, make sure we get the proper care instead of roaming around. You know, God forbid."

Heidi's invocation to God got drowned out as the lights dimmed and a loud thrumming filled the space. A helicopter appeared at the edge of the hangar, its door opened, and a bleached blond socialite whose name Maya knew but couldn't remember stepped out to wild cheering. She strutted down a long, raised catwalk to a booming bass rhythm. Her name rhymed with Slinky, Maya thought, finding it difficult to concentrate in the wind and the cacophony. Binky? Tinky? Kinky?

"C'mon, Maya, I'm serious," Heidi screamed, prodding her in the arm again.

"Sorry, this is a little distracting. Shouldn't we be paying attention?"

"Please, it'll be all over *WWD* tomorrow. So, where would you go?"

"Probably the usual, Port Authority." Maya humored her as the music died down. "With all that activity, you're more likely to blend in if you're yelling at your voices."

"I'd go to church," Heidi decided. "It's pretty, and there are all these icons you can talk to anyway. People might think you were holy."

Maya nodded, but she wasn't focused enough to answer. And she wasn't watching the celebutante's lesser-known sister, a second-string socialite named for some kind of dessert, parade the catwalk, either. She was thinking that the first place she'd really go if she had any hint of psychological instability would be Scott's apartment. Heidi loved Maya, sure. And her parents thought Maya was great, if always pigheaded and sometimes disappointing. But Scott treated her with a hint of wonder. No matter how serious an imbalance she might suffer, Maya knew that when Scott looked at her like he couldn't believe she existed, she'd be restored to her normal self. At least for long enough to find a colleague to prescribe appropriate meds.

"Ready?" Heidi asked the minute the lights came up.

"Oh, yeah. Sure." Maya blinked, disoriented by the lights, and now busy thinking through an "In Case of Psychotic Breaks" escape plan.

"We don't have to go," Heidi said, walking to the exit. "Another cupcake before I walk you home? Lucky Penny in a to-go cup, maybe?" But they were already outside, the suddenly cool fall air making them shiver like the champagne had in Maya's glass.

"What's a Lucky Penny?" Maya asked; she'd stuck to champagne.

"I don't know." Heidi shrugged. "They made it up, signature cocktail. Lots of sugar, I'm sure. Schnapps? Something for the coppery color."

"And the floating bits? They looked kind of like cranberries."

"Pomegranate seeds. They're lucky. On New Year's my dad always bashes one on the doorstep, and if the seeds scatter wicked far it's going to be a prosperous year."

"God, that reminds me." Maya leaned against a bench outside the wire fence of a basketball court, raising her voice to be heard above music coming from one of the kids' backpacks, providing a soundtrack to their game. "Want to hear something horrifying?"

"Always." Heidi sat on the bench, giving Maya her full concentration.

"During Dadiji's cremation, there was this part where my dad had to crack her skull with a bamboo stick to let her soul escape."

"No way! Unbelievable."

"I know."

"When Mom died, Yia-yia told me that back in Greece, in her

village, the priest pours wine and oil on the dead before burying them so they'll have nourishment on their way to the Other Side. After five years they're dug up, and if a body hasn't decomposed that person's a saint." Heidi turned to watch the game.

"Really?"

"Yeah. Saintly bodies are supposed to smell like roses." Heidi turned back and smiled. "I remember because Mom always wore a rosey perfume. Demi-Jour."

Heidi's mother had died of breast cancer when Heidi was seven; Maya had known this for as long as she'd known Heidi, but thinking of it now made her feel guilty, as if she'd been too maudlin about her more recent, more minor loss. If Dadiji's dying an ocean away knocked Maya's world enough to set it lopsided on its axis, how much more traumatic and disorienting must it have been for Heidi, as a child, to lose the most significant figure in her life. Heidi didn't seem lost, or even anxious. But Maya wondered if that was an impression she carefully cultivated; maybe Heidi sought out the loudest music, the brightest silk tops, the most truffle-enhanced grilled cheese sandwiches to distract herself from her thoughts. In the silence, the ballplayers' music, a dance remix of a song Maya vaguely recognized, seemed louder. "Well, when Scott's grandmother passed away, they held hands and sang hymns and made donations to her favorite charity," she offered.

"*That's* freakish," said Heidi. "Someone died, people! Let's release an emotion, even if it interrupts our singing 'Amazing Grace' and donating to the United Way."

"I think it was the Junior League."

"What did Bernard say about the skull thing?" Heidi asked.

"I can't remember; it was three champagnes ago." Maya watched the game, envying the way the kid in the red baseball hat swooped up and down the court, like a bird in flight. "But I think I didn't tell him; I'd forgotten till now. Anyway, he wouldn't enjoy it like you do. I know what he would have said." Maya fondled an imaginary beard. "Culturally informed rituals are important signifiers in the creation of our identity."

"But you told him about your dad's curse thing, right?"

"No! The residents just had a training session about how dangerous superstitions are, how people give themselves psychosomatic illnesses. He'd think I was crazy! I only told you because you already know I'm crazy. And I know you're even worse."

"Bad Maya!" Heidi said. "Holding out on your therapist."

"Besides, I don't really believe in it."

"Yeah, well, I asked Yia-yia to take the Evil Eye off you, just in case," Heidi said. "So I guess I believe in curses. And so does Yia-yia, who's fairly sane." It was true; Heidi's grandmother was as no-nonsense as they came. But then, Maya liked to think of herself as no-nonsense, too.

"What matters here is that *I* don't believe in it," Maya insisted, louder than she needed to. Sure, on some level, Maya thought there was a fraction of a chance that curses existed and that Parvati had the power to go around distributing them. But that was the seven-year-old Maya, the one who also thought there was an infinitesimal—but real—chance that Parvati actually was a powerful goddess cleaning their stove. Because she had been that seven-year-old once, Maya reasoned, she could be a tiny bit open to these possibilities while still knowing they weren't true.

The music changed to another dance tune; it seemed a little bit of a miracle to have stumbled across this music, this game, all this activity, as the neighborhood around them settled into darkness. "I can't believe in a curse," Maya insisted. "I'm modern."

"Oh really?"

"Really. My dad said so." She smiled at Heidi. "Let me try and put this in terms you'd understand . . . if our lives were a Bollywood movie—"

"Set during the monsoon?" Heidi interrupted. "Wet saris! We'd be irresistible."

"Of course." Maya nodded. "Anyway, if our lives were a Bolly-wood movie, I'd have a name like Kitty, and I'd use an English phrase every other sentence, and I'd dance to the latest bhangra. That's how you'd know; I'm modern." Maya started stomping her foot, her childhood kathak lessons coming back, then shaking her hips, then twirling unstoppably, trying to keep time to the techno beat of the unknown boys' radio. Heidi pulled out her camera phone to snap pictures, and Maya twirled, stopping when the song ended, out of breath with laughter and exertion. Applause came from the basketball court.

"You *are* crazy," Heidi said, shoving her phone in Maya's face. "I have photographic evidence." It was a horrible picture; Maya's mouth was open, so you could see the gap behind her canine tooth, which Seema had decided long ago wasn't so serious as to need braces. But she was also smiling and flushed, her hair spreading behind her, almost like wings. Looking at her heart-shaped face distorted with laughter, her eyes half closed, Maya was torn between making Heidi erase the photo, and asking her to e-mail it so she could use it as her screen saver. That way, as she wrote up patient notes, she'd have a reminder of what she looked like when she wasn't weighted down by work or worries about her patients or family, and thought of nothing but moving to the music.

"I'll bring a real camera to India," Heidi promised.

Still slightly out of breath, Maya started walking; the basket-ball boys were packing up and heading home, taking their music with them, and Scott would be at her place soon. "Since you're coming to India, maybe I'll invite Scott, too," she said. "You know, as just another friend. Safety in numbers."

"Great idea; Lamar would love it." Six years after learning Scott's real first name was Lamar, Heidi still used it whenever she could. The closest he came to acknowledging the existence of the Lamar was having L. SCOTT WALTERS, ESQ. on his business cards. He hated it, even though it was his great-granddad's name; he said "Lamar" made him sound like an evil Civil War general in a miniseries full of brothers dodging each other's bullets and mistresses. "Must get hard being the Invisible Boyfriend," Heidi mused.

"I don't do it on purpose, Hei!" Maya felt her heart rate slow, the high of the dancing fading away. "I have a lot of people's feelings to consider."

"Including his, though," Heidi said softly. "It's not his fault he's not Indian."

"I know." Maya slowed her pace. "But I sometimes wish he could do something to fix that. Think of the perfect thing to say or do to make up for it." She smiled to lighten the tone of the conversation. "Maybe write a note asking my parents for my hand in Sanskrit. Or just call them and ask in Hindi. Or Marwari."

"Three languages! Damn, you're complicated." Heidi's smile faded. "And if he never figures out the magic words?"

"He has to; I love him. And I'm lucky; I told Dr. Bernard that today."

Heidi slid her arm through Maya's as they stopped in front of her building. A light was already on in her apartment. Scott must have let himself in; he had a key. He shoved up the frame and leaned out the window, grinning so hard that Maya knew her conversation with Heidi was irrelevant; of course things would work out and they'd be together. He saw her smiling at him and yelled, *"Ciao, bellas."* Scott and Heidi had taken intensive Italian together senior year—that was how Maya had met him, waiting for Heidi outside of the language lab. After discovering him, she still spent most of every day with Heidi, but spent every night with Scott, copyediting each other's theses, taking each other out to dinner to celebrate the completion of every new draft, and savoring each walk through the quad with the precocious nostalgia of seniors who loved college almost as much as each other. Heidi and Scott were her world at Dartmouth; it made her happy, and, oddly, proud that they were still in her world now, or back in it in Scott's case, after a five-year hiatus involving law school for him, med school for her, and a number of insignificant significant others that Maya preferred not to think about now. Heidi said it was good Maya had dated other people—so when she and Scott got married, Maya wouldn't have to wonder who else was out there, she could be sure Scott was the one. But to Maya, being with him now made the other relationships feel like lies.

"Maybe your life's a Zeffirelli, not Bollywood," Heidi said, and hugged Maya good-bye. Maya waved up to Scott and walked toward her door, giving in to the pleasant, tired champagne haze until her phone started ringing, snapping her back to alertness, the bhangra tune sounding louder than ever, as if to assert Bollywood's rightful claim on her life. Priya's number flashed insistently on the screen. Priya would want her undivided attention to discuss whatever her latest purchase or domestic crisis was, would sense that Maya was slightly drunk, rushing through the conversation so that she could collapse into bed with the white man in her apartment who had no complaints about her or demands to make of her. Turning off the phone, she dropped it back into her bag and pressed the button of the elevator that would bring her up to Scott.

Chapter Five

Maya woke to the sound of Scott's slight snore, more a series of deep breaths, punctuated every third breath or so by a puffing sound when he actually opened his lips slightly to let the air escape. It was her favorite kind of white noise, so she pressed herself deeper into the curve of his body for a minute before fully opening her eyes to the light pouring in through the crack where the blinds almost, but didn't quite meet, in the window above her bed. She rose onto her elbow and pulled up the blinds.

Scott groaned, closed his arms around her waist, and pulled her back to the bed. "Make it stop," he moaned, screwing his eyes shut. "Please make the light go away." He slowly lifted one eyelid in the direction of Maya's tactless clock, which was glowing 7:17. "Is that really the time?" He sat up and felt for his glasses, almost knocking over the offending clock.

"Simmer down, the alarm's not even supposed to go off for another thirteen—twelve—minutes."

"Yeah, yeah." Scott tore the duvet off and stood, raising an appreciative eyelid at Maya's nakedness. "But I left work early last night, I should get in on time." He walked toward the bathroom, then turned back. "Of course, if the good doctor would care to join me in the shower," he said in his General Lamar voice, disappearing behind the door.

"In a sec," Maya called after him. She turned off the alarm, so it wouldn't ring endlessly in a few minutes, then lifted her bag from the spot on the floor where she'd dropped it last night, located the phone, and flipped it open. She hit Menu to start disabling the backup alarm before noticing that the screen was blank, still off from when she'd silenced Priya. Maya doused a momentary flare of guilt and pressed Power.

Piercing the soothing rushing noise of Scott's shower, her phone made its obnoxiously cheery powering-on sound, a jingle that was inappropriate under most circumstances, and undeniably garish in the halo-like light of early morning. She rang into voice mail. Five missed calls.

"Maya!" Priya's recorded voice yelled. "Where the fuck are you? Turn on your damn phone!" Maya snorted. The last time she could remember Priya swearing was in high school, when Maya had hidden behind the front door and thrown colored powder left over from Holi at Priya as she entered—unfortunately wearing her favorite white Esprit sweatshirt. "*Please* call me when you get this." There was silence, then Priya's voice came back softer, almost a whisper. "I really can't handle this by myself."

The next message was her mother. "Hello, beti. Your phone, it is still not answering, I see, but I wanted to give you the good news after those alarming messages. Your father's operation went very well. If the recovery continues so he should be—"

Maya slammed the phone shut, then flipped it open. "What happened, what operation?" she yelled when Seema answered.

"Maya!" Her mother sounded oddly chipper. "Your phone is working again!"

"Forget the damn phone! What happened?" Maya's yelling seemed to grow louder as Scott turned off the shower. He was suddenly standing in the doorway of her bathroom, naked, except for a towel wrapped around his waist, dripping on her floor. She had forgotten he was there.

"Calm yourself, there is nothing to worry about now, there is no need for bad language," Seema chided through the phone. "I tried to reach you when it happened. This is why you should have a phone in the house as well, Maya. These cellulars are not always tip-top reliable and if yours is giving you—"

"What operation, Ma?"

"Have some patience with your old mother, Maya. I did not sleep all night. I am a little discombobulated. And your phone is still not working well; there was quite a bit of static only just now."

Maya shut her eyes and made a rolling motion with her hand, trying to send her mother brain waves to speed it up.

"It was a triple bypass," Seema finally explained. "The LAD was ninety percent occluded. But, anyway, it is over now and it went very well."

"Ninety percent? Pops?" Maya was silent. Scott stepped across the carpet toward where she sat on the bed, wrapped in the comforter, but Maya turned away from him; she needed to focus. "He's always been so healthy. What happened?"

"Well, Prashant-mausa and Kruti-masi came over to see him last night, to hear about his trip." Seema would not be rushed. "Your father felt some tightness in his chest, only he thought it was caused by the stress of the journey. But Prashant-mausa had his own surgery last year, remember? So he insisted on taking your father to the ER, and it is a good thing he did. There was a great deal of ischemic tissue around the LAD, perhaps all from this single episode. The procedure had to be done immediately."

If it were anyone else, if this had happened to Heidi's dad or Scott's father, Maya would have asked for more details, partly so that she could draw her own conclusions about the prognosis, but also because she found medical terms comforting. To her, degrees of occlusion weren't new, threatening words, but descriptions in questions on medical boards, and the left anterior descending artery was a clue that could lead to a correct answer. But it was Pops in the hospital, and none of the details mattered. She wanted her mother to stop describing the particulars and explain how this could have happened, then guarantee that it wouldn't happen again. Now she knew how her patients felt when they stared at her, begging for answers she couldn't give.

"But Pops doesn't have high blood pressure, no history of coronary artery disease. This makes no sense." Maya felt something wet on her shoulder—Scott's hand—and sat very still, to keep her body from shaking it off.

"It is true, Maya, your father is very fit." When Maya heard Seema's voice, she did dip her shoulder, shrugging off Scott's hand. Sitting next to her, touching her, Scott was intruding into the conversation, and it didn't seem fair to her mother, not now. "But he is older now, he has had a great deal of stress recently," Seema continued. "And South Asian males, their narrower arteries put them at risk. Prashant-mausa sent me an article last year via e-mail."

"I know the study, Ma. Can I talk to him?"

"Not now, beti," Seema said. "Your father is resting. I will go home now, but when I come back this afternoon we will call you. If your phone is still working."

"I'll book a flight by then." Maya half expected her mother to object, to point out that she missed a day of work last week to go to Priya's, that she shouldn't bother to come home now that the crisis was over.

"All right, then, beti," Seema said. "We will see you tonight."

Maya slapped the phone shut and fell against Scott, not caring that he was wet. But when he closed his clammy arms around her, she felt suffocated. She pulled away so she could look at him. "Pops had triple bypass surgery."

"I heard, baby," Scott said. Maya looked at the carpet, with Scott's wet footprints staining a path across it. "How is he?"

"Good, Ma says. Good as can be expected, I guess." Maya stood, disentangling herself from the comforter now twined around her. "I've got to pack. I'm going to go, as soon as I can get a flight."

"I'll come with you." As Scott stood his towel fell and Maya marveled that even after med school, and years of dating, naked men still looked ridiculous to her in daylight.

"He just got out of surgery, Scott." Maya turned away from him, breathing so loudly it was almost panting. "Do you want to give him another heart attack?"

"Oh," Scott said. "Right."

At the sound of Scott's soft voice saying that short, hard word, Maya felt worse than she had a minute ago, something she would have thought impossible. She still didn't turn around but she knew how Scott would look, the same way he did when she told him she couldn't move in with him last September. He had found an apartment within walking distance of the hospital but close enough to his office, an apartment she loved. And she thought about it seriously. Until one night, just after they'd seen the apartment, they were back at his place when the phone rang while they were having sex and Maya heard his outgoing message play on his outdated machine. All she could think of was whose name would be on the message if they moved in together, or what if Scott picked up when Seema called at an off hour. The phone was a link to the outside world, which they couldn't keep from invading their hideaway. She'd told him the next morning that it was impossible, she couldn't live with him until they were married.

Scott suggested they each get voice mail, with different phone numbers, or just use their cell phones. He said he'd have all his mail delivered to work, and they could ask their doormen to warn them if an Indian couple holding Tupperware containers full of subji showed up in the lobby. But Maya knew she couldn't live that way, never having her parents visit, hiding all of Scott's clothes when they did, putting them in suitcases under the bed, banishing him and choosing them. For a minute she thought he might propose then, even though they had decided they shouldn't get engaged until her last year of residency, when he'd be farther along at the firm, and they'd both be more settled. She had been surprised to realize that if he did propose, at that moment, she'd probably say yes. But he hadn't said anything, he just sat there looking like his back teeth hurt until she put her hand on his. Then he said, "Okay." And a little later, "I understand."

Remembering this, Maya turned around, hot tears staining her cheeks and said, "I'm sorry, Scott, I—"

He had started to dress, had put on his boxers and was pulling up his pants, but he dropped them when she turned, and hugged her. She kept murmuring sorry sounds against his damp chest, and he kissed the top of her head and said, "Shh. That was stupid. I'm the last person you need to worry about right now." She nodded as best she could with her head against his chest, and he let her go. Maya started to pack; by the time she had thrown a weekend's worth of clothes into her roller bag, Scott was dressed. "I love you," he said, and kissed her good-bye. "Call when you get there."

Maya started crying once the door shut, and kept crying, loudly in the shower, and more quietly as she booked a flight to Kalamazoo for that afternoon. Then she stopped, washed her face, and started calling her Friday-afternoon patients, rescheduling the appointments she had after three o'clock.

•   •   •

At the hospital Maya moved through the day, numb but efficient, enunciating as she spoke to her patients, filling out reports immediately and elaborately, concentrating on every detail so that she could forget about her father lying in a hospital bed in Michigan waiting for her. At two thirty, she rolled her suitcase away from the hospital, hunting for a cab, then stopped when she saw a tall black man walking down the street. With a beer gut and a salt-and-pepper beard, the stranger bore no resemblance to her father. But something about him reminded her of Ajit. His open smile, maybe, so broad that it seemed impossible that it could fit on his face. And, even more so, the shiny navy tracksuit he had on resembled the outfit Pops always wore in India, along with oversized sunglasses, if it was a day he was walking around the fort or visiting a temple.

The tracksuit was his touring outfit, one she imagined he chose for its stitched-on logo, which identified him as a nonresident Indian, unmistakably American. Ajit took the concept of "sportswear" seriously, wearing the tracksuit when he felt, literally, sporty. His other Indian uniform was a houndstooth blazer, tan dress slacks, and white button-down that he wore, accessorized with a Burberry scarf and a driving cap, when he had official business, at the bank or the consulate, and needed to telegraph the air of a respected businessman. He had grinned nonstop during the auto rickshaw ride home from the bank two years ago, after the obsequious manager, who called him sir, gave him a free agenda for the new year, with his initials stamped on it in gold paint. Remembering his glee at the unexpected gift—which they had to *plan ahead* to create, given the initials—Maya felt unsteady, as if she were walking down wet subway stairs, taking care not to trip and fall. Her father's happiness, so easily achieved, now seemed precarious.

She rolled her suitcase to the newsstand in front of the hospital, and bought a pack of cigarettes. Slowly unwrapping them, she felt that they were already having a steadying effect on her mood.

She'd never bought her own cigarettes before moving to New York, but almost all her fellow residents smoked and she couldn't mooch off them forever. She tried to rationalize that smoking relieved stress, and doctors had way too much of that. But she knew that was bogus; she'd spent hours talking about her self-destructive traits with Dr. Bernard. Still, after a few puffs she was calm enough to look for a cab.

None came right away, so once she stubbed out the cigarette, she spent a minute doing her pranayama breathing, concentrating on the sound of her breath until her heartbeat slowed. Then she called Priya, who was picking the kids up from day care. She wouldn't be going to Michigan until Pops got better, Priya said, switching into Marwari to explain that seeing him in the hospital would be too upsetting for the girls, and she couldn't leave them for long.

"I'm glad you're going," Priya added in English. "Now that we finally found you."

"I turned my phone off before bed, didn't get the messages until this morning."

"It's probably better; at least you got a good night's sleep," Priya said. Just as Maya relaxed, she added, "But I don't see why you have a cell phone if it's not so we can find you in a crisis. I'm sure you'd be available if other people called."

Maya didn't ask what other people. She knew Priya was talking about Scott, although she would never bring herself to say his name. Priya had gotten to marry the man she wanted; she should be more supportive of Maya, or at least understand her situation. But it was as if she felt Maya had to marry their parents' biodata fantasy to erase Priya's own betrayal, Tariq's one imperfection—although Priya herself would never admit to feeling this way, but insisted again and again that Tariq was "just like us, culturally, where it counts." Last time they'd discussed Scott, Priya—who had been cochair of the Diversity Council in college—added, "And Tariq looks like us, too, like our kids. People see me in the park with the girls and they don't think I'm the nanny."

"I'm doing the best I can," Maya shouted through the phone, angry at the memory and the unspoken accusation in Priya's words right now. But she wasn't about to have that fight again, not today, so she lowered her voice to add, "I'll call you once I see Pops." After hanging up, Maya glanced right and left, to see if any of her patients had walked by and seen her yelling. The pavement was crowded, even at three in the afternoon, but she didn't recognize any of the faces immediately around her. A cab finally pulled up and she surveyed the rest of the crowd as she got into it, pulling her bag into the backseat next to her. Luckily, everyone she saw was a stranger. And most of them were on their cell phones, too, repeating what the doctor had told them about biopsies or protocols or centimeters dilated, the whole range of human experience from birth to death, floating in the air in front of the hospital like her cigarette smoke.

Chapter Six

Maya walked down the third floor of Bronson Methodist Hospital, her wedge heels squeaking on the linoleum. Seema had privileges at this hospital; Maya had been here to visit her mother at work dozens of times, and had done her homework on the plastic chairs in the waiting area when Seema couldn't get a sitter. She knew the best snack machine, the one with the Kit Kat two-packs, was on the fifth floor, that there was a small TV in the nurses' lounge, and that Denise was the nurse you asked if you wanted to go in there and watch it. This was the first place she had seen an old man talking through a machine he held up to his neck, and once spotted a woman with a goiter the size of an avocado just walking down the hall, chatting with Denise. But despite the strange sights and the blood-specked sheets she occasionally noticed on cots rolling past her, Maya had never found the hospital a scary place before. She slowed down, walking a few feet behind Seema, noticing how black her mother's braid was in back, although the fuzz around her hairline was now completely gray. Seema's pace was as quick as ever but her upper back looked swollen in her cardigan. Had she hunched like that for years, and Maya hadn't noticed?

"Do not be a lollygagger, Maya." Seema stopped before a door. "Visiting hours cannot last forever. We are not above the rules here." She held the door open and rested her hand on Maya's shoulder for a second before taking it back and pressing it against her stomach. Arms folded in front of her stomach was a characteristic stance for Seema, for many of Maya's aunties. It reminded Maya of the Cycladic idol Heidi brought her from Athens the year of the Olympics, a white figure with a huge, featureless head and a small body, lines representing arms carved across its stomach. Heidi called it "Minoan Woman with Really Bad Cramps," but seeing her mother make the same gesture, Maya wondered if maybe it was something women everywhere did, after they'd had kids, having grown used to resting their arms on their vast abdomens when they were pregnant.

Her father lay in bed with his eyes shut, sheets tucked up to the bottom of the rib cage, his upper body covered in nothing but a pajama top and the tubes that disappeared underneath it. Maya followed the tubes to the telemetry machine monitoring his heart functions. It was a machine she had seen hundreds of times, a normal sight, one that balanced out the unusual vision of her father with his eyes closed, his mouth slightly open, head listing to the side. Maya smiled at the machine.

"Ajit, are you asleep or just resting?" Seema asked. Maya could count on her fingers the few times she'd heard her mother call her father by his name; she usually said "your father" to the kids, and "*suniye,*" or "please listen" when she needed his attention.

"Resting." He opened his eyes gradually. "Maya. You came, foolish girl! Missing work, troubling the hospital staff." His speech was slow, but picked up speed with each word, and he grinned as he spoke, making the scolding sound like singing.

"Who cares?" Maya walked to the bed and leaned over to hug

him, careful not to disturb the reassuring tubes. "I came to see you, drama queen! Scaring us all."

"Please, drama king!" He squeezed Maya, patting her back.

"Take care with the IV," Seema said from the doorway.

Ajit let Maya go, and she sat at the side of his bed facing him, leaving the one chair open for her mother. But Seema didn't move into the room. "Kruti-masi and Prashant-mausa said they would come by," she announced.

"Sanjay, too?" Maya asked. "Isn't he home this weekend?"

"We shall see. He may be tired from his journey, or not want to bring Amrita to the hospital. One never knows with your cousin." Seema's head was wobbling again. She wasn't very close to her sister, but she adored Kruti's son. This meant she'd cook Sanjay's favorite dal pakoras every time he walked into her house, and criticize him mildly every time his name was spoken, so that anyone listening knew he was hers to improve. "His parents, they have been so, so helpful," Seema said. "I will wait for them downstairs, as I know my way." She turned to leave before Maya could protest, glancing back at them briefly through the chicken-wire-filled glass panel in the closed door.

Maya looked at her father. Pops could pass for ten, maybe fifteen, years younger than sixty-seven. His hair was still black, except right at the temples, and it was full all over. His skin was darker than Maya's, but, Seema would have been quick to point out, that wasn't so bad in a man, and anyway, it's not like her husband was dark-dark, like Tariq. But now Pops looked as if he'd faded, almost to gray at the dip in his collarbone, at the crepey skin at his eyes, and the inner bend of his elbow, where he'd pushed up his pajamas.

"How are you feeling, Pops?" Maya asked, fixing her father's sleeve.

"Fine, beti. Fine, fine. Much better. Really."

"What a shock, though, huh? Good thing it didn't happen on the flight."

"Yes, it could have been much worse." He paused. "I am not so very shocked, though. Are you?"

"Because of the study? South Asian males, smaller arteries?"

"Study, muddy! I know of no such study!" Her father took off his glasses and looked down at them. "Get me a Kleenex, beti." He nodded at a box next to the chair. Maya leaned over, her back toward him, and pulled tissues out of the box, each one making a whooshing sound as it rubbed against the cardboard, a noise that she appreciated for the way it filled the silence.

"You don't really think..." Maya paused.

"That it was the curse?" He breathed heavily, then added, "That will be enough; I only have the one pair of glasses with me."

Maya handed him the tissues and sat down.

"I considered it." He rubbed his glasses. "Heart surgery, it is suggestive."

"Why?" Maya asked, more sharply than she meant to.

"Brahmin curses affect the blood, especially." He put on his glasses, adjusting them until they sat perfectly on his nose. "Not in every case, but in general."

"That's ridiculous!" Maya sputtered. "What do Harijan curses affect, the urinary tract?"

He laughed, then coughed.

"Don't bust your stents," she cautioned. "You really believe that?"

Ajit sucked his cheeks in, then exhaled loudly. "I do not, beti," he insisted. "I was fortunate in some ways—I was home from India already, Prashant-mausa was at the house. Perhaps I was blessed, not cursed. Now the doctors say that I am recovering very well."

"You look like Mr. India," Maya promised.

"It is not polite to tease your father," Ajit said. Still smiling, he closed his eyes. "It was the stress of Dadiji's death and the strain of all the travel that made this happen. Now Denise says much of recovery depends on the thinking positively. I will do that. There is no need to speak of the curse now. It seemed quite frightening back in India, but here, it is too silly to think of."

Maya looked around the room at the telemetry machine and the adjustable bed, their shiny metal solidity making them seem like a rebuke to such vague, diaphanous fears. The door opened and Seema's voice came through it before she did. "Look at the treasure I found in the lobby." Maya resented the intrusion until she saw it wasn't her aunt and uncle behind her mother, but Sanjay.

"Ajit-uncle, look at you, kicking back, feet up." Sanjay hugged him quickly, patting him on the shoulders. "I warned you India's hazardous to your health."

"Then why are you getting married there, jerk?" Maya stood and reached across the bed to hug Sanjay hard. If her father was going to be Mr. Chipper in his sickbed, she could be upbeat, too.

"You will smother me, you both!" Pops warned.

"It's because of me," Amrita said. "It's my mother's dream to see me married in Bombay." Maya hadn't even seen her come in, but there she was at the foot of the bed. Now that Maya noticed her, she was aware of the powdery aroma of Fracas, which followed Amrita wherever she went. Seeing Amrita by her father's hospital bed, Maya felt terrible for judging her at that dinner in New York. So Amrita wasn't quick to get an in-joke; maybe that would come in time. Right now what mattered was that she was here, a calming, sweet-smelling presence softening a hard time. Maya wished she had brought Scott; maybe it would have been fine.

"How are you feeling, Uncle?" Amrita asked.

"Much better. I will be back in tip-top shape for your wedding in January."

"You have to come, Ajit-uncle," Amrita said. "Maya's going to be the star of the sangeet." Sanjay glanced at Amrita and she looked steadily back at him. It was the first time, outside of the movies, that Maya had seen a glance that actually smoldered with passion.

Maya wasn't sure she could ever manage such a look; maybe she just wasn't a smolderer.

"Sanjay, selfish boy, take the girls to the cafeteria and tell your parents they can come in," Seema commanded. "Visiting hours end in fifteen minutes."

Driving her mother home, Maya felt almost guilty. She had actually been having fun at the hospital, gossiping with Amrita about wedding plans, blowing on cups of burnt coffee. Amrita had said that in her family, at every sangeet, relatives performed a skit reenacting the couple's first meeting, and she wanted Maya to play her. She actually blushed when she asked, which made Maya accept immediately.

"My cousin Raki's playing Sanjay," Amrita had said. "They're so alike, funny, sociable." She smiled. "If you weren't dating such a great guy, I'd fix you up with him."

"I'm still hoping Scott can come," Maya said quickly.

"Maybe Raki for Heidi?" Amrita suggested. "Sanjay, what do you think?" But the wedding talk had bored Sanjay, so he ran around getting them half-price desserts from the display case on the counter, then ate all the Jell-O himself, which was fine with the girls. As Amrita said, spearing the tip of a triangle of coconut cream pie, if you're going to do dessert at all, you might as well do it right.

"It's nice that Amrita came, with all she has to do. She's not even part of the family yet, officially," Maya said now, turning off the highway. "The wedding's going to be amazing, Ma. Amrita's dad booked the Gymkhana Club and her mom's already gone to India to work on the wedding saris. Amrita showed us the mockup of the invitations—they're so fancy, all gilded. Heidi will just about die when she sees hers. I told you she wants to come?"

"That's nice, beti." Seema sounded tired; she was digging through her plastic purse for something. Priya tried to buy her designer bags, but Seema said a vegetarian with a leather bag was nothing but a hypocrite, and she had apparently raised two of those, which was quite enough for any family.

"Maybe I'll invite some other friends, too," Maya said. "Take advantage of the opportunity."

"Why not?" Seema mumbled from behind her hands, which she had raised to her face, clutching a tissue.

"Ma, don't cry! Pops is gonna be fine, he's already fine, he was so lucid."

"I am not crying, stupid girl!"

Maya pulled into their driveway and turned off the motor.

"It is only I am having a bloody nose. It happened also last week, it is not important. Your mummy is getting old. Bodies fall apart." She made the sound of a laugh.

"It's not age, Ma," Maya said. "Mohan got them in high school, remember?" She opened her door and the car's overhead light flicked on. "Oh my God!" Maya whispered, pulling off her driving glasses for a closer look.

Now visible under the light, Seema was covered in quickly drying blood. The tissue she clutched was crimson, her tan cardigan was stained rust, and the orange blouse of her sari was spotted burgundy.

"Maya, it is a nosebleed," Seema said sharply.

"Nose hemorrhage! That's got to be like one hundred cc's of blood." She grabbed her mother's wrist to take her pulse but Seema pulled away with such force that her arm slammed into her torso.

"I went to medical school, too, you know," she said, rubbing her wrist as if Maya had hurt her. "I passed the boards—twice! I am not impressed with your—"

Maya slammed the door; the motor came alive with a violent chugging.

"What are you doing?" Seema shouted.

"Driving back to the hospital. Your BP could drop any minute."

"I cannot appear at work like this!"

But Maya had already pulled out of the driveway and was halfway to the highway. Seema didn't speak during the entire ride, even though Maya was speeding; they made the return trip in thirteen minutes although it had taken them almost twice as long in the opposite direction. Maya couldn't tell if her mother wasn't talking because of anger, worry, or practicality; it must be hard to speak with a blood-soaked tissue in front of her mouth. When they arrived at Admissions, Seema finally broke her silence. "Walk in front of me," she commanded, and Maya did, blocking the stained sari from view. She saw Prashant-mausa before he noticed them. The fact that he was still there seemed like a windfall, an undeserved blessing, although she shouldn't have been surprised; it always took him at least a half hour to leave any family event, whether it was a party or a condolence call. Besides, he had privileges here, too. Denise always brought in brownies for her favorite docs, and Prashant-mausa was chewing one rhythmically, gazing at the rest of the square as if figuring out which part to eat next—walnut or not walnut? He didn't notice Maya and Seema until Denise yelled, "Dr. Das, what happened?"

Maya started to explain, but Seema waved a bloody tissue at her, interrupting, "Maya, in this hospital, I am the Dr. Das."

Prashant-mausa dropped his brownie on the nurses' station, rushed toward them, and took over. He found an empty room for Seema, paged a colleague to cauterize her nose, and insisted that she stay overnight for observation while Maya went home to sleep.

"Prashant-mausa, I'm used to sleeping in hospitals," she argued, but he put an arm around her, shoved a brownie in her hand, and herded her to the exit. "You need a good night's rest, Maya," he instructed. "It is a tiring thing when a child has to care for her parents."

"I'm twenty-seven."

"And still a child." He pointed a long, pink-tipped finger at the sliding doors. "I don't want to see you in this hospital before nine A.M. I will give Denise strict orders to have you ejected, and you know such humiliation would make your mother breathe fire."

Maya stood still for a minute, holding the brownie so tightly that it crumbled in her hand, trying to think of an appropriate argument. But none came, and suddenly, she did feel tired, whether because of the exhaustion of the trip and the dramatic evening, or because of the power of suggestion. She thanked Prashant-mausa and walked through the hospital's sliding doors alone.

Chapter Seven

Maya woke in her childhood bedroom, which still looked as if it were 1993 and she had just left it to go to a sleepover at one of her cousins'; her mother had rarely let her spend the night away unless it was at a relative's, arguing about each of Maya's friends, "That girl's parents, who knows when they are at home, not at home." Maya had gotten around her protests a few times by insisting that she had to work on a school project with a classmate. In fifth grade her mother asked what the project was and Maya said they were making a volcano for science; she had seen Peter Brady do that on a rerun, and it's not like Seema ever watched TV. She remembered the volcano that never was now, looking at the bookcase that still held her shiny orange Spanish textbooks next to the autographed photo of the *Melrose Place* cast Priya had sent away for in honor of Maya's tenth birthday.

Priya's side of the room was still intact, too, frozen in the last century. She'd gone to college before Maya started high school, but it never occurred to Maya to redecorate. She'd awakened while the sun was coming up through the blinds, and reread the titles on Priya's bookshelf so many times that she'd almost memorized them—*Jane Eyre,* then *I Know Why the Caged Bird Sings, Silent Spring,* and an unusually fat copy of *Animal Farm,* which Maya suspected was Orwell's dust jacket stretched over *Are You There God, It's Me, Margaret* or some other of Blume's oeuvre, books Priya loved but couldn't be seen reading either on the bus (too girly) or at home (too racy). When enough light flooded the room that Maya felt it was truly morning, she moved to the master bedroom to sit on her mother's bed. It was her parents' bed, technically, but her father often slept on the couch in the den; he said he liked to work late on the computer and did not want to disturb Seema. Pulling an afghan her mother had crocheted around her shoulders, Maya switched on the TV, raising the volume since no one was around to complain. She flipped channels, comparing perky local morning-show hosts, trying to find one who hadn't yet learned to contract her long Midwestern A's. Finally it was seven, late enough to call.

"You have reached Dr. Seema Das, M.D. Please leave a message." The only people who called Seema's cell were her children and siblings, but to her, an outgoing message was an official document requiring her title.

"Hi, Dr. Das, M.D.?" Maya tried to sound chipper, matching her voice's pitch to the talk-show hosts she had just silenced. "It's Dr. Das, M.D. I'm coming to get you at nine so we can discuss doctorly things. Tell your husband, the nondoctor, that I'll see him then." She hung up and dialed again.

"Ma?" Priya answered before Maya heard the phone ring. "I told you not to call so early."

"It's me, just on the house phone," Maya explained. "I know it's early but—"

"Is it Pops?"

"No, he's fine. Thrilled Sanjay came to see him last night—"

"He understands why I can't be there, right?" Priya asked, then said, "The bathing suit is for swimming class, and that's on Tuesdays, not Saturdays. Saturday is music!"

"Are you listening, Priya?"

"Why don't we pick something else?"

"What?"

"Not you, Yasmin. She dresses herself now. You can only imagine," Priya muttered. "Maybe the pink dress? You *love* pink. With the beige turtleneck underneath."

There was a pause, then Priya's breath came through the phone again. "Beige is apparently a boy's color now, you'll be glad to know."

"I'll alert the transgendered." Maya readjusted the afghan. "Just throw whatever you want on her and listen to me."

"Maya, I'm not Ma!"

"Yeah, if you were she'd be in a polyester jumper and Mohan's old T-shirt."

"Okay, I'm listening," Priya promised, but Maya could hear water running. "C'mon, Maya, I've still got to get them to eat before we hit the road."

"It's Ma; she had a nosebleed."

"That's too bad," Priya said in a tone that suggested nosebleeds were unfortunate, but not worth delaying breakfast.

"A really serious nosebleed; looked like one hundred cc's of blood, maybe more. I took her to Bronson, Prashant-mausa said it needed to be cauterized and kept her there overnight."

Priya made a noise like the sound of a tightly closed jar popping open. "I wish I were there. I mean, she'll be fine, it's a nosebleed, but still I could—"

"Did Pops say anything to you?" Maya asked. Pops said he hadn't told anyone else about the curse, but maybe, after the heart attack, in a moment of fear, he slipped? If he had said something to

Priya, she would have said something to Ma, and the nosebleed could be a somatized reaction, especially if Ma believed that Brahmin curses affected the blood. It was possible.

"What?" The water stopped running. "Nisba, get your sister, come eat breakfast."

"I don't know—about the nosebleed," Maya improvised.

"He just had bypass surgery, Maya; I know you're just a shrink, but medically, that's much bigger news than a nosebleed."

Normally Maya would have come up with a response to the dig; this banter was what they did to remind each other that no matter how the outside world saw them, between them it was permanently 1995, when they defined themselves by how they saw each other, and the one who threw in the last volley in the latest verbal skirmish was cool, while the other was a loser—until the next rematch. Instead, Maya was silent, considering whether it would be worth it to break her word to Pops in order to share the burden of this knowledge with the one other person who would understand why it was silly and frightening at the same time.

Priya's voice rose several octaves. "Don't you girls look beautiful! I *love* that dress. And Nisba, your shiny shoes!" When she started speaking normally again, her voice seemed so low in contrast that it sounded like a grumble. "What's the big deal about a nosebleed?" Priya breathed heavily into the phone. "Come on, Maya, if they're late three times in a term they lose their spots in this fascist music class."

"Nothing." Priya could be annoying, especially before hitting the Dunkin' Donuts drive-through in the morning, but Maya loved her too much to give her something else to worry about, something more sinister than the gender roles of toddlers' turtlenecks. "I'm just worried about them, I guess."

"Stop being so neurotic! Pops is a man in his sixties—they have heart surgeries; it's what they do," Priya said. "And Ma's stressed

about him and she had a nosebleed. Yasmin, no! That's Nisba's."
Priya breathed deeply, sending a crackling sound through the phone
that made Maya shiver. "Look, sweetie," Priya said in a soft, slow
voice Maya hadn't heard in years. "I know you've spent years studying every little thing that can go wrong with the human body—I
have, too, okay? But I promise, everyone will be fine."

Maya could picture her standing over the sink, brushing her
bangs out of her eyes with her wrist since her fingers were wet. She
wished they were in the same room and was about to say so, even
though Priya would make fun of her, when she heard a click that
wasn't coming through the phone line, then the swishing of shoes
along the carpet. "I think someone's in the house," she whispered
into the phone.

"Who? Why are you whispering?"

"I don't know who! Ma and Pops are at the hospital."

"Well, Sherlock, why don't you go see?"

"I'm scared," Maya whispered, but she stood and wrapped the
afghan around her.

"You're worse than the girls. I'll stay on the phone, you go."

Maya walked toward the bedroom door. "Hello?" she said
softly. The doorknob started to turn on its own. Maya stepped
back. The door swung open, revealing Sanjay standing there in a
red hoodie.

"Sanjay!"

"Good-bye, Maya; I'm going to go back to raising my biologi-
cal children now." Priya hung up.

Maya let the cordless drop onto the carpet and threw her arms
around her cousin's neck. "You scared me, rat bastard!" She pushed
him away and pulled the afghan tighter around her shoulders.

"Seema-auntie said to stop by anytime, use my mom's key."

"And just bust into her room?"

"Dude, you said hello. I mean, I barely heard you, it was like a baby whispering, but, still, I thought 'hello' meant 'come in' in this society." He frowned. "Why are you wrapped up like Obi Wan Kenobi? It's not even cold."

Maya dropped the afghan and led Sanjay into the kitchen, describing her mother's nosebleed in as calm and as comic a manner as she could, trying to convince herself that there was nothing to worry about now. "Crazy timing, huh?"

Sanjay said his dad had mentioned something about the nosebleed, but he hadn't seemed too concerned. "I thought Seema-auntie would be back by now," he said. "I had no brilliant ideas to contribute to the wedding command center at home, so I came to see her."

"I'm sure she would have made you dal pakoras if she hadn't been busy hemorrhaging at the nose—"

"Enough with the gore, Maya."

"There's some besan parathas, though." She looked around the kitchen. "And Raisin Bran."

"I'll take the cereal."

"Excellent choice; an old man like you needs his fiber." Maya started boiling chai, handed two bowls of cereal over the kitchen counter to Sanjay. The Realtor had called the counter a "bar" when they moved into the house when Maya was in third grade. But since her parents didn't drink, to the Das family the counter only served as the border between the kitchen and what Seema called "the dining room," a big square space with a table, chairs, and a glass case filled with their good china, photos of family back in India, and murti Maya brought back every January, mostly Krishna and Hanuman, who were her parents' favorite gods, although all major members of the pantheon were represented at least once. Sanjay was leaning into the cabinet, messing with the god figurines; Seema would have told him to stop fidgeting.

Maya brought two mugs to the table, setting one down at Priya's place for Sanjay. It made a squishing noise as she set it on the oil-cloth, the soundtrack to the breakfasts and dinners of her child-hood. She ran a finger along the round depression in the oilcloth that had been tamped down where Seema set her chai every morn-ing in the exact same place. When she'd gone to her friend's house for the fake volcano project, Maya was surprised that they didn't have oilcloth spread over their nice tablecloth. She had spilled a little Diet Coke—which Seema didn't even allow in the house—on the white embroidered spread, but her friend's mom said not to worry, she'd just throw it in the wash. After that, whenever Maya waited for her mother at the hospital, she watched the doctors hurry past and wondered who had oilcloths on their tables and who just threw things in the wash.

"Want to turn the plastic over?" Sanjay asked. "So that ring goes away?"

"No, I like it." Maya stopped touching the oilcloth and sat in her own chair. Sanjay, already seated, was playing with a two-inch-high figurine of Krishna the Butter Thief, making it dance on the table. "Amrita's still asleep?"

"Nah, when I left she was looking through magazines with Mom, picking out sari blouse styles for the wedding," Sanjay said. Then he was back on his feet again, opening the display case, look-ing at the other figurines. "She wants an open back, but my mother and her mother—"

"Let me guess, they want 'modest style.'" Maya looked up from her chai and saw Sanjay leaning into the case, resting his elbow on a shelf and his forehead on his hand. "Sanjay. What?"

"I overheard Amrita on her cell last night," he said, still with his back to her. "She's traveling to her old roommate's engagement party next weekend, this annoying blond girl, Kristen. I can't go because I have to work. That's no big deal, but last night I heard her ask Kristen if she was sure Darren would be there—Amrita's col-lege boyfriend."

"Wow." Maya stared hard at her chai.

Sanjay sat back down, righting the toppled Krishna. "They were on and off for a couple years before we met. But I didn't think they were still in touch. And they are. I asked her flat out."

Amrita had appeared so serene last night. It seemed impossible that she could be the cause of any turmoil, or have any dark secrets. Maybe Sanjay was overreacting. "What did she say?"

"That she felt she needed to talk to Darren before the wedding. And then Mom wandered through the kitchen and hustled us off to our separate rooms. We haven't been able to talk since. But at breakfast Amrita was all smiles, like everything's great."

"Oh."

"She still wants to marry me." Sanjay picked up the figurine and started closing and opening his fist around it, making the blue god disappear and resurrect again and again. Maya wanted to tell him to put it down. "She said so before Mom showed up. Said she didn't tell me they talk every now and then because she didn't want to upset me, didn't tell me about him coming to the party, because she knew I wouldn't want her to go without me. And she's going to."

Whatever the reason Amrita wanted to see her ex—and maybe it really was nothing but nostalgia—she had made it clear that when it came to her desire to see Darren, Sanjay's feelings were subordinate to hers, maybe even irrelevant altogether. That was the part Maya couldn't understand. And she was supposed to play this person at the sangeet, to celebrate the moment Amrita met Sanjay, whom she was clearly putting through so much pain. "Oh, Sanjay," Maya said. "You must feel so disoriented. Hurt. I like Amrita, I mean, I think I do, I hardly know her. But this is just . . . not good." That wasn't helpful. Maya knew nothing she said would solve this problem, but at least she should try to say something constructive, make Sanjay see the situation differently. "She definitely loves you, of course she does. You look like a film star. You're a consultant. You're a Brahmin."

Sanjay laughed. "Yeah. I'm the man of her mother's dreams."

"True. Okay. But she does love you. I saw how she looked at you. You can be the man of her dreams *and* her mother's. It has to happen sometimes, right?" Still, if that were true, then why hurt Sanjay, just to bid a friendly farewell to an ex? "But," Maya started, thinking out loud, "people can be complicated. Do you think it's possible that she loves him, too?"

There was a loud cracking, snapping noise. Sanjay opened his fist and pieces of the Krishna murti fell out of his hand onto the table before bouncing to the floor.

"Damn it, Sanjay!"

"Sorry." He wiped his long, thin fingers across his face. "I didn't know I was squeezing that hard. I'm really sorry."

"You didn't have to tell me, you know," Maya said. "You wanted my advice."

"No." Sanjay gripped the mug in his hands. "I wanted Seema-auntie's advice."

Maya stood, pushed her chair aside, and knelt down, picking up pieces of Krishna the Butter Thief. The wooden statue had splintered into three distinct parts—the baby god's disembodied head, his hand in the butter churn, and the rest of his blue body. This had been her grandmother's favorite incarnation of Krishna, as a mischievous toddler. Once, while Dadiji was praying, she looked up from her mala and saw a dark-skinned little boy wandering through her house. "It was the Lord, I tell you," she swore to anyone who would listen. Maya had started to believe her until Pops pointed out that the cassette player they'd brought her from Walmart had disappeared along with the Lord. Ravi-uncle got it back the following week; he'd bumped into a neighborhood boy walking down the street with the same cassette player resting on his shoulder,

"Like he was a big man in one of those films about Brooklyn or Chicago," Ravi-uncle had said. He thought the story was hilarious, but Dadiji still insisted that it was possible, the boy could have been an incarnation of the little god who meant for the tape deck to be found and restored to her.

"I'll get another murti in India in December," Sanjay offered.

"It's no big deal." Maya stood. "Anyway, about Amrita..."

"You don't have to—"

"You must put that phone call out of your head, stupid boy." Maya shook her head back and forth. "She came to your uncle's hospital bed before you were even married; she will be a good and dutiful wife. Real life is not like American TV, with roses and the moon. Amrita is a professional woman, almost thirty. You knew you were not the first boy she kissed. Stop being a crybaby and go help your bride and your poor mother plan your wedding. We are all looking forward to it, we have bought our tickets; you will not want to ruin it for us. Besides, the white horse you will ride in on is already paid for."

"Amazing!" Sanjay looked down at his soggy Raisin Bran. His shoulders and the top of his head were shaking, but it sounded like he was laughing. At the imitation of Seema or the advice itself, Maya couldn't tell.

"In twenty-seven years I had to have picked up something, right?" Maya put the pieces on the counter, unsure whether you could throw murti bits in the trash. Seema would know what to do, but Maya didn't want to call attention to the broken god; enough had broken lately. It was probably safe to bury the pieces, return the wood to the earth. And maybe they could replace it before Seema noticed. Maya walked around the table, put her arms around Sanjay's neck. "Sorry you couldn't have the real thing."

"No, this is better," Sanjay said with a mouth full of cereal. He squeezed her arm quickly, then stood up. "I got auntie-quality advice without Seema-auntie knowing what's going on. She'd be giving Amrita the fish-eye for the next twenty-seven years."

"I won't say a word," Maya promised.

On Sunday, Sanjay and Amrita insisted on giving Maya a ride to the airport. Her mother came, too. Seema had come home from the hospital on Saturday insisting she felt "perfectly fine, better than ever," and stayed upbeat through several visits to Pops. Maya had thrown out Seema's stained cardigan but put her sari to soak in cold water when she got home from the hospital on Friday, then hand washed it the next morning and hung it over the shower curtain rod to dry. Now it was pristine, and Maya's foresight had left Seema more pleased and proud than Maya had seen her since her med school graduation. Seema was still beaming when they arrived at the airport. Sanjay hugged Maya good-bye, reached into his jacket, and pulled out a packet, which he thrust into her mother's hands. "I wanted you to open it in front of Maya."

"What is this, silly boy?" Seema demanded.

"Nothing." He shrugged. "I broke one at your house, and Amrita found this at the Indian market this morning." He grabbed Amrita's hand as he spoke. She looked down at her shoes and smiled as if they pleased her. She didn't seem like a cheater.

"You should not be spending money on us," Seema chided, unwrapping the gift. "Things are things, God is within people." She hugged Maya good-bye, holding her a few seconds longer than her usual squeeze and pat on the back. Maya pressed against her mother's body. Not liking the feeling of bone at her ribs, she moved her hands down to Seema's waist, which was just nice, solid flesh. Looking at Amrita and Sanjay over her shoulder, Maya realized the list of things she wasn't telling her mother kept getting longer. Pops was right; you shouldn't seek to identify the source of sorrow. Pain would find you, it didn't need a reason. It was luck you needed to look out for.

Seema patted Maya on the shoulders, indicating that the hug was now over. But as Maya stepped back, her mother pulled her close again. "Krishna the Butter Thief is the one which has broken," she whispered into Maya's ear. "I noticed it missing as soon as I got home. And he bought Krishna with the flute." Maya felt her mother's body shake with silent laughter. "Silly boy."

Chapter Eight

Maya sat at a desk on the EPU floor, chewing a Luna bar and reviewing the interaction she'd had earlier that morning, with the parents of a seventeen-year-old freshman at NYU who had experienced his first psychotic break; he was found raving in a tree in Washington Square Park late last night, after his roommate reported him missing. Some parents screamed when you told them, or cried. But these two were very quiet, the husband asking questions—how could this happen with no family history, what did they do now? Then the wife whispered, "Why would God do this to us?"

Maya should have let it go; these questions were better considered later on, and probably would be, for as long as the couple and their son lived. It was wiser to stick with practical considerations, easily digestible bits of information, right after revealing a diagnosis. But having just seen her own father in a hospital bed, Maya wanted to be more helpful than that, more human. She knew what her attending would say—that she was this couple's doctor, not their friend. But she wanted them to know she understood a fraction of what they felt, and that they weren't responsible for what had happened.

"Schizophrenia is not an act of God," she'd told them. "It's a chronic medical condition, like diabetes; it can be controlled with medication for the most part. And the support of a loving family really improves a patient's prognosis." She searched for words that the couple would find comforting. "A family like yours is a real blessing."

"But there must be some reason," the husband insisted.

Maya could tell her words had made the situation worse, not better. So she returned to the script, promising that a nurse would take them to see their son as soon as he was fully awake, and that she would be back soon with literature on the condition and contact information for support groups. They didn't respond, but the wife cocked her head and fixed her gaze on Maya in a way that made her feel as if she had somehow caused this situation, that what had befallen their son was all her fault.

Maya swallowed the last of her Luna bar. She knew exactly where she'd gone wrong—when she'd stopped trying to inform the parents and started trying to comfort them. She meant to be compassionate but came across as weak, letting them down when they wanted answers, not sympathy. She wouldn't do it again. The break room door opened; a nurse stuck her head in and said, "Maya, the unit director wants to see you."

The nurse had looked down at the floor, not at her, as she said it, Maya realized, following the woman's silent white shoes down the hall. Somehow, her supervisor must have known about her talk with the schizophrenic boy's parents. Walking into her supervisor's office, Maya realized how much noise the rubber soles of her wedge-heeled moccasins made on the hallway floor and swore never to wear them again.

The unit director was awkward on his best days, but now, as he asked her to have a seat, he seemed almost as nervous as Maya felt, stumbling over the few steps he made to get from his file cabinet back to his desk chair. "I don't even know where to begin with this," he said, picking up a piece of paper that was folded crisply into three sections. "Legally, your name shouldn't be on the document; I don't know what possessed them to name you, list you first even—"

"Sorry," Maya interrupted. "What?"

"No, I'm sorry, I haven't been clear. I've been running this through my mind all morning," he rushed on, cutting her off. "It seems you've been named in a malpractice suit, wrongful admission to the psych ER. A Paulina Esleck."

Maya made her pranayama breaths as discreet as possible, so the unit director wouldn't notice her slowing her thoughts, trying to remember. "The borderline lady with the molting coat?" she asked finally. "Dangerous apartment? Neighbors complained?"

"That's her," he said. "Although I'd be careful about calling her borderline."

Maya tried to keep up her breathing as the unit director explained the situation; when she forgot to focus on the pranayama she felt she wasn't breathing at all. He seemed to speak very slowly, so slowly that instead of making his meaning clearer, his words were drawn out into absurd sounds that were barely recognizable, like the voice in a drive-through box. He explained that Mrs. Esleck's lawyers were charging that she didn't suffer from mental health problems but was the victim of persecution from an avaricious landlord trying to oust her from her rent-controlled apartment. Her son had happily collected a calm, medicated version of his mother when he arrived at the hospital two days later than expected. It was his sister in Florida who filed suit, arguing that if her mother was doing as well as her brother said when he retrieved her, there had been no reason to admit her in the first place. The Esleck children couldn't bother to remove mountains of cat litter from their mother's apartment, but now they were turning their guilt and sibling rivalry toward ruining Maya's career.

"What does this mean?" Maya asked. "Can I still—"

"Oh, it's business as usual for you, Maya," the unit director said, refolding the paper, which he had smoothed out as he related the story of the Esleck family circus. "Until the forms get straightened out, anyway, and this is settled or sent to trial. The EPU has malpractice insurance for all residents; since an attending signed off on the admission, you can't be held personally responsible for something like this."

Maya unlaced her fingers, which were intertwined with each other in a prayer-grip she didn't remember making. "Right," she said.

"I'd like to tell you this is nothing to worry about," the unit director said, standing up. Maya stood, too, and noticed the file folder, neatly labeled ESLECK, on his desk. "But every time the hospital gets hit with a lawsuit, it's cause for worry."

Maya looked up from the file and noticed that the unit director had extended his hand. She shook it, remembering the only other time she'd shaken his hand, after her interview for the residency program. "Thank you," she said, because she couldn't think of anything else. "For telling me," she elaborated, hoping that if she kept adding words one would be the magic sound that made him release his firm, sticky grip.

The unit director said some words of encouragement, or commiseration, or censure, or just farewell, as Maya left his office. She heard the sounds as she walked out, but couldn't concentrate on what they meant.

•   •   •

Arriving at her studio apartment, Maya unlocked her door and surveyed the tangled mess of clean sheets, dirty laundry, Xeroxed medical handouts and dog-eared *Hi! Blitz* magazines she'd brought from India, the detritus of a life that, right now, held no appeal. She hadn't told her parents about the lawsuit—there was no need to worry them yet. She told Heidi, who said life sucked sometimes, but Maya was the best psychiatrist in the tri-state area, and this would seem less tragic tomorrow, and hilarious in a year. But malpractice suits took so long to resolve it could still be going on in a year, and Maya would spend all that time feeling like a human cliff-hanger. The lawsuit made her want to believe in the curse; then none of it would be her fault. But there was no blood involved. The hospital wasn't her family. Besides, the curse didn't exist, or if it did, it was only in Parvati's hate-spewing mind. And now Parvati and Chotu were long gone. They had packed up and left the day of the fight, and no one knew where to find them.

Maya was lying on her couch in the dark watching a pirated DVD of *Omkara* when the lock turned, the door opened, and Scott appeared. She covered her eyes with her hand to block the light he let in from the hall, and moaned when he turned on the lamp.

"What are you doing?" Scott set a grease-stained white paper bag on the counter.

"Wallowing."

"Don't worry!" He bustled about the too-bright kitchen, pulling down bowls and filling them with savory-smelling food. Maya sat up a little to see what it was.

"Pad thai! You're good to me." She flopped back onto the couch. "Even though I'm incompetent."

"Baby, you know how many malpractice suits hospitals get thrown at them every day? And how many actually go to trial?"

"But none of those named me."

"This one shouldn't have either!" Scott tugged on a corkscrew he'd stabbed too viciously into a bottle of wine. "I forwarded your e-mail to this fourth-year associate who's—"

"Great, now everyone knows I'm incompetent."

Scott set the bowls on the coffee table, followed by the wineglasses he'd stashed under his arms. He lifted Maya's legs off the couch, sat down, and settled them on his lap.

"I was just trying to find solutions," he said, rubbing her feet.

"I don't want solutions; I want sympathy."

"Would it help if I offered to break the old lady's legs?"

"Very much." Maya pulled the coffee table closer to them. "Thanks for the food."

Scott nodded at the TV. "How come the sound's off?"

"I wasn't really watching, just distracting myself with the pictures." Maya sat up and turned up the sound. "*Omkara.* It's basically Othello, but set in Uttar Pradesh."

"Gorgeous." Scott leaned toward the screen.

"We can go to that market, maybe, in December, if you come. I'll ask Pops how far it is. And Heidi would single-handedly improve the local economy."

Scott opened his mouth, then shut it again, set his bowl on the table and stretched out on the couch. Maya settled into the curve his body made, resting her elbows on his rib cage. On TV, a woman with deep eyes and deeper cleavage threw herself at the feet of a man who turned away from her. The woman shouted and reached up toward him.

"What'd she say?" Scott asked.

Maya translated the woman's cries, the man's harsh reply. She translated the next line, too, and continued doing so. The translation kept her mind too busy to worry about her failures, and the warmth of Scott's body felt good against hers. Onscreen, a man knelt on some train tracks in a rainstorm, sobbing. The music swelled, overpowering the sound of the rain, but was quickly drowned out by the lively bhangra of Maya's ringtone.

She grabbed the phone, which was angrily flashing her sister's number, off the coffee table. "Priya. Can I call you back?"

"You leave a message saying your life is over and now you can't even be bothered to tell me what happened? I hustled the girls into bed so I could call."

"My life will still be over tomorrow." Maya stood and walked to the sink. Scott stopped the video; the sound of a soccer game filled the studio. "I'm watching *Omkara*."

"So watch tomorrow." Priya bit into something crunchy; it sounded like an apple.

"But Scott's here, and I'm translating it for him; it's at a really good part."

Priya made a scraping noise as if the apple had gotten lodged in her throat. "Do you want to have to do that your whole life, every time you rent a video, go to a movie?"

"That's exactly what I want to do," Maya said loudly enough that Scott looked up.

"Watering down our culture, whispering in the theater, annoying the nice Indian families?" Priya made a clucking noise with her tongue. "My sister's going to be that couple, the pushy desi with the clueless white guy pretending he's having a good time."

"Bye, Priya. Give the girls my love," Maya sang.

"Fine, talk to—" Maya slapped her phone shut before Priya could finish. She returned to the couch, to Scott, to translating the movie he had switched back on, sipping wine between sentences. I love this, helping him connect to the language, she thought. But without Priya to convince, the thought had no force. When the next dance sequence started, she cleared the table and started washing dishes.

"Dance over," Scott called from the couch.

"I'm making tea, but I've seen it before," Maya said, still hunched over the sink. "You keep watching." She turned to face him. "You know the story of Othello, right?"

Scott shrugged. "Can't we all just get along?"

"See," Maya said, turning back to the sink. "You're going to be just fine."

Chapter Nine

All Maya wanted to do was stay home, cook some dal or order a pizza, and read Agatha Christie. When she was depressed, only Christie, with her tightly plotted mysteries and cardboard cutout characters, could help. Even a Bollywood movie, despite its dance sequences and hysterical hair, makeup, and costumes, touched on too many relevant themes—marriage, usually. Family. Life. Although Agatha served up death, along with just enough teas at the vicar's rectory and dinners at the major's manse, it was death as a puzzle, one that was neatly completed at the end, with no annoying introspection. Death left no fingerprints besides the ones needed to solve the case.

But there would be no staying home to read; she was the one who arranged this evening. Actually, it was Scott who had mentioned Walker, a fellow third year at the firm, saying that he was perfect for Heidi. When Maya asked what made him perfect, Scott replied, "Single, straight, still has all his hair." Which, really, was enough, at least for dinner; Heidi swore she only met women and gay men at the magazine. She did usually have a guy she'd met at a party or through friends orbiting around her at some stage in the classic Heidi pseudo-relationship. They were always the same, starting as one-sided, obsessional friendships, with some man Heidi wasn't sure she even liked professing his good luck at having met someone like her. After months of late-night conversations and multicourse dinners that dragged on for four hours, Heidi would finally sleep with the poor guy. Suddenly four hours seemed too long for dinner, the late-night conversations became litanies of Heidi's faults, and Maya's inbox filled with e-mails whose subject lines were things like "Neurotic Megalomaniac" and text that read, *Do you think I am one? Pretend you're not my friend, just my therapist. BE HONEST!!!!!*

Megalomania was too strong a description. But there was something there. Heidi liked a guy who came on strong, wooed her. When she found one, she'd seek his attention with what Maya could now identify as object hunger. Most likely she was trying to replicate her relationship with her father, who'd been single-mindedly devoted to her and Kyle since their mother's death. Or maybe it was more primal than that, more mystical. Maya had taken a lit class at Dartmouth in which the professor insisted that naming was destiny; they read an article that posited most patricides were committed by juniors, so sick of living in the shadow of the man they were named for that they resolved to eliminate him. Maybe it was Heidi's full name that was the problem: Aphrodite, goddess of love; that had to inspire unrealistic expectations. Even the nickname, Heidi, a naïve Swiss child. Of course, the Aphrodite was really after her grandmother who'd ended up raising her namesake in the absence of her own daughter. And Yia-yia couldn't have been more practical, bustling around the house in elastic-waist pants and a black sweater, even in summer, Murphy's Oil Soap in hand. No goddess of love illusions there.

Maya owed it to Heidi to show up tonight. And to Scott. She loved it that he wanted to set up Heidi, to see her beloved, taken care of; it proved that he was the right person to take care of Maya herself, that he would be able to take the pieces of her life and make them all fit together into a kaleidoscopic, dazzling whole. Maya slapped *Endless Night* onto the coffee table and began looking for something to replace Scott's plaid boxer shorts, which she'd been wearing since she got home from the hospital.

This was better than Agatha Christie, Maya thought, looking across the table at Heidi, who was smiling so widely that the candlelight glinted off her shiny nude lip gloss. Walker was leaning over, his floppy brown hair falling over his forehead as he poured a dark red wine into Heidi's gold-embossed glass. "Your hair smells great," he said, not quite low enough for Maya and Scott not to hear.

"Well, I have started showering every day," Heidi answered, with an uneven smile that showed she was torn between appreciating his compliment and resenting its cheesiness. "You know, since the neighbors complained."

Walker laughed and Maya gave Scott's hand a quick squeeze under the table. He looked at her and the candlelight seemed to be bouncing off him, too, highlighting the rise of his collarbone, casting shadows on the dip in the middle. This was one of the parts of Scott's body that Maya had claimed as her own before he left for law school, telling him that if he dated other women at Yale, they should know that his collarbone and hipbones, the subtle protrusions that fit in her mouth, and the hollows around them, belonged exclusively to her. But she no longer had to worry about that, now that they were in the same city and had found each other again.

"That's not illegal, is it, Maya?" Heidi's voice pierced the rolling hum of restaurant noise, the low laughter and chattering, the clinking of plates.

"What?"

"If I buy dozens of shawls in India to sell to the girls at the magazine?"

"It's kind of illegal," Scott answered.

Heidi frowned. "What if I wear them all, so they're used and it's like a yard sale?"

"I don't know, Hei," Scott said.

"You're going to wear *dozens* of shawls?" Walker teased.

"She'll need them," Maya insisted. "There are going to be tons of parties for my cousin's wedding."

"Yeah, Indian weddings last at least three days," Heidi said, her voice rising with her enthusiasm. "And the groom rides in on a white horse, right, Maya?"

"It's true." She looked at Walker. "Heidi studied comparative religion in college."

"So how did you get into fashion?" Walker asked.

"I like rituals, pageantry, lots of jewelry," Heidi said. "And I'm Greek Orthodox, so the priesthood's out. No, really, I worked on the paper in college, and my first job afterwards was as an assistant at *Elle*. It went from there."

"And you like it?"

"It's fun." Heidi shrugged. "But I might renounce it all in India, grow my hair into dreds, become a sadhu, wander around naked."

"Women don't become sadhus," Maya corrected. "But I could drop you off at an ashram, help them shave your head, take some of your worldly goods off your hands."

"Maybe on the next trip."

"Scott, you going on this spiritual journey?" Walker asked.

Heidi and Scott swiveled their eyes toward Maya, perfectly synchronized.

"I hope you are," Maya said after what seemed like several minutes of silence.

"Me, too," Heidi chimed in. "We'll be a whole honky posse."

A tinkling sound arrived at the table along with the waitress, an olive-skinned woman wearing excessive eyeliner and several noisy anklets and charm bracelets that livened up the slinky black dress that seemed to be the uniform at Ephesus. Heidi had chosen the restaurant, an upscale Turkish place that had recently opened on the Lower East Side, because a publicist had e-mailed her their private reservation number.

"Dessert, after-dinner drink, Turkish coffee?" the waitress asked in an accented voice that Maya suspected owed more to Queens than Istanbul. "Okay, then," she said, looking across their heads. "Let me give you a few minutes to decide." She pulled out a mosaic-bordered tile with the day's dessert offerings written on it, dropped it on the table, then jingled away to a party of six who were clearly more organized when it came to ordering.

"I couldn't eat another thing. But you all go ahead if you want to; I'm gonna scope out upstairs." Heidi stood. "It's a hookah lounge; the publicist said it's a scene."

"I'll come." Walker stood, tossing a gold card to Scott. "I like a good hookah."

Heidi shot Maya a glance that was equal parts amusement and triumph, a look that meant *this is going well, isn't it?* but was too complex to be directed at Scott.

"He likes her," Maya said to Scott. "And she loves that."

Scott slapped Walker's card and his own into the booklet handed to him by the waitress, and waited until she undulated away to speak. "I want to come to India, Maya."

"Great." She put her hand on top of his forearm, which rested on the table.

"But only as your boyfriend." He drew his arm off the table and turned toward her. "Not as part of a honky posse, another friend from college."

"Scott, you know—" Maya started, shaking her head.

"I know this is a rough time for you, and that makes me a dick for bringing it up now," Scott interrupted. "But I can't help it. I love you, I know you love me, and I don't think we can move forward unless everyone else knows, too. It doesn't have to be now; it doesn't even have to be in India—I don't have to come. But if I do, I'm not going to lie to your parents." He paused but Maya just kept shaking her head, looking at her own hands, which were now folded in her lap. "And maybe India is the right time," he continued. "It's a happy occasion, everyone will be there. I'm not so bad, Maya. Parents love me."

The waitress dropped off the credit card receipts. Maya waited until she'd returned to the other end of the restaurant to respond, "What's not to love?"

"Really?"

"Maybe, Scott." She took a breath. "But maybe not. I have to think about this, make sure the time is right."

"But you will think?"

Maya looked up and Heidi and Walker were there, approaching the table with red cheeks and huskier voices, bringing with them the heavy odor of apple tobacco. Something about the scent reminded Maya of the way her backyard in Kalamazoo smelled on humid summer nights, although she hadn't been home for one in years.

Outside, in front of the restaurant, Maya lit a cigarette while Heidi and the guys negotiated where to go next.

"Can I bum one?" asked a forty-year-old guy in a three-thousand-dollar suit.

No, you can buy one, Maya thought, but she said "Sure" and pulled out her pack, then her beeping cell. The message turned out to be Tariq, asking her to call right away. While Heidi and Scott debated East Side or West, Maya walked to the corner and dialed.

"Maya?" Tariq sobbed, a sound she'd never heard before.

"What happened?"

"It's Priya," he said, in a soft, suddenly composed voice. "She had a miscarriage."

"No." Maya's whisper matched his.

"I came home from work and she was in the bathroom, crying," he said. "She bled a lot so I brought her here; I'm in the hospital, in the lounge. They're going to do a D and C in the morning. My sister's at the house, so I'll stay here tonight, unless the girls get upset. They don't really know what happened, just that Mommy's sick." He breathed heavily. "But there was so much blood."

"I'm coming," Maya said.

"Are you sure?" Tariq's voice rose. "Priya said it's a routine procedure."

"I think I can get the last bus."

"Thank you. Priya would say not to come, but I know she'd want to see you." He started crying again. "I don't know what to say to her. I haven't even told your parents."

"Don't worry about that now," Maya said. "I'll call you from the bus if I make it."

Having brokered a bar agreement, Heidi walked over.

"Priya had a miscarriage," Maya told her in the same even voice she would use to announce a change in her call schedule. "She's in the hospital. It's too late to fly or take Amtrak, I think, but I'm going to try to get the last bus to Boston tonight."

As Scott flagged down a cab, Maya let Heidi hug her. Inhaling Heidi's vanilla-scented shampoo, she looked over her shoulder at Walker, hating it that this floppy-haired stranger already knew what Maya felt was rapidly becoming the salient fact about her. That she was unlucky.

Chapter Ten

Maya hadn't slept on the bus; at first she tried to calm herself by remembering prayer chants, but in her mind, everything sounded tinny, fake, like the beginning of a mediocre yoga class. So she focused on identifying the darkened shapes of the ghost buildings along the highway—the onion dome outside of New Haven was a Russian church, that was easy, but the blocky factories and office parks all looked alike.

Still, she must have cried at some point; she got off the bus with her shawl damp with tears and who knew what else. She was embarrassed when Tariq hugged her and the clammy shawl brushed against their hands. But he didn't seem to mind. By the time Maya arrived she felt she had achieved some kind of fatigue-induced clarity, that she could sense the thoughts of the other passengers who got off at South Station—one had worked the late shift and was arriving, elated, to visit his girlfriend; the other had missed an earlier bus because he was drunk, and shuffled into the warm station to sleep until tomorrow's leg of the journey. The enhanced perception followed her into the car with Tariq, who had been at the hospital until now and hadn't slept either; she could tell they were both grateful for their exhaustion, which excused them from speaking.

Maya still felt numb the next morning, which she spent with her nieces, watching Hanuman romp in cartoon monkey god form. This was the fifth time she'd seen the video, and she was starting to regret having bought it in an effort to expose the girls to Hinduism and to wean Yasmin away from her *Aladdin* fixation, which was unavoidable, given her name. For that Maya blamed Tariq; Yasmin was named after his favorite aunt. But the name wasn't the issue, really; the larger problem was, how do you blend two major religions into one child? And such a small child, Maya thought, looking at the soles of Yasmin's feet as she lay on the carpet. Something about the clean, tiny feet made Maya feel shaky, powerless, and she forced herself to turn back to the movie. She was only half watching, waiting for Tariq to return so she could go visit Priya at the hospital. Tariq's sister Laila had gone home to her own kids once Maya arrived, leaving Maya as the token responsible adult in the house. Following Tariq's lead, she was going with the "Mommy's sick and went to the doctor but she'll be home soon" angle, and the girls seemed fine, although unusually quiet. She was trying to come up with magically soothing words to say to them when the phone rang.

"Iqbal residence," she said, to reassure the caller, and the girls if they were listening, that he or she had reached a house where nothing was wrong.

"Maya, is that you?"

"Mohan!" So her brother did remember his original family occasionally. "Girls, it's Mohan-uncle," Maya sang to the two prone, flannel-covered figures on the floor, as if this call from their uncle in D.C. was the most exciting thing that could happen short of a visitation from Hanuman himself. "Say hello."

"Hi, Mohan-uncle," came a mumbled chorus. He hadn't visited in at least two years; to them the cartoon monkey god was more familiar and much more interesting.

"Priya's not back yet," she said into the phone.

"Back from where?"

Maya looked at the girls and switched into Marwari, hoping Mohan's wasn't too rusty. "The hospital."

"What's she doing in the hospital?"

"You don't know?" she said in English. Maya tried to summon a Marwari or Hindi word for miscarriage but couldn't. "She lost the baby," she said finally, piecing small vocabulary words together. "Ma and Pops don't know yet; Priya's waiting until Pops gets home from the hospital this afternoon to tell them."

"I can't believe it. She was fine with the others." Although he was speaking English, Mohan kept pausing between disjointed sentences. "Good you're there. What—"

Tariq's key jostled the lock, and Maya stood, too eager to get to the hospital to soothe Mohan's disorientation. "I've got to go," she said loudly in English as she stood, glancing at the girls. "I'm going to the...grocery store...but I'll call later."

Priya was doing well after the procedure, Tariq whispered to Maya in the kitchen. They wanted to keep her for observation until six, but she could receive visitors now.

Walking into Priya's hospital room, Maya was struck by how much she looked like her daughters when they slept, a tiny bundle of a body under a white blanket, with a little hand resting above the covers, and shiny black hair sliding down the pillow. Priya's back was to the door but she turned slightly when Maya walked in; she was on the phone, crying. She didn't say anything for several minutes, just wept silently. Maya couldn't hear any words coming through the phone. Finally, Priya wiped her cheeks and said, "Okay, Ma. Maya's here now so I'll let you go. Tell Pops I'm glad he's home."

Maya walked over to the bed, climbed up, and put her arms around Priya. After a few minutes, Priya pulled away and turned to look at her sister.

"There was so much blood, Maya."

Maya nodded. On the bus last night, she kept remembering Tariq saying those same words. And by the time they'd reached Stamford, she felt, with creeping certainty, that her family was under attack. She felt guilty even thinking that the curse could have such power, as if she were rejecting Dr. Bernard personally, along with their entire profession. If she believed in the curse, she deserved a malpractice suit. But looking at Priya, whose lashes were still wet and clumped into points, Maya had to consider the possibility that Parvati's curse was more than just an angry insult. Pops had survived his heart attack, and Ma was okay, as far as she was letting on, but the undeniable fact was that they had both gotten violently, luridly sick within a month of each other. And now, a family member was lost, or a potential family member anyway. Gone. Priya had always protected and advised Maya, whether Maya wanted her to or not. Sitting in the chilly room, looking at her sister's chalky, wet face, Maya wanted to swear to Priya that she would get this curse removed, fix everything, make it better. But if Priya knew Maya was buckling under the weight of what they both normally would mock as an old superstition, then she'd end up comforting Maya, not vice versa.

"You're going to be fine," Maya said, both to calm her sister and to convince herself this was true. "You'll try again when you're ready."

Priya nodded and brushed a tear off her hand.

"But it's still terrible," Maya said. "I'm so sorry this happened."

Priya grabbed Maya's hand. "I'm so glad you're here. If the girls remember this at all, they'll think of it as the weekend Maya-masi visited. Twice in one month."

"Anything I can do for them? Or you?"

"Actually, yeah." Priya took her hand away, started twisting her wedding band around her finger. "I didn't want to ask Tariq. He's so upset, he hasn't slept." She looked down at her fingers. "When it happened, I was walking across the yard, and I tripped. I didn't fall, just stumbled on that crabgrass." She kept staring at her hand as if the lines on her palm held some explanation, CliffsNotes to the story she was reciting in a clipped, even voice. "But a half hour later, my stomach hurt. I had just put the girls down for naps, so I went into their bathroom. I saw I was bleeding. I stood up to look for my cell phone, but it wasn't in any of my pockets. I must have stood there for a while, because soon blood was all over the floor, three pints easily, maybe more. I used the girls' towels to mop it up. Then I heard Tariq come home, so I wrapped a towel around myself, and yelled for him. Laila came over and he brought me here."

Maya was crying now, but Priya wasn't. She was looking at her folded hands as if studying her manicured thumbnails.

"So, the towels," she continued. "They're still in the hamper, except maybe I left one on the floor, a pretty clean one I think." She looked at Maya, and when she started speaking again her voice picked up speed. "Can you get rid of them? Just throw them out. I know Ma would say that they'd clean up in the wash, or that the girls can use the guest towels. But they like having their own things, and they should, something with a nice design, something happy— they're kids, right? Can you just buy some other kid towels?"

"Of course," Maya said, wiping her face and pulling herself together. It felt good to have a task, something concrete to focus on. "What kind?" she asked. Disposing of the bloody, ballet-slipper-printed towels would be easy enough, but not choosing the new ones; Priya was so particular.

"It doesn't matter!" Priya pushed a handful of hair off her fore-head. "Just go to Walmart and get something temporary. They can have Princess Jasmine on them ... no, that'll piss Nisba off. They can have Hanuman for all I care."

"Yeah, I don't think Walmart has debuted their 'Pagan Idols' line yet." Maya laughed and a tear fell into her open mouth, salting her tongue. "But I'll do my best. As long as I know you'll get your real, Perfectly Priya towels later."

"Sure, mock me in my hospital bed," Priya said. But she was smiling, and she didn't cry for the rest of the visit.

Tariq was in the kitchen with his sister, cooking a special dinner. Laila was staying so Tariq could go back to the hospital to get Priya and Maya could go buy dessert; she said she'd promised the girls ice-cream sandwiches, but it was just an excuse to get out of the house; Priya would hate having anyone else be reminded of how her body had betrayed her, in a way that had been as messy as it was devastating. Maya thanked Laila, stooped to pull a trash bag out from the box in the cabinet under the kitchen sink, and headed to the bathroom.

There was a light pink towel still on the ground. Now she lifted it up and saw the rust-colored stains on the bottom of the towel, the amoeba-shaped spots on the white tiles. She took the disinfecting countertop wipes Priya kept behind the toilet and scrubbed the floor with them, her eyes burning from the chemicals. When she finished, she threw the wipes and the towel from the floor into the Hefty bag, then dumped in the crunchy towels that had hardened in the otherwise empty wicker hamper. Maya looked around the disinfected bathroom. It was perfect, except for the naked racks.

She unlocked the door and walked down the hall into the living room, where she almost bumped into her brother. He was standing talking to Tariq, stealing glances at the girls, who were staring hard at him; they were probably wondering what presents he had brought them, but Priya had raised them too well for them to ask.

"Mohan! What are you doing here?" Maya hugged him, still holding the Hefty bag in her right hand.

"I came after we talked." He nodded at the girls. "I wanted to see my nieces."

"He took the shuttle from D.C.," Tariq said, filling the silence.

"Want help with the trash?" Mohan asked.

"I got it." Maya lifted the bag up against her hip bone. "Thanks." She looked at her relatives standing in the living room like trees in a forest, little ones at the edge, big ones in the middle. "Tariq's going to get Priya, Laila's making dinner, the girls get to watch Hanuman again since they've been so good, and I'm going to Target," she said.

Mohan considered the girls looking up at him and said, "I'm coming with you."

On her way to Target, Maya spotted a Dumpster, pulled into a church parking lot, and threw the tightly tied plastic bag into it. The church was a century-old steepled brick number made even grimmer by its paint, which was the color of a scab. Walking back to the car she thought it would be nice to put five dollars in the poor box, a token in return for trash removal services. But she didn't have any cash with her, just her credit cards.

"Chestnut Hill doesn't have trash pickup?" Mohan asked when she got in the car.

"Just taking care of business." They were silent for the rest of the ride, Mohan flipping stations on the radio of Priya's Toyota Highlander until Maya pushed his hands away, grabbing the CD case from Priya's glove compartment.

As if by common agreement that the best place to talk was under fluorescent lights, inside the store they both opened their mouths at the same time, Mohan asking "How—" just as Maya started to tell him "Priya—"

"You go first." Maya maneuvered her body in between Mohan and the shopping cart. "And let me push; I know where I'm going."

"Really?"

"Sure. There's no Target near me, so I come here when I'm in town. Priya said go to Walmart—the girls need towels—but Target is my home away from home, so..." Maya rolled the cart past jauntily striped wrapping paper, red pleather ottomans, yellow bottles of dishwashing detergent, colors so bright they hurt her eyes.

Mohan cleared his throat. "I was just asking about Priya," he said.

"She's fine, as good as can be expected. The D and C was this morning."

Mohan shuddered and stopped walking; the clicking sound made by the hard heels of his loafers ceased for a minute.

"Anyway, she's going to be fine." She started walking again and heard Mohan's footsteps fall in behind her.

"They sell printer ink here?" Mohan had barely walked six steps before stopping at a rack festooned with ink cartridges like a Christmas tree showing off its ornaments.

"Have you never been in a Target?" Maya refused to stop; Mohan had to trot after her until they reached the bed and bath aisles. The colors and textures all around her, the fact that everything was new and bright, comforted Maya. Buying the girls' towels started to feel like an act of defiance, faith that everything would soon get back to normal. "Get ready to enjoy life the way the other half lives it," she gloated to Mohan, waving her hands down the aisle. "Egyptian cotton sheets! Mod print bath mats! All at low, low prices." She pulled out a towel with a friendly looking octopus on it and shook it out, freeing the folded beast's eight expressive legs. "Where does Shalini shop for basics?"

"I don't know; maybe I should." Mohan sank down to the floor in front of the bath mats, dropping his head and curving his back, as if he were whispering secrets to his knees. "Anyway, she won't be shopping there much longer."

Maya stared at her brother. He was eight years older than she was; she hadn't seen him sit on the floor since his high school graduation party. Years later, Priya had told her that he and Arjun-uncle's kids had been smoking pot in the backyard that night.

"She got this big job offer. This place called Ochsner, in New Orleans."

Maya nodded; she had a friend from med school in residency there.

"Anyway, they've got this massive pediatric oncology unit they're pouring cash into and they want her to be a part of it."

"Isn't that a good thing?" Maya asked. "You'll find work in New Orleans."

"How do I know if I'll find work or not? She totally blind-sided me."

"So you'll look into it, and if you can find something, that's great, and if not..."

"If not what? I lose my family? Maya, she didn't ask if she should take the job. She told me she's going to. She was holding the baby and she said, 'We're moving to New Orleans. I hope you'll come.' Like I'm an afterthought, like it makes no difference to her if we're married or not. I don't want my sons to grow up in the South. How many Indians live in New Orleans?"

"Bobby Jindal." Maya tried to smile. "He's governor, even."

"Fuck Bobby Jindal!" Mohan yelled. Maya laughed nervously but stopped as soon as Mohan started speaking again. "She's going whether I come or not, Maya. You get to a point in your life where you think you're an adult, you have some control, you make the decisions. But it's just not like that for me anymore. I thought maybe she confided in Priya, said something when Priya came to D.C. for that conference. That's why I called, to talk to her. But now..."

Maya saw a flash of Shalini walking toward Mohan at their wedding, her hands covered in henna, holding the gold-painted sacred coconut. Red silk twined around her body and slipped off her head just enough to show the jasmine in her shiny black hair. The white of the flowers was matched by Shalini's teeth—she was smiling broadly at Mohan, a smile so wide that Seema shook her head; it was unseemly for a bride to be so gleeful on such a solemn occasion.

Maya had only seen Mohan with one other girl. She'd met Shelley, Mohan's college girlfriend, at his graduation, had admired her shoe-boots, and made a mental note to dress like Shelley as soon as she grew up and moved out from under Seema's sartorial control. That afternoon she woke from a nap at the Quality Inn to her parents' shouting in Hindi in the next room, and Mohan answering in English, "I'm a man! I'll do whatever I want. I'm a man." There was an empty seat at the table for six they'd reserved at the Magic Pan that night, and Maya never saw Shelley again. Recently, in Dr. Bernard's office, Maya wondered aloud if the whole overheard fight had been a hallucination, something she'd invented to feel closer to Mohan, who seemed so much older than herself when they were growing up. The eight years between them mattered less now, but there were times when he still seemed like a mystery.

But she hadn't made it up. It was too vivid in her memory. Six years ago, when she saw Shalini's triumphant smile on their wedding day, Maya thought everything had worked out for Mohan, that he had sacrificed something he wanted for something even better, a doctor with the straight nose and amber eyes of a Bollywood star and a love so strong it split her mouth into a smile she couldn't control. Maya had admired that strength and exuberance, the way Shalini always knew what she wanted, and usually got it. But Priya always said Shalini was too strident, too controlling. Maya hated to think that Priya had been right about her all along. But here was Shalini, giving Mohan an ultimatum. Surely she could have found a better way to say "This is something I really want."

It couldn't be easy, to be married to such an alpha female. On the other hand, women had been expected to follow their husbands' career paths for years, this situation was just a reversal of that. Maya opened her mouth to say as much, and remembered Krishna the Butter Thief crumbling in Sanjay's fist. She had no business analyzing Mohan's relationship, what little she knew of it. Not when she couldn't succeed in making hers work, in giving Scott what he wanted, to be recognized. That request sounded so simple and it just wasn't. Maybe that was the case here, too; this conflict wasn't as clear-cut as Shalini being an alpha bitch.

In any case, Mohan wasn't her patient. He didn't want an assessment of his wife's personality. He wanted support. She spread an octopus towel on the ground next to Mohan, another around his shoulders, and sat cross-legged next to him, her arm twined through his. "You'll find a great job in New Orleans. You're the best ad exec I know."

Mohan laughed. "I'm the only ad exec you know. I can't even tell Ma and Pops what I'm working on." He snorted another laugh. "It's the K-Y Jelly campaign."

"For him *and* for her?" Maya punched her brother in the arm. "That's great, Mo! Those ads are on TV every five seconds."

"Why didn't I become a doctor?" He pulled the towel closer around his shoulders. "I could have. I'm smart. It just seemed so much like what Ma and Pops expected, you know? I didn't want to be their little robot. Now, I write copy to sell K-Y Jelly and my wife saves kids who have leukemia."

"Which is a blood disease," Maya said slowly.

"Yeah, thanks for the bulletin. I'm not that out of touch."

She let the sarcasm pass; she could hear the suffering in her brother's voice. Maya knew her family had their dysfunctions—so did everyone's. But she couldn't accept the thought that they were somehow responsible for bringing such sorrow and confusion into each of their lives, not in the span of six weeks. They had to be at the mercy of something larger than themselves. Something evil. She wouldn't tell Mohan about the curse; he needed to feel new beginnings were possible if he was going to reshape his life. So Maya just sat quietly next to him, waiting for his breathing to regulate itself. A Hispanic boy in sneakers that glowed red at the sole toddled down the aisle. "Why you sitting on the floor?" he asked before his mother came and hustled him away.

"Everything's going to be fine, Mohan," Maya said. "I promise."

"Is that what you tell your patients?"

"No."

"Maybe you should." Mohan stood. "I actually feel a little better." By the time they finished with housewares and toys—where Maya found two stuffed octopuses, one blue, one green, to go with the towels, and Mohan bought a LeapPad for Vivek and a bear for the baby—they had developed a plan. Mohan would drive Maya to the bus station tomorrow morning, then head to the airport to catch a shuttle home, where he would call Shalini and ask her to leave the boys with her parents for the weekend so they could discuss their next step. He would say nothing to their parents or Priya about a potential move, or his anger and confusion, for now, to spare them this new strain. Priya might have expected Shalini to do something like this, but even if she had, that thought would be of little comfort to her. And her parents loved Shalini, they thought she was the perfect daughter-in-law, that Mohan's marriage was the greatest success of his life. Maya had easily absorbed the shock of his news, she realized, because she had come to expect her family to suffer, had been waiting to see how the curse would impact him, too. But no one else was prepared for this extra burden.

As Maya helped her brother plan his next move, she was planning hers. She'd track down Parvati as soon as she got to India and make her end the family's suffering. Without involving anyone else, Maya could take care of this, stop it. She had to.

Mohan paid for the toys and that night, when the girls found the octopuses resting on their empty plates as they came to dinner, Maya said they were a present from Mohan-uncle. Priya flushed as she smiled at him. She was still as pale as she'd been in the hospital that morning, but at home with her family, she seemed to glow with a yellow light that reminded Maya of the mosquito candles Seema put on the windowsills in India.

Chapter Eleven

Maya stepped through JFK's sliding doors; she hadn't checked luggage and was the first person off the plane. Everyone else seemed to be following her lead, staring at their watches, calculating how late to work they'd be this Monday morning.

"Maya!" The shout made her look up, and there was Scott, waving at her and holding a pack of Marlboro Lights, although she'd never seen him smoke. "I thought about flowers, but then you'd have to deal with getting them in water before rushing to work." He shoved the pack of cigarettes into Maya's bag, then kissed her on the forehead. She wrapped her arms around his back and clung to him for a few seconds.

"Enabler," she accused.

"I've got Walker's car." He led her toward the parking lot.

"That was nice of him."

"We all want to help." Scott pointed the key at the vehicle, making it beep in greeting as it unlocked its doors. "I had to come once I saw the news this morning."

"What?"

"Oh." Scott took a breath. "I was sure you would have seen. There was a bombing in Mumbai, at the train station, maybe some other places, news is still trickling out." Maya sat in the passenger seat and shut her eyes. It had probably been on the TV monitors in the airport; India was ten and a half hours ahead, the tragedy might even have made the morning papers in the newsstands. But she had walked blindly through the airport in a fugue state, weighted down by her own sorrows, only finding relief in sleeping the minute the plane took off. She probably had a message from every member of her family, but she hadn't bothered to turn her cell on once the flight landed.

"Some extremist Muslim groups have claimed responsibility," Scott said. "It's tragic; dozens of people died."

"Hundreds, probably; the government always underreports these things." Maya looked out the window, seeking the comforting sight of Woodlawn Cemetery, all those gravestones resting companionably near each other. But they hadn't even reached La-Guardia yet; Woodlawn was miles away. And in Bombay, hundreds of people were newly dead, victims of ancient hatreds. Maya had to admit that her her sorrow for them and their families was mixed with guilt. Because she knew her grief at the news came only partly from horror at the victims' suffering. She was also devastated by a more personal, much more selfish thought—that this news could keep her from going to India to save her family.

She knew Scott was waiting for her to speak, but she would never reveal such self-focused thoughts to him, even though he loved her, and said he always would. It had to be impossible to love someone so damaged.

"I'm still going to India, you know," Maya said. "The whole family will." She hoped this was true, but she couldn't be sure, she hadn't spoken to any of them yet. She hoped that saying it out loud would help make it real.

"Of course."

"Sanjay will be upset, I bet a few of his friends from B-school will cancel their trips, but they don't get to ruin the wedding, to keep us from India."

"Right," Scott said. "If you don't go, the terrorists win." He was smiling at her when she turned to look at him, but stopped when he saw the tears distorting her face.

"You know I can't tell my parents now," Maya said. "About us. Not before India, not with all this going on. It's not just the attack; Priya's not coming to India anymore, Pops is still waiting for his doctor's okay. Who knows what's going on with Mohan? I love you, and I want you to come, but I can't ruin the wedding."

"I know." Scott kept his eyes on the road. "Maybe next year."

"But you can still come! Heidi is."

Scott snorted or laughed; Maya wasn't sure, she couldn't look at him. "Let's not plan on it," he said. Maya wiped the tear off her cheek quickly, but he must have seen it, because he kept talking, a torrent of words. "If my bonus is somehow as high as last year's, if my brother's not coming home for Christmas, if my mom doesn't freak out, if there's no State Department warning." After that, she stopped listening. Maya usually loved seeing the skyline of Manhattan rising at the other end of the bridge. But today all she could see was trash everywhere—graffiti on the buildings, litter lining the exit ramp, even garish bundles of garbage crammed onto a boat that floated in the river. She closed her eyes and pictured the garbage barge listing to one side, slowly dropping bales of trash into the murky brown water.

After that one tear, Maya didn't cry, not really, until Scott had dropped her off and she was safe in the shower, where no one would hear her. She stepped out of the shower and wrapped a towel around her shoulders like a protective cloak before pulling a brown shirtdress—modest, professional, almost invisible—out of the closet. Then the tears came again and she crumpled the dress against her chest, getting it wet from the towel and wrinkled from her grip. Still clutching it, she went to her bureau and pulled out a bra and underwear to go underneath. Priya loved that boring, stupid dress, she'd once told Maya that it made her look "like a lady." But Maya herself had never felt less in control, less polished, less like a lady before. She balled up the dress and threw it across the room at her bed, then flung her underwear along after it. The underwire gave the bra some weight and it hit the TV with a satisfying ping, but the boy shorts just fell to the ground like a sigh. Maya stomped on them once, then laughed at herself, naked, with tears streaming down her face. The curse was rounding out its work, leveling her life, too. She'd be in India soon enough. Maya tugged on her underwear, collected her bra, and pulled her ironing board out of the closet.

It was Thanksgiving the following weekend, but each member of the Das family celebrated in their own respective homes; there had been too much unexpected travel lately. Priya and Mohan observed the day with their families and in-laws and all the cardboard turkeys and construction-paper pilgrims that come with young kids. Maya's parents had celebrated with Sanjay's family. Scott had invited her home, of course, but Maya had volunteered to work; she needed all the brownie points she could amass in the EPU, and, besides, she didn't feel much like giving thanks.

The next several weeks passed in a blur of survival, an almost silent blur, as Maya doled out what she hoped looked like particularly hearty nods to colleagues who passed her in the hall and bleated, "Merry...um, Happy Holidays!" Two lunch hours a week were taken up with Dr. Bernard, in a room where it was all right to cry for forty-five minutes solid, where it might even be a good sign. Heidi went home to New Hampshire for a week of pre-Christmas festivities with her father, brother, and Yia-yia before leaving for India, and Scott was busy trying to wrap things up before the office closed, so Maya wasn't forced to socialize much at night, either, aside from the residents' end-of-the-year observances where everyone else got too drunk to notice her glassy eyes and early exits. She even managed to put on a cocktail dress and nod her way through Scott's office party, so maybe it wasn't as bad as she thought, as obvious to all that she was broken.

She picked up as many overnights as she could; it was easy with everyone trying to fob off their hours to start celebrating early. In the hospital, Maya felt controlled, at peace. Outside the hospital, she had rules about where it was appropriate to cry; the sidewalk was okay, if the crying was quiet and the street far enough from the hospital that it was unlikely she'd bump into any patients. The subway was out of bounds unless the car was empty and she had a newspaper to hide behind. The biggest threat to her isolation was Ramon, her superintendent, who sat at his desk sorting mail in the evenings when she walked in off the beautifully dark sidewalk. He got even more chatty as the time for his Christmas tip approached, inquiring about her family with a solicitude that made her bite the inside of her cheek even though there was no way he could have known that her father and sister were recovering, that she suspected from the way her mother rushed off the phone twice, mumbling, that her nose continued to bleed but that Seema would tell no one if it was possible to just lie down with a cold washcloth on her face. Maya would wipe her cheeks on the sleeve of her coat before reaching her apartment building, pull out her cell and pretend to be talking as she passed Ramon, nodding hello as she chattered animatedly to no one. In the elevator, she was fine, chatting with the Cat Guy from 4F about how Kitty liked the cold, until she could unlock her door, get under her duvet, look at her watch, and close her eyes. A feeling that approached happiness would fill her as she realized she had ten hours before she needed to see or talk to anyone.

Maya and Scott had gone to dinner on December 23. She almost offered to cook—the thought of being at home was appealing—but she took over someone's late-afternoon shift, and didn't get back in time. Still, dinner went well. She felt she had been soft and smiling, in an almost good mood. Her schedule had caught up with her; this was the skinniest she'd ever been, which made her feel like she'd accomplished something. After dinner, there had been sex; it had been good, she thought. Scott seemed to think so; he clung to her so closely that she wasn't sure whether the sweat on her body came from herself or him. Walker had lent Scott his car again, and the next morning he drove Maya to the airport while she dozed. When she woke up, they were in short-term parking.

"You don't have to come in," Maya said. "I can handle the bag." But Scott picked up her suitcase anyway. She managed to smile.

"I thought we could talk in the car, but I didn't want to wake you," he said, walking through the door under the departures sign. "You looked almost happy sleeping."

Three feet behind him, Maya stopped. "I know."

"You do?" Scott turned toward her.

"You're coming!" Maya grinned. "You got a last-minute ticket, the bonus—"

"Maya, no." Scott stepped toward her, but she knew it had to be true; there was no way he'd let her go to India like this alone. "I was going to wait until you got back."

"So you're not even considering coming?"

"I was going to wait, to see if things went back to normal in the new year, but it didn't seem fair, you being away, and me knowing."

"You're not coming," Maya repeated.

"I told you." Scott walked over to a bench just inside the airport entrance, dragging her suitcase behind him. The bag seemed resistant, its wheels turning outside of their prescribed paths, as if trying to escape. He sat, looking down at his shoes. "I told you I'd only come as your boyfriend." Scott's hand appeared in her sight-line, reaching for hers, which hung limply in his grip. "It's not your fault, the timing and everything. Your sister and dad are sick, you're worried about your job, the lawsuit; I know that. But I can't wait anymore. That makes me a jerk, I know that, too. But there's never been a good time to tell your parents. Maybe there never will be."

Maya grabbed her hand back as if Scott's palm were hot and burned the tips of her fingers. A month ago she would have been able to articulate her thoughts in the same passionate but clear voice that had made her the head of the debate team in middle school. But she knew if she opened her mouth now only a sob would come out. He was right; she couldn't think of a good time to tell her family, especially now that each of them was suffering. She couldn't even imagine a time when they'd each be happy and whole again, when thinking of her family didn't make her feel like a giant with huge hands had grabbed her rib cage and started to squeeze. She stared at Scott; he looked different, far-off, like an acquaintance she could barely place. "Is there someone else?"

"Maya, no." Scott's voice choked. She suspected he was crying but couldn't bring herself to lift her gaze up from his hands to his face to find out. She felt heat rising from her chest, anger, at him for doing this at all; at the strangers surrounding them, watching; at herself, that at this moment, as the latest tremor shook her world, she couldn't defend herself. All she could come up with was that question, a line she had heard a million times on television, trans-lating *Dynasty* for Dadiji's best friend the time she came to visit the U.S., or watching Lifetime: Television for Women with Denise in the nurses' break room at Bronson Methodist. Sometimes Maya hated herself.

"At least, not in any way that matters."

"What?" Maya whipped her head up so quickly that her carry-on bag slipped off her shoulder, hitting the floor with a thud.

"It's nothing." Scott looked down, talking to his knees. "A girl on the subway. She had pretty hair, and I said so. I wasn't hitting on her, I was just being… neighborly."

Maya snorted.

"When she left, she handed me her card."

"And where was I?" Maya tore the handle of her suitcase out of his hand. "In the hospital with my father? Or my sister?"

"This was last week, Maya." Scott took off his glasses, probably, she thought, so that he couldn't see her clearly, could consider her an out-of-focus blob, a burden to escape. His eyes filled with liquid, intensifying their blueness.

"I haven't called her. It's just—" Scott grabbed Maya's hand. She tore it back, taking the handle of the suitcase with her, causing the bag to roll over her foot. "I've thought of her," he continued. "I thought, if I called her, maybe we'd go to dinner. Maybe we'd like each other, meet each other's friends, families. It could all be so easy."

The sounds of the airport closed in around Maya, the announcements coming over the loudspeaker. She wanted to be on the plane, away from here. "I wish you luck with the easy girl." She pulled her ticket from her bag. "I hope you have a very easy life together."

"You don't let me help, Maya," Scott said, speaking too loudly. "When my grandfather's Alzheimer's got worse, you came to check out clinics. My mother stayed up talking to you, not me. But your family, with all of this, you won't let me help."

"You were helping," she said. "Just not in the way you wanted."

He didn't respond, and Maya knew he was waiting for her to go on, to list clinical explanations for his behavior, all the subconscious motives that led him to this rash, foolish decision. But she just stared. As the numbness wore off, Maya realized that Scott was right to do this, to save himself.

Scott stood and stepped toward her. "I'm not saying I don't love you. I do." He raised his hand as if to reach for her, but left it sticking out in midair. "I'm just not sure what to do with that." He put his glasses on, took Maya's ticket, and looked at it before handing it back to her. "There's still time," he said. "Aren't you going to say anything?"

"Nothing would help," Maya said, and she knew it was true. She was tired, weak after all the worry of the past few months. How could she hope to fight this inevitable loss, to save herself when she couldn't even help her family in their struggles? She envied Scott his red eyes, his shaky hand. She hadn't cried and wouldn't. She was used to this; she knew what was happening. "It's the curse," she said.

"Maya! What the hell are you talking about?" Scott yelled, loud enough that a security guard walking past them turned around and circled back.

"Nothing." Maya turned and pulled her suitcase behind her, raising her voice so that Scott would hear her even as she walked away. "I have to go; I'm going to India."

PART TWO

Chapter Twelve

"What?"

Maya pulled her eyes away from the swamps and compulsively gridded neighborhoods of Long Island receding beneath her and turned toward Heidi.

"Fifty-five what?" Heidi repeated.

"Oh." Maya hadn't realized that she'd spoken out loud. "I was figuring out my GAF. It calms me down."

"What?"

Maya focused on the tiny illuminated seat belt and cigarette with a line through it above her head, wondering how old this aircraft was; the nonsmoking sign would never go off now, it was doomed to glow dully throughout all future flights. "Global Assessment of Functioning," she said finally. "You assign numbers to a patient, based on how they manage themselves in their world, all kinds of things, work functioning, self-care, social interaction, and relationships. Sometimes I check my own."

The voice of God, if God was a tired, Swiss woman, came over the loudspeakers letting them know they were free to walk about the cabin, but implying that really, they were better off, safer, if they stayed in their own seats, seat belts securely fastened. The man in the row in front of Maya had to be almost seven feet tall; his ears were visible above the top of the seat. Maya didn't know how he managed; she was a foot and a half shorter and even she felt trapped, suffocated. She wanted to break free from the iron pod of the airplane, but the only way she could imagine doing so was if an engine exploded or a bomb went off and the plane erupted into a fiery ball, freeing and killing them all at the same time. Maybe she should offer the man in front of her one of her alprazolam, so he could relax and get through the flight. But then, he seemed to be doing just fine. Maybe it was Maya herself who should take another, enough time must have passed since the last; she had taken it as soon as she was sure Scott could no longer see her walking away, once she'd been swallowed up by the crowd of people massing to get through security.

"So, fifty-five out of what?" Heidi reclined her seat and loosened her seat belt.

"A hundred."

"That's not even a D minus, sweetie. That's failing."

Maya nodded; failing felt right. Fifty-five fit a depressed person with reduced functioning not requiring hospitalization. Maya wasn't that badly off, comparatively; at least she was good at assessing mental health, even while suffocating. And the impulse to give the freakishly tall man meds, that was other-directed, wasn't it? She felt Heidi squeeze her arm, and the hand on her limb made Maya feel smaller, protected.

"You guys broke up once before and got back together," Heidi said. "And that was after, what, a two-year hiatus? You'll get back together this time, too."

Maya shook her head; she didn't have the energy to argue, but she knew Heidi was wrong. Maya had met Heidi, fresh from the US Air Express from Lebanon, New Hampshire, at the gate, and by the time their flight took off she had reenacted the whole breakup at least three times. She couldn't start over again; the parsing of the conversation, of Scott's every intonation and possible motivation, might easily swell to fill all nine hours to Zurich and the remaining six from Zurich to Bombay. There was no room to set those words loose here, not with the flight attendants roaming the aisles with swollen beverage carts that kept banging into Heidi's elbow.

"Just try and enjoy the trip, put him out of your mind if you can," Heidi instructed. "Compartmentalize! Don't call, don't e-mail. Scott will feel you pulling away and by the time we return, he'll be begging for you to take him back."

"No." Maya pulled the pale blue pashmina she traveled with instead of depending on the germ-ridden airplane blankets tight around her shoulders.

"Wanna bet? I give it two months. Tops. March at the latest. You two are meant to be together, to get married, have babies. Dogs, maybe. The whole thing."

"No. This was it." She had ruined her relationship with Scott and was now flying to India to witness her cousin celebrate a union she was no longer sure was a healthy one. Without Scott as an example, she didn't know if she could believe any loving relationship was possible. Maybe such a thing was a lie propagated by Bollywood and iTunes.

"Maya, we'll find that bitch in Jodhpur and get the curse reversed." A woman striding down the aisle to the bathroom turned to stare at Heidi and Maya breathed heavily through her nose, an almost-laugh to acknowledge that things could have been worse, they could have been sitting in the middle section, with two strangers eavesdropping on them, instead of tucked away by the window.

Glaring back at the woman, Heidi lowered her voice to promise, "Everything will go back to normal."

"Not this," Maya said. "Scott blames me. He's never coming back."

"You don't know that." Heidi stroked Maya's hair. But Maya did know, she just didn't have the energy to explain how, so she shut her eyes. She knew she'd never marry Scott because at the airport she had looked into his eyes and saw nothing, no flicker of recognition, no spark of divinity. Maya had visited countless temples in India, and a few in the U.S. Even as a little girl she knew that the point of each visit was to do darsan, to look in the eyes of the statue, to see the divinity and to have the god or goddess see you. When she was very little, Pops would put her on his shoulders so she could see the black and white eyes of the temple deity sparkling over the heads of the crowd. And in the airport, once Scott took his glasses off, that was what she had been trying to do with him, a domestic darsan. Maybe it was sacrilegious, but it was true. She had looked in his eyes, seen him, and realized that he would never see her, not in the way she needed to be recognized. Scott had been a sort of household god to her, and now she knew he was just an ordinary man. A man who was gone.

"Tired, My?"

Maya nodded into Heidi's shoulder. "But my mind's too loud to sleep."

Heidi wriggled out from under Maya's head, dove under the seat in front of her, and came up with a huge metallic purse some PR person had given her. "Have an Ambien," she offered. "The fashion director gave me some for the flight."

"I didn't know editors could prescribe," Maya said, and Heidi's eyes flickered with such gratitude for the weak joke that she felt guilty. She couldn't let Scott or Parvati ruin this trip. She took the pill without waiting for the attendant to circle back with meal service and bottles of water, leaned against the window, and tried to shut out the noise.

From Zurich to Bombay, once the Ambien wore off, Maya distracted herself by describing her aunties and uncles, so that Heidi would know who was which when they arrived. Her father's sisters would be waiting with her mother in Dadiji's house, and when Maya said their names she could see them, Parul-bhuasa was the fatter, and Radha-bhuasa the thinner. But on the last leg of their trip, from Bombay to Jodhpur, Heidi fell asleep again, resting her head against the pashmina, which was now splashed with tomato sauce. Maya watched Heidi sleeping, leaning against the window with her mouth slightly open, occasionally emitting a puff of Altoids-scented breath. She had left her Agatha Christie in the Bombay airport bathroom and now there was nothing to do but think. She reviewed Scott's dead eyes in the airport and the events of the last few months over and over, trying to find a moment when she could have done something to change things, stop what had been set in motion. It made her feel like a moron. She spent every day analyzing the lives of others, and she still couldn't process what had happened to hers. But it was clear that the day Dadiji died was the moment everything changed; Dadiji had loved Maya completely, and with her gone, that comfort disappeared. Then Parvati spoke those furious words and in doing so, extended the family's suffering beyond just grieving Dadiji's loss. Maya, her parents, brother, and sister had all been going about their lives in their respective American cities when hate spewed out of Parvati, black and thick, and covered Maya's world. The lawsuit, Scott, everything else was just an aftershock.

Maya didn't want Parvati to apologize, necessarily, just to take back the words, reverse what she had set in motion. Even if she could convince, bribe, or guilt Parvati into doing that, would the antidote work? Would taking the words back counteract this mystical manifestation of anger? In his office, Dr. Bernard sometimes said, "You're doing good work here," when the discussion became charged. But therapy was work Maya knew how to do. Curses were new to her; she didn't know how to fight one.

The flight attendants made their last round, collecting stray trash. Maya handed over a plastic cup and the movement woke Heidi, who pulled up the window shade in time for them to see Jodhpur's airport come into view, its white pasteboard fence cut in wavelike dips and rises, probably meant to call to mind the Taj Mahal. "Maya! It's just like the glorious lost days of the British Raj!" she said, quoting the back of *Daybreak in Darjeeling,* the paperback she was now shoving into her oversized bag.

"Colonialism never looked so good, huh?" Maya hauled her carry-on out of the overhead compartment, cringing as she anticipated it falling on her head or toe. But she made it safely down the aisle, and as she stepped onto the rickety staircase that had been pulled up to the side of the plane, the dread she had whipped up thinking about Parvati shrank a little. Humid air wrapped around her shoulders, making her shawl irrelevant. Folding it into a tight bundle, Maya felt herself unfurling. At fourteen she'd come with her father to visit Dadiji, one of the times Seema stayed home to work, and brought back a shawl for her mother. Seema had shaken it out, pulled it to her face, and said, "It smells of India." Maya couldn't remember anything she'd given her mother since that had pleased Seema as much. Walking toward the airport, past the fake fence, Maya breathed in the smell of India: dust and heat, and the pomade and sweat of the men in short-sleeved shirts pushing past her. She looked at Heidi, who grinned and said, "We're here!"

Maya exhaled deeply to settle the sudden quickening in her stomach, the kind of fluttery twitch that usually made her think she was about to get her period. But maybe this time it wasn't just her uterine lining. Maybe it was hope.

• • •

After baggage claim, dragging her rolling suitcase behind her, Maya heard Nanaji shouting her name, saw him smiling and waving. He was wearing a wool jacket, because it was January after all, although it hadn't been this warm in New York since September. Maya rushed over, bent and touched her maternal grandfather's feet to show respect, then reached up and hugged him, squeezing hard. He smelled like lemon Liril soap and her childhood. "Look at you, Maya, slim and trim as ever," he said as she released him.

"Where's Pops?"

"Maya." Nanaji wiped his clean hands against his wool vest. "Your baba is not coming. It seems he has a bit of infection from the hospital."

"But I talked to him the day he left."

"Was going to leave," Nanaji corrected. "He had a doctor's visit that afternoon, he suspected something was wrong. Prashant-mausa went with him—he does not fly out until tomorrow, when Mohan will relieve him; you see, it is a blessing, in the end, that Mohan was not able to go on holiday at this time. And your baba is taking antibiotics now; there is no need to worry. If there were, your mother would go to him."

Maya wasn't sure she could handle India, all the dust and the relatives, without Pops, who saw her as calm, capable, and modern, and would be so happy to be here, back with the fellows, that some of his joy would have to rub off on her. She felt her intestines twist with what she thought was fear or anger until it became clear that it actually was a cramp. She had misinterpreted her body; this was no time for hope.

"Are you not going to introduce us?" Nanaji nodded at Heidi, who was pretending to be busy with their bags. "This will be Heidi. We are so pleased you have come."

"Nanaji!" Heidi threw her arms around his neck and he stumbled back a step. "I've heard so much about you!" She pulled away before he had time to raise his arms toward her. He laughed, a low rumble, and Maya wondered when was the last time a ponytailed white woman had flung her arms around Nanaji, if ever. Watching Nanaji and Heidi dance around each other, trying to please, Maya sensed something missing, and as she looked around the airport, she noticed that no one was carrying malas, marigold garlands to throw around the necks of long-lost relatives who had returned from away.

"The mala makers must be on strike," she said to Heidi, pulling up the handle of her rolling suitcase. "My luck followed us."

"Huh?"

"Normally, we would have brought garlands to welcome you," Nanaji explained, leading them toward the exit. "And tomorrow is Tuesday, and you know your mother likes to go to the Hanuman temple to make an offering, Maya. How she will grumble! But maybe the strike will have been resolved by then." He turned toward Heidi as they stepped out onto the parking lot, and joked, "Welcome to India!"

"It's not India, Nanaji." Maya rolled past him toward his 1983 Ambassador, which looked like he'd owned it since the glorious lost days of the British Raj. "It's the Das family luck."

Nanaji either didn't hear Maya, or pretended he didn't. "We will take the luggages in the car," he said after a quick consultation with the driver. "And after Ramu drops me at home for a little nap, he will deliver them as close to the house as he can. Mohammed will take you girls straight there in his auto rickshaw."

"Madam!" A short, slim man with a face so clean-shaven that Maya wondered if he was capable of growing a beard walked up to them nodding, his hands pressed together in namaste, his clean fingernails shining so impossibly that Maya wondered for a moment if he had polished them.

"He's going to pull us along?" Heidi asked.

"*Auto* rickshaw! You've got to stop reading that book." Maya pointed toward the vehicle, a sort of booth on wheels attached to a motorbike, which was narrow enough to navigate the constricted alleys of the old town. The cab was covered in red, white, and black leather in a playing card motif, with a heart-shaped vinyl window in back.

"It's like something out of *Alice in Wonderland*," Heidi said. She pulled out her camera and Mohammed hurried over and gave rapid-fire instructions to Maya.

"He wants a copy of the photo," Maya translated, leading Heidi inside the vehicle. As they chugged toward the Old Town, smog filled Maya's nostrils and her eyes watered. It would have been the perfect time to cry without anyone noticing, but she was nowhere close to tears, a fact that made her feel, momentarily, triumphant. She would be better here, she was sure, so she made a point of praising the dirty city she loved, showing Heidi the palace the king built as a public works project in the 1930s, and her aunties' favorite chai shop where men smashed their earthen cups on the ground when they were done drinking. In between, Heidi pointed out camels pulling flatbed trucks along the teeming highway, a woman wrapped in a blindingly green sari that would be a great color for a cocktail dress, a gaggle of ladies in burqas entering the market.

"Look! Is that a kindergarten?" Heidi pointed to a wall painted with a coloring book–like cartoon of kids flying kites under the maxim, GIRL OR BOY, SMALL IS JOY.

"No, it's a campaign against female infanticide." Maya turned toward her own window. Everything was new to Heidi, and she seemed to be enjoying it too much to notice the litter lining the sidewalk, the beggar boy in a sweater and no pants kicking a Limca bottle down the street. Had there ever been a time when Maya looked around her and didn't see the squalor at the edge of the road? Probably not. Maybe her readiness to see the unappealing side of life everywhere had nothing to do with the curse, but was an inherent part of her personality. If so, she wished they'd discover the neurochemical that made her perceive ugliness, so she could take meds to lower her levels of it.

"Over there." Heidi pointed to a temple doorway, where widows sat begging next to a pile of rotting marigolds, holding out their twisted hands. They were surrounded by holy trash, leaves that had been used to hold prasad, which the faithful had tossed onto the street after eating the offered sweet. So maybe Heidi did see the suffering.

"The abandoned flowers," Heidi said. "That's where the mala-maker would sit?"

"Mm-hmm."

"We're totally coming back tomorrow, if they're back on duty," Heidi insisted. "It's gorgeous—such a spicy shade."

Mohammed took an alley off the market into the Old Town, and now they were eye level with men sitting cross-legged in their shops, surrounded by stainless-steel pots, vials of perfume, spice packets, children's backpacks, bolts of sari cloth, and men's under-wear in neat boxes printed with faded photos of white guys with sideburns. The shopkeeper's faces, some smooth, some whiskered, and the goods surrounding them, swept past as Mohammed mo-tored the auto rickshaw down the street. In some places the alley was large enough for another auto rickshaw to pass; a family of five crammed into one glanced at them, spotted Heidi, and wrenched their necks for closer examination. But mostly it was just them and a passing cyclist, or a schoolboy in uniform walking home for lunch. At one corner, Mohammed stopped to let a teenager carrying a tray of syrupy sweets pass, and a pack of boys in red shorts, navy sweaters, and striped ties walked toward them, bags swinging. One spotted Heidi leaning out of her window and yelled, "Hello, madam!" Immediately, the others opened their mouths, too, like baby birds waiting to be fed, sending squawks of "madam" into the air.

Maya laughed, but it sounded like choking, and Heidi turned to her. "You okay?"

She squeezed Heidi's arm. She felt tired, thirsty, dirty, sore, and bloated. But not sad. "I'm happy to be here." It was true, and almost miraculous. Mohammed turned off the motor, letting out a final, victorious burst of black exhaust.

The house looked just as it had when Maya last left it, a narrow slice of chalky blue walls, with lacy carving above the massive arched doorway. But Dadiji's empty window gaped like a wound, and Parvati didn't rush out with lowered eyes to greet them. In previous years, Maya would have felt vague relief at Parvati not being there, but today the feeling was overshadowed by the other absence, which felt all-consuming.

"It's gorgeous; so old," Heidi said. "Like a palazzo."

"There's the latrine." Maya pointed to what she would have called an outhouse if it weren't—just barely—inside the entryway. "I swear it's why Priya hardly ever visits. Now we have a bathroom on the second floor, but it used to just be that."

The entryway opened onto a central courtyard, and the woman whose family rented the first floor that surrounded it rushed toward Maya murmuring offers of chai and letting her know that her mother and aunties were upstairs. Maya thanked her, explained they were tired from their journey and had to rush right up to see her family, and the tenant let her go after pressing warm besan parathas into her free hand.

"It's like a dirt pancake," Heidi said with her mouth full of the gritty dough, following Maya up the slippery, narrow staircase. "In a good way."

"Whose voices are those?" Seema yelled, undoing the latch on the wooden gate that barred the second floor landing as Maya came into view. "I thought so! You have arrived all in one piece. Two pieces, rather."

Maya stopped chewing her besan paratha; the dough seemed to swell in her mouth, and she forced herself to swallow, becoming flushed with that exertion and the hot anger of having been kept in the dark about Pops. But she could hear her aunties chattering in the room behind her mother, so she stepped toward Seema, who somehow looked younger and smaller here than she had in Kalamazoo, and hugged her. Leaving the carry-on bags on the landing, Maya and Heidi followed Seema into Dadiji's old room, a combination bedroom, living room, and dining room, which, this afternoon, was full of her father's sisters, who grew fatter and more sparkly eyed with age.

"Parul-bhuasa and Radha-bhuasa." Heidi identified each sister correctly, to their obvious delight. Their husbands were working, or busy discussing politics or having their shoes shined or engaging in some other manly pursuit, but they would all join Seema's side of the family for dinner at Nanaji's house later. Right now, aside from Heidi, Maya, and her mother, it was just Pops's sisters, women who had grown up in this place, who had assembled so many times before on all of Maya's returns and farewells, to cook on feast days and complain during heat waves. Maya wished Priya were there, Mohan, and Pops, too, to complete the picture. But the most important person would still be missing.

Seema went to get more biscuits and chai for the girls, and, after the bhuasas assured Maya that they had all spoken to Ajit and he was perfectly fine and had just been to Jodhpur for a visit anyway and was talking of coming in spring, so there was no need to worry, Maya spent a half hour answering her aunts' high-pitched questions: Had she met any special someones? What about her friend, was she engaged yet? What makes you girls so picky? "Now is the time to be having a family," Parul-bhuasa said. But Radha-bhuasa shook her head and said they should take their time finding suitable boys, adding, "Hurry-burry spoils the curry," in English, for Heidi's benefit.

It was one of the few English phrases Maya's aunts knew, so when they finally transferred their attention from her unwed self, she functioned as translator between them and Heidi. "Your friend is very pretty; many women with her eye color are, but she is especially." Radha-bhuasa wanted her compliment passed on to Heidi, then Heidi wanted them to know she found them very pretty as well, and that she thought their saris were absolutely gorgeous. The diplomacy continued over tea, as Heidi praised the house and Seema said she was lucky to have married a man with such a beautiful family home and such lively sisters. But when Seema collected the tea things and headed for the kitchen with the dirty cups on a tray, Maya decided that it was time to get on with business. She leaned forward to ask Radha-bhuasa if she happened to know where Parvati worked now, in a voice soft enough that Seema wouldn't hear it but loud enough that the aunties wouldn't think she was whispering. As the sound of Seema's steps from the kitchen became louder, Maya leaned over, letting a sheet of hair fall in front of her face, and whispered to Heidi what she had learned: when Radha-bhuasa went over to look at photos at Ravi-uncle's—he was Prashant-mausa's brother, and the proud keeper of the engagement pictures Sanjay and Amrita sent—she had seen Parvati cleaning the house.

"Have you visited Ravi-uncle's yet, Ma?" Maya asked, pulling her hair back into a ponytail as soon as Seema entered the room with a new tray.

"I got here one week before you, silly girl, I have hardly been anywhere," she chided. She set the tray on the table and the aunties rose from their chairs, each pulling a biscuit out of the tin to keep themselves busy as they walked to the homes they had married into. Maya swept her hand across their feet as they patted her head good-bye, then fell on the bed that dominated the room, next to Heidi, who was sitting by the window. The aunties' voices faded down the road, and even though auto rickshaws, bicycles with rusty chains, and shouting housewives clogged the street below, the room seemed to fill with heavy silence. Heidi stood and examined the niches in the wall, which held extra toilet paper and paper towels on the lower shelves, and photos of Dadiji's guru higher up.

"Priya and I used to call this 'the nest,' because Dadiji never left it," Maya said. "She perched here, looking out at the world." The tears she had held in on planes for two days swelled behind her itching eyes, then fell, leaving cool tracks on her dusty cheeks. Heidi heard Maya crying and turned around, but Seema was faster, already sitting next to Maya on the bed, stroking her hair.

"We all miss Dadiji," Seema said softly. "Even I."

"It's not just that." Maya pressed her head into her mother's hand, feeling Seema's swollen knuckles against her scalp, wishing she could transmit the thoughts in her head through those fingers to her mother. She wanted Seema to understand that Scott had left and taken the last unbroken thing in her life with him. If Seema took on the weight of that, even without knowing about the curse, Maya might feel lighter.

"Of course," Seema said. "You are sad your father cannot be here. And, perhaps, you are angry we did not tell you that he was sick. But he asked me to promise, he did not want you to cancel your ticket, to go see him instead. I reserved a ticket back for myself, I was going to turn right around, but your baba said there is nothing for us to do, I should stay and represent the family at Sanjay's wedding. And Prashant-mausa assures me that he is really responding very well to the antibiotics. His white blood cell count is—"

"If you say he's going to be fine, I believe you. It's okay." Maya leaned harder into her mother's hand. "I am sad Pops can't be here, but also, along with that—"

"I know, beti!" Seema took her hand off Maya's head. "Also Priya is not with us, and you girls were always a gang of two in India together. But she is still recovering, also, and should not face the strain of a journey now."

"It's not Priya." Maya's nose was now running along with her eyes, but she was too focused on her words to wipe the warm liquid away. "Or Pops. Or Mohan. And it's not just losing Dadiji. I also lost a friend, my best friend."

Seema stood, tore a paper towel off the roll on the shelf, and handed it to Maya. "Heidi is your best friend." She inclined her head toward the window where Heidi stood.

"Ma, not—"

"I know, Maya. Now, blow your nose." Maya did, and Seema put out her hand for Maya's crumpled paper towel. "Your mother is not ignorant. There was a special friend, maybe. But he was not the right one. So this loss is a gain, a blessing." She handed Maya another rough towel, which Maya kept rubbing against her face even after her cheeks were dry. So her mother had suspected Scott, or at least someone like him. And she hadn't exploded like Kali, wreaking destruction in her wake. But this quiet dismissal of him, as if he were a piece of empty, secondhand luggage with a broken latch, to be used and then replaced, this seemed worse somehow. If Maya had misjudged both Scott and Seema, then the loss of him really was her fault, not Seema's, not Parvati's. She closed her eyes for a moment to banish the thought. More likely, Seema didn't understand what Scott had meant to Maya, what had existed between them.

"But you don't know—"

"I know, Maya," Seema said. "I know what it is to suffer. When your father and I were first married, and he had to do his military service, I would write him letters saying everything was fine and dandy, and then I would write in my diary how much I longed for him. I cried while I wrote." Seema laughed, once. "My tears stained the page."

Maya looked at Heidi, who had pressed herself into the corner by the window, discreetly making herself as small as possible. But her eyes were huge, staring at Maya. She nodded quickly toward Seema, who was still looking at the floor.

"The feeling passes, Maya! I promise you this." Seema looked up, finally, then stood, walked over to a chair against the wall, and sat facing both girls. "Life is not cinema, all dancing and battles. You must learn to be strong and practical. You do not need stars and moonlight and music to build a family, to lead a good life."

Maya sat up, wiped her nose with the back of her hand, and looked out the window. She knew her mother would never understand that she was much more interested in what she wanted to lead a happy life than in what she needed to cobble together a good one. So she said nothing. Seema stood and walked toward the kitchen.

"Seema-auntie," Heidi called. Seema stopped in the doorway. "Where did you meet Ajit-uncle?"

Seema snorted, as if she, too, needed to blow her nose. "At my wedding."

"I knew it was arranged, but... you'd never seen him before?" Heidi sat on the bed and crossed her legs like a kindergartener.

"Once." Seema leaned into the doorjamb. "I was in the yard at school—it was a girls' school, of course. We wore lovely uniforms, with a dark green jacket." Seema pulled her cardigan across the front of her sari. "I was sitting and reading, as I usually did during the recreation hour, when I heard shouting. I looked up and four boys rode past on bicycles. I did not think anything of it at the time. Or, more likely, I thought they were rowdy, ruffians." She laughed again, more than once this time. It was a nice laugh, actually, Maya thought. Seema turned to her. "Years later your father told me—"

"I know, Ma, that it was him and his friends, checking you out." Maya pulled her knees up in front of her chest. Her breath was uneven from crying; the intermittent gasps were almost painful; talking helped to steady them. "His parents picked you, he thought he'd see what he was in for, and he liked how smart you looked."

"Yes, of course you know," Seema said, brushing her wrinkled palms against each other. "Only, it is that, after all these years, I am not sure if I really saw those boys or if it simply seems so because your father told me he had been there." She rubbed the uneven edges of a hole in the elbow of her cardigan. Maya looked at her mother's hand working the fabric. She had heard this story so many times, she'd accepted it as an empirical fact, was as sure it had happened as the Battle of Gettysburg, or Partition. Whether or not Seema had seen the boys changed nothing about what came next—she and Ajit married and produced Mohan, then Priya, and, years later, Maya. But somehow it made Maya's world feel even more precarious to think that her parents' meeting was as hazy and uncertain as everything else in life was proving to be.

"Perhaps it was the same day I saw the invitations," Seema continued. "There was a stack of red cards on the table one afternoon when I got home from school. I could tell it was very thick, heavy paper, and I was a curious thing. So I picked one up and saw my name and Ajit's. And I knew."

"What did you do?" This time, it was Maya who asked.

"I burst into tears. I was only sixteen. A decade younger than you girls, more. I thought I might have a few more years." She started buttoning her cardigan. "Kruti-masi told me to stop being a baby, and so I did." Seema rubbed her hands briskly, as if touching the buttons had dirtied them.

There was honking below the window, and Maya looked out and saw Mohammed march into view, pulling Heidi's hard-shelled zebra-striped suitcase behind him.

"The luggages?" Seema asked. "Go to help him, Maya."

Maya stretched; she felt cleaner having cried. But Heidi must have thought she was tired, because she said, "I'll go—it's my bag that's the big one," and left the room, turning back to say, "Thanks for the tea, Seema-auntie."

Once Heidi was gone, Seema said to Maya, "Heidi is such a very nice girl." She plucked a stray hair off of the front of her cardigan. "But she is not one of us, and I am not her auntie," she added, and disappeared into the kitchen.

Throughout dinner at Nanaji's, Maya became more and more pleased that Heidi had come along. She loved her, of course, and it was fun introducing her to India, but she hadn't realized when Sanjay invited Heidi to his wedding how useful she would be as a conversation piece and distraction. Everyone wanted to know Heidi's impressions of India, how many siblings she had, what she did at the magazine, if she'd have a chance to see the Taj Mahal on this trip, and they were so involved in interviewing her that Maya could sit quietly, forcing herself not to perseverate on Scott's desertion or Sanjay's questionable future or the lawyers in New York plotting to end her career. Instead, she planned her pursuit of Parvati, asking family members when they last saw her, slipping the questions in between discussions with the main attraction so that they went unnoticed. She had already arranged for Nanaji to book a meeting with Bauji, the family astrologer, on the pretext that Heidi wanted her chart done. It was true, she did, but Heidi did not have the same frantic need for divination as Maya, was not as desperate for assurances that the future would be better than the present. Maya needed to ask about Parvati.

Once Mohammed left them at Dadiji's, Maya convinced Seema that she and Heidi had to stop at the international calling office down the block so Heidi could let her family know she'd arrived safely; if she had called before dinner it would have been too early in New Hampshire. It was only out of respect for Heidi's father and grandmother that Seema let them traipse down the dark alley to the phone office, which was painted on three sides with the letters STD. "Standard trunk dialing," Maya explained, seeing Heidi's horrified expression. "It has nothing to do with chlamydia, herpes."

Heidi shuddered.

"Seriously," Maya promised. "I don't know what a trunk call is, but my parents made a lot of them to us back in the day."

"I'm still Purelling my hands after using the phone." Heidi ducked into a cubicle.

Maya watched Heidi through the plexiglass door as she waited for a teenager with a wistful attempt at a mustache to vacate the office's lone computer terminal. First she saw the rapid moving of the jaw that meant Heidi was telling her father about India, then the more indulgent grin that was reserved for her grandmother, and a tight smile that made Maya suspect Mr. A. had invited his girlfriend over for the holiday weekend. She wanted her father to be happy, Heidi had told Maya. Just not with that woman. Heidi perked up just as the teenager left—she must be talking to her brother, Kyle, who went by Achilles now. Maya sat and pulled up her e-mail using the longest, slowest connection she'd encountered in years, rotating her ankle back and forth. She made herself read the update from Priya before looking at her bulk folder—Scott's office e-mails often went to spam—and was rewarded by assurances that Pops was doing great and was eager to see pictures of Sanjay's wedding when she returned, Priya was fine, and Nisba hadn't gotten any Needs Improvements on her report card. *No NIs is good news!* Priya wrote. Then Maya's bulk folder opened quickly, revealing offers to enlarge her penis and notices that she'd won the Nigerian lottery, extinguishing any hope. She would be fine, she told herself. She was in India, Scott didn't belong here anyway, and by the time she got back to a city that was empty without him, the pain would have dulled. Maybe it was already doing so; hadn't she almost laughed at Heidi's shock over the STD sign? The door of the phone cubicle slammed behind Heidi; Maya looked up at her and said, "Nothing."

As they walked back to the house, Heidi tried to amuse Maya with news from home, the growing inches of snow and Kyle's changing plans for New Year's, and Maya half listened, inwardly evaluating the vast reach of the curse. It had managed to find her and her family in America and then follow her back to India, working on two continents at once, infecting both places, like the nostalgia Maya felt in each country, the heavy longing for everything and everyone who was missing.

Chapter Thirteen

It wasn't until the sun streamed through the crenellated windows in the morning, making lacy patterns on the floor, that the girls could really see how lovely their third-floor room was. After Parvati and Chotu had been banished—as Maya couldn't help but think of it now, the whole thing seeming like a horrible Grimms' tale—Pops had hired someone to clean and paint their apartment. Now it was the nicest in the house. The transformation was the one good thing Maya could find that had come out of the whole Parvati debacle, although the lovely, light-filled space was also, somehow, the source of the curse, the desired object in Parvati's mind. To be fair, it had been her home since she moved in with Dadiji; it was only natural that she'd feel attached to the place. But to consider it her own so viscerally that Parvati would seek to destroy the family that had put her here was truly twisted. In any case, there was plenty to covet about the room, which opened onto a balcony with stairs that led to the roof and its cinematic view of Jodhpur's celebrated fort. As the light came through the balcony's half-closed door, it spotlit the room's built-in cupboards with their faded green doors, the carved wall niches that were painted the same sky blue as the exterior of the house, and the beds with their block-print covers. Heidi's bed was empty, and when Maya pushed open the door and climbed up the stairs, she was already on the roof, dressed in an old salwar kameez she must have ferreted out of Maya's suitcase, photographing the fort in the distance.

"You look ridiculous, Hei!" Maya said. "Those are like capri pants on you."

"Maybe I'll start a trend." Heidi turned and took a picture of Maya, who shaded her face a minute too late. "I had nothing to wear; I feel so boring in jeans, when everyone else gets to run around in these."

"You can borrow whatever you want," Maya said. "And we'll buy you fabric in the market—you can have your own outfits made in a few days."

"Great." Heidi started snapping shots of three monkeys tightrope-walking along the power lines. "I love a makeover! That can be our first priority. Then the sari stores Sanjay told me about; I've got a lot of editors demanding fabric. That can be second."

Maya's only priority was to find Parvati. She sat on a plastic chair, letting the sun warm her neck. Looking around the old city she could see her neighbors going about the business of the morning. A woman holding a baby washed dishes with her free hand at an outdoor sink. On a lower rooftop, a heavyset older lady rose and fell, moving through her morning yoga, her fuchsia sari shattering the blue of the walls behind her.

"Chai, girls?" Seema slowly ascended the stairs holding a tray with two teacups, a plate of sliced mango, and a chipped porcelain dish full of bleeding pomegranate seeds. She never brought Maya chai when she was alone; Maya had to roll into the kitchen and reheat the pot on the kerosene burner.

"Seema-auntie, you have the best view in the city here." Heidi pointed to the monkeys jumping from rooftop to rooftop with the fortress as their backdrop. "You could turn this into a boutique hotel, rent out our room as the honeymoon suite."

"Do not say such a thing to my husband!" Seema pulled up a folding chair and took a long sip from her own cup. "He would do it immediately; he will take any excuse to spend more time here. Soon he will be saying, maybe we should renovate the next-door room, too! Then I would have to come and turn the house into a muddle trying to find the key. I am not even sure I have ever seen it unlocked myself. Did Maya tell you?"

"Not yet. I was tired," Maya mumbled with a mouthful of seeds, then bit down, crushing the sweetness out of them.

"Maybe you shouldn't," Seema teased, enjoying her tea break. "Heidi is an excitable sort, she may hear noises at night."

"What?" Heidi pulled up a chair. Seema explained that back in some remote time "still with the Britishers," Ajit's exceedingly beautiful grandmother had gone to the temple and been spotted by the king. The next afternoon, a man from the palace came to the door and insisted she follow him. She didn't return for three days.

"My husband's grandfather did not know if his wife was alive or dead," Seema elaborated. "By the time she came back, he was mumbling to himself, forever changed."

"Probably depressed, maybe with psychotic features," Maya murmured.

"So they locked him in that room," Seema continued, popping a pomegranate seed into her mouth. "That is what they did in those days."

"Not the most effective form of therapy," Maya interrupted. Seema waved her hand in the air as if swatting a fruit fly.

"He died later that year. Your Dadiji was only three or four, Maya," Seema added. "No one wanted to use that room after." She selected a few more seeds, chewing slowly. "After that, even when she was already quite old and Ajit was a small boy, the few times his grandmother left the house, she hid her face with her dupatta."

Maya visualized the locked door. This house was where the family began, after all. Maybe the curse emanated from the house itself? It seemed perverse to think something so evil could be rooted in such a lovely place. But why shouldn't it be? The monkeys Heidi found adorable were aggressive biters, probably carrying rabies. And it was her great-grandmother's beauty that poisoned the woman's life.

Maya stretched her arms in the sun as if to shake the thought off her shoulders. On some level she doubted the story was even true; it so closely resembled the plot of the Ramayana when Rama's wife Sita is kidnapped by the demon king Ravana. Maybe her ancestors had appropriated the kidnapping trope in an attempt to explain away her grandfather's mental illness, or to align themselves with the gods. She'd never know for sure; specific facts were too hard to come by, oral histories weren't precise, and after a certain number of years, the past took on the hazy simplicity of a fairy tale.

Seema stood and gathered the empty cups, putting hers and Heidi's on the tray while Maya still cradled hers in her cupped hands. "Nanaji will be coming to get me soon; Ramu is taking us to pick up Prashant-mausa at the airport," she said. "So, what is your program today, girls? Where to first?"

"I need to buy fabric, and also find a place that will make prints so I can give Mohammed his photos," Heidi said.

"The photo shops are near Ghanta Ghar; that is the Clocktower Market, Heidi," Seema said. "They are open late, so you should start with the fortress."

"No." Maya stood and brushed an errant pomegranate seed off her lap. A pink stain spread on the knee of her saffron salwar kameez. "We'll go to Ravi-uncle's first."

Seema started down the stairs with the cups, her braid twitching suspiciously.

When Maya and Heidi arrived at Ravi-uncle's, the house was full of relatives sitting on the veranda in chairs arranged in a circle around Sanjay. Maya scanned the crowd; there was a young girl, sixteen maybe, collecting the empty cups. If she was the housekeeper now, then Parvati wasn't likely to be in any of the back rooms either.

"Guys, what do you think?" Sanjay called above the heads of his aunties and uncles. He was wearing a white embroidered coat that was being hemmed by a slight man with a lush mustache who knelt at Sanjay's feet, pins sticking out of his mouth. A fat man in a black suit with gold embroidery around its Nehru collar spoke to the tailor sharply in Marwari, then said to Sanjay in English, "You could find no finer suit than this in Bombay, sir, that is a guarantee."

"It really is amazing." Heidi stepped closer and caressed the filigreed fabric at Sanjay's wrist. "I like your suit very much, too," she said to the fat man.

"Wore one just like it to a B-school friend's wedding," Sanjay said. "Huge hit."

"How much did it cost?" she whispered.

"Thirty-eight hundred rupees," the fat man answered before Sanjay could.

Heidi looked at Maya, who said, "About eighty bucks," and shrugged.

Heidi turned to the man. "Have you ever made this pantsuit for a woman?"

"Oh, madam." The fat man seemed to swell, becoming even fatter. "We have made so many formal pieces for big-big important women, many gowns."

"That means no," Maya whispered.

"Do it," Sanjay urged.

A beatific look settled on Heidi's face. "So. I'm going to be the first woman in India to have a pantsuit made by—"

"Raymond's of Park Avenue," Sanjay supplied.

"Mr. Raymond, I'd like a suit, please," Heidi told the fat man, whose name was not Raymond. The tailor whipped out a tape measure, and the relatives shouted advice and acted as chaperones while Heidi's measurements were taken. Maya winked at Heidi to let her know she was in good hands, and made straight for the kitchen, trying to look like she was wandering in thirsty or hungry. Kruti-masi was there helping her sister-in-law fry stuffed chilis in anticipation of Prashant-mausa's arrival. Each woman kissed Maya as well as the hot oil demanding their attention would allow.

"Is Parvati here, Masi?" Maya asked in English. Kruti-masi wiped her hands on a dishrag and stepped away from the pot. "No, Maya, she is gone, weeks ago. Ravi-uncle saw her in the market one day and had her come to clean the house two–three times, only to prepare for our coming to stay. He meant well, Maya. We always pitied that girl, an orphan, really, such a father…" Kruti-masi smacked her oil-shiny palms together. "But then Prashant-mausa told me that Parvati was very rude to your father, shouted at him! So as soon as I got here, first thing, I dismissed her, shoo-shoo, go-go."

"Where did she go, Masi?" Maya tried to keep the urgency out of her voice but could hear the strain when she spoke, like she had a sore throat.

"I do not know!" Kruti-masi raised her voice above the hissing oil. "Why should I care about such an ungrateful one? A girl your Dadiji took into her home, saved from who knows what? You should not either, hey? You have better things to think about! Celebrating your cousin's happiness. Finding some of your own. Choose someone, like Sanjay did! After your sister's troubles, your parents need happy news."

Maya stared at the mole on Kruti-masi's cheek; it seemed to

have grown. Maybe Maya was projecting, trying to magnify Kruti-masi's blemish, since she herself felt so noticeably marked by the curse. If only it were as easy as Kruti-masi suggested, and Maya could choose to be happy and in love. Her aunt seemed to believe Maya was alone because she wanted to hurt her family, when it was the opposite; she was alone, now, because she had tried to protect them, had, however passively, chosen them over Scott.

Kruti-masi was insensitive, but in a different way from her sister. Seema was no-nonsense, but Kruti-masi was just self-absorbed. Even so, she should get the mole checked to rule out melanoma. Maya would tell Prashant-mausa to see to it when they got back to Kalamazoo. Right now she couldn't bring herself to give advice to this woman who stood staring at her, suggesting that Maya was the reason her parents suffered. As if her own family was so perfect. Maya imagined telling Kruti-masi about her future daughter-in-law's rendezvous with her college boyfriend, drawing the name out, the thick, nasal drone of the first syllable, the clipped *n* of the last. Darren! She pictured Kruti-masi's face crumpling, or maybe she would get angry, open her mouth and hiss and pop like the oil in the pot. Alarmed by how satisfying she found the fantasy of her aunt exploding, Maya turned and walked toward the veranda, where Sanjay was unfolding silk sari lengths he had bought for Amrita, showing them to Heidi for her expert approval.

After lunch at Ravi-uncle's, the afternoon was spent playing tourist, or, for Maya, pretending to. She and Sanjay told the adults they'd be showing Heidi around; doing so allowed Sanjay to escape the cloying attention of his family and Maya to walk the alleys of the Old Town looking for Parvati. Every time she saw a small, curvy woman with a glossy braid, she walked quickly forward, finding it harder to breathe with each step until she was even with the figure and could see she was a stranger. She even asked one woman who turned out not to be Parvati for directions to the fort, although she knew perfectly well where she was going.

If she seemed preoccupied, the others didn't notice. Sanjay rattled on in English narrating Jodhpur for Heidi while her large camera's clicking shutter provided a stable backbeat to his words. She'd borrowed a serious digital model from her cousin Byron, who was in the photography department at the Art Institute of Chicago; it was his recreational camera, but its bulk made Heidi look—and apparently feel—like a serious photographer. She shot the fortress guards with their red and orange turbans and elaborate mustaches that were waxed to curve up at the ends like the scimitars hanging off their belts; the puppet-seller; the dancing boy with kohl-rimmed eyes, and the street-sweeping old woman who lived in a mud-walled shed next to the temple, cleaning for the goddess Chamunda.

At the temple, with the dusty earth warm under their bare feet, Sanjay rang the bell to get the deity's attention. Maya watched as a paundit tied red and orange string into bracelets for Sanjay, then Heidi, who closed her eyes as he wrapped the mauli around her wrist. She must be making a wish; Heidi made wishes everywhere, throwing coins in the fountain at the mall in Hanover where they'd shopped during college, and the moat that surrounds the Temple of Dendur at the Met in New York. When it was her turn to receive mauli, Maya closed her eyes, but no wish came; she felt too hopeless to ask for anything.

They put their shoes back on and walked down the ramparts past the fortress. The path Maya usually took, the back way, was blocked. A few weeks before, on Chamunda's holiday, one of the steel barricades separating the lines of pilgrims into men and women fell, and a rumor that the noise was a bomb spread through the crowd, already anxious in the wake of the Bombay attacks. There had been a stampede; several people died, Ravi-uncle es-

caped only because he was late in getting to the temple, and listened
when fleeing worshippers yelled at him to turn back. Today the
temple glowed in the afternoon light, gold against the blue rooftops
of the city below, and it seemed impossible that such violence could
take place in this holy spot.

Walking back through the Old Town toward the house where
Maya had arranged for Mohammed to pick them up and motor
them to Ghanta Ghar, they passed a teenaged girl herding her two
little brothers down the street. Catching sight of Heidi the children
turned and circled back, extended their hands and said "good
morning." Something about the whole ridiculous scene, the way
the children thought nothing of greeting a foreigner, of expecting
her to share their delight in meeting each other, made Maya want
to protect them. The kids eventually disappeared down the street,
and soon they heard a voice chirp "Hello! Up! Up!" and spotted the
girl on her balcony, leaning against a curved window frame. Heidi
turned and waved, walking backward.

"Watch out for the open sewers!" Sanjay warned.

Sanjay and Heidi chattered and swatted at each other like the
rooftop monkeys, and Maya tried to interfere enough to seem like
she, too, was alternately enchanted and disgusted with the sights
and sounds of the city, instead of consumed with the frustration of
not being able to find Parvati. Passing the cobblers who squatted by
the public toilets cutting new soles to affix to the bottoms of old
sandals, Maya noticed a Jain woman waiting patiently for her shoes.
She was dressed entirely in white, with a flap of gauze covering her
mouth so she wouldn't accidentally swallow any bugs. Maya imagined the suffocating taste of cotton on the woman's tongue and
smiled at her, thinking that the muted, muffled stranger must understand exactly how she felt.

Later, at Ghanta Ghar, Maya bought bracelets for Nisba and
Yasmin from a bangle-seller who sat on the ground surrounded by

a mosaic of her plastic and glass wares, nursing a baby on her lap through complicated folds in her sari blouse. Heidi said she looked like a Madonna and wanted to photograph her, but stealthily, in case she objected and didn't act as beatific as she looked; Maya's job was to distract her by browsing her stock. Bargaining with the vendor in rapid-fire Marwari, Maya felt savvy and capable, like her old self, as if the gauze that muffled her reactions had been torn away. She had hoped that India would heal her at once, release her from her worries, her family's health troubles, the curse. That hadn't happened, but maybe some of the water-borne parasites Maya had undoubtedly swallowed by now were eating away at her sadness. Or maybe she had entered acceptance, the fifth, and final, stage of grief over the loss of Scott. Focused solely on the minor jewelry transaction, it seemed possible that she wouldn't always be in mourning for her old life.

As Mohammed drove them to Ravi-uncle's for Prashant-mausa's welcome dinner, Sanjay pointed out that instead of bilge-gray waste, the sewers were now filled with cobalt-colored water, runoff from bandhej saris, a local specialty being made in a workshop down the alley. His mother had placed a special order for the wedding, and last week he had dropped off a deposit and seen the women working. Sanjay explained the tie-dye process to Heidi, how the wastewater ran pink, orange, green, depending on the fabric lot being dyed. She photographed the gutters, whispering, "Even the sewers are beautiful."

"But they still stink," Sanjay said, voicing Maya's thoughts exactly.

Ravi-uncle's kitchen was full of relatives, some of whom couldn't make the long trip to Bombay for the wedding and wanted to hear every detail they'd be missing.

"I'm not going to remember everything," Sanjay said. "Where's Ma?"

"Your mother is not feeling well; she is lying down," Seema said. "It is nothing to worry about, just GI complaints, a little loose stool."

"Thanks for the detailed report, Ma," Maya said, but she worried, momentarily, that this sudden malady was her fault. What if her negative thoughts about Kruti-masi had drawn bad health to her? That would make Maya no better than Parvati, although her "curse," such as it was, was unintentional, and its results minor. Maya tried to feel guilty, but failed. She would really only care if Kruti-masi told Seema that Maya had rudely stormed away from her and she had to endure Seema's loud sighs and feigned self-deprecation as she wondered aloud how she had raised such a disrespectful child. But Kruti-masi must not have said anything, because right now her mother was busy quizzing Prashant-mausa about Pops's health, asking for the names of his doctors, nurses, and orderlies, and for physical descriptions when she didn't recognize the names. "I will call the hospital when it is late enough; Ajit is a very difficult patient." Seema clucked her tongue against the roof of her mouth. "I am surprised you did not think to bring a copy of his file, Prashant."

"Ma, the man just got off a plane!" Maya said. "Cut him some slack."

As the girls walked to the kitchen to wash their hands, Heidi whispered, "She looks out for your dad. I think that's sweet. Romantic, like when she cried over him while he was in the army. She'd fallen in love even though they started out as strangers. Who knew Seema-auntie had it in her?"

"Why is it so important for you to think my parents love each other?" Maya snapped. Everything anyone said was irritating her today. But Heidi really was being ridiculous. Inquiring about a person's health didn't mean you knew anything about their soul, that you understood the person the way she and Scott had known each other.

"Why is it so important for you to think they don't?" Heidi turned off the kitchen faucet and dried her hands on her borrowed salwar kameez.

For the next three days, Maya failed at finding Parvati. The vegetable-seller Parvati swore by said he hadn't seen her in weeks, and she wasn't at the Shani temple for Saturday prayers, or on the street with her favorite spice shops. Maya had even loitered at the sari stalls while Heidi and Sanjay did business at the bandhej factory, trying to use creative visualization to conjure her up, imagining Parvati lifting up the fabrics, rubbing them between her thumb and forefinger with an expression of distaste. But none of it worked.

In between searching, Maya caught up with all the aunties and uncles who seemed to take pleasure in reminding her that next year, they might not be here for her to visit; the way they said it made Maya feel that they considered their mortality her fault. The days passed to the whirring of Heidi's camera, as they rickshawed from auntie's house to cousin's house for meals, from the National Handloom outlet at one end of town to the sister store at the other so that Heidi could buy more fabric to bring back to New York, quizzing the shopkeepers about the provenance of each printed tablecloth. Maya suspected that Heidi had her own three-pronged agenda—to personally uplift the economy of the region, to inspire jealousy in the editors back home, and to protect Maya, to be a shiny white buffer between her and the laughing, crying, squeezing, needing relatives constantly asking why she didn't have a husband, never thinking that she might have driven one away because she couldn't envision him next to them.

The day before Maya and Heidi were leaving for Benares to see the Ganges, Nanaji and Ramu escorted them to their appointment with Bauji. The pretext was to introduce Heidi to the family astrologer. But really, Maya wanted an explanation. Not of the curse; Pops had made her promise not to tell anyone about it and it wouldn't be fair to burden Bauji, he couldn't help with the trauma in her present. But he owed her answers about her past, and, she hoped, could provide inspiration for her future. There was a risk, of course; Bauji might see even more pain ahead. Or he might see nothing new, identify nothing wrong, might turn out to be a powerless old man who could make no promises about her future. If Bauji's powers of divination collapsed under Maya's scrutiny, she would have to write off his predictions as a quaint tradition, or, to borrow Dr. Bernard's phrase, a culturally based belief system. She wasn't equipped to face another loss.

"You go first, Heidi," Maya said, earning herself a few minutes of reprieve to prepare herself. "I see him every year."

Nanaji leaned back in the one armchair, and Maya and Heidi sat on a twin bed that had been pushed against the wall, opposite Bauji in his straight-backed wooden chair. Heidi glanced over at Nanaji, then at Maya, who shrugged. In India, divination was a family affair—the prophecies Bauji made, involving marriage, career, fortune, affected not just an individual but everyone who loved him or her. There was no way Maya could ask Nanaji to leave. If Heidi wanted to be considered part of the family, her future would be a matter of public interest, too. Bauji's teenaged granddaughter swished in and out, silently bringing tea, biscuits, and a bowl of foil-wrapped chocolates.

"Ramu-ji brought me your information yesterday, so I have done your janampatri and made you a copy," Bauji began, handing Heidi a piece of paper on which he'd drawn the position of the planets at her birth. "Let us begin with the academics. Your education has been quite good. You are respected in the field you have chosen, and will go on to even more acclaim. In a few years, I see an elephant in your household."

"That means you're going to be rich," Maya explained.

"Thanks." Heidi flashed a smile at her and turned back toward Bauji, her ponytail flicking. "Maybe it's the design and import business I'm trying to start. I've been talking to the owner of the band-hej factory, he speaks some English, and Sanjay helps, he's the businessman, I'm not." Heidi paused for breath and Bauji nodded as if he had understood her rapid, American delivery perfectly.

"Is there anything you would like to inquire about?" he asked slowly.

"Oh! I guess; Yia-yia will kill me if I don't ask about marriage, kids."

"I see you have had relations in the past." Bauji scanned a copy of Heidi's janampatri, which shook in his mottled hand.

"I come from a large family, on my dad's side."

"No, relations of a romantic nature," Bauji clarified. Nanaji leaned back in his chair and closed his eyes as if to nap.

"He means you've had premarital sex," Maya whispered to Heidi.

"He can see that?"

"I guess. He's never said anything to me about it, but maybe he was just being tactful." She twitched her nose toward the left, in the direction of Nanaji.

"What about in the future?" Heidi said to Bauji, enunciating carefully.

"There will be a husband, yes, and a happy marriage, but not for some time."

"Well, I've got to get the business off the ground."

"And you are manglik," Bauji said.

"What?" Heidi looked at Maya, who shrugged, then turned toward the astrologer.

"If you had married at a young age, in the early twenties let us say, it would have been quite disastrous," Bauji explained. "A grave mistake. Your friend," he nodded at Maya, "she is double manglik."

"Figures." Maya laughed from her perch on the bed, impressed at how calm she felt, at her ability to dissociate herself from the discussion of her future, the improbability of her happiness. "So I should never marry?"

Bauji laughed, his shoulders shaking even after he stopped making sounds. "No, Maya, it is just that it would have been even worse for you to have married early, the wrong person. Now, unless your friend has any more questions?"

Heidi shook her head, murmured her thanks, and began rummaging through her tote bag, pulling out a number of hair elastics, none of which seemed to meet with her approval. Maya couldn't tell if this marked disinterest was Heidi's way of giving her privacy, or if she was trying to create a distraction for Nanaji, in case Bauji got explicit.

"Before we start, I was wondering, have you seen Parvati lately?" Maya said softly to Bauji, under the cover of Heidi's noisy search.

"Dadiji's girl?" Bauji frowned. "No. But if you are needing more help around the house, I am sure—"

"No, thank you. I just hoped I might see her before I go, we practically grew up together," Maya said. It wasn't really a lie.

"So then, let us get started." Bauji consulted the paper in his hand. "Listen to me. You have lost the battle, but not the war. I see that there has been a great deal of—"

"It's December and I'm not engaged," Maya broke in, widening her eyes to keep them from filling with tears. "Last time I was here, you said that by this December, I'd know who I was going to marry." Bauji was nothing if not specific; he'd given her the month and said that the man would be from the South, which had mystified her until she remembered that Scott's mother's family was from Alabama; that's where the Lamar who had inspired his name had been born.

"This did not come to pass?" Bauji peered at Maya, who was breathing carefully.

Maya shook her head. "I know less than I ever did."

"Your last chart indicated a significant decision would be made regarding marriage; it seems I interpreted the outcome wrong," he said finally. "I did not expect this." He put down the paper, took off his glasses, and put them in an aluminum case he kept in his shirt pocket. "But I see you will be acquainted with the man who is your future by this summer. I am so certain that if this does not bear itself out, I will never read another janampatri again." He leaned against the spindly chair back. Nanaji's eyes popped open and he mirrored Bauji's movement as if they were playing a game of Simon Says. Then he leaned forward and whispered to Maya in Marwari, "I don't care who the man is; if he is a Brahmin or an Untouchable. I just want to see you settled before I die."

In New York, the worst thing Maya or Heidi could say about a friend's marriage was that she had settled. Just having that aspect of your life squared away wasn't the goal; happiness was. Were Sanjay and Amrita in love or was he settling, filling the wife slot with someone who would fit in nicely with his family, his life, sit next to him on AirIndia as he shuttled back and forth between Jodhpur and Chicago? Maya wondered if she could want that; sometimes it seemed a partner who was not a soul mate, but a companion, an appropriate addition to the family, would be so much easier to find, so much more pleasant for everyone to have around. It hadn't escaped her attention that the most extreme example of an inappropriate spouse Nanaji could come up with was an Untouchable; a white man never even occurred to him. Maya felt tired, although it was only late morning.

Bauji's granddaughter came back with nimbu paani, the liquid in the glasses shaking as she carried the tray. Maya took one, murmuring her gratitude. As she sipped the fizzy, lemony liquid, she began to feel her energy returning. She had come fearing that she'd have to write off Bauji, to lose her belief that her future was part of a larger plan that could be predicted and managed somehow. But Bauji had taken the tragedy of Scott's desertion and made it a challenge, a necessary step on the ladder of personal growth. And he had promised her—guaranteed—that she was headed somewhere positive, that she wouldn't always be this alone. It was more comforting than the best therapy session. This is why you believe, she wanted to tell Dr. Bernard. She knew what he would think, but never say; she half thought it herself. That divination was a coping mechanism for psychic cripples; not a healthy defense against powerlessness, like humor, or sublimating that feeling into productive activity, but a destructive one, a delusional lie to the self. Still, at this moment she felt both light and strong. If Bauji was right, it seemed possible she could be in love again, or at least, be happy and marry, bringing her family joy. She remembered dancing by the basketball courts in New York for no reason, when the world seemed full of possibilities. Bauji seemed to promise that someday she'd feel that again. In the meantime, she had just been given six months of peace of mind. All she needed to do was be patient.

She leaned toward Bauji. "Could the man be someone I already know?"

"Perhaps." He brought his paper close to his face. "But whatever decision was made this month will not be reversed."

Maya inhaled deeply to replace the air that had been sucked out of her body. You knew this, she told herself. Looking at Scott, you knew. The pranayama worked; she felt bruised but alive, as if she had survived a fall. If she could heal from the loss of Scott, Bauji was offering her an answer, not the one she had hoped for, but maybe something even better. Someone who could bring all the aspects of her life together. The glass of nimbu paani sweated cool drops onto her hand. She heard a whir and click and looked up to see Heidi put down her camera.

"I call it 'Lambent Chilies.'" Heidi pointed to a tray of peppers that Bauji's granddaughter had put on the window ledge to dry in the sun. They glowed red against the faded green of the wall.

After their visit to the astrologer, Heidi insisted they go to the photo shop first in their afternoon errands, so she could pick up her prints and give Mohammed his pictures before they left. She had made sets to give to Maya's relatives, to the old opium-smoker at the fortress who posed with an empty hookah for appreciative visitors, and to the breastfeeding bangle-seller at Ghanta Ghar. When she gave Mohammed his copies, he shook Heidi's hand, and, as soon as he dropped the girls off in front of the arched entrance to the market, set to work replacing one of the film star stills tucked into the heart-shaped cutouts in the upholstery of his auto rickshaw. Maya had warned Heidi not to expect such enthusiasm from everyone; the bangle-seller might not be here today, or, even if she was, might not be sitting on the same plot of earth. But inside the market, there was the woman, baby on her lap. She sat up straight, shading her eyes to look into the crowd for likely buyers. The plastic, rhinestone-studded discs spread around her made it look like she was sitting on a magic carpet, poised to fly off somewhere better.

"You give it to her." Heidi thrust the photo at Maya. "She might think I stole her soul or something by taking her picture."

"And if I give it to her?"

"You can explain that I'm a honky who doesn't know any better."

Maya walked toward the vendor with Heidi trailing behind. She handed her the photo, the woman shrieked, and a yellow-saried bangle-seller who worked beside her leaned over her merchandise to see what was causing all the fuss. Soon all the bangle-sellers were clustered around the mother, telling her how lucky she was, how beautiful she looked, like Aishwarya Rai, whom she actually resembled not at all.

"It's the first picture of herself she's ever seen," Maya translated for Heidi.

Maya watched the bangle-seller beaming at her photo, an artifact of herself at her most beautiful, of her child as an infant. The clock in the tower struck four and Maya looked toward the market gate, to see if she could spot Mohammed spreading out his prayer mat. And there, walking in with a tray full of sweets, was Parvati, swaying like a young tree on a windy day. Maya's breath quickened and when she tried to isolate which emotion was causing her heightened state, she could only identify joy. She had never known Parvati to shop here; perhaps she had conjured her, made her appear through all her efforts at searching. Or maybe Bauji had somehow summoned Parvati; maybe he was a better fortune-teller than Maya believed, had looked into her soul, found the source of her pain, and sent her the solution. Maybe the gods had brought Parvati or it was just a beautiful coincidence—there was no reason a coincidence couldn't also be a miracle. In any case, Parvati was here and relief was possible.

Parvati looked to her right as if she had important business in that direction, an urgent matter she had to focus on exclusively and immediately. But she glanced back, so quickly that her glossy braid flipped back and forth, and just in time to see Maya walking straight toward her, so that she had to turn or risk Maya running into the tray, upsetting the sweets, and knocking the entire day's profits into the dirt.

"Parvati! Wait!" Maya said in Marwari.

"Maya-ji!" Parvati smiled, not the familiar, small smile she would give Dadiji, but a huge grin as if no other sight could bring her such pleasure. "I heard you had arrived. I was planning to visit, to see you and your greatly respected parents. How is everyone?"

Maya's happiness turned to hate at the fake, film-star tone of Parvati's voice, the mockery she heard in her words. She felt her body emanating heat from the core of her abdomen. The backs of her knees started to sweat. She had been nervous around Parvati for years, self-conscious. But now she was afraid of her, and the feeling made her realize just how much power Parvati had exerted over all of them. "We have been better."

"Really? I am sorry to hear that. I am not doing so well myself since your dadiji left us, may the gods give her soul peace." Parvati's mouth turned down and her shoulders rose up, as if her body were folding itself into a symbol for sorrow. "We live behind the market now, and I hear this noise all day. Chotu is working small jobs for a shopkeeper outside the gate, a new shop, I don't think you know it, and I make a little extra—"

"Parvati, all I ask is that you remove it," Maya interrupted. She heard a sound to her right but couldn't take her focus off Parvati long enough to look at Heidi; all she could see was a bangle-covered white arm make its way into her peripheral vision.

"Remove what, Maya-ji?" Parvati let her mouth hang open in cartoon confusion.

"The curse!" Maya whispered. She knew she spat when she said it, but she didn't care. "Take back the words."

"Oh, Maya-ji!" Parvati giggled. "But you are educated! I am not, but I learned a great deal living so long in a house with modern, educated people, even if that time has come to its end. Thanks to the kindness of Mataji, even I am not so old-fashioned as to believe there is such a thing as a curse." She shrugged her left shoulder, so as not to upset the pastry tray in her right hand. Maya stared at her. Each time she had pictured this moment she'd imagined Parvati having a different reaction; crocodile tears feigning regret, high-pitched screams yelling further maledictions, words Maya didn't even recognize. But she had never anticipated this, Parvati, calm and rational as Dr. Bernard, acting as if Maya were the superstitious bumpkin. And maybe she was; perhaps Parvati was a better student of human nature than Maya would ever be, no matter how many years of analytic studies she completed. By pretending the curse didn't exist, she not only confirmed all of Maya's fears about her own sanity, but also absolved herself from removing the hex, leaving it free to work its evil. If Parvati didn't acknowledge the ability of the curse to harm her family, that implied that Maya had been living in a delusion for months, making the curse true because she believed it was so. Or maybe Maya's family was just unlucky, fundamentally flawed and responsible for their own slow, painful deterioration. Maya wanted to knock the tray out of her hand, to knock Parvati to the ground and hold her down until she admitted what she'd done and took the words back, fixing everything and proving that an end to this sorrow was possible.

Instead, Maya jammed her hand into her bag, a burlap square advertising Raju's Sari Shop, so roughly that the material scraped the skin off her knuckle. "I'll pay you to take it away," she said, trying to fight Parvati's cold rationality with practical tactics. "How much?" She pulled out her wallet, letting the bag fall into the dust. Her voice was too loud and high; a crowd had gathered. Parvati turned her cheek to her shoulder, blushing prettily, and waved her free hand in the air as if to make the wallet disappear.

"It is true that I said some things in anger to Ajit-ji; I wish we had both been more reasonable that day." Parvati looked directly at Maya. In her lovely, liquid eyes Maya saw the glint of something hard and sharp. It wasn't evil; it was triumph. As much as Parvati might need money, no amount that Maya could offer her would generate the profound satisfaction of this moment. Parvati loved seeing fear in the eyes of Maya, Dadiji's pampered, petted girl; loved the power a few well-chosen words had given her; loved that to the crowd of tourists and vendors who had gathered she seemed like the worldly lady and Maya the superstitious, ranting madwoman, great-granddaughter of the raving madman who had died locked up, a prisoner in his own home.

"And look at you, a beautiful doctor in a salwar kameez so new it still has the lines from the tailor's ironing," Parvati said, her voice like a song. "Are you not proof that there is no curse, that your family is healthy and wealthy as always?"

This was pointless. Maya hated herself for having said too much already. Seema would never have debased herself in front of Parvati, she would have thrown one fearsome look at her and Parvati would have done whatever she could to erase the memory of that stare. It was too late for Maya to save face, but she knew enough not to list the ways the curse had been successful, to expose the wounds that the Das family walked around with like so many open sores. She wouldn't give Parvati reason to go home to Chotu wearing an even bigger, more hideous grin than the one that split her face now. Maya had failed to save her family or herself; all that was left to her was to accept the consequence of her weakness with as much grace as possible. "You're right," Maya said, wiping her cheek to dislodge the dust she had kicked up while striding over. "I got carried away. In America, we don't speak to each other like that, so it made me nervous. It's odd, how easy it is to get wrapped up in a backwards superstition."

Parvati smiled sweetly at Maya. "I'm so glad, then, that everyone in America is so well," she said. "Here, take a sweet for your foreign friend." She handed Maya and Heidi each a gulab jamun. "Good-bye, Maya-ji," she said, turning slowly with her tray. "Even though we are no longer part of the same household, I wish you and your family all the great good luck that you deserve." Her hips swung like a metronome and her voice grew louder as she walked toward the covered stalls. "Next time, I hope to see you with a male friend, if the god wills it."

After a few minutes of silence, Maya spoke in English. "Pretended she has no idea what I'm talking about, like I made the curse up, like I'm crazy," she said to Heidi. "Her father warned us she was evil, but because of me Dadiji brought her into our home."

"That's her," Heidi marveled, and unwrapped Maya's clenched, sticky fingers from the paper that held the sweet. She took the pastry and handed Maya the burlap bag, which she'd picked up soon after Maya dropped it. "Parvati is almost pretty."

It was true. Parvati should have looked damaged, with horns, or scars, at least vitiligo disfiguring her cheeks, her syrup-covered hands. But she looked like any woman whose life didn't turn out as expected—a bit pinched, but attractive enough.

"Come on," Heidi said. "I have some Purell in the rickshaw." At the entrance to the market they were stopped by a beggar girl holding her naked brother at her side, where her hip would be in a few years. Heidi handed her the mashed sweet and Maya sighed, but it sounded like a gasp. Now Heidi would want to photograph the girl and her brother, who were grimy but beautiful. It would only take thirty seconds, a minute maybe, but Maya didn't think she could last that long; she needed to be gone from this place. Until today Maya at least had hope that the power of the curse could be ended. Now she had lost that, too, and as she felt herself succumbing to the power of this phenomenon she once laughed at, she sensed that her knees were about to buckle. The thought of falling into the dust was oddly comforting, as if she might sink straight through until the Indian earth closed above her. But Maya's legs held firm and Heidi didn't stop to take a photo. She just wiped her fingers on her bag and kept on walking.

"Thank you, madam," said the girl, chewing her gulab jamun as she trotted after them. "I am a good girl."

Now she did start to sink, but Heidi grabbed her elbow before Maya even realized what had shocked her. She was stunned, not because the beggar had learned this useful phrase from some long-gone tourist, but because the child sounded like her own mind. Maya tried to be good. She didn't understand how or why she had ended up this bereft.

"I know you're a good girl, sweetie," Heidi said to the child and tears started falling down Maya's face. Heidi kept walking, her hand on Maya's arm, pulling her forward. The girl gave up on Heidi and tugged at Maya's salwar. "From you, madam?"

Maya wiped the tears off her cheek with her sticky hand, and Heidi said, "Please, honey, leave madam alone."

Chapter Fourteen

Maya and Heidi were two of five women in the packed train car, and the only ones not traveling with husbands, fathers, or brothers. It would have been different on the plane—all the students in their tight jeans and silk kurtas heading back to university after a weekend home took the flight to Benares, as did the tourists, instead of the five-hour train to Jaipur, then an overnight train to Benares. They should have been Heidi and Maya's anonymous traveling companions, the people they jockeyed with for space in the overhead bin. But after seeing Parvati, Maya had forgotten to confirm their flight, so when they arrived at the airport the next morning, the stocky woman behind the AirIndia counter informed them that their seats had been sold to other passengers. It was Nanaji who thought to call the train, and did so, shouting into Ramu the driver's cell phone because he was going deaf and wearing a fur hat with earflaps that had been given to him by a visiting Russian diplomat in the 1980s.

"Isn't he a vegetarian?" Heidi asked, indicating the hat.

"It was a gift," Maya answered, and Heidi shrugged, placid. It was only on the two occasions she had called her assistant back in the office that Heidi's voice had the sharp edge to it that it often did in New York. Maya thought Heidi could have drummed up some of her assistant-scolding voice to use on the AirIndia lady, but she just stood there, flipping through her *Lonely Planet: India.*

Ramu raced them to the train station, where Seema and Radha-bhuasa had shown up with tinfoil packets full of besan parathas, and Heidi screamed from the bathroom when a rat ran across the floor, causing two security guards to rush to the Ladies'. Outside, the platforms were filled with Muslims bringing goats to their relatives, to be sacrificed for Bakr Eid, which started the next day. The bleating of the sacrificial lambs drowned out the good-byes Nanaji and Maya's mother and auntie shouted as the last chai sellers stepped out of the cars and the train pulled away.

"Take my water," Heidi said, handing Maya a plastic bottle. "I'm never going to the bathroom the entire time."

"It's twenty hours altogether."

"Maya, if the *station* bathroom had rats, I mean—"

Maya didn't answer. She was watching children playing something like King of the Hill on the trash piles that formed the back-yards of the shantytowns lining the tracks. Heidi left her own bench and came to sit next to her.

"We'll see your mom at the wedding," she said, putting her arm around Maya. "It's too bad Nanaji can't make the trip, but you'll be back in a year. In the meantime, you'll have my pictures all over your apartment."

"Thanks. Can I see them?"

Heidi returned to her berth across the aisle to rifle through her bag, continuing to do so after she'd pulled out the packet of prints and handed them to Maya, who flipped through them absently. The city was bruisingly beautiful, but Maya had never been so relieved to leave Jodhpur and her suffocating relatives. She had known, ever since she was little, before she could put words to the thought, that being happy was her job, and Priya's and Mohan's, too. Her parents had emigrated from Jodhpur to build a better life; if their children weren't happy, then why had they abandoned the people and place they loved? Heidi saw Jodhpur as fireworks—an explosion of color, light, and sound. But to Maya the city had become a reflection of the ways she had fallen short, not only of what her parents wanted for her, but also of what she wanted for herself.

She looked around at the berths. The passengers had flipped up the ends to extend them into beds, and were now lying under thin blankets, snoring or reading Bollywood magazines. An old man whose beard was orange where he dyed the tips with henna stuck his pinkie finger into a luxurious tuft of ear hair and rummaged around blissfully.

"Does he think that looks natural?" Heidi was staring at the orange-bearded man. "His ear hair doesn't match. He looks like an Oompa Loompa. Who do these guys think they're fooling?"

Maya thought she had answered but the next second Heidi was back sitting next to her, wiping the tears that were falling down her cheeks. "You'll be back," Heidi murmured. "You'll see all of them again soon, I promise."

"What if I don't?" Maya sobbed. "They keep telling me they're getting old, that they want to see me married before they die."

Heidi laughed. "Your aunts want you to be married? I'm surprised mine haven't set fire to every church in New England with the candles they light praying for me to meet my husband. Chill out; you've been single for two weeks; for me, it's two years."

But Maya knew that for Heidi it was just a matter of time; the right person would someday grab her bauble-covered hand and not let go. Maya couldn't have the same faith for herself anymore. "I get it," she said. "I'm not the only person who's had her heart broken. But what if Scott was supposed to be my husband, like Bauji said last year?"

"You think Scott would have made the bhuasas and Nanaji happy?"

"I didn't let him try."

Heidi handed her the antibacterial wipes she kept in her gold purse, which seemed to be stocked with all the tools necessary to womankind. Maya blew her nose with one and cleaned her hands with another.

"Maya, you know I loved Scott, he's a great guy," Heidi said, retrieving the plastic pack and taking care to close it securely, so she had to look down at it, not up at Maya. "But, seeing you here, I don't know if he would get it. And I think that if you were sure he could have made you happy, you wouldn't have let him go."

"I didn't have a choice."

"Well, you did, sort of." Heidi glanced quickly at Maya, then studiously out the window. "Now that you could end up with any-one, what kind of guy do you want?"

Maya crumpled the antibacterial wipe into a ball. The ear-cleaning uncle—or was it some other elderly male—was staring at her through the falling darkness. She didn't care. "I don't know," she said at last. "Someone who can be with me wherever, in New York or in India. Someone to help out with whatever curses get thrown our way; I'm not handling this right alone." Heidi stroked Maya's hair.

"It was Parvati who started this, but I couldn't get her to stop it." Maya unfolded the crumpled wipe in her hand and smoothed it out. "And if it wasn't Parvati, then we caused this. It's our fault; Par-vati just made us see it, see how damaged we really are."

Heidi turned to face her. "But how could it be your fault? You're the ones who got hurt."

"Well, Dr. Bernard might say these are all psychophysiologic conditions, a shared psychiatric syndrome. I think it's called folie à famille."

"Whatever," Heidi said. "Parvati, Satan, psychiatric shared thing, who cares who caused this whirlwind of pain? What matters is that the curse is real, at least as far as you're concerned—and as far as I am, too, P.S. All this nightmarish stuff happened to you guys and it's not fair. But since you saw Parvati, it's like you've just given up. If you all caused this, then you have the power to change it, too."

But she hadn't been able to, and this fact was just one more way Maya had failed her family.

"Besides, maybe Parvati can't stop it," Heidi said. "Maybe what she told you is true; she was just being hateful, she doesn't have the power to curse."

Maya snorted.

"And even if she does," Heidi continued, "once she said the words, the curse passed from her to your family. Whoever caused it, you're the ones who carry it around. You can find a way to remove it."

Heidi was staring at her with the same hopeful look she had when suggesting that Maya simply tell her schizophrenic patient that she couldn't possibly be Hitler's reincarnation, thus setting her free from decades of self-hatred and self-abuse, all in one quick session. "How?" Maya said quietly.

"Well, I don't know." Heidi looked into her bag. "That's what we have to figure out. But you can get the curse removed. It's not too late to save everyone. Except for Dadiji, you and your family are all still alive."

Maya winced behind the antibacterial wipe she was using to clean her face. "I know, Hei. You're right. I've been whining all over this subcontinent and you suffered more loss before age ten—"

"It's not a contest! But I do know it's up to us to make something good out of what we're thrown. You have to believe you can change this. It's not over till the fat lady sings, and Parvati was pear-shaped, but she's no plus size!"

Maya pretended to laugh as she lay down on her cot. The fake laugh had almost the same effect as a real one; by the time she was stretched out on the musty banquette, Maya felt calmer and, if not optimistic, less doomed. One point to cognitive behavioral therapy, she thought, and laughed again.

"Things can only get better," Heidi said. "And soon we'll be in Benares, 'City of Light.'" She pulled a paperback with that title out of her bag and tossed it at Maya.

"I thought that was Paris."

After more digging, Heidi came up with her *Lonely Planet India,* and opened it to the Benares/Varanasi section. She lay down to read, then sat up and reached for her Purell, rubbing the pink fluid all over her hands like she was at a sink, about to go into surgery. "This says that Ganges water contains one point five million fecal coliforms per milliliter; the acceptable amount for human consumption is about five hundred," she reported.

"Oh, that's true," Maya called from her bunk.

"The fashion director said the Ganges is one big toilet; I told her it was holy."

"Both true." Maya closed her eyes.

"It says here the whole city is a tirtha, 'a sacred crossroads where mortals rise to divine heights and gods and goddesses descend to earth to bathe in the river.'"

"Teer-ta, not tuhr-the. I hope you brought your bathing suit."

"Gross." Heidi reclined again, adjusted her new embroidered pashmina, and turned her back to Maya. She was asleep in minutes, breathing heavily, undoubtedly dreaming of sacred beings frolicking in crystal streams, which allowed Maya to use her book, and book light, guilt-free until she, too, dozed off. She woke a few hours later, when the train clanged to a stop somewhere near Jaipur, to the sound of a loud voice with a Long Island accent complaining, "All we could get was third class. Dude, you are so glad you got to stay. Next year, you're bringing Mom and Dad to this fucking pit."

"Language!" An auntie's voice pierced the dark.

Outside the Benares train station a swarm of cycle rickshaws rang their bells. Maya had never been on a cycle rickshaw; in Jodhpur they were all motorized, and she rode around surrounded by a cloud of diesel exhaust. These seemed much more civilized, but there was no way Maya, Heidi, and their luggage would fit in their narrow backseats, so she loaded her bag on top of the faux-Burberry rug that lined the trunk of a prepaid taxi.

"Good thing your parents weren't born here, huh?" Heidi said, peering out the window at shops selling mobile phones, acrylic sweaters, secondhand sewing machines. Cows chewed rotted fruit rinds among the trash that clogged the sewers. "This looks like... the parts of the Bronx you end up in when you take a wrong turn off the bridge."

"You're just cranky because you couldn't make it," Maya teased. "Held your urine for seventeen hours, but then..."

"Maya. Please." Heidi sniffed.

The city was packed with devotees of Shiva who were descending on Benares for the Kumbh Mela, their annual pilgrimage, but Nanaji had managed to secure a room at the Hotel Ganges View. After forty-five minutes of the jerky cab dodging mourners in white and sadhus in loincloths, they'd finally reached it and were now sitting on the hotel's tiled rooftop, overlooking the sacred river.

"Talk about a lucky break, hmm?" Heidi was photographing water buffalo on the riverfront below. "A restored mansion, views of the goddess-river? This is like *The Jewel in the Crown*."

Maya laughed.

"What?" Heidi asked. "I watch PBS sometimes; I like a British accent. Anyway, I feel like now that we're here, maybe your luck has changed."

"*I'm* not the one who got us in here," Maya said. She was sorry her life wasn't as entertaining as a costume drama miniseries, but she wasn't willing to have Heidi foist a happy ending on her. "It was Nanaji."

"He's part of the family, related by blood."

"Not to Pops; he's just Pops's father-in-law, related by marriage, and it was Pops's family Parvati cursed." Maya regretted the words as soon as she heard her voice speaking them. She'd been talking about the curse nonstop; Heidi must be sick of hearing it. Maya herself was tired of thinking about it, so tired, but every time she woke up it was there. And now they were in Benares; there were no more family preparations for Sanjay's wedding, no saris to be bought, and no long e-mails to write to Scott so he could experience all of this with her. All that was left was the curse, thickly surrounding her, blackening her life like a cloud of auto rickshaw exhaust.

Heidi sat down on an antique palanquin. She had showered after checking in, and her hair was drying in the afternoon sun, glowing like a halo. The rest of her didn't much resemble a saint, but she looked healthy, well rested. Maya had showered, too, but she could feel the dark circles under her eyes as if they were bruises. "Does it matter who got us the room?" Heidi picked up her camera. "It's gorgeous."

It was, with a double bed piled high with puffy duvets, and latticed shutters shading the windows. It was the kind of place Maya would have liked to have visited with Scott. Or, if she were alone, she could have stayed in that bed all afternoon, drinking ginger tea, reading, resting until she stopped feeling tired and sore. But

Heidi had insisted they come up to the roof, and now she was standing, leaning too far over the railing to photograph an orange-robed sadhu with an outstretched hand and a topknot of dreadlocks. It wasn't fair to suck Heidi into the black, choking cloud with her.

"Let's take a boat ride." Maya stood as Heidi swung around to face her, already packing up her camera. "Go see the Golden Temple."

They walked down the ghat toward the shore, past sadhus and chai stands and a group of white people about their age, the girls dressed in flowing skirts and the men in open-necked shirts. One was playing the sitar and the rest swayed to the music, sending blond, red, and brown dreadlocks flying into the air, releasing little puffs of dirt.

"What do you think they do here?" Maya asked.

"Teach yoga to tourists, English to locals. Have sex with their yogis." Heidi was carefully picking her way around piles of water buffalo dung. "Live off their parents' money. Standard trustafarian stuff."

"But why here?"

"The karma? The scenery?" Heidi waved her arm toward the river. It was wide and brown. Plastic bottles and bunches of marigolds floated onto its shores. "They must feel like they belong here."

Maya bit the inside of her cheek, embarrassed to feel so envious of the dirty expat kids, who had no one to please or protect but each other. A barefoot little girl in a too-big sweater padded up and thrust a palm-leaf bowl filled with marigolds and a candle toward Heidi. Maya smiled at her but shook her head no. A wiry man fell into step beside them, rapidly repeating "Botright, botright," until Maya realized he was saying "Boat ride." They settled on a price and he led them toward his boat, which was "very near, madam."

The boat was more like a raft, wooden boards fitted together so that they curved up slightly at the sides, with two planks laid across the middle where the vessel sagged a bit. The man helped them onto the planks, leading them over puddles on the floor of the boat, then nodded at a younger man who sat at its front with a pole in his hand. "Brother," he said, and walked away.

Brother knew even less English than his partner, but was delighted to converse with Maya in Hindi. The best times to take a boat ride were at sunset and sunrise, he said, and set off, occasionally pointing out temples in the distance. The buildings along the ghats were beautiful and dirty; pink stone palaces, marble watertowers, the occasional brick wall with an ornate Om sign or ad for a silk sari shop painted on it. From far away, the people running along the ghats, boys flying kites, girls holding hands, Europeans photographing each other, looked as enduring as the buildings. Pilgrims in the skiff passing theirs threw garlands of marigolds into the river; Heidi photographed the orange flowers floating toward the boat. Maya reached out to free a garland that had gotten snagged on a plank, waving her fingers slowly in the cool, sacred water.

"Take your hand out," Heidi said. "There's a dead dog on my side of the boat."

Maya jerked her hand out of the water, splashing Heidi.

"Don't look!" Heidi yelled. "We're almost past it."

"Even if I don't look, I still know the body is there."

"But you don't need to dwell on it. There are flowers and candles all around. Don't let one dead dog ruin it." Heidi's voice was getting higher, the way it always did when she grew irritated. Maya tried to feel guilty, but she couldn't suppress a twinge of satisfaction that Heidi had finally had to acknowledge something unpleasant; things don't get much more tangible than a bloated dog carcass.

"We're lucky it was just a dog," Maya said. "Some human corpses don't get to be cremated; snake bites, suicides, pregnant women. They're just wrapped up with stones and thrown in the river to cleanse their karma." At her darkest, Maya felt a kinship with those people, who were unlucky even in death. There was some comforting perspective, along with shame, in the thought that other people had suffered much more than she had lately. But behind those feelings Maya identified a quiet but strong yearning to find a way to cleanse her own karma, to rid herself of her bad luck or at least to avoid any risks that would contaminate her further. She could already see the smoke from the burning ghat up ahead, and leaned forward to ask Brother not to sail too close to it when they passed. He nodded, pushing them farther out as the fire came into view. "Don't take a picture, okay?" Maya turned away from the cremation site to the other side of the river, where families walked along a sandbar that looked as wide as a desert.

"Should I turn around?" Heidi asked. "Is it rude to look?"

"No, it's fine." Maya paused. "I'm just being stupid; Ma says it's not good for women to see cremation; only men go to funeral pyres. She always insists that seeing one could be bad for our woman parts."

"Woman parts?"

"I know! A doctor, and she still says woman parts. Anyway, I'm being neurotic, but no one knows what causes reproductive cancers. Six months ago I wouldn't have believed in a curse, either, and look what happened. I just don't want to tempt—"

"We're past it now," Heidi said. "Our woman parts are safe."

Maya turned around. On the ghat, the gilded dome of the Nepali temple rose above other rooftops, and old men walked and spat on the ground, children flew kites and water buffalos peed vigorously. Upriver, with the cremation ghat behind them, the water became less clogged with floating trash and Maya felt it was safe to trail a hand in the river again, as a show of faith in its holiness. "Remember that Thanksgiving I came home with you in college?"

"Mm-hmm." Heidi dipped her pointer finger in the wake Maya's hand made.

"And on Sunday in church the priest said a prayer for everyone leaving town in the snow?" Maya continued.

"Father Michael. He's big on the traveling prayer."

"Do you remember any of it?"

"Sure." Heidi took a deep breath, then mumbled, unsure of the first few lines. "Travel with us and gladden our hearts with your presence," she said more loudly. "Something, something, then 'During our journey surround us with your Holy Angels and keep us safe from seen and unseen dangers.'"

"So all-inclusive," Maya said, putting her second hand into the river as well.

The boatman shouted to three boys playing with a semi-deflated ball on the shore. They ran over and held the boat steady as the women stepped onto the riverbank. Maya led Heidi into an alley where whitewashed homes were plastered with signs advertising music shops and Internet cafés and they came face to snout with an albino cow whose pale bulk almost filled the narrow gully. Inching past the massive animal, Heidi yelped as it flicked its dung-covered tail at her. They cleared the cow and ran out into a narrow main street, stopping in front of a mustachioed security guard who stood tall, guarding the lockers that held the shoes of pilgrims visiting the Golden Temple, Kashi Vishwanath. Heidi kicked off her flats, revealing the pedicure she'd gotten at JFK. "Ginza Gold," she told Maya. "The closest I could get to saffron; I wanted my toes to be holy, sort of."

They handed over their shoes and wallets, and, at the guard's insistence, Heidi's camera, then proceeded to the gate for frisking, and down a path toward the temple entrance. Halfway to the gilded archway, a uniformed man cradling a machine gun stepped in front of them.

"Hindus only," he told Maya, nodding at Heidi.

"Ji, how do you know she's not one?" Maya asked quickly.

"Real Hindus." He popped a toothpick in his mouth.

"Is that what it says in the Vedas?" Maya asked. "Or does it say, 'The God Ram is one but he has many names'?"

"What's happening?" Heidi asked. Maya whispered a rushed explanation.

"American girl, isn't it?" The guard smiled at Maya, revealing a missing tooth almost hidden by the mustache curling over his lip. "I'm starting to wonder if you're really a Hindu, too." He cocked his head to the right, as if appealing to his gun for advice. Maya was silent, considering his question. To the guard it was so clear; she was an American girl. He was a racist jerk who was clearly in love with the murderous phallic symbol he caressed all day, but Maya still envied him his certainty. She wished she could see herself as concretely as he did. As an American girl, like the ones immortalized in countless rock songs, free and light, able to roadtrip across the world with only a backpack, or maybe a six-pack of Coke or beer to weigh them down. She'd like to feel like that, even if it would bar her entry into the occasional Hindu temple.

"Hei," Maya finally said, turning toward her.

"Yeah, I got it, I'm out of here. They could have warned us before I gave them my camera, before the guard felt me up."

"I'm not from here." Maya breathed deeply, back to her in-between status, moderating for the real American girl. "He is. I don't know what he deals with every day. Maybe foreigners defaced the temple once. Maybe he worries about terrorism, or a white woman was mean to his grandmother during the Raj and he has deep-seated resentment. If it were in Jodhpur, I'd know who to talk to, or if this were last year, before the curse, I might be able to convince him. Nothing I say to this guy now would be good enough." Maya inhaled a pranayama breath. "If you don't want to be left alone—"

"Nah, go see your temple." Heidi shrugged. "I'm used to it. Can't get into Mount Athos because I'm a woman, can't get in here because I'm a white oppressor. I'll be out by the lockers. Just bring me back a lucky flower or a magic sweet, or whatever." She started down the path, then turned toward the guard and said, "Thank you so much," flashing a teeth-whitened grin before she put her hands together and bowed. "Namaste."

As Maya walked into the temple, the shuffling sound of her bare feet on the marble made her feel like an old woman. She straightened her spine to make sure she wasn't hunched over, like Dadiji; she was too young to be stooped, bent under the burden of her failures. Maya stepped past the crowd doing darsan at the lingam, which was one of the Jyotirlinga, the twelve sites where Shiva appeared in a column of light. Dadiji had taught her that visiting a Jyotirlinga and bathing in the Ganges could bring moksha, spiritual liberation. Any kind of liberation sounded good. Maya felt her eyes swell, the imminence of tears, and was surprised that she could still cry because of beauty.

She sank to the stone floor, letting the light reflecting off the temple's golden dome wash around her, listening to someone chant Om Namah Shivaya, staring at the lingam and wondering how to formulate a comprehensive, foolproof request that would guarantee the curse be lifted. It was a short, but complicated wish, one that included so many aching desires: That her parents would be healthy. That she wouldn't be alone forever. That Sanjay would have a good life with Amrita. That Maya herself could be liberated, released from worrying about them all, from wanting what she didn't have. That she be protected from seen and unseen dangers.

She rocked back and forth on her knees, with each inhalation mentally repeating the phrase "The name of god is great" in Hindi and with each exhalation "Please lift the curse, please lift the curse" in English. She closed her eyes to hear the phrases in her head better, to will all her body's energy into the repetitions. She kept rocking until she wasn't aware of the feel of the marble or the sound of her breath, just the words.

Something landed on her foot, then sprang off, and when she opened her eyes an auntie was skittering away, blushing. Maya couldn't tell if the woman was embarrassed at having stepped on her, or horrified Maya had been on the floor, making such a spectacle of herself, needing so much attention from the god. The bhuasas would be mortified to see her in this holy place, rocking like an autistic patient in distress, maybe even like her own, unbalanced great-grandfather. She laughed out loud, causing several pilgrims to turn and look. To avoid their eyes, Maya glanced at her watch. She had no idea how long ago she'd left Heidi, alone in a world of dirty cows and predatory guards. The pandit sitting on a platform was tying mauli and Maya wanted to feel one around her wrist. She looked at the Well of Wisdom and wanted to stare into its depth until she could see something. But it was getting late, and crowded, and she had two more days in Benares, she could come back tomorrow. It was up to her; even the gun-fetishist guard had to acknowledge that she belonged here, she could return any time she wanted.

The street was full of people, but none of them were Heidi. She was gone, and when Maya checked the lockers, so was her camera, and both of their bags. In New York, Maya wouldn't have worried, but here Heidi knew no one, had no place to go. Maya asked the locker keeper about Heidi but he shrugged, and she turned around slowly, hoping that if she didn't panic, Heidi would reward her by stepping out from around the corner. "Friend!" yelled a man selling chai from a big copper pot across the street.

"Nahin!" Maya shouted, shaking her head no. She didn't want chai or sweets or conversation. "Nahin!"

"Nahin. *Friend.*" The man stood up behind the pot and pointed to Maya's right, waiting for her to understand.

She ran into the silk shop he'd indicated. It was empty and Maya could feel her heart beating fast in her eardrums. Then she heard laughter upstairs.

"Heidi," she yelled, and ran up to find Heidi sitting cross-legged on the floor while a middle-aged man in a sweater vest and two barefoot assistants unfolded squares of silk, whipping them out in the air until they became shawls and fluttered down in front of Heidi's knees. With each whooshing noise the room filled with a new color; saffron embroidered in gold, crimson printed with black elephants, turquoise, emerald, then virginal white on white, washing away all the other colors.

At dinner around the corner from the hotel they sat on the restaurant's terrace so they could watch the candles floating in the river. It was cold, and Maya thought about suggesting they go inside, but that seemed like giving up, giving in to the elements when she should be practicing detachment, mind over matter.

"Should we get champagne?" Heidi suggested. "It's New Year's Eve."

Maya had forgotten. The words made her think of Scott; she had started the last two years kissing him. "There's no alcohol on the ghats," she said. "Hindus don't drink."

"You drink."

"*Good* Hindus don't drink."

"Cheers anyway." Heidi raised her glass of ginger tea. "So. You must be glad to see the end of this year. What are you most excited about in the new one?"

Maya groaned. She wanted to think of something to please Heidi, who was here with her, champagne-less, shivering, trying to be positive. But nothing came to mind, and trying to invent something made her feel as if her brain were swelling, pressing against her skull. "I don't know," she said. "What are *you* most excited about?"

Heidi looked at her nails. "My new business endeavor, I guess."

Maya took a sip of tea, which felt faintly gritty. Maybe a fruit fly had drowned in her cup. No, with her luck, it would be a mosquito, a malarial one.

"Sanjay said Amrita's friend would look into the paperwork after the wedding so that it's all legally imported," Heidi continued. "And Ravi-uncle is going to make sure the women get their share of the proceeds directly."

"You're serious about all of this? The fabric imports?" Maya felt like she'd been drinking after all; her head hurt and she was having trouble following.

"It's more design than straight-up imports, you know; modern patterns, traditional fabrics," Heidi said. "But yeah. That's why Sanjay and I spent so long in the bandhej factory. We had to call Amrita once to translate with the manager when the owner was gone and you were busy in that row of sari stalls. And I took Mr. Mishra's card in the silk shop, he's already got a Web presence, and said he'll sell to me at his wholesale import price. I'll get the stuff in the magazine, put it in that shop in Nolita, we'll sell it for a huge markup, and the proceeds'll go back to the artisans. It'll start small, of course."

"I know you bought a ton of stuff," Maya said, trying to participate.

"Way to pay attention!" Heidi said, giggling at the lameness of Maya's comment. "Is it your analytic experience that enabled you to pick up on that fact or do you think even a layperson might suspect I like to shop?" Heidi laughed so hard ginger tea came out of her nostrils, stinging her nose so she grimaced. Her face twisted in the candlelight, making her look like a demon, and Maya started laughing, too, so hard her stomach hurt, her eyes ran, and a dreadlocked German turned to gawk at her, sending a cloud of pot-scented air her way. That only made Maya laugh more until she was left gasping.

"I always say depression turns patients into narcissists." Maya laughed again. "Now I am one!" She had another fit of laughter, then stopped, feeling as calm as if she had cried. "I'm sorry I didn't take the shopping, I mean the business, seriously, Hei."

"Big deal!" Heidi pulled her woolen shawl around her shoulders. "You've had a few things on your mind."

"Still, I'm going to be less self-centered," Maya vowed. "New year, new me."

"You sound like a cover line. Right above *365 Great Hair Days!*"

"I'm serious!" Maya signaled for the check. "We'll wake up, take a dawn boat ride, bathe in the Ganges." Maya refused to drag this heavy curse into the new year with her; it had to be possible to unload it, and if the Ganges was as powerful as everyone said, maybe she could wash off the curse, leave it in the holy river with all the other shit.

The next morning, it was half dark when they boarded the boat. Maya gouged her calf on a protruding nail and spent the beginning of the boat ride remembering her last tetanus shot, when she couldn't raise her arm above her shoulder afterward and Scott had to help her dress for the clinic fund-raiser. When the nail pierced her skin, she swore at the boatman leading her onto his craft, making some of the first words she spoke in the new year insults. She remembered making resolutions the night before, Heidi saying that the noblest thing anyone could do was to try to be happy. But Maya knew now there was no way she could keep that promise. The thin, curving line of blood that reappeared on her leg each time she wiped the scratch with one of Heidi's antibacterial towelettes was a sign that the curse didn't acknowledge boundaries of place or time. Scott was gone but the curse seemed to have entered the new year along with her.

The sun rose and soon pink and gold light illuminated everything, and the shadows along the river became visible, real people. The dhobis were washing clothes, a young man, ankle-deep in the water, had his hands pressed together in prayer, a girl was brushing her teeth, an old man lovingly bathed his water buffalo. They passed the cremation grounds, and on the next ghat, five middle-aged men in loincloths were doing sun salutations. One of them jumped into the river and swam with strong, sure strokes, as if he knew exactly where he was going and loved what awaited him there. Stopping midway to the sand dune, he turned to face his colleagues on the ghat, raised his arms and boomed, "Hah, hah, hah!" The yogis on the ghats laughed back. Heidi stood and switched her camera to video mode. The yogi in the water turned to her and laughed again.

"Amazing."

"Sit down; you'll fall in!" Maya tugged at her elbow until Heidi sat. "It's laughing yoga; there's a place in New York where you can do it."

"But it's so incredible *here*! Seeing him plunge into the river, then rise up laughing. It just made me think, I want to be that joyous every day."

Maya put her hand on Heidi's arm. "Hei, do you sometimes feel like *you're* the laughing yogi in the fetid river of life?"

Heidi brought her palms to her face and for a minute Maya wondered if she had gone too far. But then she heard muffled giggles, and Heidi put her hands in her lap saying, "You know what? Sometimes I do. Doesn't everyone?" She replayed her video and hummed softly as the boat floated along the smooth, caramel-colored water. The tune sounded familiar, but it wasn't until the boatboy started singing along that Maya recognized it as the song from the aarti, the fire-worship ritual they'd watched the night before while sailing back to their hotel. The boatboy had a high, pure voice, and he was so carried away by his song that he almost overshot the ghat that led to the Golden Temple. "Stop," Maya yelled, and he snapped to attention, rowing them as close to the shore as possible. On the next ghat over, washerwomen had spread saris along the steps to dry, turning the entire bank into a striped quilt. In their own bay, a woman in an orange sari waded, pouring water over her head from a copper pot that glinted in the sun.

"Should we?" Maya asked Heidi, who was paying the boatman.

"But, my camera."

"It's just us and that lady; leave it on the shore under your shawl, we'll keep an eye on it." Maya flung her shoes onto the land, pulled up the legs of her salwar pants, and stepped into the glowing water, sinking into the sand beneath her feet. It felt good to be the adventurous one, to take initiative without fearing what might happen next.

"You have an open wound." Heidi pointed at Maya's leg.

"Heidi, what else could happen to me?" Maya reached out her hand to support Heidi as she stepped out of the boat into the inch-deep water. "I have nothing to lose." As she said the words, Maya considered all that could go wrong as a result of her bathing in the river; a staph infection was the least of it in terms of disgusting possibilities. But the Ganges was her last hope for removing the curse. And Maya wasn't so far gone that the goddess-river would refuse to help her. She hoped she wasn't, anyway.

"Does this count?" Heidi asked. "Just my feet?"

"It all counts." Maya smiled for the first time that day, that year.

"I know I said I'd go in, but after the dog carcass and everything," Heidi apologized, stepping out of the water onto the shore.

"You don't have to; you can watch our stuff." Maya walked into the river, her pants now wet up to her knees. She looked around, and, seeing no one but the bather, the washerwomen, and Heidi, pulled off the salwar top she had borrowed from Priya, which had a V-neck so deep she was wearing Heidi's tank top under it. She tossed it to Heidi and waded to her waist. Marigolds washed up against her hip bones.

"See, Maya," Heidi shouted from the land. "You *are* a good Hindu."

The sun rose higher in the sky, angling itself toward her. Maya dropped to her knees and leaned back, wetting the top of her head like she'd seen born-agains on TV do in some Southern river. It was stupid, maybe even sacrilegious, to be approximating baptism in this Hindu river, but she hadn't asked Seema what counted as bathing in the Ganges, and she didn't want to immerse her whole torso into the murky water. Besides, she wanted to be baptized, washed clean of the original sin that plagued her family, whatever that had been—the turning-out of Parvati? The madness of her great-grandfather? The failure to be nothing but happy in the land of opportunity? Whatever it was, she needed to be free of it. She raised her wet head and the gritty Ganges water that ran from her hair left her feeling cleaner. On the shore, Heidi aimed her camera at Maya, taking several shots, but unable to find an angle that didn't send star-shaped shafts of light glinting off of Maya's rings, her knuckles, her knees, even her teeth. Calf-deep in the Ganges, Maya remembered stepping out of the bathtub as a child into the towel her mother held out for her, which Seema sometimes heated on the radiator in winter so that when Maya came out of the tub, she would be wrapped in warmth.

"Back up," Heidi yelled when Maya had almost reached the shore. "One more."

Stepping back, Maya smashed her toe on something hard and tripped, falling to her knees with a splash. She fell further onto her back, and, now that she was really in it, thought about how soft the water felt, how easy it would be to float away and remain forever in the Ganges, surrounded by holiness and filth. Pressurized air began to push out at her eardrums and so she sat up, laughing, spitting out the holy water. As Heidi ran toward her, Maya felt around in the sand, digging for what her foot had touched—she had felt something tangible in the water, and should be aware of what it was. She was up to date on all of the shots required to work in the

ER, tetanus, all the heps, so, clinically, it didn't matter much what she had stepped on. But she still wanted to know what the river had shoved at her. Looking at the object would help her interpret the sign, accept the message that the goddess-river was giving her. Maya's foot felt something that was firm, but not sharp like metal; as she reached into the river to uproot it, keeping her face above the waterline, bits crumbled off into her hands. She pulled and found herself raising a clay figure up through the water; the statuette just filled the space made by her cupped hands. It was a woman sitting on a throne, wearing a crown and raising one palm in salute. Heidi's gilded toes came into view on the shore.

"A goddess," Maya told her, cradling the statuette with both hands as she rose to her feet. "I was worried I'd tripped on something disgusting, but it's clearly a goddess." She remembered Nan-aji mentioning some annual festival when Bengalis came and threw clay gods into the Ganges; this must be one of those. But which one? Maya wished Seema were here to confirm her suspicion, to make sure she truly understood what the river was telling her. Because if she was right, then maybe she had found a way to absolve herself, to protect her family; by falling into the filthy, holy river, Maya might have, in fact, washed the curse clean away. It seemed impossible, but Maya was pretty sure that Lakshmi, the goddess of abundance, had washed up at her feet.

Chapter Fifteen

In the moist Bombay airport, Heidi kicked the metal pleats that
held up the sluggish conveyor belt, which was now bereft of luggage,
circling empty, the same seams in the plastic passing by again and
again. "First the flight's delayed," she started.

"But only an hour," Maya interrupted. "That's early for India."

"And now this. All the Benarsi silks I bought were in that bag."

"It'll turn up eventually." Maya was determined to bring the
joy of Benares into the new year. She felt good. And a little guilty
to be so glad Dr. Bernard wasn't here to nod and clear his throat and
ask, good in what way, and since when, and did this good feeling
differ from other good feelings she'd had in the past? For now, Maya
didn't want to look back or forward, just to face what was in front of
her. She walked toward the information desk, where a woman with
too-light powder flaking off her face was studiously ignoring a French
couple yelling increasingly loud, nasal phrases. In Jodhpur, she
might have had Heidi talk to the flight attendant, see if the vestiges

of colonialism still carried any weight with SpiceJet, but being fair and lovely didn't seem to be helping the French couple, and Heidi was in no mood; she was caressing the one Benarsi shawl she had wrapped around her neck and humming a mournful little keening sound. She looked at Maya. "What are the chances that when you bathed in the Ganges, the curse washed off and tainted water splashed me?"

"I lost a suitcase, too, didn't I?" Maya stepped in front of the French pair, who were now fighting with each other, and confronted the SpiceJet lady, wobbling her head back and forth, flicking her shawl over her shoulder, and cutting off the woman's sentences without raising her voice, employing all the tics she'd picked up in a lifetime as Seema's daughter. Every few minutes Heidi would lean in and demand, "What?," and Maya would turn to her, make a "tsst!" noise with her tongue while brandishing her pointer finger, then turn back to the attendant, who was even more cowed with each hiss at Heidi. Only when the woman handed Maya a pile of bills, then put a second set in her other hand, did Maya nod, say namaste, and hustle Heidi toward the door.

"The plane was too heavy, so they took off four bags," she reported when the drone of the French husband finally died out.

"Without telling us?"

"Or that couple, obviously." Maya moved briskly, her rolling carry-on making a comforting clicking noise on the dirty rubber floor. "They'll come tomorrow, but I explained we're here for a wedding, the mehndi is tonight, and our party clothes were in the bags." She stopped on the curb. "So they gave us a shopping allowance." Maya pulled a wad of cash from her pocket and shoved it at Heidi. "Four thousand rupees. Each."

"Eighty bucks?" Heidi grinned for the first time since landing. "Hello, Lakshmi!"

"Even in Bombay this'll buy a bunch of fabric; the goddess must be investing in your start-up." Maya redirected her suitcase toward the prepaid taxi kiosk.

Amrita had warned them her parents' driver would be busy ferrying aunties back and forth to the Intercon to prepare for the evening festivities, so the girls were responsible for getting themselves to the flats her family had rented for Sanjay's relatives. They were only blocks away from the apartment Amrita's parents lived in half the year, which was conveniently located across from the Turf Club, the maidan where the wedding would take place. Her father probably bought the place for Turf Club proximity alone; Mr. and Mrs. Gupta had been planning Amrita's wedding since she was born. At least the white horse wouldn't have far to travel; after a few blocks in the Bombay smog he'd probably turn gray, which couldn't be a good omen, and, given what Maya knew about the bride's questionable commitment to the groom, she wanted Sanjay to have all the luck he could get.

"Seema-auntie!" Heidi rushed into the flat and hugged Seema as if she hadn't seen her for a year. "Some of our bags were lost, but not really, and SpiceJet gave us money for clothes, even though we totally have things to wear tonight, because a statue of Lakshmi washed up at Maya's feet in Benares."

"Well!" Seema took a step backward, toward the kitchen. "It sounds as if you two had quite the time in the holy city. Although Lakshmi, praise the gods, may have one or two concerns besides lost luggage."

"Sanjay!"

Maya's cousin loped out of the hallway in a blue button-down frayed at the wrists, madras shorts, and flip-flops. She had always envied his obscenely long eyelashes, teased him that they made him look like a girl. But right now Sanjay looked like a prep school kid on a Saturday, and she wanted to tell him that he had no business getting married, especially to such a complicated, grown-up lady, that he was grounded for his own good and he'd thank her later.

Heidi threw her arms around his neck as Maya stepped into the kitchen to give Seema a quick hug. "We got money from Spice-Jet," she heard Heidi tell Sanjay. "Do you have to do groom stuff or can you chaperone-shop?"

"I'm so there. FabIndia. Neemrana. You'll probably want to do Colaba Causeway. Amrita showed me Bombay by credit card last year." Sanjay hugged Maya, lifting her off the ground. "Besides, I've got nothing till dinner with the guys." He looked over his shoulder at Heidi as he deposited Maya back on the floor. "No men at mehndi."

"I knew that! I'll hit the bathroom and I'm ready." Heidi walked down the hall.

"I'm going to change, too, I'm all plane dirty." Maya started toward the bedroom but Seema grabbed her arm, squeezing at the elbow.

"No, beti," she said. "You are to attend the dance preparations for the sangeet."

"Oh right, Amrita said to tell you, there's rehearsal at her parents' place," Sanjay said. "But you're a good dancer, I'm sure her friends can teach you tomorrow morning."

"Absolutely not!" Seema tightened her grip. "We are here to represent Sanjay's family, not to shame him. Amrita is your sister-cousin now, you will dance for her at the sangeet, make us proud. You can go to prepare now; Sanjay will show Heidi the shops."

"But Ma!" Maya folded in on herself, crumpling into Seema, who half hugged her, half pushed her away. Heidi appeared in the hallway, smelling of sandalwood soap.

"Don't worry, Amrita's friends are fun. Sort of." Sanjay turned toward Maya, grabbing Heidi's hand and pulling her out the door.

Maya breathed deeply to keep from overreacting; her neck flushed at the thought of wasting a precious day in Bombay celebrating a woman she wasn't sure she could trust. She felt the weight of Seema's hand on her shoulder. "I know, beti," she said, her voice so heavy Maya wondered who told her about Amrita's Darren. Or did Seema's all-knowing perception extend beyond her own children to her nephew's future spouse?

"Someday, it will be your turn to be entertained at your sangeet, this I promise you," Seema continued. "When I return to Kalamazoo, I will do a special puja, eating no grains on Thursdays, so that the gods will send you the right man."

Maya knew the ritual would give her mother comfort; that's why people create them. But she hated the thought of Seema depriving herself because her daughter had wasted years in a relationship she couldn't sustain. After all that time with Scott, fearing Seema's reaction and considering her the small-minded enemy, Maya felt nauseated to think her mother wanted the same thing she did all along, and apparently just as badly—someone who would fit into Maya's life and make it better, who would expand her world instead of dividing it. "C'mon, Ma," she said. "You don't need to do that."

"The gods will listen; the right Brahmin will come." Seema patted her shoulder and walked to the sink. "Do not 'C'mon' your mother. You c'mon. You will be late." She turned on the tap; the rush of water muffled the sound of the door shutting behind Maya.

A woman in too much eye shadow and too little clothing was barking orders at Amrita and four girls Maya had never seen. "You're late," she said, when Maya walked through the door to the Guptas' living room.

"Just one minute, please," Amrita said, moving toward Maya. "I think we all need a tiny break."

Amrita hugged Maya and whispered, "She's kind of a witch but she's a real Bollywood choreographer so…" Amrita released Maya and shrugged. "I just want everything to be perfect. The weather, the dancing, everyone's toasts. A wedding is kind of a nightmare for a control freak." She laughed.

Maya laughed, too, looking at Amrita. She appeared to have lost five pounds—which she didn't need to—since the last time Maya had seen her. Was she suffering, having doubts? Regretting her decision? "My mom would say, 'You can only control your own behavior, that is all,'" Maya said, slipping into her imitation of Seema.

Amrita laughed again; this counted as giddy for her. She was too skinny, but glowing brighter than Maya had ever seen her, her eyes clear, her smile wide.

"Oh, I have," Amrita said. "I mean, maybe not how Seema-auntie means. But I've been eating right, exercising."

Maya suppressed a laugh. Had Amrita ever had a conversation longer than two sentences with Seema? These concerns would have been at the bottom of Seema's list—no, they wouldn't even have been on there.

"I haven't been doing puja, that's probably what she'd want," Amrita continued. "But I've been tying up loose ends, preparing mentally, and I guess spiritually." She leaned closer to Maya. "I just want—"

"Break over!" the choreographer yelled and by the time she'd finished the phrase Maya had lost Amrita to a gaggle of twirling girls.

Maya looked around the room at the ladies gathered for the mehndi, thinking she might be inspired by the latest Bombay fashions and develop an idea to contribute to Heidi's new venture. But she kept getting distracted by the throbbing in her thighs. Her legs hurt, whether from the four hours of grueling dance rehearsal that afternoon or the kneeling position she'd been holding for twenty minutes now, with her arms stretched out in front of her as if she were having blood drawn. She shifted a little, stretching her calves out to the side, and the girl applying mehndi to her left wrist glanced up at her with glossy eyes.

"Please do not smudge," the girl said, then lowered her head as Maya tensed her right hand, already covered in flowers and swirls, waving it a little in the air to help the patterns set. The mehndi painter's Hindi had an accent; she must have come from some village, with her parents probably. She looked young, younger than Maya by ten years maybe, but she wore the bindi of a married woman. Maybe her husband moved her to the city. What was he doing while his wife worked this party, spending the evening on her knees, adorning other women's limbs? Maya opened her mouth to ask where she was from—in New York, she'd had dozens of conversations with her Korean pedicurist, and the one time Heidi dragged Maya to her bikini waxer, before they went to Scott's beach house last summer, she could not stop chattering to Monika. The Polish woman probably didn't even understand, but Maya kept up a running commentary to drown out Seema's voice in her head asking why a daughter of hers would pay for such torture, and what kind of humiliating bathing suit required that she degrade herself so completely to wear it? But now, even though she was clothed, something about this girl gently squeezing henna out of a tube onto her arm made Maya shy, and the words were slow to come.

"Thirsty?" the girl asked, then shouted to a waiter who stooped with his tray of soft drinks and champagne. Maya wasn't thirsty, but she reached for a ginger ale, which the mehndi painter snatched off the tray herself, then put up to Maya's lips so she wouldn't smudge her right hand. Normally, there wouldn't be any kind of alcohol, sparkling or not, at a mehndi, but then, normally, the party happened in the afternoon, at the bride's home, with aunties fluttering around, roughly shoving bangles up the arms of the unmarried girls. At Priya's mehndi, Maya had spent most of the afternoon stuck on a footstool while an unsteady auntie marked her with patterns that were more ticklish than artistic, with too much glop squeezed out of the tube here, not enough there. She had been eye level with Priya's graduation photo, and was able to study the details that added up to her sister's beauty, the white teeth, neither too big nor too small, the gently curved nostrils, the slightly almond eyes that made her sister look like a Bollywood movie star, at least when she wasn't in scrubs or some suburban mom terry-cloth sweat suit. Looking at the photo Maya had felt feverish, jittery and hot, and she told herself that it was joy at her sister's upcoming wedding that was making her flush, not jealousy. She hadn't even started her residency then, or therapy, so it was easier to convince herself of such things; she had been born with a talent for building defense mechanisms. But she knew now that it had been envy that warmed her, and wondered if that envy was a powerful enough force to attract sorrow to Priya years later, to drill holes into her shiny veneer. She wished Priya were here now, whispering in her ear about how low-cut Amrita's mother's sari blouse was, how Amrita's Bombay auntie who had married the diamond merchant sounded like a chicken when she spoke English.

"Maya, help me out here." Heidi, sitting next to her on the blanket-covered platform where a half-dozen women were having their hands painted, stuck a leg out to the right, kicking Maya gently in the shin. "She's asking me something."

Heidi's mehndi was being applied by a rotund woman with a braid that merged from orange, where she hennaed the roots of her hair, to black at the end, the hair that had been with her since she was a little girl, a tail so narrow and fine that she could have used it as a paintbrush to decorate Heidi with designs, if she worked with an artist's palette instead of a tube full of mehndi. The woman was pulling Heidi's upturned left palm back and forth, consulting with her fellow artists.

"Speak Hindi, girl?" she barked at Maya.

"What else?"

"I have applied mehndi to four other white women, friends of brides who live in America or U.K. Never have I seen such a fine, blue line." She pointed at Heidi's wrist.

"It's the visible veins," Maya told Heidi. "On your wrist. They fascinate her."

"Really? Tell her she should see my left breast. No, don't."

"I want to use the vein in my design, as the branch of the bougainvillea," the woman explained to Maya. She had already drawn a few blossoms growing off the vein at the base of Heidi's wrist. "But she's not the bride; I can't go too far up."

Maya nodded, considering. "Draw whatever you like, auntie," she said finally. "I'll tell everyone it's the first time Heidi got mehndi, and she insisted you keep going."

The older woman grinned, nodded, then slapped Heidi on the wrist, saying, "Beautiful," in English six times in rapid succession.

"This is so gorgeous; it's a sin that it fades," Heidi said to Maya. "Everyone in this country is an artist, absolutely everyone. Today I saw a woman sweeping the street who paired the most amazing peacock-colored shawl with a bright purple salwar suit."

Heidi went on describing her afternoon with Sanjay, the block-printed tablecloths she'd bought, the embroidered saris, all whose provenance she knew, all the work of artisans she planned to make rich and famous, or less poor and less obscure, when she returned to New York. Maya felt electricity running through her veins and wondered if the bacteria she'd undoubtedly swallowed in the Ganges were starting to fight back. If so, what horrible timing; with the sangeet tomorrow and the wedding the next day, she couldn't spend the weekend running to the bathroom, lying on the couch drinking nimbu paani and eating Saltines her mother smuggled in from Kalamazoo. But although Maya's pulse was jumping, her stomach felt fine. More likely it was envy again. Of Amrita, who was the focus of all this attention, who was loved by enough people to fill this room, drinking champagne and making flourishing hand gestures to show off their suddenly interesting wrists? She didn't think so. Amrita was too wound up to be envied. At least it seemed that way. Mrs. Gupta had shown up to oversee the end of dance practice, so Maya hadn't gotten a chance to finish her conversation with Amrita, to ask how exactly she had readied herself to marry Sanjay, and assess what those preparations cost her. Amrita had been perfectly nice all day, but Maya was still a little suspicious of her; her swirl-covered fingertips were still the ones that had dialed her friend to make sure she'd see Darren, her patterned hand had waved away Sanjay's words when he confronted her.

No, it wasn't Amrita. Maya realized it was Heidi she envied, who got to spend the afternoon shopping instead of practicing an elaborately choreographed lie, who got to see India as a subcontinent full of artists and opportunity, a country she could make better, not a place she had already failed by being herself, unmarried and unlucky. Perhaps Lakshmi had been floating toward Heidi when Maya found her, Heidi who had a business plan and a blue vein, who seemed to think happiness was a possible, even normal, state. Maya felt lighter and calmer than she had in months, but despite having washed off the curse in the Ganges, she still felt dark around the edges, as if a shadow of it remained.

The young girl finished the mandala she had been creating on the part of Maya's hand where her thumb ended and her palm swelled like a turkey drumstick. She moved on up the arm and as the henna paste tickled Maya's wrist her body remembered, before her mind could quite figure it out, the feeling of Scott's hair, wet from the shower, rubbing against her arm as he crawled back into bed. Maya shivered and the girl looked up at her with curious dark eyes.

"Out! Shame on you, cheeky boys," Amrita's mother shrieked from the door across the room, which was suddenly silent; even Heidi had ceased chattering. "This is so improper, really, this must—" Her shouts were drowned out by a rumble of male voices.

"Get ready," Heidi whispered to Maya. "Sounds like the crazies might have followed you from New York."

"And here I am without my Haldol and ancillary staff," Maya murmured.

A guy's voice rose above the rest of the chatter. "Please, auntie, Sanjay isn't with us, we've already dropped him at the flat."

"Raki!" Amrita suddenly appeared at the door, sideswiping her mother and throwing her arms around the man's neck. In her celadon sari she seemed to levitate toward him, floating a few inches above the ground. Maya had to admit that Amrita would be a beautiful bride. "They can come in, Mummy, can't they? It's just Raki and some of the cousins, and their schoolmates, right, Raki?"

"Just family, yaar," the man said, as if he were talking to a buddy, not his aunt. Mrs. Gupta probably liked being called "pal," but Amrita should warn this guy not to try that on Seema. Maya scanned the room to find her mother, but she was busy talking to Mr. Gupta's sister on the other side of the hall.

Amrita folded her arm through the ringleader's and soon he and a dozen other guys were all over the room, having infiltrated it by diffusion; there was a back in an embroidered kurta by the buffet, here were two jean-covered butts raised in the air as their owners leaned over to examine the mandap where the sangeet performances would take place tomorrow night. And now there were two feet in front of Maya, black leather shoes untroubled by buckles, looking as if they'd just been shined. Next to them a toffee-colored toe twitched in rhinestone-studded sandals, disrupting the beige calm of a nude pedicure. On the third toe of the woman's left foot a silver ring shimmered; Maya hadn't taken Amrita for a toe ring wearer.

"This is Maya, Sanjay's cousin, and her friend Heidi," Amrita said, as Maya nodded and Heidi raised both of her drying hands in greeting, looking like she was the victim of a holdup. "Rakesh lives in New York, too, he works at Goldman."

"First time in India, Heidi?" Rakesh asked, and his voice

surprised Maya; it seemed unusually high for such a solidly built man. "Amazing, yaar?"

"Unbelievable." Heidi flashed a smile, then glanced at her mehndi painter, who had finished but still lingered, enjoying the show, and raised an eyebrow back at Heidi, making Maya wonder what kind of private jokes those two could have concocted in the past half hour without a language between them besides the word "beautiful."

"C'mon, Raki, I see that thousand-year-old waiter, and this is probably his last run." Amrita tugged at her cousin's arm. "We'll get you the champagne you came for."

"I came for you!" Raki insisted over Amrita's clinking laughter. "See you at the sangeet, Heidi." Raki turned to Maya. "I'll get your mobile from Amrita, so we can make plans in the morning; tomorrow we fall in love, yaar?" Raki laughed, and the glow from his shoes seemed to spread all the way to the tip of his head, causing his shiny black hair to glint blue in places. As he followed Amrita away, Maya raised her hands toward her face, but the mehndi mistress grabbed her elbows, arresting her arms midair.

"I guess he's playing Sanjay in the sangeet skit," Maya explained to Heidi, who must have been staring, along with her new best friend, the mehndi-auntie, although Maya couldn't bring herself to raise her eyes to meet theirs. She had forgotten she'd have a partner in reenacting the moment Amrita met Sanjay.

"He seemed nice to me," Heidi said. "Friendly."

"Sure," Maya said. Maya imagined Heidi was shrugging, but she still had her eyes trained on Heidi's gilded toes, and wouldn't lift them to see her face. She waited for Heidi to make a joke, to congratulate her on regaining her power of speech, since Maya had gone mute so suddenly and dramatically in the presence of that slick-haired stranger, just like junior year when she couldn't speak in front of the gorgeous biochem teaching fellow. But she said nothing, and when Maya finally looked up, Heidi was blowing on her forearms while the mehndi-auntie tried not to laugh. Maya slowly rose to her feet, keeping her arms out at her sides like a model indicating cars in an auto showroom.

The next morning Maya was sitting on the veranda of the flat, drinking chai with her mother, still wearing one of Seema's housecoats, when Heidi bounded through the glass doors, fully dressed. She threw her head back and stretched out her arms. "It's amazing to feel the sun on your skin in January."

"Sit and have some chai," Seema instructed.

"Thank you, Seema-auntie, but I'm late." Heidi fished through her bag.

"For what?" Maya and Seema demanded at the same time. Seema's head was already tilted to the right, threatening to start wobbling back and forth. Whatever Heidi's answer would be, Maya could tell Seema wasn't going to like it.

"I'm meeting those Canadian friends of Amrita's from last night at the Gateway to India; they arranged for a guide, some walking tour of the city. Amrita's driver is probably already downstairs to pick me up."

"I'll show you the city." Maya held the mug close under her chin.

"You are going to spill," Seema scolded. "And this is not Jodhpur. You have spent how long in Bombay in your life, Miss I Know Everything about Everything? One week? Ten days? A fortnight? Who will show the city better, you or a professional?"

"Besides." Heidi finally pulled her sunglasses out of her bag, triumphant. "You've got to do sangeet stuff today, dance rehearsal, meet with Amrita's cousin."

Seema slurped her chai, staring at the terrace tiles as if examining them for cracks.

"I'll be back around five to get ready." Heidi swooped in to kiss Maya, then walked toward the door, pausing behind Seema's chair.

"Have a lovely day," Seema said, grabbing Heidi's vine-covered wrist. She reached into the pocket of her long, shapeless cardigan and pulled out a hundred rupees, then pressed them into Heidi's hand, saying, "Get yourself a nimbu paani."

"But I changed money yesterday."

"Do not be silly, it will be quite hot today." Seema stood and started to tidy the tea things, taking Maya's cup from her hand before she was done with it. Maya opened her mouth, then shut it again. "Go on, Heidi, do not insult Amrita's family by having the driver wait," Seema scolded, but the force of her voice was diminished by the smile fighting for life at the corners of her mouth. When the sound of Heidi's heels clacking through the apartment faded, Maya stood. "I guess I'll shower."

"Do not leave your cellular on the table." Seema nodded at the Indian cell on the table, a hand-me-down from Sanjay. "I cannot spend all day playing at being your secretary."

In the shower, Maya slid the sandalwood soap over her body, breathing in the scent. In New York she smelled of Suave shampoo, a jasmine shower gel Heidi gave her from the magazine's beauty closet, and a water lily attar she had bought last year in Jodhpur that she found sexy, mysterious, but which a bipolar patient told her made her smell like a livery cab driver. Today's clean, musky-smelling body was a lie, it was Maya in India, Maya after the goddess of abundance washed up at her feet. The Maya who had been cursed, who'd spent the last three months crying, wasn't visible anywhere, except, maybe, in the hollow of her newly flat stomach, and that was the one blessing that had come out of this; she now looked like she did Pilates every day. Gazing at herself in the bathroom mirror, Maya snorted a laugh. Her body was as slim as it had been in college, her skin the same as ever, halfway between the goddesses Kali and Parvati in color. It felt wrong that the curse had left no scar or bruise, no visible mark. Both the cut from the protruding nail in the Ganges skiff and the scratch on her big toe where she'd stumbled onto Lakshmi had healed. It didn't seem right that when she looked in the mirror, Maya should like what she saw. And that she wished Scott could see her, too, and smell her strong, soapy scent. It was unfair that Raki, a stranger, should see her at her best.

She squeezed the water out of her hair and the thought of Raki out of her mind. They would meet, in the living room, probably, or maybe on the veranda if Seema didn't keep bustling in and out of the kitchen, to discuss their skit and figure out how to transform the real story that Maya knew—Sanjay and Amrita, probably both drunk, hooked up at a bar night in business school. But the sangeet was a family affair, so liberties would have to be taken. This was nothing to be nervous about; she and Raki had a joint project, and the entire meeting, including a rehearsal of the five-minute skit, would take, maybe, forty-five minutes.

But she only said a total of four words when Raki called, interrupting her blow-drying. "Hello," then "Yes," she would meet him downstairs in a half hour, "No," she wasn't afraid of motorbikes, yaar, and "Great" after he told her he'd see her soon.

Twenty minutes later, with blow-dried hair and balm-covered lips—she wouldn't let herself apply any other makeup, this was not a date—she sped through the flat and called, "Bye, Ma," hoping to be out the door before Seema made her way from the sink, noticed her smooth hair and shiny mouth and asked where she was going and what did she know about this boy and how well did he know the city and when would she be back, then said that she should behave and give him the respect he deserved as a member of Amrita's family, however distant. But Seema shot out of the kitchen, saying, "Wait a moment, why are you flying off so?" She reached into her cardigan, pulled out a bill, and stuffed it into the pocket of Maya's jean jacket. "I do not want you to feel left out. You should get nimbu paani, too, when you are done with the sangeet business."

"Thanks, Ma," Maya mumbled.

"And one more thing."

"Ma, I'm going to be late; it's rude."

"Let him wait a minute so you can speak to your old mother who will not be here always." Seema took the end of her braid and swung it over her shoulder behind her back, then reached toward Maya as if she were going to touch her face, her shoulder, her arm, but her fingers couldn't decide which body part to land on. "You are a smart girl, and you have a big personality," Seema said, finally tucking her floating hand into her own cardigan pocket. "Just, maybe, you can show that personality bit by bit, not all at once."

Maya heard Dr. Bernard's voice in her head saying, "Don't react, just take it in."

"I should go now, Ma," she said finally.

"Yes, well." Seema turned and padded toward the kitchen so that Maya could barely hear her saying, "Have a nice time."

Repeatedly, over the course of the last decade or so, Maya had promised Seema that she'd never ride on the back of a motorcycle. "At the hospital," she'd say to her second cousins in Jodhpur, drawing out the word "hospital," mocking Seema's accent, "the nurses call them donor-cycles!" Then her cousins would laugh so hard their mopeds would shake beneath them, and Maya would jump on the back after making sure no one they recognized was strolling down the dusty alley. But that was in Jodhpur, where the streets were clogged with cows and auto rickshaws and little boys with the maroon knit ties of their school uniforms flying as they raced each other home.

Here in Bombay, on the back of Raki's bike, Maya zoomed

down the coastal road excessively fast, bugs hitting her cheek and dust flying into her eyes as she watched BMWs and Mercedes dodge crazy taxis, enterprising beggars, and reckless magazine vendors peddling copies of *Hi! Blitz* to bored socialites who rolled down their window to exchange cash for trash and flip through the pages, noting which of their friends had made the issue—there was Queenie with her daughter Princess right on the cover!

"Best city in the world, isn't it?" Raki shouted at a stoplight. "Gorgeous weather, friendly people. Unparalleled street food." Then the light flipped to green and he sped off again, as Maya became convinced that this ride would end with her a pulpy mess on the side of the road; maybe the Ganges had been a false promise and the curse was coming to claim her now. She tried to turn her terror into calm, closing her eyes and pretending she was back in Jodhpur, puttering to the fortress behind one of her second cousins. But then she'd force them open again, despite the dust and the flies, the stray pieces of Raki's hair that poked at her face, not wanting to miss the crowds strolling the beach, the Muslim pilgrims in the distance walking to Haji Ali mosque, the fashionistas getting in and out of cabs in the latest salwar suits, with narrow pants and a preponderance of Lucknow embroidery that she hadn't seen anyone wearing last year.

The air smelled like salt and whatever gel Raki put in his hair; she couldn't fault him for that, not in India, everyone wore gel here, and maybe he didn't back in New York. Same with the Egoïste Pour Homme; one of Heidi's boyfriends used the cologne all through college, and Maya could never get the stink out of their common room. It smelled different on Raki, though, and his chest felt hard and reassuring under her arms, so she refused to read too much into the name. Instead she inhaled the scent and held on to Raki and to the slow-growing realization that she was having fun, and how relaxing it was to be taken on a journey, however short, instead of leading someone, or everyone, else. It was worth risking her life to feel this protected.

"This is the best bhelpuri in Bombay," Raki announced, pulling up to a street vendor, who scooped the snack onto two plates made from leaves. Maya fumbled for the money Seema had shoved into her pocket, but Raki waved his hand at her, saying, "C'mon, yaar! You can buy me a pretzel back in New York." The bill grew moist and soft in her hand; it was a five-hundred-rupee note, Seema's way of letting Maya know that even though she gave Heidi pocket money, too, she had her priorities in order.

"Why're you smiling?" Raki asked, but Maya didn't know if she was still grinning about the bill or his Bombay boarding school accent.

"No reason. It's too bad Heidi's not here to try this."

"We'll get her some on the way back, when we pick up the bike," Raki said. "Friend here is going to keep a watch on it while we work." He led her to the beach, where they sat on a bench and rewrote the story of Amrita and Sanjay's beginning. In between, Maya was grateful for the bhelpuri and the way its crunch filled her silences.

At the sangeet, once she and the girls had finished their over-rehearsed raas, Maya stood watching the men perform a bhangra, still breathing hard from the exertion of dancing. Raki managed to look graceful and strong at the same time; he was the best dancer of all of them, and would probably have said so himself. All day he'd been spouting hyberbole, praising the most spectacular weather he could remember in Bombay, the coolest book he'd just read, the funniest idea she had about their skit. When a patient spoke like that, Maya saw it as a sign of insecurity, an overcompensation. But on the beach, Raki just seemed sure of himself, appealing.

Maya grabbed a Limca off a waiter's tray, hoping the soda

would cool her down, steady her breath and still her heartbeat, which was so strong in her chest it was almost painful. Maybe if Scott had been more like Raki, more emphatic, if he'd insisted on being recognized by her family, if he'd shown up at the airport with a ticket to India and won everyone over, they'd still be together. If Scott had known what he wanted, been strong enough to make it happen, she wouldn't be without him at Sanjay's sangeet, expending a fair amount of mental energy thinking about a stranger who wore an awful lot of cologne. Instead, Scott had just given up. Raki would never do that. Of course, he wouldn't have to; if she called the U.S. to say she was dating an Indian guy, Pops would get out of his sickbed and jump up and down on it until Priya made him stop. And Priya would bake a seven-layer cake, or whatever it was she did to express boundless joy.

The Punjabi music stopped, and Maya felt Raki looking at her. Sanjay and Amrita's friends had already danced and lip-synched, and so had their more distant relatives. It was time for Maya and Raki to perform their skit. She stepped onto the mandap to join him as the other boys disappeared. One of them advanced the CD and a Bollywood lament began playing. Amrita's other boy-cousins began stepping onto the stage, glasses in hand, stumbling and eye rolling, clutching their stomachs as if about to vomit. "There were many well-educated men at the business school happy hour," one of Sanjay's friends read from the script they'd written on the beach as this guy and that mock-pawed at Maya. "But none of them was quite suitable for Amrita."

One of the men lunged at Maya while the narrator read a mock-biodata of the type found on suitablematch.com. "Ravinder is twenty-nine, an economist by training, and an alcoholic by avocation." "Ravinder" passed out at Maya's feet and she gingerly stepped over him. Startled laughter bubbled up all around her.

"Shankar is a thirty-two-year-old venture capitalist who

spends his free time eating meat and drinking beer," the narrator intoned. "Shankar" gave a raucous burp and Maya did her best imitation of Amrita's mother in disgust, scolding, "Chee-chee-chee!"

"Ajay is thirty-five, a diplomat's son, and eager to support a wife who promises never to work, nor travel, nor speak if not spoken to." "Ajay" stepped forward and twirled the lush fake mustache he was wearing.

"Then one night, a networking event Amrita decided to attend at the last minute ended, and the lights went up." The narrator paused. "That's when Amrita first saw Sanjay." Raki stepped toward Maya, extended his hand, and said, "Can I buy you a Coke?" Suddenly a joyous love theme started playing and Raki and Maya began dancing, hiding behind the other men who joined them onstage, peering out around the bodies that surrounded them like trees in a wooded grove to catch glimpses of each other, flashing their eyes from side to side, and generally acting like young Bollywood in love. At every move they made, laughter filled the room, bouncing down off the ceiling and up from the floor. Maya could make out Sanjay's deep rumble, Heidi's ringing blasts, and then, as she turned and turned toward the sound of a high, clear giggle, she noticed Seema, her face contorted by the effort of laughing, her eyes closed behind her thick glasses.

The morning of the wedding Maya watched as Heidi stood like a mannequin, her arms out, while Seema folded six yards of blue and green sari fabric into pleats, tucking them into Heidi's petticoat.

"These colors flatter you," Seema said. "The colors of water." Her fingers moved rapidly back and forth, like the paddle extension on the standing mixer she rarely used but kept in a place of honor on the counter in Kalamazoo; the fabric doubled onto itself like whipping cream. Seema secured the material at Heidi's waist with a safety pin, then did the same at her shoulder, giving it a brisk pat before walking over to check Maya's attempts at wrapping her own sari.

"And the colors of fire suit you," she said, pulling out Maya's tentative pleats and starting her fingers dancing through the fabric.

"Make it tight so I can dance during the baraat."

"Are you sure I can be part of the groom's parade?" Heidi asked. "I'm not Sanjay's relative."

"You practically are; you know he would want you to be included."

Seema pulled a safety pin from her mouth. "Neither of you will take part in the baraat, Maya; Amrita asked that you come to her house, since she has no sisters or girl cousins. Of course Heidi will go, too."

"Ma! You can't agree to something like that for me." Maya jerked away from her mother, sending the pallu of her sari cascading off her shoulder onto the floor.

"Stand still, Maya!" Seema shouted as she bent to pick up the fabric. Folding it again, she spoke more softly. "You would have agreed to it, too. It is an honor that she wants you to walk her to her wedding. She has no one her age."

"But Amrita's not my cousin yet, Sanjay is! I've waited my whole life to see Sanjay on a white horse. I'm sure her friends from dance practice will go with her."

"Friends! What are friends?" Seema jabbed the safety pin through the layers of fabric, pricking Maya's shoulder. "Friends are flighty, come and go. Amrita wants to walk to her wedding with someone who will be in her life forever. She is your cousin now, too, Maya. Stop acting like a child." Seema turned away from Maya toward the mirror, examining her own ensemble, smoothing the part in her hair. "You will see Sanjay on his horse when he arrives at the Turf Club."

Maya was still figuring out how she felt about Amrita. But she knew how she felt about Sanjay, and she was willing to do whatever was necessary to be at his baraat, to support and celebrate him as he rode in as a groom. She glared at her mother's reflection. "If you knew what I know about Amrita—"

"I would have the good sense to keep it to myself," Seema said, and left the room.

In Amrita's parents' apartment, the bride sat in state on an over-stuffed couch, looking as if she feared she might break. That was how her parents had raised Amrita, as their fragile, precious trea-sure. And now they had dressed her up like an expensive doll from a collection showcasing international costumes, one of the "Brides of the World" series Priya would tear out of magazines when she was a child, even though Seema always said they were too expen-sive and china dolls didn't belong in homes with boisterous chil-dren. The rest of the family was paying homage to the porcelain princess; overstuffed aunties sat at Amrita's side and feet, singing mournful songs and draping her in gold. *"Raja ki aayegi baraat, ran-geeli hogi raat, magan mein nachungi,"* one corpulent woman keened, kneeling with surprising dexterity to shove three gold bangles onto Amrita's wrist. The words were happy: "Raja's baraat will come, it will be a colorful night, I will dance in the courtyard," but the aun-tie's tone was that of a lament.

On the wall, next to a painting of the Taj Mahal, hung a two-foot-by-three-foot Sears photograph of Amrita standing behind her seated parents, Amrita at about thirteen, grinning smugly as if she were wearing her first public eye shadow. Her mother was primly staring straight ahead, but her father was smiling as if in perfect happiness, his hand on top of Amrita's, which rested on his shoulder. Today, balder, thinner, but recognizably the man in the photo, her father was smiling the same way, with tears already stain-ing his cheeks.

"Maya, come sit closer," Amrita called. Maya leaned over to Heidi, who was snapping photos of the weeping, singing aunties, and close-ups of Amrita's mehndi-covered, bangle-adorned forearm, and whispered, "Spotlight effect."

"She's not your patient," Heidi muttered back.

Maya sank into the space Amrita had cleared for her on the couch, pressed thigh to thigh with an auntie who was angry at being displaced. For a moment, Maya felt she was back in New York and that the subway must be passing underneath them. Then she realized it was just Amrita, bouncing her knee next to her on the couch, rippling the surface of her smooth sari; she managed to hold still only for the few seconds it took Heidi to photograph them, then started bouncing again immediately.

Maya put her hand on Amrita's knee to steady it. "Are you okay?"

Amrita laughed. "I'm just eager to get this damn show on the road!"

Maya must have looked as startled as she felt at hearing Amrita swear for the first time; Amrita was giggling at her expression.

"Look, it's a really momentous change," Amrita said. "And all these people are watching so I guess that's making me a little nervous. I mean, I saw you looking at our portrait and it made me think about how things were and how everything that came before today is changing. But I'm ready for it. It's just the waiting that's killing me!"

"You won't lose your family," Maya said. "It's just, from now on, Sanjay has to come first." Maya was talking softly, so the aunties couldn't hear them, but she made sure to enunciate clearly so that Amrita couldn't miss her meaning.

"I know," Amrita said. "Sanjay is amazing. I know sometimes he seems childlike, maybe, but it's not immaturity. I really think it's his purity of heart. His sweetness. I'm not like that, that warm. But still, I know I'm going to make him happy." She looked at Maya and leaned closer to her. "So I made sure to fix the things in my life that needed changing. To really move on, so I'd be ready for this new phase. I was kind of ruthless about it. I couldn't really explain it all to Sanjay, he wouldn't get it; but I even—"

"It is time, beti," Amrita's father interrupted, rising from his chair below the family portrait. "We have to be there to welcome the groom."

"Yes, Baba." Amrita stopped her knee jiggling. She turned to Maya and said, "It's starting."

Maya felt as if her body were swelling, filling with the sorrow and splendor of the moment. All of Amrita's past, whatever had happened, had led her to this moment, this choice. The Darren situation wasn't Amrita backsliding, it was her moving forward. She was right, Sanjay would never really understand that. But Maya knew all too well what it meant to give up the last vestige of an old reality in an attempt to build a new, better one.

Maya took Amrita's hand and held it as she helped her off the couch, kept holding it the entire walk down the stairs and across the street to the Turf Club, where silken tents awaited them. Amrita's fingers vibrated in hers and when Maya looked down at this bridal hand, covered in ink and emeralds, she noticed how much smaller it was than her own. Beneath the nail polish and the mehndi and the jewelry it was still a child's hand, the one resting on her father's shoulder in the Sears portrait. But years had passed since then and Amrita had lived a whole life before Sanjay. She was a grown woman, except for her hands, which still needed protection. Maya regretted having hated her for making Sanjay worry, without once thinking that saying good-bye to Darren was something that had caused Amrita pain as well. Darren was a part of Amrita, just as Scott was a part of Maya, as were Seema, Ajit, Priya, and Mohan. You carried all of the people you loved into your present and future, even if just in a small way. Sometimes the people Maya had loved felt so heavy; maybe Amrita and Sanjay had passed through one of those times. Right now Maya felt that both she and Amrita were so light, they would float away if they didn't have each other to hold on to.

As they entered the tent Maya smelled the incense and saw the faces of Amrita's relatives, each one a world filled with hope and envy, regret and optimism. She wasn't a bride doll after all. Even as Maya held her hand she felt Amrita changing every second from a spoiled princess who toyed with her cousin's emotions into a person, a part of the lives that hummed all around her.

She was still holding on to Amrita when they heard the shouting of the baraat, and when Amrita squeezed her fingers Maya looked up and saw Sanjay in the achkan he commissioned from Raymond's of Park Avenue. It looked even more regal now, as he rode in on a white horse, high above the shoulders of the musicians, his parents, and all his friends, a sea of bobbing heads, some bald, some turbaned, all moving to the music. He was laughing and singing but when he spotted Amrita he stopped. In his embellished coat, he no longer resembled a prep school student; he seemed like a man, and when he looked at Amrita his eyes glowed like the silver thread in his jacket's embroidery.

Maya spotted Kruti-masi dabbing her cheeks with a lace-trimmed handkerchief; her round face was wet with tears that had the unexpected effect of making her appear lambent, not ridiculous. All Maya's relatives looked like their best selves, the way she remembered them before the curse, from when she was a child. Or maybe she'd never seen them look this way at all, but was now able to imagine them younger, happier, whole. She was becoming more and more convinced of the possibility she'd been nervously entertaining since her immersion into the Ganges: that the curse had been washed away. She was finally here, watching these two people, each of whom were profoundly loved by the others crowding around them on the lawn, masses of relatives for whom today was a fulfillment of painfully held hopes.

Kruti-masi dropped her handkerchief and Maya saw her mother bend slowly, pick it up, and wave it to brush off the dust. Seema handed it back to her sister without looking at her, staring instead at Sanjay, who was being helped off the horse. She was dryeyed but with the tiny, almost-suppressed smile that was the outward visible sign of her rare moments of inner joy. Maya wished she could give her mother something, everything, to make her smile fully. If she ever had her own wedding, Maya knew now, the promise of the future would heal the pain of the past, and the scars the curse had left on her family would fade.

An auntie lifted Amrita's heavy veil, and she looked back at Sanjay with no gold-embroidered netting to block her view. This was the experience Maya had tried to have in the airport with Scott, a domestic darsan. It might have been the incense or the exhaustion or the sound of the drums that made the earth vibrate beneath her, but Maya swore she could feel the divinity pass between Amrita and Sanjay as they recognized each other. She had misread their relationship. Or the part she had interpreted correctly was just one fraction of the whole, one small part she dissected and magnified, like a cell on a slide.

Sanjay proceeded to the mandap, where the pandit waited to perform the ceremony and sat down, cross-legged in front of the fire pit, surrounded by his relatives. Someone handed Amrita a golden coconut. Clutching it, she began walking toward Sanjay and the future. Maya fell into step behind her and Heidi leaned in and whispered, "It's the first time she's smiled. What's up?"

"Nothing." Maya knew Heidi expected her to have a criticism ready; as the wedding approached, mocking Amrita's self-absorption had become their favorite sport, what Seema and the aunties would call a "time-pass." But Maya couldn't do that now. "It's a serious occasion," she explained. "Brides aren't supposed to be all giddy."

Heidi shrugged. "I guess it's a good sign, then. And Sanjay looks amazing."

"I'm going to sit on the mandap," Maya said. "You'll be okay?"

"Are you kidding?" Heidi gestured around the maidan, where men in red turbans circulated holding trays of bright juices, and guests ignoring the long ceremony browsed a table laden with delicacies. "This is the best wedding I've been to."

Sanjay's cousin on his father's side left the mandap and Maya settled in her spot, watching as the pandit said prayers over the fire and wafted incense over Sanjay and Amrita, who leaned in to each other every now and then to whisper something, and sat straight the rest of the time, rigid with concentration. Then they stood and started walking around the sacred fire. Maya tried to keep count; it would be a total of seven circles, three led by the bride, three led by the groom, with the two of them walking together, side by side, on the last one. But she lost track, first watching their feet, then their hands, then their eyes. With each round they seemed to inscribe their own world, to create a circle of protection. It was impossible to really understand what went on between two people, Maya knew now. This was true even if you were one of them, as with her and Scott, and even more so if you stood outside their sacred circle.

Maya felt a hand on her shoulder and knew that Seema was standing behind her. The marriage Maya had observed most closely in her lifetime was her parents', using it as a template of everything she didn't want—a mere partnership in the business of building a family. She had seen no overt affection, no cherished, shy glances. But now she had to acknowledge that in all those years, she was still just outside the circle Ajit and Seema formed. And because of that, her parents' marriage would always remain a little bit of a mystery. If she had to rethink what she knew of their relationship, what did that mean for what she wanted in her own, going forward?

Maya leaned back into her mother's body, returning the pressure of her hand. Out in the crowd she saw Heidi drinking pomegranate juice and talking to Raki. Maya wished Pops and Priya and Mohan were there, and wondered if she could ever give her family this, if there would ever be a time when everyone she loved would be together in one place. A breeze lifted the incense into the air, and it mixed with the smell of the dishwashing liquid on her mother's hand. Maya said a prayer of thanks to Lakshmi for giving her so many people to love, for helping her family survive the curse. She watched the smoke curl into the air and disappear, and Parvati and her words felt far away, farther than Priya and Mohan and Pops, even though they were all across the ocean. The chatter of the crowd rose to match the chanting of the pandit into the microphone and the afternoon sun shifted, hitting her through the fuchsia silk of the tent. Maya felt sweaty and calm and full of possibilities.

Chapter Sixteen

The reception that night was at the Gymkhana, a country club where Europeans once floated on their backs in a pool whose water was guaranteed to be untainted by brown bodies. Now all you needed to get in was money, and Maya could tell by the way Amrita's father walked, as if he were about to tip forward, that he remembered, each minute, that everyone assembled knew his presence here meant he had it. Yesterday, after the dance practice, when she heard Amrita's mom discuss the Gymkhana while her father nodded to the crisp sound of his wife's voice, Maya had found Mrs. Gupta grasping, sharp-edged, and him soft and pathetic. But tonight she felt the urge to hug them both, so she went up to Mr. Gupta, wrapped her arms around his swollen midsection, and said, "Welcome to the family, Uncle."

His body temperature seemed to rise in the seconds she held him, and she thought he might be blushing, but he was too dark-skinned, and the glow from the strings of lights around the pool bar too dim, to tell. Mr. Gupta patted Maya on the back and passed her off to his wife, who fluttered her arms, sari fabric billowing, before squeezing her firmly.

"Have you been drinking already?" Heidi whispered as they walked to the edge of the lawn, where Seema stood looking at the Arabian Sea. "You can't stand those two."

"Couldn't," Maya said. "Maybe I'm maturing now that I've started seeing Dr. Bernard twice a week."

"Twice a week? You're practically dating." Heidi stopped to pick a samosa off a tray. "You see him more than you see me!"

"Also, I think I'm different since being cursed, then saved."

"Saving yourself," Heidi said through a mouth full of potato and pastry.

"What?"

Heidi swallowed. "Not to get all *Glamour* on you, but like Oprah told Katie Couric last month, you've got to acknowledge your own agency."

"But—"

"Parvati didn't remove the curse; bitch refused."

"Quieter," Maya said as they neared Seema.

"You took the train to Benares—"

"To see the river. Because of Dadiji's ashes."

"You ducked into the Ganges, and survived, and that—"

"You girls look very grand this evening," Seema said as her eyes focused through the darkness. "Not quite as pretty as this morning in your saris, but still lovely." Maya was wearing a black halter dress that she thought made her look a bit Bond girl when she bought it, but seeing Seema with her pallu wrapped around her against the night breeze she wished she were swathed in a sari too, or, even better, still small enough to sit on her mother's hip, wrapped in hers.

"Amazing view," Heidi said, looking at the moonlight on the bay.

Maya put an arm around her mother. "Are you thinking that the moon is brighter in India, Ma?"

"I am not a silly old woman yet, Maya," Seema said, shaking free of her arm and readjusting her sari. "I was thinking of the patients I will have to see when I return, how Nisba and Yasmin go back to preschool next week. I should really be there to help your sister, but with the practice having been minus one..." She shook her head and noticed Maya grinning at her. "We have a moon in Kalamazoo, too, do not forget." She turned to Heidi. "And you must come to visit sometime with Maya."

"You're going already?" Heidi asked.

"Oh yes. My flight leaves hours before you lucky girls—and I have two plane changes ahead of me! I will go to prepare my baggage." She kissed each of them on the cheek quickly, as if she'd be seeing them again in a few hours. "And now you can have some champagne." Seema giggled as she walked off to find the bride and groom, and Maya resisted the impulse to run after her with messages for Pops and Priya and Mohan, to grab her hand and not let go until they were both on the same flight traveling together somewhere. But where would that flight be going? Not to New York via Zurich. To London, then Chicago, then a Kalamazoo that didn't exist anymore, now that her family was scattered in different cities?

"You'll see her soon," Heidi said.

"True." Maya grabbed two glasses of champagne from a passing waiter and led Heidi toward one of the small round tables in between the two buffets; Amrita's parents had insisted that there be a meat table for guests. They spent a few minutes trying to decipher which buffet was which based on the crowds lining up for them, until Heidi inevitably started pointing out visible panty lines and poor hosiery choices.

"I mean, why wear panty hose at all; it's like eighty-five degrees," she was ranting. "And there's no way those are control top, they're just cutting into her waist causing all kinds of backfat. Sad, really. She needs a friend. Or a stylist."

"You're already reacclimating to the magazine," Maya said. If Heidi were her patient, she'd have called her comment "mirroring," paraphrasing what she heard the patient say to make her hear her own statement. Apparently, Maya was already shifting her focus back to New York as well.

"Yeah, I'm just itching to get back to saving the world, one panty line at a time." Heidi drank the last of her champagne. "Everyone looks so much better in a sari."

"Not everyone." Amrita glided by in a body-skimming white slipdress.

"Thinks she's Carolyn Bessette," Heidi whispered. "Sorry, I forgot you love her now."

Maya looked around, doing a quick auntie-check, then reached into the beaded bag she'd borrowed from Heidi and pulled out her cigarettes. She lit one and sighed.

"You haven't smoked this whole time," Heidi said.

"I'm getting reacclimated, too." The tobacco smelled sweet and strong. Maya still had another day of not having to work, her mother was healthy and heading home, her father doing much better in Kalamazoo. It seemed like she really had washed the curse away. Her siblings' sorrows, the malpractice suit, Scott, and his cruel removal of himself, all still had to be faced when she returned to New York, but those were just traces of difficulty still clinging to her, and she could find a way to banish them, too.

"Mummy's gone?" Raki set a plate on the table and pulled a chair around to face the laughing girls. "What's so funny, yaar?"

"Ma being called Mummy," Maya said as Heidi choked on her champagne.

"I'm surprised to see a doctor smoking." Raki pulled out his own pack.

"Unfiltered," Heidi observed. "You must be a real man."

Raki looked at Heidi, expressionless, for a long moment. But then he smiled and said, "Don't be fooled by the immaculately manicured hands," before lighting up.

Maya disguised her sigh of relief with an exhale. "All residents smoke on occasion," she said. "Death wish resulting from too many overnights in the psych ER."

"You don't indulge?" Raki asked Heidi, still staring at her.

"Please, I'm a fashion editor." Heidi flourished her mehndi-covered hand at her raw silk shift in a *ta-da* motion. "I would never do that to my skin." She looked at the vein showcased on her wrist. "Not all of us have melanin to help us out, you know."

"Sorry," Raki said. "Didn't mean to be racist." As he looked for an ashtray, Heidi raised an eyebrow at Maya and mouthed the word "funny." Maya flushed, hoping Heidi couldn't see her color rise through the smoke and the night and the melanin.

"I'm getting another drink; anyone want anything?" Heidi stood and smoothed her dress, then, when she didn't get an answer, walked toward the bar. Maya became aware of the hum of the party around her, the spikes of laughter and the rumbling dips that followed them. An image of her father's EKG screen flashed into her head.

"Heidi was in the modern dance company in college," Maya said, in order to say something. "She taped a cocktail thing we had in our common room and choreographed a dance to the party noise. Not a dance, a piece, I think she called it a 'piece.' "

"Very avant-garde. We didn't have a dance company at boarding school here, but I was dragged to a few performances that sound like the type at university in London."

"Another time she had me read out loud from *The Great Gatsby* and made a piece to go with that." Maya laughed at the memory. "She should have been in the sangeet."

"I'm glad it was you," Raki said, and she saw his hand flicker by his plate, as if it weren't being allowed to move. He was fairly dark-skinned, and she liked that, liked that even if he was an Indian boy, he wasn't the perfect Indian boy with an M.D. and a "wheatish complexion" her mother would have conjured by fasting. Maybe she wouldn't have to fast now, Maya thought, looking at the ridged surface of Raki's nails and wondering if he'd really had a manicure. Probably; they're dirt cheap in Bombay.

"Hungry?" Raki asked. "I could fix you a plate." She looked away, embarrassed at herself for thinking that she should have offered to fix him a plate first. On his dish she noticed chicken korma, lamb vindaloo, some shrimp dish she couldn't identify.

"My father started eating meat when he went to university in Birmingham," he said quickly. "But we are Brahmin."

"Then I guess you can sit here." Maya put her hand on his sleeve to show she was joking. For a minute she thought she could feel his pulse through his jacket, but she knew that wasn't possible.

"Cheers!" Heidi emerged from the dark, raising a glass of champagne at them.

"Heidi, something to eat?" Raki asked.

"No, thanks. I'm actually not feeling so . . . fabulous."

"Headache?" Maya asked; Heidi had been prone to migraines in college.

"No," Heidi said slowly. "But in the bathroom now I looked in the mirror and was surprised at how pale I am. Do I look pale to you guys?"

"Not any more so than this morning," Raki said.

"Feel my head." Heidi leaned toward Maya.

"I'm a doctor, not a mom." Maya pressed her hand against Heidi's proffered forehead, which felt cool compared to Raki's sleeve. "You're fine; temporary identity crisis caused by being exposed to brown faces for a prolonged period."

"I wish you were a real doctor." Heidi took a sip of her drink.

"Actually, the champagne does settle my stomach. Like Coca-Cola I guess."

"Good," Raki said. "Let's go elsewhere for the next. They'll close up soon."

It had been an unexpectedly lovely day so far, filled with the pleasure of the wedding, and now of Raki. Maya didn't want to ruin it by being greedy. "Maybe we should call it a night if Heidi's not feeling well."

"But it's her last night in Bombay, yaar!" Raki protested. "She can't leave without seeing Indigo."

"I read about that place in *Hi! Blitz*! At the hair salon," Heidi added when Raki looked at her, surprised. "I know all about Queenie and Princess, Ash and Abishek. Come on, Maya." She reached out a hand. "It's my last night in India." She pulled her up so forcefully Maya almost crashed into her, then whispered, "At least until you get married."

Maya sat between Raki and Heidi in the back of the cab and every time it plunked into a pothole she was pushed closer to one or the other of them, the hem of her dress riding higher up her thighs. She felt unreal somehow, as if she were in one of those early morning reveries that are part dream, part fantasy, part controlled mental exercise, visions that feel clear at the time but recede into a haze after waking. She had shared so many cabs with Heidi and Scott in New York, detouring downtown to drop off Heidi before they returned to her place because Scott didn't want Heidi riding home alone at the end of a long, boozy night. To steady herself, Maya put her hand on Heidi's, which was resting on her stomach. Then, to remind herself that it was Scott who had chosen not to ride in cabs with her anymore, Maya put her other hand on Raki's arm.

Maya admired the grace with which Raki paid the driver, led them past the crowd massing in front of Indigo, and, shaking hands with a large, dark, elegantly suited man at the door, into the court-yard. She wondered, briefly, if she was just telling herself she ad-mired Raki's suaveness and all the other qualities he had that were so different from Scott, or if she genuinely liked him. But then she pushed the question out of her mind. As far as she knew, Scott wasn't sitting around thinking of her right now. He'd already taken up enough of her mental energy. He didn't get her last night in Bombay, too.

"That's creepy," Heidi said, pointing. Trees all around were hung with lanterns in the shape of stars and pots of gardenias stood on either side of the door, but in between them sat a large placard printed STAY ALERT, MUMBAIKARS! INSTEAD OF READING THIS, SHOULDN'T YOU BE LOOKING AROUND FOR SUSPICIOUS OBJECTS?

"It's getting me a little paranoid," Heidi admitted. Maya mur-mured in sympathy, but she wasn't worried at all; she felt safe, in-vincible.

Leading them inside, Raki explained that after eleven, Indigo morphed from a restaurant into more of a lounge, with a whiskey-and-cigar cottage on the rooftop. Whiskey aside, he said, the roof deck was worth seeing. As they made their way through the crowd to the stairs, Maya kept spotting people she recognized from the Indian clubs in New York and pointing them out to Heidi. "See the tall woman kissing the Punjabi-looking guy? She has a white fiancé in the city."

Heidi was quiet. Maya assumed she was taking in the reinter-pretations of Indian fashion all around her, memorizing the bra top made of antique sari fabric here, the salwar altered to be skintight and worn with no pants there. An egregious reveler inspired Heidi to mutter, "Not everybody has to be a blond," but otherwise she was silent as they climbed the stairs to the roof. Maya was about to ask how she felt but then they reached the top and Heidi gasped. The world opened up, with the moon and stars visible above the frangipani trees strung with fairy lights. The perimeter of the deck was ringed by a narrow reflecting pool, spotlit from below, dotted with floating water lilies.

"I'm going to sit here and make wishes," Heidi said, sinking into a chair by the water and pulling change out of her minaudière. "You all mingle."

"Are you—" Maya started, but Raki already had her hand in his and was leading her toward the bar, calling back to Heidi, "One champagne for the lady, coming up."

The bar was topped with glass and underneath it someone had slipped postcards of the wonders of India: the Taj Mahal, a beach in Goa, the Benares ghats. Maya stared at them, trying to think of something clever to say.

"Have you been to Tirupati?" she finally asked Raki, tapping on the glass above the image of the temple.

"Not personally. But my mother's from Tamil Nadu originally, and she had a bit of a hard time conceiving, so she made a pilgrimage there, vowed that if she had a son, she'd come back and shave her head, leave her hair as an offering of gratitude."

Maya felt an instant kinship with this woman who had also been shortchanged by fate until she, too, took matters into her own hands, maybe even changing her biology with the power of her beliefs. "It worked!"

"Here I am!" Raki shrugged. "I suppose it's a bit crazy?"

Maya laughed, a short, hard sound. "A few months ago, someone told my father that she cursed our whole family. Twelve days later, he had a heart attack. In the next two months, something horrible happened to each of us, really. Everyone I work with at the hospital would say it's coincidence, or a self-fulfilling prophecy. But I know . . . I think . . . it was bigger than that. I came here to get it removed. Do you think that's crazy?"

"I think you must be quite brave." Raki handed her a flute. "And the curse?"

She didn't know him well enough—yet—to tell him about the

Ganges, that she thought dipping herself in the filthy river had cleansed her of the curse, that at that moment she had felt a bit like Achilles being lowered into the River Styx in search of immortality. She wouldn't let herself get cocky; even Achilles ended up dead, and the curse could just be lying dormant for all she knew, ready to return and suffocate her at any moment. "I'm not sure," Maya said finally. "But it seems like my luck might be changing."

She lifted Heidi's glass of champagne off the bar so she could look at the bubbles rising in the pale liquid instead of at Raki. If his mother was from Tamil Nadu, that made him South Indian, or half South Indian anyway. Maybe Raki was Bauji's shot at redemption, he was right about her marrying someone from the South, and Scott and all the Lamars on his mother's side of the family were just a blip, a distraction.

"It's a shame, though," Raki said, looking through the crowd. "My mother had such beautiful hair in photos. After it grew back, it was never the same."

Maya laughed—that had to be a joke, it was such a shallow, and almost Oedipal, thing to say—but Raki's expression was blank, his eyes focused on the crowd before them. His face twitched and, as if the twitch had conjured her, a woman appeared in front of them. She was half a foot taller than Maya, with hair that was lush and wavy in a room filled with the flat and shiny.

"Ashoke said you're leaving a day early, naughty boy." The woman, who was tapping at Raki's stomach as if he were the Pillsbury Doughboy, sounded like Princess Diana, soft-voiced and expensive. "Are they cracking the whip at Goldman?"

"Maya, you must know Indira from New York," Raki said, and the woman looked down at Maya as if noticing her for the first time, then swooped in to kiss the aura that apparently emanated from her.

"You do look familiar," Maya admitted.

"Mmm, but I don't think we've met." Indira took Raki's Scotch out of his hand and sipped from it. "Are you coming to Goa, too, then?"

"No." Maya nodded toward Heidi's table. "My friend and I head back tomorrow."

"Pity." Indira's voice came from high above Maya, so that Maya had to suppress the urge to rise onto her tiptoes to hear her better. This tall, whispery woman made her nervous.

"We're just having a last drink; I should bring this to her." Maya pivoted and slid through the bodies to Heidi's table. All the remaining chairs had disappeared, so she sat on the edge of the fountain and handed Heidi her champagne. Maya meant to ask Heidi how she was doing, but she grew distracted as she watched Raki battle his way through the crowd toward them; he was stopped at every step by a man in too-expensive jeans shaking hands and clapping him on the shoulder, or a woman wearing what could easily pass for lingerie kissing him where his cheek met his jawbone. Someone bumped into him and he spilled Scotch on his jacket and grimaced. Maya laughed.

"You should come, you know," Raki said, arriving at the table. "Both of you. To Goa." He stepped to the next table to negotiate the release of two chairs, pushed them over, and sat in one.

"Raki, you must know where the ladies' room is?" Heidi asked.

"Next to the gent's, inside the whiskey bar; actually, we'll lead you." But by the time he stood, abandoning the hard-won chairs, Heidi was already gone. Raki grabbed Maya's hand and led her up three steps to a tiny, private patch of roof hidden behind the walls of the little cottage that held the bar. "You can book dinner for two up here," he said, leaning against the cottage's back wall. "If you stay we could come tomorrow, then join everyone in Goa." He grabbed Maya's other hand as well. "Change your ticket, yaar." He leaned closer to her. "We've got really the most beautiful hotel, and it's a big crowd, guys and girls."

"I have to get back to the hospital." Maya struggled to think of a joke, something to neutralize Raki's obvious disappointment. "I work with psychotics; they might riot if I don't return."

"Someone can cover you." He managed to keep sulking as he spoke, and the gesture was rapidly tipping from cute to annoying.

"Seriously, Raki, a lot of these patients have trouble with boundaries. It's a big deal when the therapist goes away; I have to honor the terms I've set." A breeze passed and Maya took her hands back to rub her arms. "I can't ditch them to party with a bunch of strangers I could see in New York next week at OM."

"Forget them." Raki grabbed her right hand with both of his. "And Goa. We could go anywhere, just us. We could go to Tirupati, put the nail in the coffin of the curse for good. Please, Maya. We could get to know each other."

The word "curse" sounded odd coming from his mouth. Maya shouldn't have told him about the curse, and her family. She'd been so discreet until she blurted this ridiculous thing to a near stranger. He wasn't Heidi, he wouldn't understand. And his acknowledging the curse revived it in a way, made it seem even more real. "We live in the same city," she said. "We can get to know each other in New York."

He dropped her hand. "In between leaving the office at ten week-nights, and hitting the clubs at midnight on weekends? We can *survive* in New York. But we could create something amazing in India."

"I don't know if it's the kind of ticket you can change," Maya mumbled, but when his fingers reached for hers again, she twined her hand with his. The smog had cleared and the stars seemed somehow brighter than before. It would be different in New York. Raki probably wouldn't even call. He'd be too busy with Indira and the rest of the accent brigade. If she saw him again it would be in a crowded club some night when Sanjay visited and dragged her out, not on a private roof deck in the starlight, holding hands like they were starring in a Bollywood movie. If she let him go, she'd be alone.

If Raki could fill the emptiness left by Scott, if he could be the man her mother prayed for, then perhaps *he* was the antidote to the curse.

"Maybe we can just enjoy tonight," Maya said, and kissed him. He had been drinking Scotch on the rocks and his cold tongue was such a pleasant shock that Maya wished she could kiss him for the first time again.

"I've been wanting to do that for two days," Raki said.

"I saved you the trouble," she said, acknowledging her agency; Oprah would have been proud.

This time Raki kissed Maya, wrapping his arms around her tightly. The heat rising from his body was stifling after the cool of his mouth, and his stomach was softer than Maya remembered from the motorcycle. But it wasn't the ice that had made him a good kisser, and the breeze blew up around them again, making her think this was the most perfect last night in India she'd ever had. She could feel her heart beating faster in her wrists, the backs of her knees, in her chest as she pressed against him. This was good adrenaline for a change and she wanted to feel this light and strong always, wanted to bring this feeling of being desired rather than pitied, harried, or worried back with her to New York. She wanted to make Raki hers, to bind him to her so he'd never leave her like Scott, could never even suspect that she was capable of being depressed, or weak, or cursed. She wanted to be as confident as he was, and India was giving her that bravado tonight.

Raki whispered her name and started kissing her neck, twisting his torso around hers. She clutched his back and her fingers found the top of his pants. She slipped her right hand past the waistband, through the elastic of his boxers, and then her left hand, until she found his skin, smooth and firm, surprisingly so compared to his stomach, but of course he'd probably played some rich person's game like rugby all through school, still played it on the weekends.

His buttocks were so unlike Scott's flat behind that Maya couldn't stop touching them, sliding her hands across them, cupping them when she could dip low enough, wrapping one of her calves around his, all the time kissing him and, when her mouth was free, laughing quietly at the sound of his moans. Even his body proved it; he was the man of substance she needed, strong enough to ground her and protect her. She felt the back of her Bond girl dress being lifted, the breeze on her legs, and laughed out loud as she thought of her ass exposed to the air of India. Raki's thumb found its way into the top of her thong and she felt the lace inching down.

"Good Lord!" A voice came from behind Raki and Maya ripped her hands out of his pants and pushed Raki in front of her, trying to use his body as a shield. "I'd say I hope I'm not interrupting, but obviously I am." The voice came from a chubby man who, if it weren't for his receding hairline, would have given the impression of a chubby boy.

"Ashoke, I'm glad to see you, man, just not now," Raki said, turning toward him.

"I know. But I've been sent to find, um, you." Ashoke looked over Raki's shoulder at Maya, who had been doing her best imitation of an invisible person. "Your friend's a bit... under the weather."

Maya raced past both of them to the steps, glad of an excuse to get out of there. She heard one of them say, "Who knew doctors could be so much fun," as she ran down the stairs, but their voices were so alike she couldn't be sure who had spoken. It had to be Ashoke, she thought, her cheeks burning with embarrassment, her underwear still bunched below her hip bones. She was sure she'd talked to him at the sangeet, told him she was a psychiatrist. He and Raki went to school together, probably had the same snooty British-sounding teachers, of course they spoke alike, and Ashoke was obviously a crass jokester, he even looked like one, an Indian Benny Hill.

At the wall by the reflecting pool, Heidi's hand was shaking so quickly that it seemed to blur her mehndi. She rested it on Maya's shoulder, sending vibrations through her body. "There was some controversy in the bathroom."

"Vomit? Diarrhea?"

"Maya!" Heidi shushed. "Both."

"Loose stool or full-on diarrhea?"

"The term 'explosive' comes to mind," Heidi said. "I felt terrible; people were banging on the door. There's nothing left, but still, I've got to go. If you want to stay—"

"Of course not!" Maya wrapped an arm around Heidi's waist and started propelling her toward the stairs. "We'll get you hydrated, a little saline, maybe a nimbu paani. I've got Cipro, which is good. Let's just say good-bye." Maya looked for Raki; he was now in the middle of a crowd, surrounded by a throng of people massing around him like ants crawling on a piece of candy that had been licked and discarded. Maya could see the top of his head; if she reached out she might even be able to touch him, but she'd have to push away a number of his well-dressed pals first.

"Your friend all right?" Maya looked up and saw Indira, bestowing on them a look of pity, affection, and disgust such as a kindergarten teacher might give a child who'd just peed on the rug. "Upset stomach?"

"Will you tell Raki Heidi's sick and we had to go?" Maya asked. "And that I'll see you both in New York?"

"Of course, darling." Indira was already walking toward Raki's table.

"I think I'm gonna hurl," Heidi said.

Maya looked around frantically for a bucket, a glass, a potted plant.

"I meant that figuratively, *darling*; that woman. She makes me sick." Heidi shuddered. "Anyway, I'd rather blame her than the Ganges."

• • •

Maya managed to drag Heidi out of the cab and into the apartment without waking Seema, who was sleeping behind the closed door of the master bedroom. Pretending to sleep, more likely. Her flight was in a few hours, so she was probably already up, wrapping jars of mirch in Ziploc bags in case the spices escaped, and rolling them up in her trouser socks, zipping and rezipping each compartment of her suitcase, not wanting to miss the driver when he called. Maya was grateful that Seema restrained herself from coming out of the room at the sound of their stumbling in; she probably assumed they were drunk, and didn't want to confront them. The whimpering moans Heidi kept emitting as Maya put her to bed would only confirm that impression. She had gotten Heidi to drink a salty nimbu paani and take some Cipro, and was now packing in a dual attempt to be efficient and to keep from reliving the minutes on the roof when Ashoke had interrupted them. What must he think of her? Maya pulled off her T-shirt; it was hot in the bedroom. Who cared what Ashoke thought, he was a buffoon. But what must Raki think? Scott would have liked it, her being more aggressive. But good Indian girls weren't supposed to go around grabbing strangers' asses, and Raki knew that, no matter how modern he was. She should have left earlier while he was still enthralled with her.

Maya attacked a pile of clothes on the floor, trying to puzzle out which paisley shawl was hers and which was Heidi's. She was too jittery to sleep, too preoccupied wondering what Raki was doing at Indigo, with whom, how well he knew Indira, and if she was being self-defeating, pushing him away when he could make things better. A more grounded person, who put herself above her job and hadn't cultivated a martyr complex to rival her mother's, would have gone to Goa with him, wouldn't have risked losing her lucky charm to a club-hopping Amazon.

A clanging parade march erupted from the floor, Heidi

moaned, and it took Maya a good fifteen seconds to recognize the
noise as the ring from the cell phone Sanjay had left with her. It
continued its strident tune until Maya deconstructed a pile of
shawls and found her evening bag. She fumbled the phone, flipping
it open accidentally while trying to silence it, then managed to
put it on vibrate, throwing it onto her side of the bed. She hadn't
refolded one shawl when the phone started convulsing on the
blanket.

1st you ditch me, then you hang up on me, read the text from what
she already recognized as Raki's number.

It's too late to talk. Heidi is sick + sleeping, Maya wrote back.

The phone whirred again, sounding like a hand mixer, churn-
ing Maya's nerves. *U could have said goodbye,* the screen accused.

I asked Indira to; it was too crowded. If Indira was too absorbed in
partying to relay the message, it was natural that Raki felt abandoned. But Heidi was sick; Maya was already taking care of her, she
was in no mood to placate him. Maybe his insistence was an only
child thing, the miracle son's need for attention. But everyone has
problems; it's a question of finding the ones you can tolerate. Once
that thought appeared in Maya's head she tried to isolate the voice
she imagined speaking it: Her mother? Dr. Bernard? Oprah?

Heidi stood and stumbled toward the bathroom. Three minutes later, the toilet flushed, water ran, and she reemerged, tripping
over the doorjamb. "Is it time?" she muttered. "I thought I heard the
alarm clock."

"No, sweetie," Maya said. "Go back to bed."

"I was dreaming of all these hands grabbing at me." Heidi
pulled the sheet up to her neck. "When Sanjay and I were shopping,
every time he turned around a little beggar kid would grab my elbow, or throw me a flower she wanted me to buy. I wanted to help
them all, but I also wanted them to go away and leave me alone."

Maya put her hand on Heidi's hot forehead. "You'll be home

soon," she said. "In New York, where the homeless don't touch you. And your business will help so many women, and they'll help the children." It felt good to be the one doing the comforting, the calm, healthy friend. Hearing her own soothing voice, Maya felt confident that she would be a good doctor, that she was one already, regardless of what Mrs. Esleck's lawyers said. "It's a new year, full of beginnings."

Heidi smiled faintly and turned onto her side. Once Heidi's breathing slowed, Maya picked up her phone and thought about what to text Raki that would seem nice without being an apology. The warm metal felt alive in her hands, about to start pulsing again. *Have a good time in Goa,* she typed quickly, then powered it off.

Each time Heidi flushed the toilet throughout the night, Maya woke up, but drifted off again when Heidi seemed to sleepwalk back to the bed. When sunlight was just starting to cast bars through the blinds, Maya heard the sound of wheels on marble and crept out of the room in time to see Seema pulling a huge suitcase behind her.

"Let me get that, Ma." Maya tried to grab the handle with her decorated hand, but Seema wouldn't relinquish control.

"You cannot let the driver see you this way." Seema surveyed Maya, up and down, skimming over the sweatpants, but shaking her head at the braless tank top.

"I'll get a jacket." It was cold in the living room. Maya felt stupid for getting up at all; Seema would be fine, she always was. There was no reason to miss her already.

"No, you stay here. Your mother is not so old that she needs an orderly." Seema smiled. "It was a good trip. Next year we will come all together."

"Give Priya and the girls a kiss for me," Maya said. "And Pops. Make sure he—"

"Your father is fine, Maya, do not be silly. We are all fine." She hugged Maya so quickly that Maya barely had time to wrap her own arms around her mother's ever-tinier frame. "You girls have a safe flight. The gods protect you."

"We'll need it. Heidi's in bad shape."

Seema leaned toward Maya and whispered, "She drank too much?"

"Too much nimbu paani with ice, maybe."

"Traveler's stomach; it happens to everyone. You gave her amoxicillin?"

"Yes, Doctor."

"You have the Cipro I gave you in Michigan?" Seema opened the door and started wheeling toward the elevator without waiting for her daughter's reply. "You will take good care of her, Maya," she said as the elevator doors slid apart. Seema stepped into the machine and as the doors closed Maya felt abandoned, the sole Michigan Das still left in India. There were only three floors in the building, but Maya watched the light at the top of the elevator hit each one as her mother descended away from her.

Inside the airport five hours later, Maya loaded their bags on a cart while Heidi looked for a bathroom to run some cool water on her wrists. She was already at the front of the line checking in when Heidi returned, hunched over and swaying back and forth.

"Didn't need a bathroom," Heidi reported. "But I still have shooting pains."

"Madam," the man at the desk said. "The blue bag is overweight by one–two kilos."

"You're probably having colonic spasms."

"No, the pain's up here." Heidi pointed just below her ribs.

"Madam," the man repeated.

"The colon goes all the way up, could cause pain to your whole thorax."

"Thorax?" Heidi groaned. "What am I, a grasshopper?"

"Madam, why not take one–two kilos out of the bag and put it in the others, or in hand luggage?" the man suggested cheerily. "Go make adjust and bring the bags back to me."

Heidi pushed the baggage cart, looking like the hunchbacked old women Maya saw in New York, curved over their wire grocery carts. Maya opened the offending suitcase and set about repacking; it was Heidi's, full of fabrics she planned to use to start her company. Maya wondered if Sanjay had begun the paperwork before leaving on his honeymoon or if she was abetting the illegal exportation of goods, but Heidi was too busy moaning, "Make it stop, make it stop, Maya," to be questioned. Squatting on the floor, surrounded by shawls, Maya saw a familiar pair of black shoes running toward her. They were dustier than she remembered.

"Maya!" Raki yelled. "I was worried you'd have gone through customs." He dropped to the floor so that he was eye level with her.

"We'd have waited," she said. "Why didn't you call?"

"My phone got smashed last night." He shook his head, laughing. "I dropped it and Ashoke set his chair down on it, that fat bloke who . . . I mean, you saw the size of him. I'm glad I caught you. I just wanted to say good-bye."

"Sorry we left without—"

"No worries," Raki answered. "We'll have nothing but time in New York." He grabbed Maya's hand and she looked down at his knuckles so that he couldn't see just how pleased she was that, somehow, he was still enthralled, might still be the beginning of something new, something both safe and exciting.

"Maya, it's freezing." Heidi, now sitting on the grimy airport floor, was shaking, shuddering like a cell phone on vibrate.

Maya shoved most of the remaining shawls into her own suitcase, wrapping two around Heidi. "It's not that cold," she said. "You probably just have a fever. We'll get on the plane, wrap you up, give you some Tylenol PM to knock you out. You'll be fine."

"Here, take this." Raki shed his jacket, the same one he'd been wearing last night, and draped it around Heidi's shoulders. "I'll get it in New York when you're feeling better," he said over her protests. "Give us a kiss good-bye." He bussed her cheeks.

"I'm sick," she said.

"But not contagious," Maya soothed. "I promise it's just something you ate."

"Madam, it is time," the man at the desk called. "Please to bring the bags."

She stood, and so did Raki, pulling Heidi up off the ground before turning to her. "I'll see you in New York, too," he said, and leaned toward her, his face hovering in the air for a minute. Maya kissed him quickly on both cheeks, then hugged him hard. Passing through security, she regretted not really kissing him. It was a little late for modesty now.

As they walked through the first-class cabin toward coach, a blonde in a fuchsia terry-cloth tracksuit noticed Heidi shaking, her teeth chattering, and said, loudly, "Oh my God!" Maya glanced at the flight attendants passing by, but they were too busy preparing for takeoff, distributing blankets and stowing ill-fitting luggage in the overhead compartments, to notice Heidi or care that she seemed to be detoxing.

"Thinks she's J. Lo in that old-school tracksuit," Heidi said as they passed through the curtain dividing first class from coach. "Bet she chose it because someone told her pink is the navy blue of India. But it doesn't do your butt any favors."

"You sound like you're feeling better," Maya said, but Heidi just kept muttering about the outdated tracksuit until she swallowed two pills, and, swathed in Raki's jacket, three shawls, and a blanket, fell asleep well before takeoff. Surrounded by passengers, with Heidi sleeping beside her, Maya was now alone. Usually, at takeoff in Bombay, she breathed into her shawl, inhaling India, and wondered when she'd be back, and if all her relatives in Jodhpur would still be there the next time she came, until she forced herself to start thinking about all she had to do in New York upon returning, finally pulling out a pen to make lists. But this time, she didn't even look out the window, didn't replay the image of Sanjay on his white horse, of Nanaji and Bauji puzzling over her astrological chart, didn't think about the EPU and the overnight shift that awaited her on Tuesday. As the plane rose, all she could see was Raki's face floating in front of her before she'd swooped around and kissed his smooth cheeks.

PART THREE

Chapter Seventeen

Maya walked into her apartment and thought, for a second, that she had opened the wrong door. The place looked as it always did, but too much so, it was too perfect, like a display in a furniture store, a set for an imagined life, one much tidier than her own. Nothing had changed in the time she'd been gone. Three and a half weeks, almost a month, half of the trip belonging to last year's vacation time, days she had stolen from long weekends that could have been spent with Scott, or helping Pops deadhead the garden in Kalamazoo, or babysitting Nisba and Yasmin so Tariq and Priya could get away somewhere. The second half of the trip belonged to the new year, days she had yet to pay for, people she had yet to miss. And the smug apartment had ignored it all, as if none of it had happened, Sanjay's wedding, Raki's kisses, Parvati's insults, and the holy, dirty Ganges, where she had been washed clean. Her coffee table was empty, except for the stack of junk mail she had just dumped on it. Her block-printed bedspread was smooth, the blue elephants, trunks raised for luck, calmly marching around the border as if she had just made the bed that morning.

But she hadn't made the bed the morning she'd left, had barely been able to cram clothes into the suitcases, slapping in some colognes for the relatives in Jodhpur, before Scott arrived to take her to the airport. Not knowing what was coming at the time, she'd thought his picking her up was sweet, a favor, and hadn't wanted to make him wait. There had been piles of rejected clothes all over the floor and when Scott reached toward the elephants to pull up the bedspread, Maya, eager to get to the airport and be on her way to India, told him to just leave it, she didn't want him to get a parking ticket, or, worse, cause Walker's car to be towed. "Fine, let's go," Scott had said, dropping the blanket and pulling Maya's suitcase toward the door, picking his way through the refuse on the rug. "I just didn't want you to have a mess waiting when you get back."

But now the floor was spotless, and when she lifted the bedspread, Maya found clean sheets on the bed. She leaned over and inhaled the scent of Tide. She had once told Dr. Bernard she wished the detergent weren't so sticky, so she could dab it on her wrists, smell it throughout the day. There was no more comforting scent, or at least not one that she could create without the help of Seema and several spices she could never distinguish properly by herself when she went to the specialty shop in Curry Hill.

A wet dot appeared on the clean blue sheet. Maya brushed away the next tear before it fell. Moving to her dresser, she opened the bottom drawer. Usually she had to shove it back and forth a few times to free the yoga pants and scrubs trapped in wrinkled masses. But now the drawer slid open smoothly, and the clothes that had been in mounds on the floor when she left were folded, neatly stacked, filling the space where Scott used to keep his gym shorts, socks, some boxers and T-shirts. She slammed the drawer shut.

Kneeling, Maya looked under the dresser. Scott's backup work shoes were gone. The overstuffed closet's door, which she kept open even though Heidi's grandmother swore it was bad luck to leave a closet ajar, was primly shut. Maya knew if she opened it, Scott's blue-and-white-striped shirt would be gone from the far right, his gray pants wouldn't be waiting on their hanger. She swept her hand across the top of the dresser, feeling for his key, but only grasped a few hair elastics, and when she stood and looked she saw nothing but her bottles of perfume, an old deodorant, a few picture frames.

Violent honking erupted on the street and Maya turned toward the window, half expecting to see Scott leaning out of the door of Walker's car, yelling for her to come down so they could go somewhere and talk. In the second or two it took her to snap her head toward the street, she silently berated herself, telling herself not to be so delusional, he'd never come back, and if he did, she might not—didn't—want him anymore. Down on the street, the honking started again. A blue Prius was trying to get around a cab that was dropping off one of Maya's neighbors and the woman's elaborate stroller. Maya roughly scraped another tear off her face, punishing her cheek because she was angry at her mind, at her own foolishness in thinking that the honking might mean something, that it might be for her.

On the windowsill, the altar where she did puja looked undisturbed. Sinking in front of it she smiled back at the grinning photo of Dadiji, at the handsome stare of Nanaji. The movement diverted a tear, which fell on her bottom lip. It tasted salty and delicious; she hadn't eaten since Switzerland. In front of the tin box that held all her objects of devotion Maya noticed an intruder, a folded piece of notebook paper. She stared at it for a few seconds, willing it to make its contents known. When she picked up the square, Scott's key fell into her lap. She unfolded the paper, holding it by the ragged edge. "Thank You" were the only words on it, floating slightly above the line in Scott's spiky handwriting. She crumpled the note in her left hand and threw it toward the bed. Then she crawled after it, smoothed it out, and placed it under the tin.

The hollow feeling she thought she had escaped in the past week came back, emptying her. Unzipping her suitcase with the same force she'd used to crumple the paper, Maya dumped out all its contents and spread them on the floor. The apartment was full now, the floor covered in Maya's dirty clothes, some of Heidi's T-shirts that had crept into the wrong bag, and Raki's crumpled, stale-smelling jacket. Maya was surrounded by silk and cotton, wooden gods and clay goddesses, spices and attars, color, scent, hope. She made a small leap over a pile of gifts, and landed on the bed, settling in between her clean sheets.

Maya put her clothes away little by little, an eighth of them on Monday morning before she went in to work an overnight, a third on Tuesday night after she returned. She filled her days, and every third night, with work, extra shifts to combat the credit card bills that would come soon, filled with reminders of the trip. Two lunch hours each week were taken up by sessions with Dr. Bernard and her evenings were packed with sleep, work, or launches she attended as Heidi's plus one. In nine days her sleep patterns were back to normal, her bank account was swelling slightly, and her apartment was starting to feel empty again. So when Raki returned, she brought him back to her place, to scatter his pictures of Goa over the coffee table, and fill the air with his cricket-commentator voice.

They had met at his favorite Indian restaurant at ten thirty, the soonest he could safely leave work, and by the time they finished dinner the owner's pregnant wife was sleeping in a chair by the door, as the owner swished back and forth on the loud synthetic carpet, asking if there was anything else they needed.

"We should go; we're acting like my borderlines," Maya said.

"Borderline?" Raki asked.

"You know, personality disorder? Axis II, Cluster B— dramatic-erratic? They don't understand boundaries and limits." She nodded at the owner, who was flipping the *Sorry, We're Closed, Come Again!* sign back and forth in the door. "He's been trying to tell us, in the nicest way, to get the hell out of here already."

"We're paying customers, he'll bloody well wait," Raki said. But he pulled out his wallet, waving away Maya's attempts to reach for hers. "Anyway, I'm leaving a forty percent tip, so he'll be pleased; poor sod's probably been working since lunch."

When the owner picked up the check and Maya saw his grinning reflection in the mirrored wall above the cash register, she suggested to Raki that they go just around the corner to her place, to look at his photos for a bit. Even as she heard her voice inviting him she was promising herself that it didn't mean anything, this was just a welcome distraction to keep her from thinking about Scott for another half hour. Maybe her new, post-curse life would be full of such pleasant diversions, and if she surrounded herself with distractions they would act like a shield, deflecting new assaults from any potential unknown evils. The truth was, she wasn't really sure what she was doing; it had been so long since she'd been out with a man who wasn't Scott. Heidi had told her, her voice ringing through the cell phone while Maya waited for Raki, that she should by no means go back to his place before the third date. Now here they were, leaning over glossy images of paradise, filling her apartment with the sound of their words.

"Gorgeous," Maya said. "I haven't been to Goa since my nephew was one; I sort of acted like a nanny for my brother and sister-in-law that trip. It was my brother's last visit to India."

"Mohan?"

"Good memory." Maya felt her stomach swell as if she'd just drunk something overly carbonated. She had called Mohan to see how he was doing, but Shalini answered the phone and stayed on the line listening to Maya's play-by-play of Sanjay's wedding, so they hadn't been able to talk. When she asked her mother if Shalini and Mohan were staying in D.C., Seema had sputtered, "Of course— where else would they go?"

"Is that him and his wife?" Raki pointed to an eight-by-ten black-and-white that hung on the wall to the left of Maya's altar.

"No, those are my parents, before I was born." In the photo, her father stood behind her mother, his head on her shoulder; the only clue to the era was his ambitious sideburn. Seema was in a sari, of course, and you couldn't tell from the photo that it was probably inflammable polyester. Ajit seemed to be whispering something in her ear and Seema was laughing, her head thrown back, her mouth open so you could see a filling in her back teeth. She looked lovely.

"Can't really see your mum's face."

"Mmm, that's why you didn't recognize Mummy." Maya elbowed Raki softly. He grabbed her arm and pulled her closer to him. "I am jealous I couldn't join you all," Maya admitted, looking back at the photos.

"Next year we'll go together."

Maybe it wasn't too late for Maya to salvage the evening, play a little hard to get. "How can you be so sure?"

"Because I wouldn't go again without you." Raki kissed her, and he tasted warm and peppery like the wine they'd been drinking. "I promise Ashoke won't barge in this time," he said when they finally split apart.

The thought of the rotund banker barreling through her front door made Maya laugh. She liked the unfamiliar sound of her own laughter, liked feeling this light and normal. So she leaned forward and kissed Raki again. She had barely pulled away from his lips when words started rushing from his mouth. "I knew we'd end up here, I knew when Amrita said your name, and again at the sangeet when we danced and you looked round Shankar's crooked arm at me, and on the roof above Bombay."

Maya felt lost in the sea of his certainty, and soon they were in her bed, shedding outer layers, abandoning his shirt with its faded-cologne smell onto the floor, shoving her underwear into the depths of the bedding so it tangled with the mashed top sheet, until there was nothing between them and the clean linens Scott had put on the bed. Maya thought of Scott's hands pulling the corners of the fitted sheet tight over the mattress and grabbed Raki's fingers, which were clasped around her breast. She pulled away from his mouth, her lips making a rude smacking sound, so she could watch her hand trail down his chest, slide around his thigh, her hand paler than his skin but not by much, as if their bodies were poured from the same batter. The rich tone of his skin, its nearness, made hers seem more beautiful, feel warmer, and when he unrolled the ugly yellow condom, Maya hated the contrast of the dusty, sticky plastic against his warm, dark skin. She kissed his thigh before lying back and pulling him on top of her.

The next morning, as the sun streamed insistently through the window above the bed, Maya opened her eyes and saw the top of Raki's head lying next to her breasts. She felt her face heat up, but couldn't tell if she was embarrassed for herself or him. What did she know about him, really? He was related to Amrita. Which was good in that he wasn't a total stranger, but risky if he confided in Amrita about last night and she even hinted about it to her parents; every Indian person over forty should think Maya was a virgin until she married. He danced well. And he did wear hair gel even in New York. She'd felt it crunching between her fingers when she caressed his scalp last night. She ran her left hand through his hair again, with less difficulty now that the gel had worn off, and he stirred, turning back into a person. He reached for her hand and pulled it in front of his face, kissing her palm. "All I could see was the top of your head and your hands when I first met you," he said. "While the mehndi painter worked, you were looking down at your wrists as if you were making an offering."

The mehndi had taken place almost a month ago; the patterns on Maya's hands had faded, the only ink that remained was in random splotches stuck to the wrinkles in her wrists. She rested her palm against Raki's cheek. The most important thing she knew about him was that he saw her this way, as something good that was fated, inevitable. As a gift from the gods, almost, a blessing. The sound of bells ringing came from the coffee table, where Maya had left her phone, somewhere under one of the photos of the beach.

"A bit early to call, isn't it?" Raki asked, stretching alongside her.

"Ignore it, it's my mother's ring." Maya stretched her arms above her head, looked at the alarm clock. "Seven forty-seven; I have to be at the hospital by nine."

"Bollocks." Raki leapt out of bed and crawled around the floor, looking for his boxers. "I have to be at the office by nine, and I've got to go home and shower first."

"You could shower here." Maya cringed as Raki pulled the duvet onto the floor, exposing her naked body, as well as his underwear, which had migrated to the far corner of the bed. She rolled over onto her stomach, shy in the morning light, wondering when she'd last shaved her legs.

"Love to," Raki said, slapping her butt before reaching for the boxers. The sting of the strike made her yelp. Raki kissed the red mark left by his hand. "But I don't have clean clothes here, and I can't be wearing the same suit and shirt as yesterday."

Maya pulled the duvet up over herself and turned to look at Raki, now tucking his shirt into his pants. "Who would have guessed you'd end up staying over?"

"I did." Raki grinned, then leaned in, pulled down the duvet, and kissed her collarbone. "But I thought it would look presumptuous to bring a toothbrush." He put on his jacket, while Maya tried to decide whether she was insulted or amused. "Maybe I'll bring a few things over after work tonight," he said, walking to the door.

Maya arrived at the hospital pleased to be only seven minutes late. She had taken too long in the shower, washing a body that looked different, as if she'd never seen it before. She had shaved her legs now that there was someone to notice, and lingered too long, fascinated by the curve of her calf, the way her second toe was longer than her first. She had wanted to touch up her chipped toenail polish, to call Heidi and tell her about last night, but she refrained, and now here she was, practically on time.

"Unit director's looking for you," a nurse said as she picked up her paperwork, and Maya was suddenly aware of her still-wet hair, leaving damp marks all over her blue button-down. She had bought the shirt because she thought it looked professional, and it did, but not with a wet streak like an arrow pointing to her left breast. She pulled a cardigan over her shoulders to camouflage any spots and knocked on the unit director's door.

"Maya," he said. "Come in." He didn't stand up behind his desk and she was glad there would be no shaking of his clammy hand, wondering when it was safe to pull her fingers away. "Late start? Jet lag a problem I'm sure, what with being gone so long."

"I've been back almost three weeks." Maya sat in the chair at which he'd nodded. "My internal clock may be just a little off from all the overnights I've been working."

"Yes, well, it's important to always be one hundred percent, top of our game," he said. Or at least that's what Maya thought he said, it was one of his favorite phrases. But she couldn't be sure those were the actual words. She was distracted by the soreness between her legs, the kind of ache that didn't hurt but made her feel strong, like when she worked out harder than usual. Crossing her legs, she looked up at the unit director and noticed that he'd stopped speaking. He had taken his glasses off and was staring at her, his lips slightly parted, waiting for her answer, just as he had during their interview after asking her what her strengths and weaknesses were. It was clearly her turn to say something. Maya nodded and opted for, "Well, yes."

"I thought you'd be more pleased." He rested his hand on his chin, his pointer finger along his nose; it seemed to be his thinking face—he must have made it all the time back in medical school.

"I'm just taking it all in," Maya responded finally. The unit director still said nothing. "So when did this happen?" she added.

"It became official this morning, but our lawyers say the Eslecks' counsel has been recommending this for weeks. Seems the building went co-op in the new year and this litigation could be grounds to kick Mrs. Esleck out, rehash all the reasons she's a problem neighbor. Took the daughter this long to see it's in her best interest to make this lawsuit go away."

"It's settled?" Maya stood, then sat again when she saw the unit director staring up at her. "Permanently? No malpractice?" Maya saw her professional future return, just as swiftly and surprisingly as it had been threatened.

"That's what I've been explaining, Maya. It was a frivolous lawsuit, completely without merit. I don't know what possessed those people. But still, it was a serious allegation, so it's a minor miracle to have it gone." He stood now, and glanced at his watch. "And a good reminder that we can't let ourselves get overtired, we must be in top form to make the kind of decisions we do, in the interest of our patients' mental health." He extended his hand; Maya grabbed it between both of hers and stood clasping it, neither of them moving their conjoined hands up or down. "Yes, well," the unit director said, pulling his hand from between hers. "I trust from now on we all will strive to be—"

"At the top of my game, yes, of course. Thank you." Maya stood again. "I'm very pleased." On her way out the door, realizing it was true, she said, softly but aloud, "Although, I must say, not entirely surprised." Aware of how smug that could sound, Maya turned to look at the unit director, to make sure he hadn't heard her. But he had put his glasses back on and was reassembling the materials in a folder marked ESLECK. His head was bent over his work, revealing a bald spot on which Maya felt strangely compelled to plant a kiss. She hurried away, closing the door behind her.

It was as if by repeating the words, the unit director had been intoning a spell that did put Maya, finally, at the top of her game. Or maybe it was just a post-sex high, the dopamine and oxytocin sailing around in her brain circuits. Or the thrill of this most recent proof that the curse was really, truly gone, a thought she kept repeating in her mind, again and again. Either way, her shift seemed to pass in a few blissful seconds, as if Maya were starring in a movie montage about a competent "lady doctor" as Pops would call her, floating through a benevolent institution healing people to the tune of some bhangra soundtrack. She had briskly dispatched with patients from therapy appointments to med consults, then, on her way home, efficiently ducked into Whole Foods, where she surveyed the aisles, buying ingredients for tonight's dinner and talking on her cell phone.

"How much heeng in the gutta recipe?" Maya asked her mother. She could hear popping through the phone lines, which meant Seema was deep frying, pakoras probably. Maya could picture her frowning at the vegetables in the pan as they spat hot oil at her.

"A tiny bit only. Much more haldi, for color. But you will find it too difficult to roll the chickpea flour, Maya," Seema said. "Get gutta at a Rajasthani restaurant; Indian food is so plentiful near you.

And not at all expensive. Why waste your time? Cook something you know, like aloo mutter."

"Good call," Maya said, pulling turmeric off the shelf, and heading to the snaking line with all the ingredients for gutta in her basket.

"So it is now that you remember you have a mother, when you want help," Seema continued. "I leave a message in the morning, you do not call until you need my tips."

Maya laughed; she had never heard her mother use the word "tips," which sounded so women's magazine, so Food Network. Had her parents gotten cable?

"I went in early." Maya didn't stammer as she usually did when lying to Seema. "But, listen, the best news, the malpractice suit has been dropped."

"That was something ridiculous anyway." Seema sighed; she must have finished her task, and would be turning off the stove, pulling two plates down from the cabinet, one for her to eat off of now, one she'd put in the oven for Pops to retrieve when he was done reading the paper. "It could not have succeeded in court."

"But it still would have been a nightmare." Back in the dark days after Priya's miscarriage, Maya's work at the hospital was the only thing that had made her feel she had a purpose. She hadn't let herself think about how much the possibility of her job being taken away would have devastated her, wiped out all those years of school, all the people she had tried to help, and those she still wanted to. Even now it made her pulse rate rise to think about it. She needed to focus on something happier, like dinner. Maya placed her ten items or less on the checkout counter, confident that the teenager with three earrings in one ear wouldn't notice there were really eleven. "I should go to that temple in Queens and leave something at the Lakshmi altar."

"This would be a nice thing, to go to the temple." Seema paused.

Maya waited for the criticism or the warning, whatever Seema might choose to deflate the joy of the moment. "But?"

"But nothing. There is no but."

"Everything's okay? You're sure you're all right; Pops, too?"

"Perfectly fine, the both of us. Do not be so dramatic, Maya! Life is not a movie." Seema swallowed something, water maybe. "Will you go to Queens alone?"

"It's not far."

"It might be nice to bring a friend."

"Like Heidi?"

"Heidi. Or a friend who might be going to a temple anyway." Seema chewed, making a satisfied noise, as if she were pleased with her handiwork. "When is Amrita's cousin due back, the one you girls were so friendly with at the wedding?"

"Cousin? You mean Raki?"

"Yes, that is the one."

Maya bit her lip to keep from laughing. "He's been back, Ma. We've actually had dinner already." Maya waited but Seema said nothing to fill the silence, and she wasn't going to speak herself and risk making a misstep.

"Perhaps the next time you see him," Seema said finally, "you should let him walk you home, offer him a chai, not march straight into a cab, hurry-burry."

"Do you think so?" Outside the store, Maya leaned against the cold glass wall to concentrate; she had to record this exact conversation in her mind to repeat to Heidi later.

"Maybe," Seema said, stretching it out as if it were two words. "An American boy might... mistake the invitation. But he is a relation of Amrita's, he would not do something disrespectful." The sound of Seema chewing filled the phone lines for a few seconds. "And you are my sensible girl. You would not do anything stupid."

"Maybe I will, Ma. May. Be," Maya said. "I'll let you eat dinner." She walked through the February air, warmed by her mother's statement, which was almost a compliment.

•   •   •

"Amazing," Raki said later that night, carrying the empty bowls from the coffee table to the sink.

"Ma said not to bother, I'd never be able to do it." Maya stretched on the couch.

"She knows you were having me for dinner?" The dishes clanged.

"She knows I've seen you," Maya said. "And she knows I eat dinner."

"Aah, it's the 'having me' part she doesn't quite want to acknowledge." Raki walked over to the couch and knelt on the rug so he'd be eye level with Maya. "No problem, keep me in the dark; I understand. It's too painful to think of her precious baby alone with a dashing gent like myself, plying her with wine well after midnight."

"Is it that late?" Maya stood and walked to the bathroom. "I've got to get up early tomorrow; the unit director's keeping an eye on me."

"Why?" Raki appeared in the door, speaking loudly so she could hear him above the running water as she washed her face. "You said everything was fine now. No lawsuit brought forth by a diseased old crone in a cat's hair coat."

Maya patted her face dry with a washcloth so that she wouldn't have to look at him. She had told him all about the EPU over dinner; she was so excited that the lawsuit had been dropped, and she wanted to impress him with how competent she was, how she dealt with serious, life-altering situations all day, and wasn't some flighty sitcom character who made a habit of jumping into bed with strangers when she wasn't saving lives or cooking gourmet South Asian cuisine. But she'd wanted him to be quietly impressed, not to store her successes and failures, other people's tragedies, for his *Fawlty Towers* quips. Maya tossed the washcloth into the hamper and turned off the water.

"The lawsuit has been dropped, hasn't it?" Raki said.

"It has." Maya spread toothpaste on her brush. "But you know, somehow, it's still my fault. My name was on it." She shrugged and started brushing her teeth until Raki rested a hand on her wrist, gently pulling the brush out of her mouth. Maya spat in the sink, not knowing what else to do.

"Do you want me to talk to the director?"

Maya put down her toothbrush. "No!" she said, almost yelled, at the thought of the unit director turning his parted-lip listening face on Raki. She knew she should tell Raki that she was a big girl, that she could handle this herself. That it was none of his business. But she wanted it to be his business.

She had come home crying once in fifth grade, after Sister Theodore explained where unsaved souls go. Maya didn't want to tell her parents about purgatory—they probably hadn't learned about it in India, didn't know what was going to happen to them—so she told Seema she was upset because she had a difficult religion class. "Did you misbehave?" Seema asked. "Talk back to your teacher?" Maya had shaken her head no. "Did you try your best?" Maya had nodded yes. "Well, then," Seema said, chopping a potato, "there is not a thing to cry about." Later, Maya told Priya what happened, and Priya said Sister "Theo-whore" had dementia, and that wherever Maya went after she died, none of them were saved so at least the whole family would be together. But not even Priya had ever offered to go into school to stand up for Maya.

"Thank you, though," Maya said to Raki, abandoning her toothbrush in the sink.

Chapter Eighteen

Saturday night at OM, Maya spotted Heidi as soon as she walked through the door. She was wearing a loose halter-neck dress made from silver-embroidered purple sari fabric; the parts a tailor in Jodhpur would have used to make the blouse's armbands Heidi had fashioned into a mandarin collar.

"Is Walker coming?" Maya kissed Heidi on both cheeks.

Heidi shrugged. "You know how I said he's been so busy lately?"

Maya nodded.

"Well, I'm getting the picture that it's going to be a permanent situation; he's always going to be polite, but just a little too busy to see me."

"He's an idiot," Maya said, putting her hand on Heidi's arm. And he was, especially if he was dropping Heidi out of some eighth-grade solidarity to Scott. And if he was, then this brush-off was, a little bit, Maya's fault.

"I totally know what happened," Heidi announced.

"What?" Could Heidi, too, think this was Maya's fault? Or that it pointed back to last year's losses, when Parvati took away everything that was new and good? Maya was trying to move forward, onward and upward into a better future. She wasn't prepared for Heidi to dredge the curse up out of a past she'd rather forget, not now when everything was going so well.

"The last time we talked he said I was too preoccupied with the business." Heidi caressed her collar. "And I realized, he wants a mannequin, not a designer. Christie Brinkley, not Coco Chanel." She shrugged and Maya put her hand on Heidi's shoulder; she looked so confident, as brave and bright as Maya herself was beginning to feel. "Some men just can't handle a woman with talent."

"Then he's an even bigger idiot." Maya touched the embroidery at Heidi's neck. "This is amazing."

"You like it? It's a prototype for Syma. We're starting the line small, but I can get a whole travel wardrobe out of the fabric for one salwar suit—dress, top, and capri pants, and the dupatta goes with both ensembles."

"What did you call it? The line?"

"Syma." Heidi shook her head at Maya as if she had told her this countless times, and started muscling her way toward the bar. But Maya knew she hadn't forgotten, been too distracted by her own preoccupations, this time. She'd spent hours talking about the line with Heidi, suggesting advertising venues in desi magazines, lending her Bollywood videos for inspiration. No, the name was definitely news.

Maya grabbed her elbow. "You're naming the line Seema? Like, after Ma?"

"With a *y*. S-Y-M-A," Heidi said as if speaking to a particularly slow child. "Partly for Seema-auntie, and partly for my paternal grandmother, Asymina."

"But Ma only wears lab coats or cardigans—and they're usually stained!" Maya buttoned and unbuttoned her velvet blazer, repeating, "Lab coat. Cardigan. Lab coat."

"So?" Heidi asked. "She's a strong woman. And it sounds vaguely ethnic. I'm going to branch out if this takes off, Mexican embroidery, crochet from Greece. Cooperatives everywhere." She sucked on her cocktail straw. "Delusions of grandeur?"

"No!" Maya insisted. "Brilliant business plan." And it was, even if Heidi didn't seem to appreciate that it was Maya who'd introduced her to India, not Seema. The line could have been named Maya, which was poetic after all; it meant illusion! Maya liked to think she had her own distinctive style, the best she could do given the constraints of her job and income. At least, she thought as Raki walked toward her, grinning, someone seemed to like her look.

"Here she is!" Raki threw his left arm around Maya's shoulder and kissed her.

"Right by the bar, as usual," Maya said.

"Vijay, this is Heidi." Raki pointed his glass in her direction and nodded toward the light-skinned guy at this side. "And this is my girlfriend, Maya."

At the word "girlfriend," Heidi's eyes widened and Maya took a sip of her vodka tonic so she could lower her gaze. Girlfriend. So she wasn't a cheap slut after all.

"Maya's a doctor, you know," Raki said. "Shrinks heads; better be careful what you say to her." Vijay laughed. "She had this one patient who thought she—"

"Drink, Vijay?" Maya asked; good girlfriends were accomplished *and* solicitous.

"Black Label if they have it, thanks. And a Cosmo and a G and T if you manage to get the barman's attention—the girls are trying to nab a banquette. They sent me up, but it's impossible for a guy to get a drink here."

"I hate this place," Raki agreed.

"But since we can't go to World anymore…" Vijay slapped Raki's shoulder.

"I love World!" Heidi said. "Great DJ."

"Yeah, but ever since Raki punched the bouncer—"

"He started it, yaar," Raki said, taking a sip.

Maya studied him from behind her drink. Was the punch a onetime thing or was the aggressive acting out part of an ego-syntonic pattern? Maybe there was a genetic component? Raki's mother seemed sweet and meek, the opposite of Amrita's mom, she was the middle sister if Maya remembered correctly. But she wasn't sure she had met the dad; he ran some factories in Chennai and had only come for the day of the wedding. What went on with that side of the family? Now that Raki was her boyfriend, these things mattered. She had to be clear-eyed about this, she couldn't let the fact that she was making love to him trick her into thinking she was actually in love with him already. His South Indian mother, his certainty, Seema's approval; all signs pointed to him being the one, but she was too savvy to let herself be completely convinced this early in the relationship.

"Hmm." Vijay accepted a drink from Maya while Raki signaled the bartender to put it on his tab. "I don't remember him taking a swing at you."

"No, but he called Indira a trashy bitch, didn't he?" Raki said, helping Vijay collect the glasses.

"A *trampy* bitch, I believe." Vijay cracked up. "Her fault for dating the help."

Maya laughed, too, not at Vijay's snobbery, but at her insta-analysis of Raki, as if he were a patient brought to the EPU by the police, when it turned out all he'd been doing was being chivalrous, standing up for a friend.

They didn't get back to Maya's place until after four in the morning. Heidi had left at two thirty or so, after chatting up Vijay and several girls who seemed excited about the thought of being muses, guinea pigs, and potential clients for Syma. Maya would have happily headed home then, too, but Raki seemed to be having such a good time with Vijay and Indira, and she didn't want him to have it without her. Even when they got home he was in high spirits, lighting candles around the apartment to create what he called "ambience," repeating the word again and again in a funny French accent.

"What's this then?" Raki asked as Maya was slipping on a silky nightgown—one of three she'd bought in the last week, after Heidi insisted that the new, post-curse Maya had to dress for her new, romantic life. When she turned he was standing by her window, having lit the candle in her altar, holding the statue she had tripped on in the river.

"It's Lakshmi," Maya said, smiling mysteriously to mirror the expression on the statue. "She removed the curse."

"Of course she did, darling."

Maya couldn't think of a nice way to tell him she hated being called darling, it made her feel like Princess Di, and look how she ended up.

"No, really, she did. I found her on New Year's Day, or she found me. She washed up to me in the Ganges. And look what's happened since." Maya took a step toward Raki. As if her movement had somehow triggered the motion, he dropped the statuette on the floor. Maya knelt over Lakshmi, feeling like she was going to throw up although she had stopped drinking hours ago.

"So sorry!" Raki crouched down to her level. "I twigged for a moment. That river's filthy, this probably has all kinds of flesh-eating bacteria in it."

"She was bringing me luck," Maya said, running her finger down Lakshmi's face.

"Darling, you don't need to believe that." Raki stood and walked behind Maya, put his arms around her, and started lifting her off the ground. "You did med school, you're a proper doctor. You can't really buy into all of that silliness." He squeezed her a little tighter. "Besides, you don't need Lakshmi for luck now, you've got me."

Maya let herself be lifted. She did have him now. That much was true, and different from her old life. Better. He kissed her and she told herself that a living, breathing protector was better than a hundred made of clay and bacteria.

"Let's get it back in the window and go to bed." Raki reached for Lakshmi, but Maya stepped across the room to wrap her in a T-shirt and place her in the bottom drawer of the dresser, which had some room in it now that Scott's things had been removed.

"Let's not put her back yet." Maya brushed her thumb against the stump where Lakshmi's upturned hand had shattered on impact with the floor. "She needs fixing."

The next morning, when Maya finally woke, close to noon, Raki was gone. In the silence of the apartment, the realization came to her: she had scared him away with her curse and her craziness. She'd been trying to hide the truth, but he wasn't stupid, he obviously realized that she was diseased, or, at best, temporarily damaged, like the Lakshmi statuette. She heard footsteps in the hall and wondered which of her neighbors were coming home after a night at their significant other's. Her neighbors were functional people; they could maintain relationships. Then her lock clicked and her door opened and there was Raki with a cardboard tray of coffees and a crumpled paper sack in one hand and a glossy gift bag in the other.

"Bagels," he said, putting the bag on the table. "And coffee for the lady." He handed her a paper cup with pictures of statues on it; Greek goddesses. One was missing her arms from just below the shoulder; she was even more maimed than Lakshmi, but still worshipped, sort of. At least in delis and diners.

"I would have made you coffee here, silly." Maya took a sip and the warm liquid flooded her esophagus, along with her gratitude that he'd returned.

"But then I couldn't have gotten this." Raki handed her the gift bag.

The box inside was covered in white paper and had a sprig of dried rosemary tucked into its matching white bow. White was the color of widows' saris, but on this glossy box it looked minimalist, expensive. Maya never paid for gift-wrap, just took boxes home and wrapped them herself in bright orange and fuchsia paisley paper that was appropriate for any occasion.

"Don't just stare at it; open it."

"But why?"

Raki shrugged. "I felt bad about last night."

Maya tore off the paper, opened the box, and lifted out an orange enamel Buddha. It felt cold to her touch.

"The woman at ABC Carpet and Home said it was their bestseller. Like it?"

"It's lovely." She stared at the Buddha, willing him to warm up in her hands. "But," she added, slowly, "I'm not Buddhist."

"'Course not!" Raki kissed the top of her head. "You're my own Hindu goddess. I just thought it'd add color to the windowsill." He lifted the figure out of her hands and set it next to her altar, where Nanaji seemed to stare at Buddha quizzically from his photo.

Chapter Nineteen

At South Station in Boston, Maya asked a businessman furiously texting on his BlackBerry if he'd be willing to watch her bag while she went to the bathroom. He'd nodded, but hadn't even looked up from his thumbs. Someone could easily swoop in and take her wallet, the gifts for the children that were already wrapped, making them look so much more desirable than the meager puzzle and spin-art kit no thief would want. Raki should have been here with her. One of the best things about being part of a couple was having someone to share the business of life, to watch your bag at the train station. But Raki said he had to work late on Friday, and it would be too tiring to go to Chestnut Hill for just one night. That may have been true, but it was also an excuse; she'd heard him on his cell, making plans with friends from B-school who were flying in for the Holi party at OM on Saturday; the club had an event to celebrate the festival of colors each spring, and for the expat elite it was unmissable.

"You'll be so busy, you won't even notice I'm not there," he said last night, when it became clear he really wasn't coming. "And I'll spend every Holi for the rest of our lives with your family." That's when she'd stopped arguing. They'd been together over two months, three if you started counting from the night on the roof at Indigo, which Maya did. Maya counted every day that passed, hoarded each one as proof that this relationship was something real, her happy ending. She'd told Priya he would probably come; that was a bit premature, she saw now. He wanted to come, of course, it was just bad timing. She shouldn't have been so presumptuous, but she was eager to introduce Raki to her family, to fit him into them and make them complete like when she and Priya used to play Lincoln Logs and Priya would let her drop on the cheery red chimney as a finishing touch to their creation.

The businessman couldn't even bring himself to nod when Maya returned, but everything was still in her bag. She pulled out her phone. There was a text from Raki saying, *Hope you had a nice ride. Love you.* On the curb Tariq sat waiting in their tan Highlander; he started honking maniacally as soon as she stepped out of the terminal.

"I've had to circle four times," he said, hugging her and throwing her bag in the back. "Your sister's been calling nonstop, she's holding dinner for you."

"It's not my fault the train left late. Ma didn't come?"

"She's watching the kids while Priya finishes cooking."

"Pops?"

"Holi-proofing the basement in case it's too cold for the yard tomorrow; we devised a great plan." Tariq rattled on about plastic tablecloths and water-soluble dyes until they pulled up to the house, but Maya was too anxious to listen to him. She hadn't seen the whole family together since before the curse. It felt as if they had all been through a war, but fighting on different fronts; they had won, but she didn't know who would be scarred and how seriously. She wanted to ask Tariq about Pops's energy level, if Priya seemed depressed, but they were already pulling up to the house.

"Maya-masi!" Nisba yelled when Maya cracked the door. As soon as she got it open, a spray of fuchsia powder hit Maya in the face, leaving a trail of alien stab wounds down the front of her off-white coat.

"Nisba!" Maya yelled and dropped to her knees in the doorway, grabbing her niece so that the hot pink powder the five-year-old held in a little round tin fell all over her dimpled arms, her Little Mermaid pajamas, and Priya's beige carpet. "You don't play Holi until everyone else is ready! Look what you did. Now you have to wait until tomorrow to get the present I brought, to show me you can be patient."

Nisba burst into tears as Yasmin skittered around the corner in an Aladdin nightgown. "Do *I* get my present now, Masi?" She leaned over and kissed Maya on the cheek. Pops appeared from the kitchen door and picked up the bawling Nisba. "Your masi didn't mean it, beti," he crooned, covering Nisba's tear-stained face with kisses.

"In or out," Tariq's voice boomed from behind Maya as he tried to enter the house with her bag. She followed Pops and the girls into the kitchen.

"Maya!" Priya stormed in and flung open the cabinet under the sink, ignoring Maya's open arms. "You're here five minutes and already my kids are sobbing and my house is destroyed."

"So's my damn coat!" Maya followed Priya into the foyer, her arms full of spray bottles.

"No D-A-M-N in front of the little ones," Pops said, still carrying Nisba.

"We'll dry-clean your coat," Priya huffed.

"Damn straight."

"Language!" Pops yelled as Yasmin, clinging to his leg, giggled.

"It looks like Barbie threw up on me. And I don't have a fancy private practice to buy myself extra coats, or a husband to run my things to the cleaners."

"Oh, shut up, Maya." Priya threw a dish towel at her. Maya picked it up and started scrubbing the foam-covered floor while Yasmin jumped up and down, shouting, "Daddy!" But Tariq had gone back to encasing the playroom in plastic; the occasional reassuring click of a staple gun could be heard from the basement. Standing at the top of the stairs, Yasmin yelled, "Mommy said 'shut up.'"

"They're overexcited because of all the guests," Priya muttered.

"They have no impulse control because no one gives them boundaries," Maya countered. "They've been trained to expect immediate gratification."

"When you have kids—*if* you ever have kids"—Priya scrubbed the floor even harder—"then you can give advice."

"Right, it's not like I study human behavior all day every day or anything," Maya said. "I'm just a mental health professional, not an all-knowing *mother.*"

"Oh, and I'm sure withholding gifts and affection is the latest behavior modification technique."

"Maya!" Seema's voice rang from the top of the stairs, where she appeared in a clean, if faded, sari, her cell phone slung into the waistband of its petticoat, within easy reach, the off-duty equivalent of the stethoscope she kept tucked into her lab coat's pocket at the hospital. "You have arrived. Come give your old mother a hug." She started down the stairs, shaking her head back and forth as she surveyed her granddaughter, hands still covered in fuchsia powder, sobbing in her husband's arms, and her daughters on their knees attacking a frothing patch of carpet. "I leave these girls alone for two minutes to rinse my face and—"

"You didn't have another nosebleed?" Wiping her hands free of foam, Maya walked toward Seema and threw her arms around her.

"Not for months, silly girl." Seema patted Maya's back three times to indicate the hug was over, then stepped back and started unbuttoning Maya's stained coat. "We will soak this in the tub until it is time for the girls' bath," she said. "And *if* they are well behaved during dinner and bathtime, afterwards, Maya, you will give them the gifts you have brought. Only if."

Maya glared at Priya, triumphant, but Priya was smirking right back. "That's right, just ask Dr. Spock," Priya gloated. If Seema was on board with Maya's child-raising techniques, they must be damaging, or, at the very least, outdated.

Seema took Maya's coat and turned down the hall. "Ajit," she said with her back to her family. "Put down that child; you should not be lifting."

After dinner, after the girls had had their baths and their gifts, after one aborted crying fit on the part of Nisba, who seemed to be going through a needy phase and insisted on sitting on Ajit's lap throughout the meal, and Maya's conciliatory reading aloud from *Everybody Poops,* Maya went to check on her coat. It was hanging from the shower curtain rack in the master bathroom, restored to all its creamy glory, as Seema passed up and down it with a blow-dryer, gripping the appliance with two hands, raising it above her head to reach the collar. Maya didn't think she'd ever seen her mother wield a blow-dryer before. She had never used one herself until the sixth grade when Priya gave her a cast-off, having bought a fancy new dryer at the salon. And she knew Seema believed in air-drying; on Saturday mornings when Maya was very little and everyone else was asleep, she was allowed to help Seema unwind her braid before she washed her two and a half feet of hair in the tub. Then Seema would bustle about, cleaning the house, cooking lunch, with her hair drying in long black ribbons. Maya had forgotten how powerful her mother had looked then, with her hair free, like a goddess, invulnerable, a divine being who would never bleed.

"Good as new." Seema patted the front of the coat. "Why pay for a dry clean?"

The creamy front was pristine, but Maya suspected that the coat would smell of wet wool from now on. "It's great, Ma," she said, sitting on the lid of the toilet while Seema continued to inspect the coat, buttoning its buttons.

"Your friend from the wedding was not able to come?" Seema asked.

Maya stood and faced the bathroom mirror to inspect her brows; she had stopped by Lovely Perfect Shape Salon two nights ago after work, and had them threaded by a woman who reminded her of Seema. The technician tapped her roughly on the cheek if Maya didn't hold her eyelid tight enough, and patted her on the shoulder when she was done, blowing on Maya's eyebrows to make the lotion dry quicker. "No. He really wanted to, but he has cousins in town for Holi."

"They could have come also!"

"To this madhouse?" Maya turned to reach for the coat, but Seema was folding it carefully, her back to her daughter.

"But you are still... spending time together?"

"Yes, Ma." The bathtub was full of water the color of cheap rosé. Maya didn't want her mother to have to put her arm into the pink pool, so she plunged her hand in and yanked out the plug.

"I'm glad." Seema placed a towel on the radiator, and the coat on top of it.

"Because he's Indian."

"Because I want you to have someone." Seema leaned against the sink. "I do not like to think of you alone in that big, dirty city. Alone in your life."

Maya looked down at the swirling bathtub and used both hands to push the water toward the whirlpool at the drain. "I know, it's your karmic duty."

"Out of all my children," Seema continued as if she hadn't heard Maya, "you were the most easy in the world; you talked to people, laughed the most. Mohan and Priya were so quiet when they started school, all big eyes, you would think they had no mouths at all to speak with. But you . . . I thought it was because you were born here, the first real American. But your father said it was due to his bringing me a pomegranate every week when I was pregnant with you, so you became like the seeds, sweet and abundant."

Maya looked at the tub as the last trail of pink water swirled away, then picked up a sponge and started scrubbing, although it had barely left a ring. She knew if she spoke, she'd cry, but she didn't know if it was because of affection or anger. Dadiji had seen her this way—confident, easy with people as Seema said. But when Dadiji died, that version of Maya seemed to die with her. When her mother looked at her, Maya always felt Seema was seeing someone who came up short, didn't wear the right salwar or use the correct spice in the dal. She assumed Seema considered her the opposite of easy. Why had her mother never told her about the pomegranates before? That even before she was born Seema was trying to guarantee that Maya's life would be full of sweetness. If Maya ever had a child to think such thoughts about she would tell her, every day.

"I never predicted you would be the one to have difficulty finding someone to share your life with," Seema continued. "But it has been so. You will be thirty in not so long. And now—"

"Now that you've found someone, hurry up and snag him!" Priya crowed, coming into the room. "I know Ma says she met him, but this guy is like Snuffleupagus. Wasn't he supposed to be here? You say my girls are whiny brats when they don't get what they want, but maybe the apples don't fall far from the auntie?"

"Lovely," Seema said, making the nickname sounded like a warning.

Priya lifted the coat off the radiator and shook it free from its folds. "Are you trying to start a fire?" She leaned in the doorway, glancing at the label inside the collar and then back at Maya, who sat on the edge of the tub, the sponge still in her hand. "Such drama over a stupid Forever 21 coat. Who buys a white coat anyway? No one with kids, no one who has a husband to cook for, dishes to do."

Maya glared at her sister in her too-snug velour tracksuit. "Yeah, about the cooking," she said. "Maybe it's time to look into low-cal?" She glanced over at Seema, expecting to see the warning head wobble, but her mother had covered her hand with her mouth and started shaking.

"I'm not fat, Maya." Priya started laughing, too, had to lean against the towel rack her body was shaking so hard.

Maya blinked and looked at her sister. "Really?" She stood up. Priya nodded.

"Really?" Maya asked again. She took a breath. "How far along?"

"Sixteen weeks."

Seema put her hand on the edge of the sink to steady herself; she seemed to be giggling. "*Second* trimester," she clarified, as if both her daughters weren't doctors.

"We're waiting to tell the girls until we have to." Priya glanced down at her abdomen. "Which, apparently, is soon. But everything looks good so far."

Maya dropped the sponge into the bathtub. So it wasn't just herself whom the Ganges had purified; for Priya and their parents, the curse had ended. This was proof.

"Maya!" Seema said sharply. "Are you not going to hug your sister?"

"Oh!" Maya rushed toward Priya, her hands still trailing pink drops.

"The coat!" Priya yelled, holding it out in front of her. "Watch out for the precious coat." Maya hugged her with such ferocity that Priya finally let go of the coat, which fell to the tiled floor. It only rested there a minute before Seema rescued it, folded it tight, and carried it out of the room.

Dressed in almost-outgrown clothes, Nisba and Yasmin were still eating their pancakes when the doorbell rang on Saturday morning. Priya looked up from the griddle, then over at Maya, raising her perfectly shaped brows.

"I'm going." Maya pushed her chair back as loudly as she could. She opened the door to see Mohan holding Vivek on his hip, smiling at his son, whose fist was raised, ready to rap at the door again.

"Vivek!" Maya kissed her nephew's tightly curled little hand and lifted the two-and-a-half-year-old out of Mohan's arms.

"Yasmin?" the boy asked.

"In the kitchen." She set him down and he toddled off.

"Well, he's thrilled to see me." Maya hugged her brother, who still smelled of his son's oddly pleasant, sour-milk breath.

"Yasmin sent him some of her old toys, that's all. We've been practicing saying thank you." Mohan shrugged. "Sharing is hard."

"Sharing *is* hard," Maya agreed. At first she thought Mohan's hair must have gone grayer, he looked so much older than the last time she'd seen him. But no, he still had just the same subtle sprinkling of gray that made Heidi call certain men "silver foxes"; it was the deepening line between his brows that aged him.

"No more bags in the car?" Maya asked, following Mohan into the foyer. "You left the baby in D.C. with Shalini?"

"I'm right here," said a voice behind Maya. She turned toward her sister-in-law, who was toting the baby in a car seat as if it were a basket of muffins.

Maya wanted to glance at Mohan to get some sort of clue as to what their next move as a couple—or individuals—would be, but Shalini was too clever not to notice something like that. She swayed in place for a minute, almost imperceptibly, then stepped toward Shalini. "You look amazing," she said, kissing her sister-in-law's jutting cheekbone. "And the baby!" Maya reached toward the sleeping infant.

"Don't," Shalini said, in a firm, low voice. She smiled at Maya. "I've got to bring him to my saas and sasur first."

Maya stared at Shalini to see if she looked older, too, but no, her face was flawless as ever, her waist was tiny again and her breasts were huge. She didn't even look sleep-deprived, she had that hormone-flushed glow of certain thin and impeccably dressed mom friends of Priya's whom Priya pretended to like but whom Maya knew she secretly hated.

"So where are they?" Shalini asked again.

"Out back. In the yard, getting ready for Holi."

"Thanks! I'll bring the baby back soon." Shalini strolled past Maya with her precious cargo. "Just trying to be a proper Indian wife!"

As soon as Maya could no longer hear the click of Shalini's pumps on Priya's hardwood floors, she stepped closer to Mohan. "It's all systems go with the move?" she whispered.

"Obviously," Mohan said. "I'm looking for work in New Orleans. If I find something okay, we'll relocate. If I don't right away, she'll move first with the kids and I'll come when I get work. What she does is so much more important, on all levels."

"And you're sure that—"

"That what, Maya? That I want to watch my kids grow up? Yeah, I'm sure." He started walking toward the kitchen.

"But—" Maya grabbed his elbow.

"This is a good thing." Mohan let her hand rest on his arm for a minute before heading toward the kitchen again. And Maya told herself he was right. After all, even in a post-curse world, life couldn't be perfect. It was enough for it not to be horrible.

An hour later, wearing faded yoga pants and a T-shirt destined for the bag of cast-offs in her apartment waiting to be taken to Bellevue, Maya threw a handful of orange powder at Priya. Seema had decreed that it was warm enough to play Holi in the backyard, at least for a little bit. Holi had been Maya's favorite holiday as a kid, the one time it was safe to make a mess, run around, stop acting like a good daughter. Priya's daughters seemed to feel the same way, pelting their mother with peacock-blue powder, their dad with emerald green. Vivek stumbled after them, too little to throw anything, raising his hands in the air to catch the miraculously colored dust. Nisba steered clear of Maya at first, until Maya called her over, revealed her secret weapon—the Tupperware containers she had filled with water—and showed her niece how to mix in the powder so she could douse her parents and grandparents with gem-colored swathes of liquid. Now the girls were splashing everybody, and even Shalini was laughing, hiding behind Mohan for protection. Covered in orange, Mohan looked smooth and young again and Maya remembered how he'd mix Tang for her when their parents took them to India, telling her it was what the astronauts drank.

Running toward her, Priya slammed a sticky hand on Maya's chest to stop herself. "Seems like…you're the cool…aunt again," Priya panted. "But I…taught you…the water trick…first."

"Take it easy," Maya warned. "It's not a race."

"Life's a race." Priya grinned and put her hands on her knees, leaning forward to catch her breath. "Anyway, we're out of water."

Maya looked at the yellow handprint her sister had left on her shirt, and was shocked at how small Priya's palm was, only covering the WA in the WALK FOR WOMEN'S HEALTH emblazoned across her chest. "I'll get more," she said, and ran to the house, dodging color sprays and picking up discarded empty Tupperware.

A few minutes later, Maya walked barefoot through Priya's spotless living room, trying not to spill the water, which was already stained pink from the residue in the container, and stopped short in front of the sliding glass doors. Her hands were wet, splotched with red, yellow, and blue, purple where the colors ran together, and her mouth felt gritty, full of colored, and probably toxic, powder—these were store-bought Holi powders, the Ayurvedic ground herbs her parents had used in India were hard to find here and wildly expensive. She looked down at her stained T-shirt and splattered legs, then around her at the perfect living room, which was all in shades of cream and tan, a café-au-lait minefield that was off-limits to the girls, who were usually relegated to the basement rec room. She couldn't put the containers down anywhere, and if she touched anything here, Priya would never let her forget it. Maya peered through the glass, willing someone to notice her, open the door and let her out. Then she shouted her relatives' names in order of age. The effort strained her throat and made her neck throb, but it was pointless; Priya had splurged on double-glazed panes and Maya could barely even make out the children's shrieks.

On the other side of the glass, Priya had Vivek in one arm and was helping him throw yolk-colored powder at Mohan, who was still doing his best to shield Shalini, who stood on tiptoe like a Barbie awaiting her stilettos. Yasmin and Nisba were attacking Seema, who was openmouthed, shaking with laughter that Maya couldn't hear, but which she suspected was the glorious bursts she remembered so well from the sangeet, not Seema's usual nasal huffs. Pops was chasing after the girls and Maya wanted to tell him not to run so fast, he'd stress his heart, and to make Priya put Vivek down, to warn her to think of the baby. She wanted to freeze her family behind the glass, so she stopped shouting and watched, willing them to keep playing. Soon someone would fall, the children would start crying, and Seema would herd everyone inside. But right now they were riotous, gorgeously reckless, as if they'd forgotten they'd ever been cursed at all. If Raki could see them now, out of breath, splattered in Technicolor stains and dust, he would want to know them, to help her protect them. She wanted to feel that it was his loss, missing this vision, but it felt like it was hers, that if only he'd come she could have given him to her family and shown this perfect version of her family to him, permanently securing his love for them, and for her.

But Raki hadn't come and the moment was already over; Mohan had noticed her and was making his way across the lawn. The water jiggled in the plastic containers and when Maya stepped toward the door a splash leapt over the edge, washed over her hand, and landed on the beige carpet, leaving a tiny, hibiscus-colored spot that clung to the pale carpet fibers and, as much as everyone tried, could never be removed.

Chapter Twenty

"So we're all delighted, you know, at the prospect of a new baby, a new family member," Maya said. "And to me the baby, and Raki, all these new beginnings prove that now the curse is over, and we're moving forward."

Dr. Bernard brought his hand to his face, seeming to push his nose into it. Did he have to sneeze? Was he hiding, laughing at her like she feared he would when he learned about her belief in the curse? She had told him about her triumph in the Ganges shortly after her return; it was too important a moment, an epiphany, not to examine in therapy. And, to be honest, she wanted him to share in her victory, to recognize her ingenuity, how proactive she'd been, how brave. He had said he was pleased she was feeling more positive, but that was it. Maya hadn't seen any recognition of the weight of the moment in his eyes. And he hadn't brought it up since, although it was clearly the most significant turning point she'd mentioned in their sessions so far. She had obviously overestimated his capacity to understand. Better to stick to everyday family dramas, the same type of things he heard from everyone else. "And I'm so glad Priya's having another child; this one will be closer in age to my own kids."

"You haven't mentioned starting a family before." Dr. Bernard cocked his head to the right. It was a judgmental sort of slant. Maya swore she would never tilt so acutely with her own patients.

"I meant someday, in the future," Maya said. Dr. Bernard tilted his head even more sharply. "But why shouldn't I be thinking about having kids?"

"I'm not here to make—"

"You think it's too soon, that Raki and I haven't been together long enough." The truth was, she had never considered Raki as the future father of her children before. He was so ... emphatic about work and his friends and OM, it was impossible to picture him in a tan Highlander, or using a staplegun to Holi-proof the basement. But if he really was the one to end the curse, join her family, and give her the kind of protection and partnership she'd seen in Sanjay and Amrita's circle around the sacred fire, she should start to see him that way. And if Dr. Bernard couldn't, he was just being short-sighted. He didn't even know Raki. Besides, as Heidi had pointed out when Maya hesitated about telling Dr. Bernard how quickly Raki had essentially moved in, it wasn't his job to judge her. After all, he was an old man, Heidi had added, and romance is like prostate cancer—it moves slowly in old men. It's not like Maya cared what Dr. Bernard thought, not that much anyway. "We met right after New Year's," she bargained. "In two weeks it'll be four months. In India, we'd be married in four months, four weeks. Four days, even."

Dr. Bernard cleared his throat.

"I know, we're not in India. If we were, we wouldn't be dating. Definitely not sleeping together. But even here, people are getting married faster these days. If you've read *Us Weekly* lately ..."

Dr. Bernard scratched his nose again. He had to be laughing at her; it was a cool spring this year, still too early for allergies.

"People leave it in the waiting room at the EPU sometimes," Maya explained. "Anyway, with Scott, I was in no rush, I kept telling myself we were waiting for the right time. But there was never going to be a right time, see? With Raki... I just feel like right now is a cosmic reward after the misery of last year. It's like the song says, 'It's been a long, cold, lonely winter.'"

"Here Comes the Sun." Dr. Bernard nodded and scribbled something, but he was humming to himself, which Maya took to be a good sign.

"So if the 'winter' is over, why the urgency to start a family?" Dr. Bernard's head listed left this time. "What makes you think you can't enjoy the 'sunshine,' so to speak, at a pace that might differ from your sister's family planning?"

"There's no urgency," Maya said. "It might be as simple as I found what I want."

"Raki?"

"Raki," Maya echoed. But a part of her still wanted Dr. Bernard to understand completely. "And, to be in love and happy again. And, if I'm being honest, an end to the curse. If we keep adding to this family, then the curse didn't harm us. Part of me does feel that it could come back at any minute. Priya could lose this baby, too, and Pops's heart is a time bomb, and Ma, she knows something's going on with Mohan and Shalini, but she'll never admit it, she'll give herself an ulcer one of these days; if her family isn't making her bleed out of her nose, she'll have to puncture some other organ."

Dr. Bernard nodded. "So the curse itself is over, but the fear of its power still remains?"

Maya sucked the inside of her bottom lip into her canine teeth. He was talking to her like the curse was all an idea in her head. Like she was any other patient, like he thought she was foolish, or worse, crazy. Dr. Bernard returned her stare. There was a red spot in the middle of the otherwise perfectly blue iris of his left eye, just above his pupil. Straight down from it, a constellation of crumbs sat in his beard. She wouldn't tell him.

"You don't get it," she said. "It's not just fear that remains, it's more tangible than that. It's like the curse was a massive tree, and I cut it down. Now it's gone, it's just a stump, but it has roots and who knows how deep they extend and how far they reach?"

Dr. Bernard nodded. Finally, he spoke. "What kind of tree, Maya?"

She laughed. "Dr. Bernard, even Barbara Walters knows that's a ridiculous question now. I don't know, an elm? A birch?" She laughed again. "I guess since it's in India, a peepal tree. No! A banyan. But that would be terrible, its roots grow up as well as down. A tulsi! They're venerated by Brahmins."

"And it was a Brahmin curse." So Dr. Bernard had been paying attention.

"Right! And they affect the blood especially!" Maya beamed at him like he was a particularly bright pupil and she a dedicated kindergarten teacher. And she forced herself to keep smiling, even as she realized what he had been hinting at—a family tree. He thought the curse was her family, that they were the roots that tangled around her, dragging her down. Was he suggesting she abandon her roots to their own, solitary futures? Lock them up in old-age homes and move on with her own shiny new life? Or was he saying that whatever happened to them, bad or good, it was their karma, their fate? No, Dr. Bernard would never think in such mystical terms, he wasn't capable of it. He'd be more likely to believe the horror of last year was the result of their actions and behavioral patterns, that they were a twisted network of individual branches, and roots attached to a diseased trunk, and, ultimately, each of them could do nothing but try and grow straight and strong on his own, even if it meant blocking sunlight from the others.

Both of these options—that the pain and sorrow they had suffered was the result of their inescapable collective fate or their self-destructive tendencies as individuals—were unthinkable. Maya had spent so much time, expended so much energy, on saving her family from their problems, that she couldn't bring herself to consider that they, each of them, had caused this, that they had brought such pain down onto themselves and each other. It was cruel of Dr. Bernard to suggest it. It was one thing if he refused to believe in the reality of the curse; it was another to make her question all she knew. She was eager to end this line of discussion, to get this session over with, so she forced herself to keep smiling at this man whom she now, for this moment anyway, hated.

"I guess I do feel more... urgency, I think you said, today."

He smiled back at her in encouragement.

"And I think it may be because you came to the waiting room for me a full seven minutes early." Inspired, Maya was speaking more rapidly.

"The patient before you canceled." Dr. Bernard leaned back so forcefully that Maya was surprised he didn't propel the chair back to the floor with his weight. "I was reading, I finished an article, it seemed close to the time."

"But you disrupted the therapeutic frame." Maya looked at him the way she would at Nisba if she tracked mud into the house after being told not to play in the puddles. "If the patient before me is the type to cancel, he must have done so some other time. But you've never come early for me in the past. Why today?"

"I don't know," Dr. Bernard said. He was clearly absorbed in pondering, he was about to rub that beard right off his chin. So Maya had won, had made him forget her complicated, even suffocating family dynamic, and, even better, had pointed out his own fallibility. "Perhaps my—" He glanced at his watch, then reconsidered. "You're right, my action may have contributed to a sense of urgency on your part." He looked above Maya, at the trustworthy wall clock with implacable black numbers. "And I should be on time for my two o'clock. Let's continue this next session."

The next morning, Maya felt bruised and a little ashamed, as if she had been sniping at Priya. The sun came through the window behind her bed in insistent beams, and Raki tightened his embrace around her, burrowing his face into her chest. She stroked his head and wondered if she had been too defensive with Dr. Bernard. He was just pushing her to explore her feelings, examine her assumptions. Dr. Bernard was right to press her; it was what he was supposed to do. And she did question her motives, all the time, to make sure that she really felt this connected to Raki, that she wasn't just going through the motions because he was the available Indian guy at the significant moment in her life. Dr. Bernard was just giving her a safe space to discuss her thoughts, and if she had gone along with it, he would have understood her point of view, would have seen that Raki was the right person for her to build a life with. But at the time it had felt like he was questioning too much, trying to make her reject her family and Raki, her past and her future, trying to take this light and warmth away from her and trap her in his dark, musty office that always seemed stuck in the silver-gray glow of a gloomy afternoon. This morning, however, she was able to consider the possibility that the suffocating anger she felt yesterday was just a product of her own resistance. Dr. Bernard was good at what he did, and kind. And he liked the Beatles.

She'd been stroking Raki's head for so long that the gel had softened, given way, and his hair felt soft and thick, as deep as its blue-black color. She started to hum, then to sing "Rocky Raccoon" softly. The words flowed automatically, like sounds that had no meaning, no purpose beyond giving the jaunty tune something to hang on to. She hummed the bars whose words wouldn't come, until they appeared in a rush. "Said Rocky you've met your match, and Rocky said—"

"It's only a scratch." Raki's voice joined hers and he turned to look at her, propping his chin up on her rib cage. "And I'll be better as soon as I'm able" he sang alone, his strong, clear voice filling the sunlit room with sound.

Chapter Twenty-one

On Sunday afternoon Maya was claiming every last minute of her free time, standing on the corner of Forty-fourth and Broadway, holding Raki's hand and leaning into his side. Times Square, with its dazed herds of tourists, was her least favorite part of the city, except on Sundays when the cinema in the Virgin Megastore ran Bollywood movies for a one-day showing. Today was part of a monthlong homage to Shah Rukh Khan, and she was waiting to see *Kal Ho Naa Ho*; she'd missed getting tickets when it was first in town, and worried it would be sold out again. But she was already close to the theater, near the front of a long line of people who looked like her and sounded like her parents.

"Maya!" Heidi called from across the street.

"Heidi? She's coming?" Raki was clearly surprised—and, Maya sensed, not thrilled—to see Heidi, but at least he was polite enough to whisper, although there was no way Heidi could hear him over the lanes of traffic.

"I told you she was coming!" Maya insisted as Heidi darted through cabs like the frog in the arcade game Mohan used to play.

"They're not sold out, are they?" Heidi asked, kissing them both hello. "I'm so ready to learn some new moves." She stood perfectly still and began flashing her eyes from side to side, then wobbling her head a bit to go along with it, humming her favorite Bollywood song. Maya mirrored her until Heidi stopped dancing and swatted at Raki's stomach. "Come on, Raki," Heidi urged. "I know you can dance; I saw you at the sangeet!" At the mention of this seminal moment in their romance, and the reminder that the three of them had been there, together, at the beginning of it, Maya leaned into Raki and reached for Heidi's arm.

"So what's the movie about?" Heidi asked, taking in the slow-moving line.

"There's this Indian girl in New York," Maya started.

"I love it already."

"Her life's tough, dad's dead so absent father, mom's business is failing so depressed mother, grandma's an old bitch, probably resents being hauled to America."

"They always do." Heidi shook her head like a disapproving church secretary.

"Anyway, the girl has this best friend from business school and he's in love with her, but she falls for this mysterious older stranger who moves in next door—that's Shah Rukh—and tells the BFF about it. BFF reports back to mystery guy, mystery guy tells the girl he's married and convinces her to love BFF. Eventually, she meets the older guy's wife, only she's really just his doctor."

"No!" Heidi gasped.

"Yes! See, he's dying of heart disease, and he goes around bringing people together because 'Tomorrow May or May Not Come.' That's what the title means."

"So she marries the B-school guy she doesn't love?" Heidi

grabbed Maya as she moved forward in line so that she would turn and attend to her question.

"You American girls and your true love!" Maya imitated Seema before lapsing into her own voice. "She loves him enough. The other guy's dying. And this guy loves her. It's her karma."

"Tragic!" Heidi said. "I can't wait."

"I think you just saved me three hours; now I no longer need to see the movie." Raki smiled, but it came too late to soften the sharp, curt tone in his voice.

"Come on, the plot was in every movie mag." Maya put her hand on Raki's arm by way of apology. "I want Heidi to be able to follow along."

"The theater's filled with ABCDs," Raki said. He looked at Heidi and explained, "American-Born Confused Desis. There must be subtitles?"

"Of course!" Maya somehow felt she had to defend the Virgin Megastore.

"Good. There's nothing worse than sitting next to someone doing simulcast translation for their seatmate." Raki shuddered.

"Oh, I don't know," mused Heidi. "I can think of a few things. Famine maybe."

Maya laughed and pulled Raki forward with her. "Genocide," she said, and tapped him on the butt, to show she was just teasing.

"All right, all right," Raki said. "Global warming?" He brushed his hand against Maya's cheek.

"I like to know the plot in advance so I can concentrate on the clothes," Heidi explained in the voice she used when she represented the magazine on TV. "As an up-and-coming designer getting ready to launch her long-awaited line, I've got to watch how the women tie their saris, what flowers they tuck into their braids."

"But this takes place in modern times," Raki pointed out. Heidi raised her eyebrows but Raki didn't notice, so Maya supplied the "And?"

"And the only women in India who wear braids anymore are the street-sweepers." He stepped ahead as the line moved forward.

Heidi stared at Raki, then at Maya, then back at Raki, a grotesque reinterpretation of the giddy dance she'd performed a few minutes ago. Maya knew what the look meant and could sense the heat rising to her neck; it made her feel itchy, prickly, how impossible they were both being. Heidi was such a child sometimes, having to explain everything to her was like babysitting Nisba or Yasmin.

"Except, of course..." Heidi paused, staring at Maya again.

"Well, my mom wears a braid, sweetie," Maya said finally.

"But that's totally different!" Raki stood still. "I meant in India! Your mum's lived here forever, she's just being practical."

Heidi kept walking, closing the growing gap in the line.

"I love the way your mum looks," Raki whispered to Maya.

Maya refrained from saying that she was surprised he could remember what Seema looked like, it had been so long since he'd seen her; that would be too mean, and he'd definitely defend himself, and there was no need to get into this now, in front of Heidi. "I know what you meant," she said, instead.

They had almost reached the front of the line when Heidi pointed across the street and yelled, "Stay Alert, Mumbaikars! Look, Raki, that guy from Indigo is here and he's not an ABCD; he has that snotty accent." Ashoke was lumbering toward them, staying neatly within the crosswalk, and, this time, Maya was grateful for his interruption.

"Ashoke! Over here, yaar!" Raki called. "God, he's even bigger than before."

Ashoke kissed the girls and hugged Raki, patting him on the back with bearish thumps. "I see you survived India," he said to Heidi. "Last time I saw you, you were quite shaky. And greenish."

"Let's not talk about it." Heidi flashed her healthiest grin at him.

"You got the transfer?" Raki asked Ashoke.

"Just a six-month project to start."

"I guess Raki will have to keep a close watch on his phone," Maya joked. Ashoke scrunched his lips together so that they protruded from his face, ducklike. Maybe she'd offended him; he was so large and awkward he probably broke things all the time.

"That's right!" Ashoke said finally. "I forgot!"

"It was just an accident, Maya, really," Raki interrupted.

"You wouldn't pick up the phone! Raki kept ringing and finally just threw it at the wall." Ashoke chuckled at the memory. "Would've been fine, but the thing bounced and splashed smack into that stupid reflecting pool. I keep telling the owner he's got to fill it in, the rubbish people throw in there, it's disgusting."

The line kept moving but Maya stood where she was, looking at Raki.

"Excuse me, madam?" A man old enough to be Pops tapped Maya on the shoulder. "The queue is going forward."

"You told me Ashoke broke the phone," Maya said to Raki.

"I broke it?" Ashoke looked from Maya to Raki to Heidi.

"We'd just met, Maya," Raki protested. "I didn't want you to make a big fuss, get the wrong impression. I was piss-drunk."

"I think my friends might be waiting for me inside, I'll just check, shall I?" Ashoke said. "No point in paying twice!"

"Please, madam," the man behind Maya said, and she could hear his children murmuring behind him. "Are you going to go forward?"

"Oh, shove off!" Raki yelled.

"Sorry, go ahead, I'm not watching the film." Maya slipped past the stranger.

"Maya!" Raki started to follow but the man propped a hand on his chest and said, "Look here, there is no need to use such language. I am more than willing to call the usher if you do not apologize."

"Sorry, Uncle," Heidi said, and the stranger's tiny wife, whose bindi barely came up to Heidi's chin, stared up at her. Heidi grabbed Maya with one hand and Raki with the other and pulled them back to their rightful place in line. "Simmer down," she said. "Let's just watch the movie." She stepped ahead to the box office to secure the tickets.

"That happened a long time ago, love." Raki laced his fingers through Maya's. "I wanted you to like me. I barely knew you then, so it hardly counts as a lie."

In the darkened theater, Maya's hand began to sweat in Raki's grasp, but she felt she had to keep holding his, at least through the first big dance number, to show him, and Ashoke, and Heidi, that she wasn't mad about the phone incident, which was no big deal, really, just something that happened long ago on a boozy night in another country. The song in the scene was a Hindi remake of Roy Orbison's "Pretty Woman," set in Queens, with kids break-dancing against the backdrop of an American flag. Maya looked at Heidi giggling in the dark, and tried to convince herself that she was enjoying the movie just as much. But she couldn't help but notice that the mean old grandmother and the dowdy, bedraggled mother were the only women wearing braids as they watched the neighborhood hijinks. Standing between them, the ingénue turned her back on the singing and dancing; she was a serious girl.

"She looks like you right now," Raki whispered. "Same specs."

Maya reached up and touched hers, which she only wore for distance, at the movies or driving. Not that Raki had seen her driving; he still hadn't been to Kalamazoo to visit her parents, or even to Chestnut Hill to help babysit the girls so that Priya could take it easy during this pregnancy. The girl on the screen, Preity Zinta, did have very similar, rectangular-shaped, silver-framed glasses, befitting her status as a serious MBA student. But behind them she had caramel-colored eyes and light skin the color of the biscuits Seema served with tea to guests she wanted to impress. Maya looked nothing like her, she had nothing in common with this heroine who romped through Central Park with the male lead, sharing an apple and throwing sticks to a dog.

The truth was, Maya probably had more in common with the dowdy old women in braids annoyed at the ruckus the neighbors were causing. Or even with Raki. In the seventh grade she had prayed for her mother to cut her hair and dye the gray that was becoming more noticeable every day. She wanted a mom who picked her up from school, waving from the front of the station wagon, running her fingers through her glossy bob, like Shilpa's mom did, or scrunching handfuls of her sassy body wave like Kalpana's mom. But even at thirteen Maya knew she could never ask Seema to change her hair. She wasn't worried about hurting Seema's feelings; at that point, she wasn't sure her mother had any, and if Seema did, Maya was certain that nothing she could do would have the power to affect them. But she didn't want to disappoint Seema, let her know she'd raised a daughter who cared about things like hairstyles, a daughter who was ashamed of her.

Up on the screen the heroine was now dancing in the engagement party sequence, glasses off, frolicking in a sleeveless, crop-top sari between the two men who adored her. And it wasn't just the ingénue—all the women at the party were swathed in filmy chiffon saris and the dowdy mother had somehow morphed from resembling Seema to looking more like Raki's mom had at the wedding, all groomed eyebrows and heavily lined lips. Maya couldn't be those women. And she couldn't surround Raki with women like them, even if there was still a small, seventh-grade part of her that wanted to do so.

Maya pressed her abdomen, trying to isolate the cause of her stomach pain, but when she took her eyes off the screen she was distracted by the people around her, sitting in the packed theater, smiling up at Preity Zinta. Most of the audience looked like Maya, her parents, Priya if they were lucky or had a three-year-old squirming on their laps. But every ninth person or so she'd come across someone who looked more like Raki or Indira, sleek and glossy, as if they walked around with a personal lighting designer who made them resemble the people they were watching so intently up on the screen. Heidi looked like no one in the movie, of course. But when Maya imagined her own engagement party in her living room in Kalamazoo, it was easy for her to picture Heidi in a borrowed sari with Yasmin on her hip, clapping as Seema and the aunties sang a wedding song, braids swinging. It was hard to see Raki there at all.

When the hero finally died, Preity cried prettily and married the best supporting actor. The movie ended and everyone in the theater blew their noses and started clapping, except for Maya. She stared at the screen, thinking how glad she was that Raki hadn't come home for Holi. Because if he had been standing next to her on Priya's carpet, holding plastic pans full of colored water and watching her family romp behind the glass, he might not have wanted to protect them after all. Her family loved him already, at just the description of him, the sound of his name. But even if Raki had watched them in their boldest moment, there was a chance that he might not love them at all.

Outside on the sidewalk, Ashoke suggested they all go to the bar upstairs at Taj, meet up with everyone for drinks. Maya said she had work to do at home but urged Raki to go and have fun, and kissed him like she meant it so that he would. Heidi offered to walk her home, and it wasn't until they reached the corner, where the streetlight turned green, that Heidi realized Maya was counting, adding up numbers.

"Your GAF?" She grabbed Maya's hand. "Why? The phone? It's immature, but—"

"Not the stupid phone." Maya started to walk downtown as soon as the light turned red. "I don't care about that." Raki didn't have a violent streak, latent anger management problems, or a chemical imbalance; his flaws were less sinister and more common-place, and couldn't be regulated by prescribing the right meds. He was just shallow, wrapped up in his own world, which was so differ-ent from the one Maya inhabited. He'd never be interested in the life Maya wanted. Nor, really, would she want to share in his glossy, soft-lit existence; it was too sleek, too unreal. But after spending four months convincing Heidi, and everyone else, that Raki was her savior, she couldn't bring herself to admit that she'd been wrong. She had convinced herself that his existence was proof that she had van-quished the curse; if he wasn't her happy ending, did that mean that she'd never have one?

Maya stopped at the corner and turned to Heidi. "This might not work." She ran across the avenue, trying to beat the flashing hand telling her not to walk. Heidi followed right behind but they only got as far as the median before the traffic started rushing past.

"It might not," Heidi said. She grabbed Maya's hand, making her stand closer to her, away from the traffic. "Raki is a bit—much. I'm glad he came along when he did, when things were so dark. But, I mean, Scott was so solid and sweet, maybe a little boring, even. And Raki's so…Euro, even though I know that's not the right word."

"You don't understand," Maya pleaded. "This has to work. He knows the words to 'Rocky Raccoon.'"

"The Beatles? So what?" Heidi dropped Maya's wrist, the traffic slowed, and Maya strode east again. "I know the words to every Bon Jovi song! 'It's My Life'! 'Livin' on a Prayer'!"

"But he's Indian!" Maya stopped, turned to Heidi, and burst into tears. At the movie, sitting in the dark with her thoughts, she'd realized that she didn't know if she wanted Raki, or someone like Scott. All she knew was that she wanted to be happy, and it seemed so simple but so impossible at the same time. And if it was impossible, then the curse had won after all. Heidi wrapped her arms around Maya and held her until a taxi honked as it zigzagged past, the driver shouting at them in a language neither girl understood. Then she released her grip, took Maya's hand, and led her to the curb. For the remaining three crosstown blocks, and the nine downtown, neither of them said anything. They continued holding hands despite the disapproving glare of a Hasidic mother walking with a child on either side of her.

"I just want to be done," Maya said when they reached her door. "I thought Raki was going to be the solution."

"To what?"

"To my life," Maya said, laughing and wiping her nose with the back of her hand.

Heidi hugged her and offered to come inside. But Maya said Heidi might as well go home; she was exhausted and all she wanted to do was sleep. She kept insisting she was fine until she succeeded in getting Heidi to leave; she didn't want Heidi to be there when Raki showed up. No matter how many blocks she walked, crying to Heidi, nothing had changed for Raki as he sat next to her in that darkened theater, nothing was changing for him now as he drank eighteen-dollar gin and tonics in a dimly lit lounge. Even though his shirts were more expensive than everyone else's in the theater, his shoes soft to the touch and perfectly shined, during the movie he had been laughing and clapping with the rest of the audience. He had no idea what Maya was thinking. He was sure to come over tonight, like he did every other night, and Maya wanted to be alone when he did, pretending to be asleep, so that she wouldn't have to decide anything, or even to look at him and know that none of her problems were likely to be solved any time soon. She was no longer sure there was a cause for her unhappiness, a curse to conquer. And that thought left her feeling too lonely and unsteady to consider losing Raki, too.

Chapter Twenty-two

Maya heard her cell phone ring and lifted her foot off the iron railing that lined the riverwalk, stomping it on the ground to dislodge any dirt that might have rubbed off on the heel of her new sneakers. She had been stretching before going for a late-afternoon run, and admiring the white of her sneakers against the pink sky and the gray river, thinking how it would make a good Nike ad, when the phone started up. She shoved her hand into the soft pouch of her sweatshirt to retrieve it; the front pocket was fleecy and reassuring. It was a Yale sweatshirt, a leftover from Scott. She had found it the week before, shoved under the bed, when she pulled out the plastic boxes with her spring clothes, envisioning the trips she and Raki would take this summer. A week ago, before her last session with Dr. Bernard, before that cheesy Shah Rukh Khan movie, she'd almost brought Scott's sweatshirt to the Bellevue clothes drop. But now, slipping her free hand back into the soft warmth of the pocket, she was glad she hadn't thrown it away.

"Hi, Ma," she said into the phone.

"You have seen the number?" Seema's voice was so loud and strong that Maya always had to turn down the volume when she called.

"No, I'm psychic."

"Ha ha, quite the comic," Seema said. "If you are so psychic, guess where I am."

Maya rested her leg on the rail and stretched again. "Let's see; at the practice."

"No!" Seema packed so much glee into that syllable that Maya grinned wider than she had in days. "I am at Priya's. It is the spring vacation, I came to help. I told you."

Maya switched legs. "Right. Say hi for me."

"Only I am not with them just right now; I am walking the new puppy."

"But you hate dogs!" Maya's voice rose. "You said dogs are dirty and belong outside!"

"I was right, and you were too busy with school to care for a dog," Seema said. "But that was my household. This is Priya's. The girls love Crumble."

"Crumbs, Ma. Priya told me the dog's stupid name is Crumbs."

"And where are you?"

"Along the river. About to go for a run."

"Along the river?" Seema breathed heavily into the phone. "Is it a safe place?"

Is any place? Maya thought. But she said, "Of course, Ma. Lots of people run here." The runners looked so powerful as they jogged past her, creating a rush of air. Maya had been jogging more often since she returned from India, because she had felt like one of them, strong and active; vanquishing the curse made her feel omnipotent, goddesslike, Maya the Destroyer. Until Dr. Bernard suggested she hadn't really done anything at all. Why couldn't he accept that there might be a moment in life when things were perfect, instead of shining a light on all the mistakes with which she'd surrounded herself?

"Running, all this running, and toward what? Is it so hard to be still?"

Maya sat on a bench, giving up on stretching altogether. "How's everyone there?"

"Your sister is fine," Seema said quickly. "And the girls are okay, too. They miss their Maya-masi. I was thinking, maybe we will come to visit you on the weekend. Just stay for the day, go to Tariq's mother in New Jersey for the night."

Maya imagined going through her apartment, clearing out all traces of Raki's presence, any proof that most nights she had a man in her bed. "It's not the best time."

"We would not stay long. And we could have lunch with your friends. Heidi. Amrita's cousin." Seema never called Raki by his name; it made Maya blush that her mother felt the need to be so formal, so timid, about someone she herself knew intimately. Or had thought she knew.

"I'm not sure Heidi and Raki want to have lunch together," Maya said, eager to pin her uncertainty on someone else. "She told me she thinks he's a little ... overenthusiastic. Maybe not the perfect guy."

"Heidi!" Seema made clucking noises as if herding hens; Maya wasn't sure if they were meant for Heidi or the dog. "Heidi is a nice girl, but that kind ... every day Dr. Nath sees a girl like Heidi who would not so much as look at anyone who was not 'perfect' but is now only too-too happy to rush to have an embryo implanted."

"Ma!" Coming from Seema, the word "embryo" seemed dirty.

"It is true! The IVF is a rapidly growing field, Prashant-mausa says that—" Seema's voice was drowned out by barking. She began yelling and Maya wondered what Priya's neighbors thought of this woman with her long gray braid, in a sari and cardigan, probably topped by three shawls, running after an English bulldog, chiding it in Hindi.

"Ma." If Maya could wrap up the call now, while Seema was distracted, maybe the visit would be forgotten in the commotion.

"I am only saying, you are not Heidi; you need not take her advice. You are not an alone-type person, Maya."

"But that doesn't mean I should be with just anyone." Maya hated how whiny her voice sounded. She pulled her sneakered feet onto the park bench, tucking her knees up to her chest. There was dirt on the sneakers again, but she didn't bother to wipe it off. She hadn't even gone for her run and already her muscles ached; she wished Seema were here to stroke her back. "What if Raki's not the right one for me?" she said finally.

"Right one! Right one! Do you think that your father or I asked if we were each other's 'right one'?"

Maya sat up and started kicking the asphalt; the air-filled sneaker made her heel bounce off it satisfyingly, so she kicked harder. She didn't want her feelings to be erased, lost in everyone else's misery. "I know, you and Pops aren't happy, maybe Mohan and—"

"Maya," Seema interrupted. "I have never wasted your father's time or mine sitting about wondering whether I was happy."

Maya wanted to scream at Seema that she should want more for herself, or at least for her daughter. She wanted to throw the phone into the East River, to distance herself from her family and their bad luck, and small ambitions, in love and life, to escape their misfortune. The thought of tossing her BlackBerry into the dirty water, after the scene she had made about Raki and his little mobile-throwing tantrum, made her laugh.

"One minute you are unhappy, grumbling, and the next you are giggling away." Seema chuckled into the phone. "You are still the same as that messy-haired little girl pulling on the end of my pallu."

"I'm going to go run now, Ma, before it gets dark," Maya said. She hung up, and it wasn't just to escape the sometimes heavy burden of her family. She wanted to end the conversation now, knowing that there had been a few moments, even if they were years ago, when she had made her mother happy.

Maya watched Raki bite his mini Kobe beef burger in half; ketchup, mustard, and a charred bit of meat squeezed out of the back of the bun. She tried to concentrate on the delicate way he chewed, how elegantly he held his wineglass by the stem, but all she could smell or see was the beef, which he would taste like when he kissed her later. When they started dating he had offered not to order meat when they ate together, and she said no, she didn't want to deprive him of anything. Still, she had assumed he'd eventually taper off, and by the time they married he'd be vegetarian. She only cooked vegetarian food. And, in the moments when she convinced herself she could make this work, she assumed that, of course, their children would be vegetarian.

But what if Raki thought it was enough that they not eat meat at home, if he snuck the kids out to McDonald's while she was seeing patients and got them complete Happy Meals, not just the fries and the toy and a bun with cheese and pickles? A Jewish classmate of Maya's once told her that she never ate pork, except in an egg roll. Maya had been impressed at the time, envious of how the girl could order her world, chop it up with borders, erecting boundaries between lands where things were forbidden and others where they were permitted. Now, a decade later, it seemed manipulative. Or maybe it was just sad. Did Maya want to raise kids who were so skilled at sharpening fine distinctions, extracting permission to betray her in bits and pieces? She tried to picture what a child of hers and Raki's would look like, but she only got as far as a winning smile and a lot of hair gel; a kid from a TV sitcom. When she started dating Raki, just the fact of him being Indian made it feel like they had so much in common. Now, sitting across from her, Raki seemed more foreign than Scott or Heidi or even Dr. Bernard.

Maybe Maya was letting her family define her world too much; in their suffocating company, anyone would seem like an outsider. She should resist that urge; Dr. Bernard would say that she had to tell Raki what she wanted, what he should do to make her feel at home with him, she couldn't expect him to read her mind. Still, if Raki just paid attention, he'd be able to figure it out; he wasn't a moron. She could say something about the burgers now, but he'd made such a big deal about the Kobe beef, how he'd had it in Japan. If she did object, he would stop eating. He'd been on good behavior since that night at the movies, he must have sensed she was having doubts. But once he stopped eating, he would be annoyed, and smiling and touching her all night to hide it. It was too muggy tonight to have an arm constantly around her shoulder. On the other hand, if she sat there with his arm around her, like a good girlfriend, maybe she would start to feel like she was in love again. That was the theory behind cognitive behavioral therapy; make the patient take certain actions and those practices could alter his thoughts eventually. Was that all this was? Had Maya acted her way into believing she loved this person, because it was better than the alternative, not loving, or being loved by, anyone?

"Good dumplings?" Raki asked.

Maya smiled; it was nice of him to ask. She nodded, stuck a fork in one, and handed it to him. Instead of taking the end of the fork from her hand, he opened his mouth and swallowed the dumpling whole. Maya glanced around to see if anyone had noticed her feeding him. She would be embarrassed to be seen acting that way, like a poor man's Preity Zinta. But back in Bombay, when Raki had reached over and brushed a crumb of bhelpuri off her cheek, she had hoped someone was watching; there was something so erotic about the gesture that it made her feel sexy herself and she wanted all the urbanites strolling the beach to notice her. She couldn't identify what had changed since then, or decipher how to change things back.

"These are good," Raki said.

"Have the rest," Maya offered. "They're not very big. We can order more."

He nodded, but when the waitress came he ordered another gin and tonic and forgot the dumplings. Maya didn't bother to correct him; the sooner they got out onto the street the better. It was stuffy in the restaurant, and her spine ached from the backless banquette. Who ate dinner sitting on an ottoman? She looked at him, wishing he would say something perfect, something that would make everything like it was when they first got back to New York. Or in Bombay, before they knew each other, when they were full of possibilities. But Raki just smiled at her and kept eating his burger.

"My mom called today," Maya tried.

"Hardly unusual," he said, then added, "I hope you said cheers from me."

"She's at Priya's. We could go tomorrow to see them, come back Sunday."

"You go, darling." Raki smiled at her. "I can't, really. You know there's Ashoke's party tomorrow. I said I'd go; mustn't hurt his feelings."

"What about my family's feelings? Ma asked about you specifically, wanted to come into the city to have lunch with you."

"She was being polite!" Raki insisted. "Your mother doesn't want to spend time with me; none of them does. Later, when there are kids, we'll have more to talk about. Right now, you're all we have in common. They want time alone with you just as I do."

It was useless. "Who'll be at the party?" Maya asked as Raki scanned the passing waitress's trays.

"Vijay." He raised his hand to let the waitress know she was bound for the right table; she was Eastern European, barely spoke English, and she had messed up their order twice already. Maya was annoyed by her, by her spy movie accent and her incompetence, but she was annoyed by everyone lately. She tried to keep reminding herself that the girl was probably a refugee, that she may have worked her way over from Moldavia selling fruit or cigarettes, dodging immigration officials and sex traffickers. "Maybe Shankar," Raki continued, pausing to take a long sip from his drink. "Indira, for sure."

"The trampy bitch."

"What?" He put down his drink.

"Isn't that what the bouncer called her? Or was it a trashy bitch? No, Vijay said—"

"Trampy bitch is correct, but that bouncer was drunk and vile."

"Mmm." Maya tried to make the noise sound agreeable.

"And I'd be careful about calling people whores, darling."

"I didn't say whorish, I said trampy. And I wouldn't repeat it to Indira directly," Maya insisted. "I just thought it was a funny thing for a bouncer to say."

"I mean, you did have sex with me on the first date."

Maya stared at him for what seemed like several minutes while he sipped his drink. It was exactly what Seema would have said if she had any idea what had happened, that Indira was a brazen girl but her own daughter was no better. Raki thought he had so little in common with Seema that they'd find nothing to talk about over samosas on a Saturday afternoon. But, really, they were so alike, each so sure of who he or she was, what they wanted, and how they felt. They were so full of certainty, so different from Maya. She wished she could be like them. Maybe her curse was that she wasn't.

Right now, all she knew was that she couldn't look at Raki anymore. It was rapidly becoming clear that his confidence in himself was his only similarity to Seema; he wasn't strong like her mother or fiercely loving, just sure of who he was; a rich, social, would-be Bollywood hero.

"I'm going to go." Maya stood and dropped her napkin on the stupid ottoman.

"But. No. Don't be like that," Raki said, with his mouth full. "You're acting a little borderline, baby, seeing things so black and white like that. Don't you think?"

"You don't even know what borderline means!" The couple at the next table turned and stared at Maya. She sat back down.

"Course I do, you talk about work all the time, to me, to Heidi."

"No I don't." Maya spoke in a low voice so the people at the next table wouldn't hear, but her soft words sounded like pleading. "That would be unethical." She had mentioned a few interesting patients to Heidi or Raki, that was true, but she never named names. Heidi seemed to really care about her patients' problems, to find the clinical therapeutic terms useful; hearing about Maya's work broadened Heidi's understanding of the world, of herself. Maya was just trying to help. And Raki was so impressed by her job, she told him things because they made him happy to be with her. Now he was using her words against her. He made "borderline" sound like a joke. Or a curse.

"We just see things too differently, I think," Maya said. It was true, but also less complicated than what was now becoming clear to her; she had created this relationship in her mind, conjured it maybe, out of the strength of her yearning for a perfect partner, her desire for a happy ending to the drama of the last six months. But she wouldn't talk to Raki about projection or denial, she would do this using his language, not one clinical term. "And I'm sorry, because I really wanted—"

"Is it about Indira?" Raki leaned toward her over the table of food and rested his hand on top of hers. "I didn't mean to imply—"

"It's not that; I don't care about her."

"Then what?" Raki reached for her other hand and whispered, "Tell me what happened and I'll make it better."

"I don't know," Maya said, taking her hands off the table and folding them in her lap so they wouldn't shake. "I don't want to spend my life at clubs with your friends."

"Love, you don't have to." Raki leaned back again and picked up his G and T; he seemed relieved that this was so easy to fix. "I don't have to be with you every time you go to your sister's, and you don't have to be with me all night at every club."

"But you used to like being with me as much as with your friends," Maya said, and at the sound of her own voice thought how much she would hate that girl if she were seated at the next table, overhearing this eternal argument.

"I still do, Maya, I do." He reached over and put his hand on her knee. "I love it that you're a homely girl."

"Homey." Maya crossed her legs, shaking off his hand. "Not homely. Homely means something different here than in India."

"You obviously know what I meant, Maya." Raki went back to his drink.

"And I'm not that homey, either."

"No, come on. I love it that you cook and are happy to just lie in bed of a Sunday. And that you're a brilliant psychiatrist. My mother says that my dating you is a sign I'm maturing. You're my first girlfriend she's ever approved of."

"I'm glad your mummy approves." Maya put her hand back on the table in case he wanted to reach for it again. "For the record, mine does, too."

"Well, I didn't think she wouldn't." Raki laughed and signaled for the waitress.

"Is problem?" the waitress asked.

"No," Maya said. "No problem. I think the gentleman's ready to pay." Her muscles hurt and she felt incredible fatigue, as if she had the flu. "I'll just go to the bathroom," she said to Raki, who was studying the bill he'd been handed while the waitress watched, waiting for his inevitable question, to find out what she'd done wrong. Maya walked away from them slowly, descended the stairs to the ground floor, and didn't start running until she got to the end of the block.

She could have stayed at Heidi's, but seeing her would require a long conversation, and relating the story of fleeing Raki would make it real, solidify it. Maya was a little ashamed of having abandoned him like that. But at least she was trusting her emotions like Dr. Bernard would want her to, instead of sitting back and analyzing. It may have been cruel to leave without a word, but being rude didn't embarrass her as much as having been sitting there in the first place, enacting the delusion of their relationship.

So she came to the hospital in order to be anonymous and to extend the nice parts of the delusion a little bit longer. So far, no one else knew what a mistake Maya had made; no one else knew she had failed. Her family still thought she'd finally found her partner, her friends had that mix of delight, jealousy, and wonder that arises when a loved one discovers someone else to love more. She wanted to keep it that way; even if it was just for tonight, she wanted to be a person someone was in love with for a few more hours. To-morrow she would go to Heidi's, she thought, hanging her slippery silver dress in her locker and changing into a set of scrubs. She'd given her super four hundred dollars, fresh from the ATM, and asked him to let the locksmith in, take both sets of new keys, and keep the change, if there was any. "Call my cell if you need me," she'd told him. "I'll be at the hospital, I'm on overnight."

Ramon looked her up and down, from her strappy stilettos to the beaded V-neck that framed her cleavage. She should have gone inside first, gotten some new clothes, but she was worried Raki had somehow beaten her to it, realized quickly that she was never going to return from the ladies', and gotten a faster cab. Finally, Ramon raised his hands in the air and his eyes to the sky and said, "Don't even tell me! I don't want to know."

Ramon was a coward, not wanting to get wrapped up in the domestic dispute of a tenant, one who was even browner than himself. It was the police or the courts he was worried about, not Maya. But he was also right; the less he knew, the more convincing he'd sound when he spoke to anyone, including Raki. Raki had already texted twice, but Maya wouldn't let herself read the messages; it was too late, she was too tired, too raw, too weak. At the hospital, she turned off her phone, curled up on the overnight cot, and inhaled the disquieting scent of institutional detergent.

After the first night on the EPU cot, Maya spent the rest of the weekend at Heidi's, and by the time she came home from work on Monday night, the roses Raki had sent on Saturday had already started to turn brown at the edges. Ramon had kept them on his desk, still in their plastic shroud, until she returned.

"Your friend came," he said, holding the vase in his hands, but not passing it on to her. "Twice Saturday. Once Sunday. I said, he come back, I call the authorities. Let me ask you something: he's legal?"

"What?" Maya asked. The plastic crackled in Ramon's hands.

"A citizen? He's got papers?"

"Work visa, not citizen." Maya turned the keys Ramon had given her around in her hand. They were perfect, shiny and scarless, but almost too bright; they looked fake.

"He won't be back." Ramon smiled. "He don't need trouble with Immigration."

Maya nodded and started walking toward the elevator.

"Your flowers," he called.

"Keep them." Maya could see Ramon's smiling reflection in the steel door of the elevator, and she wondered if he'd give the roses to his wife, or to the broker in 5D who was often chatting with him in the mornings as Maya left for the hospital, describing some problem with her apartment that she needed him to come up and take a look at later. The elevator doors opened and Maya stepped inside, where it was safe to start crying as long as she did it quietly. Ramon would be too busy unwrapping the flower arrangement to watch her in the closed-circuit TV. She looked away; she didn't want to see the brown-edged flowers again, even in a reflection. Their slow decay made her feel that the ugliness of the curse was creeping back into her life.

Chapter Twenty-three

The knocking had started softly. In her dream, Maya was back at Amrita and Sanjay's wedding, following the musicians, walking in step with their drumming and feeling a cold stream of sweat trickle down her spine, staining her sari blouse. Then the knocking turned to banging and brought her back to her room, which was a comforting sea of blackness, with only a few islands of possessions illuminated by the sun forcing its way through the chinks in her drawn blinds. The clock flashed 6:17; she'd only been home from the hospital for an hour. Maya propped herself up on her elbows and started counting, curious how long Raki would bang before giving up and going away. If he started screaming she'd have to let him in or risk the neighbors interfering. She heard the whir and click of the lock and saw light fall on her scarred wooden floor as the door opened. Her jaw moved to accommodate any sounds she might make, but no words came. The door swung wider, revealing a hulking figure she had to squint through the dark to see; for a few seconds, she was sure that this was the curse in human form coming back to finish her off. As the being spoke, her eyes adjusted and she saw him.

"She called the front desk," Ramon said, cordless phone in hand. "Your mama. Says she can't reach you, got me worried you died up here or something. Call her, okay?"

Maya nodded and the super shuffled back into the hall, muttering into the phone.

"Mr. Martinez said he found you with all the lights shut off," Seema said after picking up on the first ring. "Why would you be sitting in the dark?" Maya dutifully flicked the switch above the bed, flooding the space with painful brightness. "And so lazy as to be asleep at this time? Even Yasmin has an hour before it is her proper bedtime."

"How did you get him to come up here? He's never around when I need him."

"Mr. Martinez knows me. When Priya and the little ones and I stayed last year, we were always ready with the tips."

"You promised him money?" Maya swung her legs out from under the covers; she was wearing only a tank top and her underwear, and it made her uncomfortable that it was a black mesh thong, as if her mother could see her through the phone line.

"Sometimes you must put in oil to make the gears work faster," Seema said. "But I only bothered Mr. Martinez after I grew even more gray hairs waiting for you to call me back. I left a message every day, all week."

"I haven't been checking." Maya lay down and rested her forearm over her eyes. Her skin was nice and cool. "I don't want to hear Raki's messages. We broke up, Ma."

"But he is still calling?" Seema said quickly. "So you are the one who ended it."

Maya was glad her mother wasn't in the room to see her face. "He was calling for a while; I could see his number," she admitted. "But not yesterday, I don't think. Definitely not today."

"Perhaps you should listen to what he has to say." Seema took a long, deep breath. "Every person deserves a second chance."

Maya got up and walked over to the sink, which held four nights of dirty dishes. If she kept her hands busy, maybe it would distract her from the conversation. "That's what I'm worried about." Maya started to cry, squirting detergent onto the moldy sponge. "That I'll hear what he has to say, give him a second chance, and spend my life wondering when he's going to look at me like that again. Like he thinks so little of me." The truth was that Maya couldn't tell who Raki was anymore, and what his absence or presence in her life would signify. She felt shaky again, as if the sorrow and uncertainty of last year were creeping back, but she couldn't identify exactly how evil would manifest itself—was it losing or gaining Raki that would be a curse?

"Maya, you are always so very dramatic!" Seema sighed. "And now you have thrown away your chance."

"But it wouldn't work, Ma. He would never have wanted to be part of our family." A curved blue glass from the Museum of Modern Art broke in her hands, and Maya dropped the pieces into the sink. "He said only street-sweepers wear braids."

"That is nothing but ridiculous! I wear a braid. Kruti-masi, Radha-bhuasa—"

"Exactly!" Maya turned off the faucet and squeezed the wet sponge, forcing out any water. "We wear braids."

"So you give up a husband and children, a life for a hairstyle? I will change my hair for you, Maya." Seema breathed desperately, so heavily it sounded like a snort. "You cannot blame this on my braid. You threw away a perfectly good man for stupid, silly reasons. You want a rajah from a fairy tale! Someone who doesn't exist."

"I don't, Ma. That's not what I want." Maya dropped the sponge and sank down to the kitchen floor, the linoleum tiles sticking to her bare legs.

"Then what do you want?" Seema asked in a voice that was so soft it seemed she might actually care to find out.

"I don't know, Ma," Maya said, and laughed once, an awkward puff of air and sound. She had brushed her teeth after lunch, but her own breath smelled foul. "I'm starting to know what I don't want." She counted four breaths in the pause that followed.

"But you are still alone, sitting in the dark!" Seema said, a cross between a moan and a shout. "Like a...a...Dracula!"

Maya said nothing.

"Your sister is in the kitchen, feeding my granddaughters, tottering around, carrying my grandson," Seema continued. Grandson? Was it possible that Seema or Priya had already told her that the baby was a boy? Maya didn't think so, but maybe they had, she felt as if she'd been sleepwalking all week. No, she'd have remembered; even now, she couldn't be that narcissistic. This was huge for Priya, for Tariq. That baby would be their chief mourner some day, send them off to a new life. He would be left to miss them.

"And they will arrive in an hour," Seema was saying. Maya grabbed the sink and pulled herself up to standing, forcing herself to pay attention to her mother's words.

"They have a big announcement to tell, but it is not another baby, I have already asked. Still, it must be good news, something tip-top; Shalini is bringing a cheesecake she made, all the way from D.C.," Seema continued. If Maya had known her brother was coming to Chestnut Hill with his family, perhaps for the last time before they moved far away, maybe she'd have gone, too. Someone should have informed her. "I told Shalini I don't take dairy, but she insisted on making this cheesecake anyway, for the children." Seema paused and Maya hoped she was done, but she was only readying her final assault. "And what are you doing? You are sitting alone in the dark, too selfish even to be getting ready for Heidi's dress party."

"That's tonight?" Maya had gotten the invitation to Heidi's launch, a postcard inspired by antique sari fabric, two weeks ago. She had written it in her planner, thought about what to wear. But that was before.

"It seems so; Heidi called here just now to see if Priya knew where you might be, if you are planning on going. You are not even answering the phone for your best friend? And this is a very important night for her! You should be there, wearing something new, to be auspicious," Seema said. Maya laughed; she hadn't exactly been shopping much lately. "Heidi's clothing line is named for me, you know."

"Half for you!" Maya shouted, but the words were hollow. She wanted to feel angry at Seema for blaming her for her own unhappiness instead of sympathizing with her, for insisting that Maya did everything wrong instead of promising that everything would be all right in the end. But she was too tired to feel anger. "What if it's my fate to sit alone in the dark, Ma?" Maya asked.

"First this is my fault, then it is the gods' fault. To be alone is not your karma, Maya. I know your life's purpose. Who do you think gave you life? I did."

Maya was startled by the sound of her own laughter. "I bet you regret that now. I'm not the daughter you want."

"Want?" Now Seema laughed. "You are quite a smart girl, Maya, but sometimes you say the most idiotic things. You are my karma. That is better than want." Maya heard a loud sigh, but wasn't sure if she had made the noise, or if it was Seema, breathing through the phone again. "All this talk about want! You have made your decision," Seema continued. "If you are now sitting alone in the dark, worrying your old mother and even large men like Mr. Martinez, it is only because you want to."

After Seema hung up, Maya tried to go back to sleep. But she could see the sunlight coming through the shades and it embarrassed her somehow, the fact that it was still light out made her feel as if someone were watching her lie there, wide awake, half naked, half crying, half laughing at her mother, at her life. She wanted everyone to stop watching. And, besides, Heidi had supported Maya in India; Maya owed it to her to witness her launch, a new beginning. She wrapped the comforter around herself and walked to the bathroom to wash her face.

Maya stared at herself in the mirrored steel of the elevator doors. Having rubbed color into her cheeks, drawn kohl lines to distract from the red blood vessels in her eyes, she looked almost normal. The bell rang, the doors parted, and she saw Ashoke, sweating through his shirt, arguing with Ramon, leaning close to the super as if it were possible to make his bulk look intimidating instead of ridiculous. He shouted, "I insist you ring up."

"Ashoke," Maya said. "What do you want?"

"So you were in." He glared at Ramon, who was already engrossed in the soccer game on the mini TV at the reception desk. "This man said you were out, and Raki thought you might have gone away. He's rung you."

"I don't want to talk to him."

"You think he wants to talk to you?" Ashoke stepped close enough that Maya could smell him. "The girl he dated at school became Miss India. Did you know that?"

"He mentioned it."

"All he wants from you is his stuff. He could buy another iPod, but those suits he had custom made."

"I'll leave them down here tomorrow morning," Maya said. Ramon glanced up from his game, changed his mind, and looked back at the screen.

"This has gone on long enough, Maya, let's go get them now, then." Ashoke started stalking toward the elevator, then paused as if he were going to take Maya's hand, but found the idea of touching her too repulsive.

"I'm already late," Maya said, and Ashoke looked at her, noticing that she was dressed up. She was wearing the same black Bond girl dress she'd had on when she first met him, on the roof at Indigo.

It was probably more formal than the occasion called for, but it was the first clean thing she had seen in her closet, still encased in dry-cleaner plastic, which almost made it count as new and auspicious. Maya hadn't realized until seeing Ashoke that the last time she'd worn it was in Bombay. Maybe that was a good sign; she was giving the dress another chance. She turned and walked out the door and to the corner, where, for once, several free cabs seemed to be sailing by. Momentarily, she loved New York.

"I have to go," Maya said to Ashoke, who was trotting up behind her. "But if you can, get Ramon to let you up."

"I don't want to disturb him."

"Please do," Maya said, getting into the cab. "He'll be happy to help." He'd be happy to shoo Ashoke out of the building, ask if he wasn't ashamed of himself, harassing a young lady for his thug of a friend, and why was he so fat, anyway, a guy like him who could afford any gym in town? Let him face Ramon.

"Right, then, I'll collect the suits tomorrow; have them downstairs first thing." Ashoke's voice trailed off as the taxi pulled away, leaving him sweating in the heat.

As the cab sped toward the Chelsea piers, it passed the Indian restaurant where Maya had first eaten with Raki, or pretended to eat; she hadn't wanted to get saag in her teeth in case he kissed her later. A few blocks on, they drove in front of the store where she'd helped Scott shop for bedding for his new apartment, the one she said she couldn't move into just then, but would, she promised, once they were engaged. She remembered slipping her hand inside the plastic envelope so she could feel the sheets, wondering how long they'd last, if they'd still have them when they moved, someday, into a real house. It wasn't just the cabbie's route; all of New York had become a map of her failures. Even on the six-minute walk from her apartment to the hospital, each time she turned a corner it seemed she walked into her past, a place where she'd once rushed down the street, thinking she was about to be happy.

"Such a pretty madam should not be looking quite so sad," the driver said. He sounded like Pops's old boss; must be Gujarati.

"I'm fine, thank you," Maya said. "Just thinking."

"Married, madam?" he asked, and Maya almost wanted to tell him the whole truth, that no, she was alone and felt like there was a very real chance she'd always be that way. Instead, she gave her usual answer: "No. But I need to get married soon; I'm Canadian, I need to find a guy with citizenship."

"Even I, madam!" The cabbie laughed. "Even I am looking for the green card." After that, he turned up the bhangra on the radio, and Maya opened the window to let the air rush in and cool her eyes so tears wouldn't fall and ruin her makeup. They were stuck in traffic funneling toward the West Side highway. The party began at six and it was already seven. Soon they would start the show. And in twenty-two minutes Mohan and Shalini's train would arrive in Boston and they'd join the rest of her family. Shalini wouldn't be pleased to be there, she'd rather be saving lives. But at least Shalini knew how her own life had turned out; she had a worthwhile career in which she got to wear a lab coat daily, and two children, beautiful ones with shiny eyes and small hands that grabbed at everything. She had a husband who was a good person, even if he wasn't a miracle-worker. She even had cheesecake pans. Shalini knew what had happened to her, how she ended up; there had to be some satisfaction, some contentment in that.

"Your friends, madam?" The driver turned down his music. "They are married?"

"I'll just get out here." As Maya ran across the highway toward the waterfront, the honking of the car horns sounded like music accompanying her frantic dance.

•   •   •

In the parking lot, marigold garlands strung velvet-rope-style created an aisle Maya ran down, through a red and gold tent and then onto the pier itself. Lengths of fabric lined the pier under Maya's shoes and seeing them unfurled, with the gray river on either side, reminded her of early morning in Benares, when the washerwomen spread saris out along the ghats to dry. Somehow the memory made Maya feel strong, as if she had washed hundreds of saris in a holy river just that morning.

"Maya!" Heidi grabbed her hand and pulled her to a cocktail table where she had rested a clipboard. "You came! You look great." She fished a hibiscus out of a bowl of floating flowers on the table and tucked it behind Maya's ear. "Perfect." Heidi turned to the dark-haired man at her left; Maya hadn't even noticed him. "You can have one, too, so don't start whining, crybaby." Heidi placed a hibiscus behind his ear, tangling it in his dark curls. It had only been four days since Maya had last seen Heidi. Was it possible she'd met someone she clearly cared for so much, felt so comfortable with, in such a short time? And if so, what was wrong with Maya that she couldn't do the same?

"Byron cries if you don't pay enough attention to him," Heidi explained, turning back to Maya. "This one time, we were all visiting Theia Rania in Athens and—"

"I was seven!" He pulled the flower out of his hair and handed it to Maya as if it were an offering. "I swear I haven't cried since... this afternoon at least." He smiled, his face wrinkling so that Maya noticed his eyes were green, like Heidi's. "It's not like this one's so calm and mature. Call her 'Afro' instead of Heidi, see how she likes that."

"Call me whatever you want, at least Aphrodite didn't have a club foot and probably syphilis like your namesake."

"You're little cousin Byron?" Maya asked. "With the camera?"

"The one and only," Heidi answered for him. "And he just got this amazing grant to go to Pakistan for a month and photograph this tribe—"

"The Kalash," Byron supplied. "They're supposed to be descendants of Alexander the Great. It's for this exhibit, 'In the Footsteps of Alexander,' that the Art Institute is having in October. You should come." He smiled again. "Chicago's a great city."

"Chicago's a great city," Heidi parroted. "How come you're such an idiot when you get around a beautiful woman?"

"It's my one fatal flaw." Byron shrugged. "So, Maya, I'm thinking I might be able to swing over to India while I'm there and I was hoping you'd give me some advice."

Heidi looked at her watch. "Now's not the time, By. You've got to grab a good spot before the show starts. Aren't you supposed to be covering this landmark event?"

"At the after-party then." Byron lifted his camera off the table; it looked even heavier than the one he'd lent Heidi. "I'm glad you made it." He raised his camera in a farewell salute. "Heidi wasn't sure you would."

Once Byron had dissolved into the crowd, Maya turned to Heidi. "I'm sorry I've been M.I.A. and that I'm so late. I can't believe I almost slept through it; I've been so tired. But this is really exciting, Hei. I'm so proud of you."

Heidi blushed. "We're running late anyway; this wiccan group had the pier before us for some May Day Spring Equinox ritual, and you know I don't discriminate on the basis of religion, but they just took their sweet time, lobbing all this fruit in the water, for fertility, one of them said. I didn't want to rush them; hey, I might want fertility someday. So we didn't start setting up until an hour before everyone got here." She scanned the pier, a small smile rising on her face. "It came out pretty good, right?"

"Amazing," Maya agreed. It was the golden hour, just before sunset, and everyone in the crowd looked impossibly radiant, golden themselves. She spotted a few of Heidi's friends she'd met over the years. And there, leaning against the bar by the edge of the water, she saw him. The sun shifted, staining the sky a deeper pink, and she felt everything might suddenly make sense, like the humiliation and disappointment of the last week might have had a purpose, and it was to lead up to this moment.

"Scott."

"That's why I called so many times," Heidi said quickly. "I mean, to make sure you were coming, but also to warn you that he was. I Facebooked WALTERS awhile ago to ask for a lawyer who could help set up the company, he looped Scott into the message, Scott got me Jason, the lawyer, and Jay invited him."

Maya could hear Heidi's rapidly falling words but she wasn't listening; the sound of her pranayama breathing was echoing in her head and a jumble of possibilities rattled through her mind, things she should say to him, questions he could ask of her, scenarios of what might happen next. She should have considered these options, rehearsed this moment, before. But she hadn't seen Scott since the airport, had tried not to let herself think of him. Each time he rose into her mind she forced herself to concentrate on something else, work, or cleaning the apartment, or Raki. Usually Raki. It was her own form of cognitive behavioral therapy, the only way to stop herself from second-guessing all the little decisions she'd made, the things she'd said or hadn't said or done, the thousand tiny choices that led up to Scott's huge decision, to leave her alone in the airport.

At the memory of that moment, how shocked and hurt she'd felt that he was able to leave—that it seemed *easy* for him to leave her—Maya's eyes grew hot and angry tears began to percolate. She had felt numb at the time, but the foggy, weary depression had hidden something molten; she had also been so angry. That anger was part of what drove her to Raki, to the promise of someone who had yet to disappoint her. But now Raki was gone, and maybe this was why, to make room for Scott. Scott had hurt her by leaving. Somehow that almost seemed like an endorsement now: with Scott it was his absence that wounded and rankled; with Raki it had been his presence. The sun grew brighter before sinking into the Hudson. Scott averted his eyes from the glare, turning his head her way. He'd seen her, now, too.

"I couldn't tell him not to come, he's been so helpful. I've known him for so long," Heidi continued; apparently, she'd kept talking this whole time. "And originally I thought you'd be here with—"

Then it was too late, Scott was standing in front of them. Maya felt strangely calm. "It's just you," she said, then looked down, embarrassed at her own stupidity. She breathed deeply and looked up again. "I mean, I thought it would be weird to see you after all this time, but it's still you."

Scott grinned and she wanted to grab his arm and squeeze it like she did to Yasmin when she said something particularly adorable.

"So it looks like you two had a pretty successful trip to India." Scott gestured his drink at the crowd around them. "Heidi was telling me she picked this place because it's the closest you can get to the Ganges."

"Filthy and holy?" Maya asked.

He laughed. "I guess. You know, I saw a documentary about India on TV and..."

A documentary? The first time she'd seen him in five months, the first time all year, and he was talking about public television?

"It showed the Ganges, the corpses and candles. It was creepy, but beautiful."

"It's really something you have to see in person," Heidi insisted.

Scott shrugged. "I think the Hudson might be more my speed."

Was that a dig directed at her? Was Scott saying he'd made the right choice, that he was better off without Maya and her filthy, holy rivers?

A girl wearing a headset and wielding a clipboard tottered over and Heidi mumbled something, excusing herself. Scott nodded at her as she left, then looked back at Maya, still smiling. It was a real smile, not a smirk that would follow an insult. He wasn't the snide one anyway, black humor had always been her department. And if his words had been an unintended dig on a subconscious level, maybe he was right.

"I'm sorry, you know." Maya was surprised at the sound of her own voice. "That I didn't fight for you. It was never you I was unsure about, it was—"

"I know. The ending wasn't, maybe, our greatest moment..." He pushed his glasses farther back onto the bridge of his nose. "I'm sorry about that, too."

But there had been great moments along the way, even if she'd forced herself to forget them. He hadn't finished his thought, so Maya silently supplied it for him.

"And I'm glad. Not that you're sorry, you don't have to be sorry. Just that we both are, that we feel the same way." He took a sip, finishing his drink. "Anyway, I just wanted to see you, say hi." Scott set the empty glass on the table. "I'd better be heading back." He glanced at the bar and Maya noticed a redheaded woman who seemed to be watching them; she looked away the second Maya saw her. The girl had such pretty hair, Maya thought, staring at the back of her head.

This redhead was the reason he was being so friendly; she was the one who would make his life easy. Or if not her, then the next girl with pretty hair. In any case, this girl was the reason Scott could feel sure everything had worked out for the best, no harm, no foul.

Scott put his hand on her forearm; his fingers were so much cooler than her skin. "You look great, Maya," he said. "It's really good to see you."

"It's nice to see you, too." Maya rose up to her toes to kiss him on the cheek, slowly drawing her heels back to earth as she watched him walk away. She made herself look down at her chipped nails before he reached the bar, so that she wouldn't have to see how he greeted the girl, if he kissed her or not. He had moved on awfully quickly, she thought, then snorted, laughing at herself. She had moved on even faster, had enacted a whole, serious relationship, start to finish, by now. Efficient as always. If she mentioned having just gone through a breakup to anyone, even Heidi, they'd think that she was referring to Raki. But seeing Scott made Maya realize that she didn't miss Raki, just the idea of him, of her perfect, happy ending, which gave everything else meaning and made anything that came before it all right. Scott was always so calm and rational, never demanding, always polite—the opposite of her family. But that had proven difficult, too, or maybe just not familiar enough. Then Raki appeared and was appealing just by virtue of not being Scott, by being brash and confident and Indian. Maya saw now what Dr. Bernard had clearly felt all along—that Raki was a reaction, not a step forward, but a response to the past.

"What happened, what did Scott say?" Heidi appeared next to her, threading her arm through Maya's. "He had to know you'd be here, he must have had something he wanted to tell you, that's why he came."

"That it was nice to see me. He said it was nice to see me."

"That's it?"

"That's something." Maya looked over at Scott, who was laughing at the girl with the pretty hair. She was telling a story, waving her hands around for emphasis, the last rays of sunlight reflecting off the tips of her nails.

"They're not touching," Heidi said. "It's a date, maybe, but it doesn't look like she's his girlfriend."

"It doesn't matter." Scott was a good guy, a kind person. And he was right, the Hudson was more his speed. With him, Maya couldn't build the transcontinental life she now knew she wanted. Not that, by the look of things, she had the option to try to do so anymore. "I'm okay," she promised. "I want him to be happy. Really."

Heidi gave Maya the look she reserved for women who wear denim shorts with high heels.

"But I don't need to *watch* him be happy," Maya admitted as bhangra music started to play. "I'm sorry, Hei, but there is no way I'm going to the after-party."

"But—"

"Let's just enjoy your show." Maya raised her voice over the music and nodded toward the stage. Heidi put her arm around her, spreading out her paisley silk shawl so that Maya was cocooned in it, too. The bhangra got even louder as women stepped out of the two mini-tents flanking the catwalk; they were taking turns walking the runway, which looked like the mandap at Sanjay and Amrita's wedding. Instead of models, Heidi had stayed true to her "real women" mandate and dressed the other women she worked with in her creations, clothing twelve different bodies in embroidered silks and pleated tie-dyes. There was the strawberry blond girl who worked for the articles editor looking like an expensive parrot in a wrap dress made of jade green sari silk, then the brunette who did the fashion credits swathed in a cobalt strapless minidress ringed in silver embroidery, and the copy chief, who was pregnant, in a bandhej smock. Each looked more beautiful than Maya had ever seen her when she'd visited Heidi at the office. And they all looked somehow the same; they were barefoot, with rings on their fingers and toes, and all of them had been given hair extensions woven into a long braid down the back. The blonde reached the end of the runway and twirled, her braid swinging out above the sound of the crowd applauding. A rope of green crystals had been twined through her hair; the sun hit one and threw its light onto Maya. The health editor, a Pakistani girl with whom Maya had once shared a cab from Heidi's apartment, paraded next, and at the end of the runway she struck a pose from classical dance, her palms raised to receive the blessings of the universe, her eyes flashing from right to left.

"She looks like you," Heidi said. "When you performed during Senior Week."

Maya stared at the girl and wondered if she had ever looked that strong and bright, if light had ever jumped off of her into a crowd as strangers smiled back at her, if she'd ever upturned her palms, expecting the universe to drop blessings into them. The woman striding down the silken runway alone looked like she could do anything.

"You know what this means, right?" Heidi said. "I can write off trips to India on my taxes. I want us to go to Kerala next. Then hill stations, someplace in the mountains. What about you?" Heidi glanced from Maya to the runway to Maya again.

Maya had been so busy fearing what awaited her in the future that she had yet to consider the question: Where did she want to go next? Seeing Scott made it clear she had no one keeping her here. Once her residency ended in two years, she could go anywhere she wanted. If only she wanted something.

"Maybe Bangalore," she said eventually. "Psychiatry is getting pretty big there; Priya sent me an article."

"You could work in India! Live there; that would be amazing."

She had just mentioned Bangalore to have something, anything, to say, to play along. But Heidi was right; it could be amazing. Maya could stride around in a lab coat helping develop psychiatry in Bangalore, and her family would visit, watch her reclaim their homeland. Maybe in all her time sleeping, she had been closing her eyes to possibilities that always existed; she just had to figure out how to claim them. Everyone else seemed to be moving on to the next steps in their lives; it was time to choose hers.

"If you moved to India, I'd come all the time," Heidi promised, but her words were drowned out by applause. The research editor was ending the show in a sliplike wedding gown with a perfectly simple cut and masses of gold embroidery winding around the white silk. As the applause intensified, Heidi slid out from under the paisley shawl, tucked the free end around Maya's shoulder, and made her way to the stage. A model threw a marigold mala around Heidi's neck and a cocktail waitress in a gray sheath appeared next to Maya and flung a garland over her head, too. "Bombay Sunrise?" asked her sidekick, wearing the same gray dress stretched over much larger hips, and brandishing a tray of pinkish orange drinks. Gray-clad sylphs had infiltrated the crowd and were tossing malas over the heads of the reporters, editors, and buyers. The marigolds' warm light reflected onto the faces of the party guests all around Maya, making them appear even more healthy and joyous and whole. She made herself glance over at the bar where Scott and the redhead stood talking. Pain flared up in her stomach, almost choking her, but then it was gone; like cauterizing a nosebleed, it seared her, then closed the wound. Or so she hoped.

Maya heard Heidi's voice in the distance; she was accepting congratulations and answering questions amid a cluster of garlanded guests as Byron snapped away. Heidi seemed flushed, happy, but still nervous; she was playing with the mala around her neck. Watching her, Maya reached for her own mala; the marigolds were smooth and rough at the same time, and as she rubbed a petal between her fingers, she knew exactly what to do with them. She would make an offering of the garland in gratitude for Heidi's success, and for the few minutes when she was so absorbed in the show that she forgot Scott, Raki, and the fact that the curse had ever existed, and felt nothing but joy.

• • •

Maya scanned the pier for the most inconspicuous place. At the edge, where the red and gold tent ended, a metal fence section on wheels bridged a gap in the steel railing. She slipped behind the tent, pushed back the rolling fence, and rested a hand on a red concrete bollard that was oddly familiar. She'd been here once before, at an engagement party for one of Scott's friends, when they'd boarded a yacht tied up to this post or another like it. She added Scott to the wishes attached to the garland, trying to believe that it really was possible to want him to be happy without her, and that one day she might be able to think of his happiness without feeling sick.

Taking the garland from her neck, she threw it into the Hudson. It floated to an oil spill and rested there, tangled with some witch's fertile fruit, cherries, a peach pit, an overripe pomegranate that had split in the middle. Maya waited for the oil to ruin the marigolds, to coat them with blackness, turn them ugly. But instead the flowers transfigured the spill, making it somehow beautiful, highlighting the opals of iridescence in the black pool.

As Maya leaned closer to witness the transformation of the flowers, Heidi's silk shawl slipped from her shoulder and into the river. She stood on the step just below the pier for a very long second, watching it sink, its fringe spreading out on the surface of the water. She remembered the first time she'd seen it, had found Heidi kneeling as multicolored shawls floated down around her in the silk shop in Benares, the holy city. The shawl looked holy itself, and Maya almost wished she were floating along with it.

Stretching her arm toward the fabric, Maya saw she couldn't grasp it. She leaned forward to extend her reach farther, felt her weight shift, and let herself fall. Her fingertips touched the river first, and the water was cool and refreshing on her hand. But once her body splashed into the Hudson, she was shocked by the sharp cold of the river, still frigid in May. She curled her fingers around the shawl and felt herself being sucked deeper into the Hudson. The water pressure pushed her left shoe off of her foot and she wriggled her freed toes.

Maya felt her body settle in the water, righting itself, as her hair fanned out around her. The Hudson was as thick as the Ganges, but gray instead of brown. Scott had claimed it as his river, but there was something comforting, familiar, about the grit and the different weights of the fluids wrapping around her body, embracing, then releasing her. It felt like she belonged here, too, like she could stay under forever, floating in the holy, filthy river, never having to see Scott laugh with the girl who made his life easy, or to come up with answers when Heidi or her mother asked what she wanted to do next.

Her mother said all rivers were holy, all rivers were part of the Ganges; if Maya stayed in the water, maybe she could float all the way to the Ganges, her river, to be surrounded by Dadiji's ashes and clay statuettes of gods and goddesses. It seemed easy to exist underwater. Seema had said Maya was easy in the world, but Maya hadn't felt that way herself, not for a long time. Still, she'd never known her mother to lie. Was the comment a sincere, but misplaced, observation? Maybe it was what Seema wanted for Maya, the life she hoped for her. Her mother, her sister, all of her family, even Heidi, they wanted so much for Maya that their yearning was palpable; she could feel the weight of their hopes pressing down on her. It wasn't just losing Scott, or Raki, that made her feel so weary. It wasn't the absence of love at all, but the abundance of it, the suffocating feeling of having so many people want so much for her, of knowing there were so many hopes that only she could fulfill. What if she could never give them what they wanted, would never again feel easy in the world? It might be simpler not to have to try.

The shawl floated in front of her face and Maya pushed it

back, grasping it tighter in her hand, a hand that looked so much like her mother's, except for the Om-shaped ring she had bought in Benares from a tray the assistant at the silk shop had displayed to distract her while Heidi deliberated between this shawl and twelve others. Maya's hand was larger than her mother's now, but in her mind it would always be tiny, wrapped in Seema's firm grip as her mother hustled her through the supermarket or the spice store, always sure of where she was going, what she needed to do or find. Maybe Seema's observation wasn't just a comment, or a request, a desire. Maybe by describing Maya as being easy in the world, Seema felt she was taking action, trying to conjure that reality just by saying those words. Maybe it was not a demand, or a curse, but a blessing.

Maya stretched her toes farther but there was no sandy bottom, no goddess to be found. She looked up at the sun glinting off the surface of the river above her and saw her garland, the marigolds glowing saffron in the light. As the water swirled around her, certainty flooded her. She knew she didn't want Raki, and she didn't want Scott, either, although what she had with him had been real. Eventually, she wanted to be with someone she loved not for what they weren't, but for who they were. And with or without that person, she wanted to feel easy in the world again. For now, though, she wanted to be up on the pier with Heidi and Byron and the possibility of a future as a psychiatrist in Bangalore or as an Indian dancer in New York, with palms upturned toward the sun, or even, someday, as a pregnant woman in a bandhej smock. Maya kicked her legs and, feeling the river buoy her up, rose through the fetid water, laughing.

She was still laughing when her head broke the water line. She pulled Heidi's shawl up after her and it grew lighter in her hand as something heavy drifted down from it. Treading water, Maya looked at the city beyond the river. She could see a man sitting on the bank. He was surrounded by blankets he had spread out underneath him, but he was sitting up, watching her. His clothes were dirty and tattered and his hair was matted; he reminded her of the sadhus meditating by the Ganges. In the distance, he nodded at her and she threw the shawl onto the dock.

As she swam to the pier, her knee bumped something. She grabbed for it, hoping for a goddess, but when her fingers closed around the slick object, she realized it was only her own discarded shoe, the sinking patent leather pump; its heel must have gotten caught in the shawl's fringe, and been freed when she pulled the fabric up through the water. She tossed the shoe onto the pier and grabbed the step below it with both hands, raising herself up, feeling her arm muscles strain beneath her as she swung her legs onto the dock. Beyond the tent the party sparkled on; she could hear laughter and the sound of ice and glasses clattering against each other.

Heidi would laugh when she saw Maya, at her sopping hair, her dripping dress. But then she'd worry, and unnecessarily; the Hudson was filthy, but no more so than the Ganges. She'd tell Heidi she tripped and fell in, reaching for the shawl, and now it was twice blessed, having come from Benares and been baptized in the Hudson.

She'd go find Heidi now, to let her know that she was going to come to the after-party, she just had to go home and take a quick shower, then change into some auspicious new clothes; maybe Heidi would lend her the parrot-green dress. She had to be nearby, Maya swore she could smell Heidi's perfume; her senses seemed keener since her nose and ears and eyes had filled with the river water during her immersion. She knew that was magical thinking, but that didn't make it any less true; she had sunk into the dirty river and emerged cleaner, sharper, and wiser.

The Bond dress was plastered to her and Maya was shivering, her arms wrapped around her torso as if held in place by a strait-jacket. She would look crazy to the party guests. But she felt strong and healthy, the wet black silk rising over the swell of her thigh muscles, the exposed flesh of her upper arms slowly growing warm under her rubbing hands. Looking down at her drying, smelly dress, Maya remembered Heidi saying that she wanted them to be wearing wet saris in the Bollywood movie of their lives. She kicked off the one shoe she still wore, laughing as she raised her right arm in the air, and did a quick, turning step, shrugging her shoulder, flashing her eyes back and forth. When she stopped twirling, the scent of Heidi's perfume was even stronger, nearer; it was time to go find her, and to get ready for the rest of the evening, for whatever came next. Maya grabbed the shoe near her feet, then walked over to retrieve the other, abandoned heel from where it had landed on the pier. She turned it over to dump out any excess water. Shaking it, she sent dozens of pomegranate seeds scattering wide.

Acknowledgments

Other Waters attempts to describe the struggle of being caught between two cultures. But I hope it also expresses the joys of being exposed to a number of different worlds. I want to thank the following people who revealed new worlds to me, making my life so much richer.

First, my parents, Nicholas and Joan Gage, for bringing me into the world in the first place, and for their insightful advice on an early version of the manuscript. To Joanie, and my sister, Marina, for careening through India with me via plane, boat, and camel, and to my extended family, especially Eleni and Efrosini Nikolaides, for their ever-present support and for accompanying me through Greece countless times.

Next, thanks to my beloved college roommate, Neela, for revealing India to me over half a lifetime in cahoots. Thank you for the inspiration, the fact-checking and correction of every draft, for introducing me to my husband, and for taking me to see a murti that brought us all the blessings one could only otherwise accrue by circumnambulating the globe three times. And thanks to your family (or, as I like to think of them, my extended-extended family) as well.

Many thanks to everyone at Columbia University's School of the Arts for guiding me through the strange new world of fiction, and special thanks to those instructors who provided essential advice on early drafts: Jonathan Dee, Stacey D'Erasmo, Binnie Kirshenbaum, and my indefatigable thesis adviser, Katharine Weber. Also, to my classmates and friends in the program, especially Glenn Michael Gordon, for their support and input.

Barnard professor Jack Hawley's "Introduction to Hinduism" class inspired my first trip to the Ganges. Thank you to him and to all the unbelievably hospitable people I met in India, mostly in Rajasthan and Bombay, for showing me aspects of a culture and a country that surpassed anything I could have imagined.

Endless thanks to those who navigate the ever-changing realm of publishing on my behalf, starting with my brilliant and glamorous agent, Stéphanie Abou, for extending her unbridled enthusiasm to include and champion my writing. My eternal gratitude, a second time around, to everyone at St. Martin's Press, but especially to my editor-turned-dear-friend, Nichole Argyres; it is an honor to collaborate with you and to know you. And to my dear-friend-and-invaluable-publishing-resource Katherine Fausset for her comments, advice, and untiring support. Thanks also to Laura Chasen for keeping all of us in line and tying the mess that is a manuscript into the wrapped present that is a book.

Finally, thanks to my husband, Emilio Baltodano Oyanguren, for showing me Nicaragua, bringing me into his family, and giving me my own. I always worried that marriage would make my world narrower, not broader; you have shown me how wrong I was. To Emilio, and to little Amalía, who came into this world a few months before *Other Waters* did and after a much shorter gestation period, I can't wait to discover what new worlds lie ahead of us.